Unexpected Bliss

Other Books by Lexi Blake

ROMANTIC SUSPENSE

Masters and Mercenaries
The Dom Who Loved Me
The Men With The Golden Cuffs
A Dom is Forever
On Her Master's Secret Service
Sanctum: A Masters and Mercenaries Novella
Love and Let Die
Unconditional: A Masters and Mercenaries Novella
Dungeon Royale
Dungeon Games: A Masters and Mercenaries Novella
A View to a Thrill
Cherished: A Masters and Mercenaries Novella
You Only Love Twice
Luscious: Masters and Mercenaries~Topped
Adored: A Masters and Mercenaries Novella
Master No
Just One Taste: Masters and Mercenaries~Topped 2
From Sanctum with Love
Devoted: A Masters and Mercenaries Novella
Dominance Never Dies
Submission is Not Enough
Master Bits and Mercenary Bites~The Secret Recipes of Topped
Perfectly Paired: Masters and Mercenaries~Topped 3
For His Eyes Only
Arranged: A Masters and Mercenaries Novella
Love Another Day
At Your Service: Masters and Mercenaries~Topped 4
Master Bits and Mercenary Bites~Girls Night
Nobody Does It Better
Close Cover
Protected: A Masters and Mercenaries Novella
Enchanted: A Masters and Mercenaries Novella
Charmed: A Masters and Mercenaries Novella
Taggart Family Values
Treasured: A Masters and Mercenaries Novella
Delighted: A Masters and Mercenaries Novella
Tempted: A Masters and Mercenaries Novella, Coming June 27, 2023

Masters and Mercenaries: The Forgotten
Lost Hearts (Memento Mori)
Lost and Found
Lost in You
Long Lost
No Love Lost

Masters and Mercenaries: Reloaded
Submission Impossible
The Dom Identity
The Man from Sanctum
No Time to Lie
The Dom Who Came in from the Cold

Masters and Mercenaries: New Recruits
Love the Way You Spy, Coming September 19, 2023

Butterfly Bayou
Butterfly Bayou
Bayou Baby
Bayou Dreaming
Bayou Beauty
Bayou Sweetheart
Bayou Beloved

Park Avenue Promise
Start Us Up, Coming August 8, 2023

Lawless
Ruthless
Satisfaction
Revenge

Courting Justice
Order of Protection
Evidence of Desire

Masters Of Ménage (by Shayla Black and Lexi Blake)
Their Virgin Captive
Their Virgin's Secret
Their Virgin Concubine
Their Virgin Princess

Their Virgin Hostage
Their Virgin Secretary
Their Virgin Mistress

The Perfect Gentlemen (by Shayla Black and Lexi Blake)
Scandal Never Sleeps
Seduction in Session
Big Easy Temptation
Smoke and Sin
At the Pleasure of the President

URBAN FANTASY

Thieves
Steal the Light
Steal the Day
Steal the Moon
Steal the Sun
Steal the Night
Ripper
Addict
Sleeper
Outcast
Stealing Summer
The Rebel Queen
The Rebel Guardian

LEXI BLAKE WRITING AS SOPHIE OAK

Texas Sirens
Small Town Siren
Siren in the City
Siren Enslaved
Siren Beloved
Siren in Waiting
Siren in Bloom
Siren Unleashed
Siren Reborn

Nights in Bliss, Colorado
Three to Ride
Two to Love

One to Keep
Lost in Bliss
Found in Bliss
Pure Bliss
Chasing Bliss
Once Upon a Time in Bliss
Back in Bliss
Sirens in Bliss
Happily Ever After in Bliss
Far from Bliss
Unexpected Bliss

A Faery Story
Bound
Beast
Beauty

Standalone
Away From Me
Snowed In

Unexpected Bliss

Nights in Bliss, Colorado, Book 13

Lexi Blake
writing as
Sophie Oak

Unexpected Bliss
Nights in Bliss, Colorado Book 13

Published by DLZ Entertainment LLC

Copyright 2023 DLZ Entertainment LLC
Edited by Chloe Vale
ISBN: 978-1-942297-84-0

Sign up for Lexi Blake's newsletter
and be entered to win a $25 gift certificate
to the bookseller of your choice.

Join us for news, fun, and exclusive content
including free Thieves short stories.

There's a new contest every month!

Go to www.LexiBlake.net to subscribe.

Acknowledgments

I've been planning this trip to Bliss for a little while. If you look back at the Lost Boys books, there's talk about a woman who looks a little like Mel and that rumors have swirled in certain intelligence circles. So Elisa's story has been a long time coming, but I didn't expect to tell it quite like this. I expected to tell the story of a relatively hardened woman who comes looking for her father and spends the book learning how to love someone and someplace that at first doesn't make sense to her. She fights and closes her heart and has to be coaxed out.

Then 2022 happened and I chucked that idea right out the window.

I knew I would process some of what happened when I had cancer through Elisa, but it became more than that. It became a story about me processing what I've learned in my (at writing) 52 years on this earth. I put Elisa in a room with Mel Hughes—my wacky, might be crazy, started as a throw away for laughs character—and could not allow her to reject the love he has.

So her journey became softer and still infinitely stronger. It became learning to accept love and friendship, to accept that we are not at fault for the bad things that happen to us, that we are stronger for getting up off the ground and trying again.

This book is dedicated to the people who helped me up and dusted me off and told me my new boobs looked pretty.

To Kim and Liz and Lee and Margarita and Jillian and Rebecca. To Jeremy and Courtney. To Esta.

To Rich. We've only been married for thirty years but I've loved you my whole life.

Prologue

Elisa Leal stared in the mirror and wondered when she would feel like herself again. It was odd to have lived in a body for almost thirty-five years, to know it so well, and now to have it changed utterly. She felt like she was looking at someone else.

Someone with more scars than she'd had before. Her chest looked like someone had taken a baseball bat to it.

That skin was outward proof of how she felt inside. Bruised. Battered. Brutalized.

She knew she hadn't been. The people who had taken care of her had been competent and kind. Well, as kind as she would allow anyone to be to her. There had been no true violence and yet she felt assaulted.

"It won't take long for you to heal," a soft voice said.

Her sister, Sabrina, didn't care that she was standing half naked in front of the big mirror in what used to be their mother's bedroom. When their mother had died the year before, neither had moved into the large but stark room. Sabrina had stayed in the little apartment over the garage she'd moved into after she'd come home from college years before. Elisa had stayed in the room she'd grown up in. She'd only moved back because her mother had been sick and Sabrina needed help taking care of her.

Then Elisa had been the one who was sick.

When she'd known she was going to have surgery and then a

long rehab with radiation and chemo, they'd decided it was easier for Elisa to stay in the large room downstairs no matter how crappy her memories of the place were.

Now she had new crappy memories of this room, so yay her.

She reached for the surgical bra she'd come to hate and gingerly slipped it over her arms and around her shoulders. She couldn't be out of it for longer than it took to shower and change and stare at the state of her body. She wouldn't even think about the state of her soul. "It doesn't feel like it."

Sabrina set down the tray she was carrying. It looked like she'd made a sandwich and some soup and a big glass of iced tea. "That's because you, sister dear, are in crisis."

"In crisis?" She zipped up the bra and wrapped a robe around her torso. She didn't want to eat, but she would force herself to since Sabrina would worry if she didn't. "Since when did you become a therapist?"

In her world, a crisis was the house being on fire or an enemy combatant coming for her unit.

Her former unit. That part of her life was over now, too.

"Oh, this is not a professional opinion." Her sister had more than the tray. She held a large envelope in her hand. Her expression turned distinctly thoughtful. "Or maybe it is. I'm not a professional therapist, but I'm an expert at being in crisis and keeping all that pain shoved way down where Mom thought it should be. You know she's not around to be a terrible role model when it comes to mental health, right? We're free to seek healthy ways to deal with stress and change."

Sabrina was right about one thing. Their mom's version of dealing with pain was to utterly ignore it.

Toughen up, kid. I'm giving you a lesson in how to survive. Don't ever admit weakness. Not to anyone. And if you trust a man, you learned nothing from your childhood.

She probably did need therapy, but that would be admitting weakness.

Damn, Sabrina was right. Her mom was kind of still here, still living in her head. "I'm fine. And you're right. I will heal quickly, and I'll get used to the new me. According to Dr. Lowell, I've now got eighteen-year-old tits. I'm not sure they go with the rest of thirty-five-year-old me."

"The skin will heal. I'm not worried about that. You're going to look even more fabulous than before—not that you know it. It's the inside stuff that concerns me."

Elisa sat down at the small table they'd set up and took a sip of the tea. It was still strange for it to be the two of them back in this house they'd spent years in. Strange and a little sad because the truth was they'd both tried to be out in the world, to leave this house behind. They'd failed. Elisa had divorced, and Sabrina hadn't been able to get out from under their mom's grip. She'd dated a bit but concentrated on her teaching career and taking care of their mom and let her own life pass her by.

"The inside stitches dissolve," she assured her sister.

Sabrina groaned. "You are so literal. I was talking about your feelings. Note I used an *s* because you're supposed to have more than one."

She had feelings. Anger. Regret. The need for vengeance on her enemies.

Loneliness.

She shoved that one aside because she couldn't process it. She needed to do what her mother had taught her. Put one foot in front of the other. Keep moving. Keep going because stillness meant death.

Was that any way to live?

"Brina, can you honestly say you're different? I'm not trying to be difficult. I'm trying to understand." If there was one thing she did know, it was that she loved her sister. Since they were young, she'd watched out for Sabrina, protected her as best she could. She hated the idea that Sabrina would think she was fucked up. Even when she knew she was fucked up.

Sabrina sighed and sat down across from her. "I'm trying to be. I'm seeing someone. Not like dating. Like helping."

"You're seeing a therapist?" It would explain this whole emotional rigamarole she was going through. "Why do you think you need a therapist?"

Sabrina laughed, an oddly unamused sound. "Oh, let's see. Cold, ambitious mother who moved us around from base to base with no regard to what we needed. A father who walked out and never once looked back. Childhood trauma I don't like to talk about. Adult trauma I don't like to talk about. Watching Mom die. Being so afraid I was going to have to do the same with you." There were tears in her sister's eyes. "I'm going through some things. I wish you would understand you are, too."

"You think I don't?" The words came out far too harsh. She hadn't meant them that way. It was habit that brought out her brusqueness in the face of her sister's pain. Her sister had been through a lot, and she'd faced it all with grace and kindness.

"I think your marriage and your career are over and you recently had to face your own mortality." Sabrina's words didn't waver. "And you haven't cried about any of it. I'm worried you're going to break because you never once learned how to bend, and what I've realized is I can't face a world without you in it."

A deep weariness swept over her. "I'm not going anywhere."

"And that's the problem. I'm worried if I don't push you, you'll stay here in this house and never get out in the world."

Her sister was forgetting a few truths of her life. "I've been in the military since I was eighteen years old. I've seen the world."

Sabrina's head shook. "No, you've seen the military, and mostly you've seen what Mom taught you to see which was duty and responsibility and not a second of real love. You married a man because he was there and you thought it was time. You didn't love him. You thought he made logical sense."

"He did make sense." They'd had the same goals and complementary careers. He'd seemed reasonable, like a man she could build a life with, and three years into the marriage he'd found someone he liked having sex with more and left her.

"I don't think life always makes sense," she said quietly. "I don't think we can logic our way through a lot of things. I think we're still paying for the mistakes Mom made. Instead of dealing with them and forgiving herself, she passed them on to us, and if we're not careful, we'll pass them on to our kids, too."

"I'm not having kids," Elisa said with a sigh. "All I would pass on to them is a gene that's a time bomb in their bodies. I don't have anything for a kid. Mom shouldn't have had kids."

"But you always wanted a kid." Sabrina put a hand on the envelope she'd carried in. "It's why you got married. You wanted a kid more than you wanted a marriage."

That had likely been part of the problem. Dennis had wanted more than he could get from her. He'd thought once they were married she would warm up, but she hadn't because she'd always been waiting for him to leave.

Now that she looked at it, she'd walked right into her mother's life, tried to recreate it.

Wasn't that fucked up?

"Well, I've realized between our mom and dad we didn't have any actual parenting, so I have no idea what it means to love a child because I never felt it myself." That was what she told herself. It made it easier to walk away from that particular dream.

"And that is where you're wrong."

"Wrong?" She wasn't sure where her sister was coming from. "Like I don't know my own personal history?"

She nodded. "You don't. Mom lied. When you did the genetic testing on your cancer, I did mine, too."

"I am well aware." They'd wanted to know if Sabrina had the BRCA gene that Elisa had, the one that led to that tiny lump that caused so much chaos in her life.

"Well, I talked pretty extensively to the genetic counselor, and she called you my half-sister," Sabrina said.

That had Elisa sitting up straighter. "What?"

"We have different dads," Sabrina explained. "I didn't tell you because I wanted to figure out what had happened. So I searched the attic where Mom kept all the records and I found a set of old journals."

"Mom kept a journal?" She could hear the hitch in her voice. This was important. Whatever was in that envelope was important. She'd thought she was on one path, the one she'd been on her whole life. The one that always led back to this house.

But what if she was at a crossroads?

"She did for a couple of years," Sabrina confirmed. "She had a lot of secrets. When she was younger she worked in intelligence."

"I am aware." Her mother had gone far in the military, much further than Elisa herself.

"I think she worked with the CIA."

Elisa had to snort at that one. "Sure she did."

Sabrina slid the envelope her way. "Here are the records I've

17

managed to pull together and some people you can talk to. The important part is Mom worked with a man for about a year on several secret operations. Finding out that guy's name was one of the hardest things I've ever had to do, and I'm pretty sure I'm on a couple of watch lists now. I think that man is your father."

Her world tilted a bit. Did it honestly matter who provided the paternal DNA that had created her? How would opening that envelope truly change her life? Her mother had lied because she was embarrassed she'd had a baby out of wedlock. Her mom was rigid that way. Whatever information her sister had dug up meant very little.

"He's alive," Sabrina said. "He lives in this small town called Bliss, Colorado. I'm almost positive he didn't know about you. Mom talks about how she cut off all contact with him when she found out she was pregnant. She didn't love him but he was… I don't want to go into that. She was overly specific about things I didn't want to know about her. Let's say she enjoyed one aspect of their time together, but she thought they wouldn't be compatible in a real relationship."

"Was he cruel to her?"

"I think he was the opposite. I think he was too nice. And there was something about aliens, but I didn't understand all of that. I think he was writing a book or something," Sabrina said with a frown. "I thought you might want to meet him. He's your dad. Honestly, I kind of want to meet him."

He wasn't her dad. She didn't have a dad. "He was a sperm donor."

"Was he?" Sabrina seemed intent on pushing her. "Mom didn't give him a chance to be in your life. Maybe you could. And the town sounds lovely. I mean you can't go until you're done with radiation, but it might be a nice vacation for you."

"I won't be done for weeks and then you know I have to find a job."

"Why? You've got money saved up and this house is paid off. You could take some time." Every word out of Sabrina's mouth sounded like temptation. "You don't have to rush into the next thing. What if you could talk to someone and they could help you figure out what you want for your post-military life?"

They were back to therapy. "I don't know how comfortable I would be."

"A therapist isn't there to tell you things. They're there to help you figure things out. You talk and they listen without any kind of judgment. You can say anything to your therapist, and it's weird how opening those doors frees something inside. You are a person who likes to fix things. You don't flinch from it. When you got the cancer diagnosis, you did what you had to do."

"My childhood wasn't a cancer." But the minute the words were out of her mouth, she was questioning them.

"It's eating away at your potential for happiness, so I think it is, and you need to treat it." There were tears in her sister's eyes now. "I hope you will, and I hope that you open that envelope and it leads you somewhere new. But here's my promise. Even if you don't do any of those things, I will be here. I will love you. I will be your sister no matter what you decide. Now eat your sandwich and I'm going to get your meds."

"I can..." Elisa stopped. She could get her own meds, and the impulse to view her sister's offer as an offense was what pushed her over the edge.

Did she want to live her mother's life? The one that allowed no kindness and harbored no real love?

"Thank you, Sabrina." She reached for the envelope. "I appreciate it. And let me know if I can help you with dinner."

A smile spread across her sister's face. "I will. Maybe we can watch a movie. I'll be back."

Sabrina walked out with more bounce to her step than she'd had in months.

Therapy wouldn't work. One didn't get a do-over because they talked about their problems, but if it made her sister happy, she would try it.

As for this whole Dad thing, well, that wouldn't work either. It didn't matter that she might have a father out there who'd wanted to know her. He was probably some uptight military guy who was as cold as her mom. She didn't need more rigidness in her life. He would be in his sixties or maybe older. Likely he'd married some perfect military wife and they'd had a couple of kids who hated them, and they'd retired to a small town where everyone was miserable and nothing ever happened.

But if it made Sabrina happy, she might at least read the stuff she'd dug up.

Elisa sat back and opened the envelope.

Luthor Melvin Hughes.

Her dad. A normal name for a normal dude who would probably resent her for screwing up his normal life.

She sighed and started to read, picking up the sandwich because now she was kind of hungry.

* * * *

Sylvan Dean looked around the cell he found himself in and wondered if Hale would even have the cash to get him out. The rent on their tiny apartment had been paid last week, and that usually took most of what they had. Van wouldn't get paid again until the end of his job.

Of course the real problem might be in Hale finding the will to bail him out.

His head ached, and it wasn't even from a damn hangover. He'd sat up all night, his brain racing with absolutely every shitty thing that could possibly happen to him in here. His gut was rolling, and that wasn't from a hangover either.

No. It was losing the fight he'd started.

Not started, exactly. That dude had started it when he'd put a hand on Melanie and then called her a slut who wanted it.

Unfortunately, according to the police officer, since that asshole hadn't thrown the first punch, he wasn't responsible for the assault. Van was, and no one seemed to care that Melanie hadn't wanted to get groped. That had been completely ignored in favor of the cop arresting him.

To his left a guy who looked like he could murder the world was snoring, and Van hoped he could get out of here before the dude woke up because he was probably going to be cranky.

Damn it. He let his head sit back against the concrete wall, pure despair threatening.

He was twenty-seven years old and he had nothing to show for his life. Nothing. No real home. No formal primary education since his parents believed driving around the country in a motor home was education enough. No relationship that lasted more than a couple of months before something happened and he decided it was time to move on.

He wasn't even living his father's life since his father had a wife by this time and a couple of kids. He might have been roaming the continent, but he hadn't been alone.

He had a lot of problems with his parents. They could be irresponsible, forgetful, easily changeable. What neither of them had was an arrest record, and Van was starting to have a nice one.

The door at the end of the hall opened and one of the police officers walked through. He was a tall man with a stern look on his face. Van put him at roughly fifty, and he walked with the force of long years of authority behind him.

Damn it. That wasn't a mere officer. He was in charge of something, and that was bad for him.

"Sylvan Dean? What the fuck kind of name is that?" The officer had his hands in fists on his hips.

"The one my momma gave me. In her defense, she was likely under the influence of some kind of natural pain killer at the time." He wasn't good with authority figures. He might have been able to get out of the arrest in the first place if he hadn't mouthed off.

He waited for the guy's head to explode, but the lawman merely chuckled. "That would explain it. You have some powerful friends, Dean. I'm letting you out, and if you talk to your brother and agree to his terms, I'll talk to Mark and get him to drop the charges. He's my cousin, and he can be a complete dick when he gets drunk. I'm going to handle him and make sure he understands he can't behave that way again. But he was not all of the problem. You've got issues, kid. I hope your brother can help you solve them."

He did a double take inside. What had he said? His brother? He had several, and not a one of them knew where the hell he was.

Hale. Hale probably talked his way out of this, which was weird because of the two of them, he was the charming one. Hale didn't usually bother to talk unless he truly liked someone.

It was a mystery he wasn't going to solve in here. He stood as the guy with five hundred tattoos all involving murder of some kind turned and started to yawn.

21

He moved a bit faster and was happy when the door shut behind him and the officer led him to a small room.

The officer opened the door and nodded to whoever was in there. "Mr. Dean, he's here. Let me know if he gives you any trouble."

Van stopped before he could see in the room.

Mr. Dean? None of his brothers would go by Mr. Dean. Except for one.

Hale wouldn't...

Maybe jail wasn't so bad. A lot could be learned in jail, and there were guaranteed meals.

"Sylvan, you might as well come in."

Yep. That was his big brother. That was Jake Dean.

He wouldn't have been afraid of facing his father. Or his mom. Or anyone else in his family.

Of course, the truth was no one else in his family would have bothered to show up. They would have sent out thoughts and prayers that the universe would show him the way. They might have told him which commune to go to in order to reset his chakras.

They wouldn't have come to suburban Oklahoma City to get his ass out of jail.

He stepped into the room, and sure enough there was his brother in all his authoritative glory. He wore a dark button-down shirt and slacks that had been pressed to perfection. His brown hair was still in the same military-style cut he'd had the last time they'd seen each other a few years before. Van had been going through Dallas and gave his brother a call. The couple of days he'd spent with Jake and his best friend, Adam, had been amazing, and then he'd moved on and they'd only talked a few times since.

Jake had gotten married, and Van had been surfing in Baja at the time. He hadn't gotten the invitation until it had been forwarded to him two months late. His cell had changed numerous times, but Jake's number had apparently remained the same.

Hale stood behind the small table where Jake's best friend and...partner...sat. Adam Miles had been Jake's best friend since they'd met in the Army, and they'd worked together for years. Now they lived together, worked together, and shared a wife.

He didn't think they were bi. Not that it would have bothered him. He wasn't sure how the whole thing worked, but it was a relationship that made his brother happy and that was all that mattered.

"Hey, Van." Adam was the only one smiling. "How was jail? Did you make any friends?"

"Adam." Jake frowned his partner's way. Kind of like Hale was frowning his.

Hale looked tired, like he'd been up all night, which he probably had. His T-shirt was wrinkled and his jeans had paint on them from his last odd job.

Those odd jobs would be their only job because Van had also gotten fired the night before.

It was definitely time to move on. Time to find the next good time until it wasn't fun anymore and they started all over again.

None of which was his brother's problem. "Jake, I'm sorry Hale called you."

Jake's jaw was pretty stone-like as he stared. "Who else was he supposed to call? Our parents? Do they even have phones right now or has Mom decided they give the world bad vibes or something? Hale was alone and knew damn well you wouldn't be able to make bail because you're broke."

"Jake." Adam was the one staring now.

Jake and Adam seemed to have a whole conversation through a series of looks and light growls—all those came from Jake.

Meanwhile Hale was leaning back against the wall, a sullen look on his face. Like he was sure Van was about to lose his shit, and he would be the one who took the brunt of it.

Or like he was just tired of all the fucking drama.

Since they'd headed out on their own it had been adventures broken up with time spent making enough money to have some more adventures. The thing was the adventures had started to wear thin a long time ago.

"Adam, Hale, can I have a moment alone with my brother?" Jake asked, the silent argument seemingly over.

Adam stood, straightening his stylish shirt. "Of course, but remember why I came."

"You came because you're nosy," Jake accused.

"I came because I understand where you are, and I hope you

23

handle this situation so you come out as well as I did." Adam walked out, glancing Van's way. "And you remember that he's here because he cares about what happens to you. He's solid, and while he can come off as an arrogant asshole, he's the best man I know."

"That actually sounds a lot like Hale," Van admitted.

It did not escape his notice that Jake and Hale both rolled their eyes at the same time.

Shit. He was the Adam.

And that suddenly didn't seem like a terrible thing to be. If he didn't have Hale in his life, he would be sitting in a jail cell. He would be alone.

It might be time to start thinking about what Hale needed.

Security. Stability.

Roots.

Hale started to walk out behind Adam. Van stopped him. "Hey, man, thanks for calling my brother."

Hale's dark eyes hooded. "I thought you would be mad, but I didn't know what else to do. We don't have any cash. Or credit. Or anything."

And that had to change or he was going to lose his best friend. He could see that now. Hale was at the end of his rope, and he needed to build something.

It was kind of what he did. He built things. Furniture. Houses. He fixed things, too.

Van needed to find a way to stop breaking things.

The door closed, and he was left alone with his brother.

Jake started to take a deep breath that would likely lead to a long lecture.

"I'll do whatever you think I should do." Van would avoid the lecture and get down to where this conversation needed to go.

Jake stopped, obviously expecting some kind of argument. "I'm going to tell you that if you want to live this way you should drop Hale. He is not meant for the kind of life our parents live."

Jake hadn't been either. He'd left as soon as he could to try to find some stability in the form of the US Army, and boy hadn't that freaked their parents out. "I know."

"I'm going to be honest. I know Kaelin and Jessa are happy living in a nomadic way, and the younger kids seem cool with it, too, but I thought you would settle down." Jake stared at him like Van was a puzzle he was working through. "When you left with Hale, I thought you two would find a place you liked and try to start a life. I was surprised when I found out you've moved twelve times in the last eight years. And this isn't the first time you've been arrested."

Nope. It was his fourth, though it was his first assault charge, so he was moving up in the world.

"I thought I would, too, and then I find myself in some kind of tight spot and my impulse is to leave," he admitted. "And I'm quite excellent at giving into my impulses."

Jake sighed and sank down to the table, gesturing for Van to join him. "Look, I know we haven't been close, but you are my brother and I care about what happens to you. The older I get, the less angry I am with Mom and Dad. I've even talked to them in the last couple of months. The truth is it's hard to be a parent, and it's even rougher to keep holding on to anger that does nothing for me. Seeing Adam get close to his brother has been…I get a little jealous that he gets to be close with someone he grew up with."

"You were twelve when I was born. I don't think I was an important figure in your life," he said softly. "Not that I didn't want to be. You were my hero when I was growing up. And I know Mom and Dad were shocked about you going into the military, but mostly they were scared."

"I know. It's something we talked about when they came through town." Jake frowned. "In their broken down camper, which they parked on my street and freaked out the neighbors with." He suddenly chuckled. "I tried to get them to stay in the guesthouse, but Mom wouldn't hear of it. And she set up a compost station. In the front yard."

"Hey, at least she didn't insist on a dry toilet in the garage," Van pointed out.

"Serena put her foot down." Jake got serious again. "We don't all get the childhoods we want, but becoming a parent has made me look differently at ours. And you. I don't think you're happy, Van. If you can look me in the eyes and tell me this is what you want and need, I'll head home and we can go back to texting every now and then when you have a phone. If you can't, I'd like to offer you something more."

"I thought you were done with all of us."

"Like I said, I'm older and softer than I used to be. Or maybe I shouldn't put it that way. Maybe I'm older and far stronger than I used to be. I watched Adam befriend a brother who had literally turned his back on him. I can help out my dumbass brother who just needs a hand."

His brother was offering him a lifeline, and he would be stupid not to take it. "I am not happy and neither is Hale, and I don't know where to start fixing things."

Jake reached out and patted his shoulder. "The good news is, I do. Come back to Dallas with me for a couple of months and then we'll figure out where you want to go next. I have a couple of ideas."

Something settled inside him. Jake was in charge, and that was a good thing.

For a little while.

Chapter One

Bliss, CO
Eight months later

Hale Galloway tapped on the door to the Movie Motel's room number seven and hoped it was his lucky number and whatever was behind that door would be super easy to fix so he could still make it to Alamosa. The faucets he'd ordered had come in and he was eager to get to work on the bathroom. Not his, of course. His client's. Any bathroom he actually owned would be shared with his best friend, who would have zero interest in claw-foot tubs and antique brass handles. He loved the guy, but Van had the taste of a kid who'd grown up in a glorified camper. Which—in his defense—he had.

And it wasn't like Hale was really interested in how luxurious that bathroom was going to be when he was done with it. The client being happy with how it turned out and the fact that he might make enough to put a down payment on a cabin of his own was all that mattered.

Their own.

At least he thought maybe they would get a cabin up here. Sometimes Van mentioned going back to Dallas but when Hale tried to talk to him about it, he changed the subject. It was typical Van behavior. Something got serious and he turned his attention back to whatever TV show/pop culture thing he was currently interested in.

Van was starting to get that look in his eyes, the one that let Hale know he was getting restless. When Van got restless, he inevitably ended up finding some new cool place for them to go visit.

Hale kind of thought Bliss might be the be-all, end-all of cool.

He could think here. He could be here in a way he hadn't when they'd been living in Dallas all those months.

Was he going to have to choose between the only family he had and staying in the only place that had ever brought him any peace?

"I'll be right there," a feminine voice said. It was on the deeper side, a little throaty and sexy.

Not that the sexy part mattered. He was here to work and fix this lady's shower, and that was all. The last thing she needed was the handyman hitting on her. Also, what the hell was up with his libido that he was contemplating how sexy this woman would be from her voice? He wasn't that guy. He didn't view women as sex objects. So why was he so damn interested in whoever was going to answer that door? Especially since she was a tourist, which meant she was likely here with a husband and kids or a boyfriend she was taking to the Winter Festival.

Still, he found himself straightening his coat as the door opened.

Damn that voice matched the magnificent Amazon of a woman who stood there in nothing but a thin robe, her short hair plastered to her face. She wore no makeup, but there was a glow about her. He stood there for a moment, staring. Like a dumbass.

A brow rose over her eyes. "Are you here to fix my shower or to serially murder me? I'll give you a moment to decide."

And she was sarcastic. He loved the funny ones. He held up his tool kit. "Shower."

She nodded. "A man of few words. I like it. Well, come on in. I suspect you can find the shower in my palatial estate." She stepped back and allowed him to enter the room. Her teeth chattered slightly as she closed the door behind him. "I'm not sure what happened. The showerhead came apart and water went everywhere. I turned it off as fast as I could. I've still got shampoo in my hair. Not that there's a lot of it. The sink's too small to rinse it out in. I only called this in a couple of minutes ago. Do you live on site?"

He moved toward the bathroom because she needed him to work quickly. "Nah, this is kind of a side gig. Gene used to do this work himself but since he found out I can pretty much fix anything, he calls me in when he can. I happened to be dropping something off at the front desk when you called. It's how I got here so fast."

And hopefully he would fix the shower and leave just as fast. Get to Alamosa so he could spend the evening installing fixtures.

Or he could go to the party that was happening out at the fairgrounds. He'd seen a bunch of the locals out decorating the big gym at the townhall. It was new, he'd been told. The construction had been finished a few weeks before he and Van had moved here. He'd overheard a group talking about how nice it would be to have a warm place for the Winter Festival gathering. The annual festival featured skiing and snowboarding competitions, tons of crafts, and food and activities for the kids.

He was pretty sure there would be some kind of protest by the Flanders' family, but he hadn't figured them out yet. He hadn't figured out much yet, and that was refreshing. Most of the time people were easy to figure out or they were easy to ignore. Not so in Bliss.

He rather thought that was why Jake had offered to send them up here while Van was in school. There had been lots of choices in Dallas, but Jake had included Adams State University. It was close to Bliss and the lodge they'd both originally worked at.

"Well, I appreciate it." She picked up a towel she'd draped over her neatly made bed and ran it over her hair. "I'm afraid I'm new in town, and my first day here has not been a great success."

He moved into the tiny bathroom. Normally he didn't like to make small-talk. He wasn't good at it. But she was awfully pretty. She was only an inch or two shorter than he was, with curly dark hair that barely brushed the tops of her ears. That hair framed a face with high cheekbones and brown eyes. It was her lips that really got to him. They were full and dusky pink. He forced himself to focus on the task ahead of him. The pull he felt was odd and disconcerting.

He was a man who could focus on a task. Sometimes way too much. He could tune out the world in a way that some people found annoying. It was one of the things he liked about this town. When he missed social cues, the folks around here simply shrugged and tried again or moved on without judgment. He'd already heard someone saying that was "just Hale." He liked being "just Hale."

This woman was distracting him, and he wasn't used to being distracted.

He needed to focus on the shower. He wasn't going to take the bait because it would lead to nothing but him making an idiot of himself. Van was the smooth one. When they had a woman with them, she was almost always into Van and put up with him because…well, he could focus on a task, and that included sex.

The sex had gotten hollow. He wanted to connect with someone, but it wouldn't be this gorgeous goddess of a woman.

So he moved to the bathroom and picked up the showerhead. She'd placed it on the sink with her neatly put-together makeup bag and a familiar-looking medication bottle. Prescription from a national chain. It was facing out, and he immediately recognized the name of the drug. Tamoxifen.

His heart constricted. His aunt had used that medication for years after her first round of breast cancer.

"Why would you say it's been unsuccessful?"

Damn. He hadn't meant to ask the question. He was supposed to be disengaging. Maybe she hadn't heard him. Maybe she was ignoring him because he was the weirdo handyman. He opened his tool kit and pulled out a Phillips-head screwdriver.

She stood in the doorway, but she'd wrapped a heavy sweater around her robe. "Well, I'm here to get in touch with a long-lost relative, but when I went out to his last known address, there was no one there. I asked a neighbor and they told me they'd never heard of him. Said the lady who used to live there was in Dallas with her sons."

This was going to be a short job. It looked like someone had played around with the showerhead and left it loose. At some point one of the screws had come off and likely gotten cleaned up by the housekeeper. Over time and use, the showerhead had worked its way off and bent the second screw that held it on. "Who are you looking for? We have a surprising amount of connections to Dallas. My partner's family is from that area."

"Oh," she said with an odd sigh. It sounded almost disappointed. Maybe she didn't like Texas. "Uhm, I'm looking for Luthor Hughes. He used to be in the military. He was an SFC."

He'd never studied military stuff. He was more interested in construction. "I'm not sure what that is, but I don't know a Luthor. I know there's a Hughes here, but he was definitely not military. He's on the kooky side but nice enough."

"Oh, sorry. I still haven't quite left military life behind. Luthor Hughes was a sergeant first class," she explained. "He worked with my mom in intelligence."

Hale snorted. "Then it's definitely not the same guy. I can't imagine this guy being in the military. Nice enough, but do not get him talking about aliens."

"Aliens?"

"Yeah, like little green men, although he will tell you that is a myth put out by the aliens themselves," he explained as he located the right screws. "The green part. According to him they're more gray."

"Huh. Well, I guess Hughes is a pretty common name," she allowed. "Maybe this was all a big bust."

That was a good place to leave it. He would be done in ten minutes flat and he would be on his way and she on hers. "Where did you come from?"

Who the fuck was this chatty guy?

"North Carolina. I've lived there since I was a kid," she admitted. "My mom was in the Army and when the time came, I went in, too. So I've kind of lived a lot of places, but I always came back to Jacksonville, North Carolina."

"You're a soldier? I thought the haircut was from breast cancer." Fuck him. Yep. He was just being Hale, and Hale was an idiot who couldn't help what came out of his mouth, and he didn't have Van to smooth things over. He faced her, and his gut tightened because her eyes had gone wide and there was a flush to her skin. "I'm so sorry. I shouldn't have said that. I noticed the meds. My aunt took them for years."

"The hormone blocker." She nodded. "Yeah, I started on them after my radiation course was over. That was after the chemo, which was after the surgery. The last year of my life has pretty much been all about cancer. Is your aunt okay?"

"She died when I was fourteen," he admitted. "Despite all the meds, it had metastasized to her bones by the time they found it."

"I'm sorry," she said quietly, her gaze softening. "I've been told I'm lucky. I had an aggressive cancer but they caught it early. They threw everything they could at it and now we hope it doesn't come back. As for the hair, I did lose it via chemo. It used to be super straight. It's coming back curly."

He couldn't help but smile. "Chemo curls. Same thing happened to my aunt. She actually loved it."

She reached up and touched the dark curls. "I'm getting used to it. My name is Elisa, by the way."

"Hale," he replied and remembered his manners—which were so easy for him to forget. "It's nice to meet you."

"So how long have you and your partner been together?" She seemed to relax all of the sudden, the sadness he'd seen replaced with ease. "Can I help you with that?"

It would be easier with another set of hands. The showerhead was big and bulky. "Can you hold this on while I screw it back in?"

Her lips curled up. "Sure."

"And we've been together since we were kids," he said, enjoying how comfortable he felt being around her. Something in the way she held herself made him relax, made him want to pay attention to her instead of the work he was doing. "I met him when we were eighteen. I'd recently aged out of foster care and I was living in a camper with four other kids who'd gotten the boot."

"You lived in a camper?"

"Yeah, but not one that was attached to anything." He started on the first screw and realized he would be done in five minutes flat and he didn't want to be. "We rented a campsite but the one car we had among us would never have actually moved that sucker. It was nothing more than a place to sleep. Anyway, I met him when his family was coming through. They stayed at the campsite a couple of weeks because his dad was doing some seasonal work and the company paid for the site. He worked, too. He'd been saving money, and we got to be friends. When the job wound up, between the two of us we had enough for a used truck, and we were kind of nomads for a long time."

"That's funny because when you think about it, being military is kind of nomadic in a way," she mused. "I say I've always lived in North Carolina, but that was just a base even when I was young. The house had been in my family for over fifty years, but my mom would rent it out when she was on assignment, and we went with her. My sister and I, that is. Just the three of us. I've been all over the world and yet I don't feel like I saw much of it. I was either in school and my mom was working too hard to take us anywhere, or I was working and I was too serious to have any fun."

"I had way too much fun," he admitted. Way too much, though he was playing fast and loose with the word *fun*. They'd had wild times. He wasn't sure he enjoyed being wild. He liked it better here than those communes and youth hostels they would stay in when they were younger. Even when they'd gotten an apartment for six months here or a year there, no place had felt like home until he'd walked into this town.

The months they'd spent with Van's brother had done what he thought Jake had meant them to. They'd shown him how nice it was to have a stable family and friends who they could count on. He'd enjoyed being around the kids. They tended to be open and honest and told him when he was being a weirdo. He appreciated honest feedback.

He kind of wanted a couple. He wasn't sure he would be a natural paternal figure, but he could learn. He could study and find his way through, and Van would be there if he fumbled.

Except he'd started to wonder if Van *would* be there. He was starting to wonder if Van was planning on going back to Dallas and leaving him behind. He might have outgrown the need to have his best friend at his side. Hale wasn't sure he had and had no idea how to deal with it. He also didn't know how to broach the subject without sounding like a whiny man baby.

She moved in, bringing her hand up to hold the head in place. Yes, that was much easier than trying to hold it on and shift the screws around. They were tricky. An extra set of hands helped.

But then he'd discovered that early in life.

"I wouldn't say my years in the military were fun," she said, her eyes on the showerhead as she watched him. "But they were rewarding."

"My partner's brother is ex-military. So are a lot of his

33

friends. They're good people." He locked in the first screw and moved to the next, shifting his body slightly. His hip brushed hers. "Sorry."

She glanced up at him, a grin on her face. "I think it's okay. Close quarters and all. And yes, lots of great folks in the military. Though I think most of the people who worked with me would say I was not a fun person."

"Are soldiers supposed to be fun?"

She chuckled. "I assure you fun can be had, but probably not if you worked under me. I was very serious."

"And you're not now?"

She seemed to think about that for a moment. "I don't know. I'm trying. Not to be less serious but to find more joy. That's what my therapist says. I need to be more open to joy. It turns out it is possible to fear happiness."

He'd never heard it put that way before. He stopped and stared at her for a moment. "Why would you fear happiness?"

"Because I don't understand it. Because it's not my default state. I think I distrust the emotion," she explained.

"Huh. I need to think about that. That's kind of deep."

"You think so? It seemed pretty apparent to me once I thought about it. I have now spent almost eight months in therapy, and if I've learned anything at all, it's that fear is pretty much at the heart of everything that drags us down as human beings."

"I thought it was anger. For me, that is."

"See, anger is how some people process fear. Most people, really. Not like normal irritations," she continued. "Like if I'm mad at the dude who cut me off, that's irritation. Anger, though, is different. It's funny how much easier it was to deal with life once I started using the proper names for things."

"So you think that the low level of rage I walk around with all the time is actually fear." He finished off the final screw.

And she stepped back, a bit of trepidation in her eyes now. "Well, I'm not a therapist myself. I'm sure you know your own feelings."

He softened his expression because even he could see she was anxious now. She'd likely tried this new information out on people— men, mostly—who got offended with simple truths. He knew some men who got their backs up the minute anyone said they could possibly have ever felt fear. "Not at all. You've kind of blown my mind, and I need to think about what you've said. It makes sense. Now let's see if we can get you back in the shower and maybe the day will turn around."

"Thanks." That momentary wariness was gone again.

He turned on the shower and the head held. "You're all set. I'll let you get back to your day."

"Thank you. Uhm, I'll be around for a couple of days. Maybe a week," she said. "If you want to talk more. Maybe have dinner. With your partner, of course."

When the hell was the last time a woman had asked him out? He couldn't remember. Maybe never. Especially one as gorgeous and glowy as this one. He liked her. Sure, he was attracted to her, but he could ignore physical attraction. He was attracted to her in a way he might never have felt before. Something about this woman pulled him in. And she had asked him out. *Him.* She obviously hadn't figured out he was a complete weirdo, and he might be able to hide it for at least a couple of days. "Yeah. I'd like that a lot. There's a place called Trio."

Her eyes had lit up. "Yes, I saw it earlier."

He was going to be bold. He was never bold. "Seven o'clock tonight sound good?"

"Yes. That sounds perfect. I'll meet you there," she said with a smile. "And my hair will be shampoo free thanks to you."

He kind of liked her any way she came, but he thought saying that might scare her off. Damn. He could learn. Max Harper had started trying to teach him how to blend into what he called the "boring world," and some of his tutoring included punching his arm when he said stuff that was "too intense." It might be working. He suddenly remembered she'd come here for a reason. "Oh, and if you want to ask about your relative, there's a festival going on in town. Everyone knows everyone else here. You can ask around."

"That won't be seen as rude?" she asked.

He chuckled. "As long as you ask politely no one will mind. This place is different. I know a lot of places say that, but it's true here in Bliss. The people are great. But if someone tries to get you to take the beet, you should probably run. Cassidy thinks she can cut the dirt taste out with rotgut whiskey. Then it tastes like dirt and potential death. I don't care. The aliens can take me. Oh, and don't worry about the murder rate. It's overblown."

"What?"

He walked out feeling something he was sure he hadn't felt in a long time.

He was looking forward to the day.

* * * *

Sylvan Dean looked over the fairgrounds and wondered at the vague panic he felt.

He liked Bliss. He felt…right…here. But he was going to graduate in a few months and then he was supposed to go back to Dallas and work for his brother. It was the deal they'd cut. Jake would pay for his college and he and Hale would handle living expenses, and at the end he would come out of it with a business degree in marketing and a job at his brother's company.

It was a sweet deal, and he genuinely loved his oldest brother, but he wasn't sure if he left that Hale would come with him.

He shook off the feeling because it wasn't something he needed to deal with now. He had lots of time. He wouldn't graduate for months and months. Live in the moment. That was his motto.

So planning for the future was weird for him, and yet it seemed like the future was all around him. There were kids running all over the place, giggling and bringing their energy to the world. The amount of throuples was somewhat shocking.

He counted three in his line of sight alone.

Max, Rye, and Rachel Harper were playing in the snow with their kids. Well, Max was being used as a jungle gym by their two kids, and Rye and Rachel were looking on indulgently.

Cameron Briggs was standing with the wife he shared with Rafael Kincaid. Laura Niles handed Cam a hot cup of coffee while Rafe held their daughter, Sierra, in his arms and let her look up at the big brightly colored Christmas tree. The girl was three and stared up with wide eyes at all the pretty ornaments.

The third trio included his boss who owned and ran the appropriately named Trio. Zane Hollister operated the small-town pub with his wife Callie, while Nate Wright ran the sheriff's office. Both Nate and Zane had a toddler boy in their arms. Their twin sons. They had names, but Van wasn't sure what they were. There were a lot of kids and they all had names.

The funny thing was Hale would remember. Hale was good at stuff like that.

"Hey, can I get a coffee?" Henry Flanders walked up to the booth Zane ran every festival to represent his pub. The booth contained a pared-down bar that served some of Trio's most popular winter drinks and treats.

Van felt his eyes narrow because coffee was served everywhere and for way cheaper. "Coffee isn't on the menu. I can serve you a virgin Irish coffee."

"Which is just coffee," Henry pointed out.

"A coffee that costs as much as an Irish coffee," Van countered.

Henry frowned. "You know I can get a coffee over at Stella's booth."

"And I can get fired for passing out Zane's precious coffee for nothing. It's a special blend he swears mixes with the whiskey and makes some kind of magic." He knew his boss. Zane was cool, but he had his rules and very specific ideas about how to make a drink at Trio.

"I seriously doubt Zane will fire you," Henry replied.

"And I doubt all you want is a cup of coffee." If there was one thing he'd learned over the course of his months in Bliss it was that Henry Flanders never ordered a cup of coffee without asking about how that fucker had been sourced. If Henry was willing to risk imbibing a non-sustainably sourced cup of joe, he was hunting far bigger game.

Henry was a blandly attractive man in his forties who—if rumors were true—used to be a spy. According to Jake, this guy—who wore Birkenstocks with socks sometimes—had trained Jake's boss, who was the single scariest man in the world. "All right. I was hoping to get you to talk to Hale for me."

Yep. There it was. This was about Hale's new job. "Why when you can talk to him yourself?"

"Hale is surprisingly good at avoiding me," Henry said with a huff. "And ignoring me. He can ignore Nell. Even when she's chanting."

That was his best friend. Hale was a stoic grump who could sleep with his eyes open through almost anything. Nothing fazed Hale when he decided not to let it. Van had met actual Tibetan monks who couldn't meditate the way Hale could when he didn't want to listen to someone. Of course Hale wouldn't call it meditation. He called it blanking out his brain.

Which was meditation, but Van wasn't going to argue with a master of the craft.

"I'm sure he's not avoiding you." Hale was totally avoiding the Flanders family. Even their baby seemed slightly judgmental. He'd seen the kid get a look when he missed the recycling bin. "He's been busy."

"Yes. That's what I want to talk to him about. I need to talk to him about some of the plans he has for the renovation of the old Jones homestead."

"You mean the cabin Ian Taggart bought." He did not understand why a relatively small three-bedroom cabin would be considered a homestead. It apparently was also considered some kind of landmark. "The one you should have told him was haunted."

Henry's eyes rolled ever so slightly. "Don't be ridiculous."

Van didn't think he was being ridiculous. "Sometimes at night I swear I can hear the sound of something creaking. Like a swing or something. And there are moans."

Henry coughed suddenly, putting his hand to cover his mouth. "I'm sure it's nothing more than normal settling. Look, haunted or not, I'm worried about Ian's construction material choices. I understand the security upgrades on the doors and windows. Given Ian's business, it's for the best. But the interior is a completely different thing. I think Hale should gently guide him toward more earth-friendly materials. Ian's a friend of mine. I was his mentor."

"Did you teach him how to look at a man in a way that makes the man feel like he's the dumbest dumbass in the history of time?" Because the man his brother called Big Tag was good at that. Van was fairly certain the man didn't know his name since he constantly called him "Dean's Little Brother who can't even make a lemon tart."

The man liked lemon tarts. He liked lemon everything except

the one thing Van could make. When he'd offered the dude a lemon drop martini, Taggart had stared at him like he was an idiot and went back to drinking his super-old Scotch.

"Oh, I think he was born with that ability," Henry affirmed. "But he wasn't born with the willingness to erase his carbon footprint. I heard a rumor that Hale was planning to expand the main bedroom's bathroom and install a shower with multiple heads."

It appeared Henry was still good at gathering intelligence. "Yes, apparently Mr. Taggart wants to get hit from all sides with super-hot water. He also said something about wanting to be able to basically hose down his kids with it."

"Has Ian considered a low-flow single showerhead?" Henry asked.

Henry was getting that "I'm going to lecture you" look on his face. Also, he'd seen those kids. He wasn't sure anything low flow could get those kids clean. "This feels like a you and Big Tag talk. I think Hale's just trying to do his job. This is a big job for him. It's pretty much what he's always wanted to do. He gets to renovate a whole house. With what they're paying him, he can buy something else and reno that, too."

Henry's jaw dropped. "He's planning to do this all over the valley?"

Oh, he'd stepped in it and likely gotten his best friend in serious trouble. "I did not say that."

"This is worse than I thought." Henry backed up. "Let Hale know we should talk."

He watched Henry practically run away. He didn't want to tell Hale anything. Hale was living his dream of renovating a house that might or might not be haunted. Sometimes Van could see the HGTV show playing out in his head. *Hale's Haunted Reno*. It could include a whole episode where Van used the skills he'd learned at the commune in Vermont to sage the space. He'd also learned how to make cider and braid friendship bracelets, but it looked like freeing trapped spirits would be the one that stuck.

"Did Henry find out the coffee beans aren't organic?" Sheriff Wright stepped up to the booth.

Normally having law enforcement approach him kind of made Van nervous. Nate Wright was different. Policing in Bliss felt different because the cops knew everyone. They lived in Bliss and raised their families here. He was comfortable with Nate Wright. "No. He's upset about the new…old Jones homestead."

The sheriff visibly relaxed. "Good. Listen, I do have something I wanted to talk to you about."

Damn. Had the sheriff figured out he had a record? Was he about to get the whole "we don't want your kind around town" talk? Was he going to get fired? He shouldn't have left the lodge. The boss there knew about his record and didn't care. "Yeah."

A quizzical expression came over Nate's face. "You okay?"

"Am I about to get fired?"

"Why would I fire…" Nate sighed. "You think Zane would send me to fire you? He would do that himself. What have you done that you would be fired for?"

Now he was really in it. He shrugged and got busy cleaning the counter. "Nothing. Just joking."

Nate stared at him for a moment. "You know I know about the arrests, right? We all know."

Van felt himself flush. "I can explain."

"No explanations needed. Van, if we ran everyone out of town who had a record, there would be no one in town," Nate explained. "Alexei alone can fill a book, though I think Max has him on sheer number of arrests. Most of those are misdemeanors, and I think he gets arrested to get out of shit Rachel wants him to do. Hope came to Bliss because she thought she murdered her husband. It's okay. We taught her how to make sure the fucker's dead next time. She teaches a class at the community center. My office manager got arrested for assaulting a fellow lawyer and stealing her hair. It's why I keep mine short. Hell, Trev McNamara's rap sheet is available on the Internet. No one cares that you got into a couple of bar fights. If you need to get into another one, do it at Hell on Wheels. Now, I wanted to talk to you about a break-in at the cabin on Old Timber Road."

He breathed a little easier. He should have known Zane would run a background check on him.

"The one Hale fixed up?" It had been a quick job, not like the months they would spend at the Taggart cabin. It had been the first time they'd moved into the place Hale was renovating. They'd been there for a month, and then moved into the Taggart place and would likely be living there until mid-spring. Van was looking forward to trying that mega shower.

"Yes. The owners are using it as a short-term rental," Nate explained. "Yesterday, the caretaker they've hired walked in and found someone had trashed the place."

Okay. The sheriff had said he was cool with his record, but here he was wanting an alibi. "We haven't been out there in weeks. We left and didn't go back once the job was done."

"You are so touchy," Nate said with a shake of his head. "I don't think you did it, Sylvan. I found something that makes me worry. Who knew you were living there?"

"You found something?"

"A note. It was yours and Hale's names written on a page from a notepad along with directions to the cabin. The notepad was from the lodge," Nate said.

Shit. He searched his memory, trying to find a name or face and finding way too many. "If someone was looking to beat the crap out of one of us, it was almost surely me, Sheriff. Hale's never been in trouble. He barely talks to people. There might be a couple of exes who are upset with him, but that's mostly because he has no idea how to break it off with a woman. He's supremely bad at it. Honestly, he's pretty bad at getting together with them, too. I'm more likely to start a relationship."

"So if it's a woman, she's pissed at you. If it's a guy, he's pissed at you."

Well, that pretty much summed it up. "Yeah, probably. If someone's mad, it's usually at me."

"Because Hale's a saint?"

Van wouldn't put it that way, but the sheriff had a point. "He doesn't piss people off the way I do."

"You know you can do therapy online now," the sheriff offered. "Or there's a therapist in Alamosa."

The sheriff was kind of an asshole. "Is there anything I can get you, Sheriff?"

Nate sighed and straightened his Stetson. "Let me know if you think of anything. I'm going to send Cam out to the lodge to find out if anyone's been asking about you. I suspect some people up there knew where you were staying."

He'd made a couple of friends while working at the ski lodge as a bartender. "Yes, and I left that cabin as my forwarding address. I probably should have gotten a PO box, but I don't get a lot of mail. I'll let the lodge know to forward everything to my brother's place in Dallas. I don't know where we'll be this time next year."

Nate looked surprised. "I thought Hale was looking for a cabin. I saw him talking to Marie the other day and she had her realtor face on."

Marie Warner was Bliss's all around everything. She and her wife, Teeny, ran the all-purpose store called the Trading Post. It sold everything from groceries to sporting goods. They also ran a tea shop, a bookstore, and when property got sold in the area, Marie handled that, too. "Hale is looking for a project after he finishes with the ones he has lined up. That's all. He wants to try his hand at potentially flipping a cabin. Hopefully one that's not haunted."

Nate grimaced. "He should be careful then. Lots of murder around here. Well, I hope you two stay for a while. And when you get tired of bartending, there's a deputy spot open. A couple, really, since Cam wants to go part time."

Nate turned.

There was no way he was going to be a deputy. "Did you forget about the whole rap sheet thing?"

Nate didn't look back, simply held up a hand. "Nope. Just don't care."

He watched the sheriff walk away. He would not be a good deputy. Not in any way. But he had started thinking about what he could do here in Bliss if they stayed.

The idea of letting his brother down gnawed at him. He'd promised Jake he would come back.

All of his life he'd truly only had Hale and Jake to count on, and he felt like he was going to have to choose between them at some point.

"Hey," a voice whispered from behind him.

He turned but no one was there. Shit. Could a booth that moved around be haunted? "Uh, hello?"

"Keep it quiet, son. You never know who's listening."

"Yeah, well, right now I don't know who's talking, and it's

kind of freaking me out."

The door at the back of the booth slid open slightly, and he was facing an older man in a trucker hat. Mel Hughes was a slender man in his sixties. He'd recently adopted a big dog with floppy ears and the look of a hunting breed. He claimed the dog could detect alien beings, and Van had been glad when the dog merely accepted him because he wasn't sure he wanted to know what happened when an alien was detected.

"It's only me and Ripley," Mel said with a nod to his hound. "Something's happening and I need you to back me up. Someone from the government is going to come and ask you about me."

"They are?"

"They are." Mel's tone was low and grave. "Sent out a woman this time, but I can tell she's military. Even looks a bit like someone I knew back in the day, so she could be an alien taking another form. You should tell her you don't know me. Never heard of me."

He barely knew the man, was the tiniest bit scared of him because while everyone told him Mel was a sweetheart, he also seemed like a dude who knew how to handle various weapons and maybe shouldn't have any weapons at all. "Will do."

Mel nodded and slipped back away, Ripley wagging her tail behind him.

He probably wouldn't get this weirdness when he was working at the business offices of DMW...WDM...it was a lot of initials. His brother's company was a whole bunch of initials, and he would never get that right and how could he work a nine to five and...

Oh. Well, that was a gorgeous woman. Damn. She was pretty and he'd never seen her before, so she was likely here for the festival.

She had a phone to her ear but she smiled as she slid it back into her pocket. She looked adorable in a puffy jacket, dark curls peeking out of the knit cap on her head. She looked around, pausing at the smaller tree that stood near the big Christmas tree the town put up each year. In addition to the tree, there was also a display of all the other holidays to be celebrated at this time of year. The lovely symbols for Hanukkah, Mawlid al-Nabi, Rohatsu, and the winter solstice weren't what the pretty lady was staring at. Nope. It was the smallish tree decorated in carved beets she was examining.

Yeah, that would likely require some explanation. Maybe an explanation he could make over dinner.

She turned his way and seemed to make a decision.

He stood up straighter because she was making a beeline for him.

She gave him a bright smile as she looked over the menu. "Could I get the boozy hot chocolate?"

"Absolutely." He smiled back, hoping he could still find some charm. He had that. He'd lived off his charm for years. "How are you doing today?"

"I'm good. Are you from around here? I'm looking for a man named Mel Hughes. Do you know him?" she asked.

Oh, here was the crossroads. She was the military person looking for Mel? He could follow Bliss law that stated plainly "thou shalt not allow the government in"…or he could go with his dick.

"Sure do."

Yeah, he was going to get kicked out, but when she smiled, he thought it might be worth it.

Chapter Two

Elisa looked around the charming fairgrounds the hot handyman had guided her to. The whole place was set up like a winter wonderland with snow on the ground and on the roofs of the buildings. Steam puffed out of the small shops vendors had set up. Children were playing all over the place, their parents looking on. Family seemed important to these people because she'd counted several obviously expanded families enjoying the day.

"So what's it like?"

Sabrina had called mere moments before. "It's a beautiful town. It's kind of like being inside a snow globe. Or maybe a Hallmark Christmas movie. The bad news is I haven't found any trace of my dad. I went out to the address we found but no luck. I then learned there's a man with the same last name as my dad and I went to his place but there was this weird note on the door. Something about a bunker." She hadn't understood but had noticed the woman's name on the note. The note had claimed that Mel and Cassidy had taken to the bunker along with Ripley—who might be their kid. Cassidy was the same name of the owner of the house she'd looked for her father at. "Apparently the Cassidy Meyer person isn't in Dallas. Unless the bunker's in Dallas."

"You know the records list his middle initial as *M*," Sabrina pointed out. "Are you sure they're not the same person? Lots of people go by their middle names."

"I'm not sure at all, but I have to find the guy first. Or his bunker. He seems to be some sort of prepper. I left a note," she explained. "But I'm starting to think he might not call me back. It's weird that so many records surrounding him are classified. I'm wondering if I shouldn't back off. I might be stepping into something I don't understand."

She'd been thinking about it all morning. Well, when she hadn't been thinking of the hot handyman. Mostly ruing the fact that the only man who'd caught her eye in a long time had a partner. Of course even if he hadn't, there was a good chance he wouldn't have looked at her the same way. He could be bi, but probably had pretty set sexual preferences.

"Absolutely not," Sabrina said. "You are not quitting. You just got there. Give it a couple of days to find him and then decide if you want to get to know him. You are in…"

She knew exactly where her sister was going because this was well-worn ground. "…a unique position to explore the road not traveled. Yes, I know. I've even seen a couple of *help wanted* signs that look like seasonal work. I would have to find a better place to stay than the motel, but there are a couple of cabins for short-term rental."

While she'd gone through the last of her treatments, she and Sabrina had talked about this trip, about how good it would be for her to get away from their childhood home for a while. Obviously if her dad turned out to be an asshole, she would cut the trip short and go back home to start her new life outside the military. But if it seemed like a relationship they both might want to pursue, she'd decided to hang out for a while. Get a job, rent a place, get to know her dad.

Mostly she wanted to see what else was out in the world for her.

"Excellent because I want to come out for holiday break and spend time in the mountains," her sister said. "I think it will be good to spend Christmas somewhere else. Somewhere new."

She would make it fun for her sister. The holidays the last few years had been dreary affairs, surrounded by death and illness, and she wanted to sit by a fire and drink hot toddies and enjoy time with her sister. "Yes, it will. It will be lovely, and I am going to find us a nice place."

"I'm looking forward to it." Sabrina sounded happy, and that was all Elisa wanted. "Now how are you going to find this Mel guy who might or might not be your dad?"

"Hale thinks I should ask around the festival, so I'm down here now."

"Hale?" Her sister asked the question with an expectant air.

She shouldn't let that go on too long. "He's the handyman at the motel, though I suspect that's a side job for him. He fixed my shower this morning and he was delightfully weird, so naturally I'm having dinner with him tonight. Before you get excited, I'm having dinner with him and his... I don't know if they're married or if it's a dating situation, but it seems like they've been together for a long time."

A disappointed sigh came over the line. "Well, it's good you're making friends. I've got to get back to class. You keep me up to date. Love you."

"You, too." She hung up the phone and slid her cell into her pocket as she caught sight of... Was that a beet? There was a beautiful display of all kinds of holiday symbols, from Christmas trees to a menorah to some kind of Yule altar. But it was the smaller Christmas tree that looked like it belonged in a Charlie Brown special since it was skimpy on the leaves but heavy on... Yep. She was almost certain those ornaments were carved from beets.

Weird place, but it was kind of cool. She was absolutely certain that even a year before she would have missed all the quirky touches of this town, seen only what she needed to see and blown through here without bothering to soak it in.

She was trying to be a different person. A person who opened herself up to joy, to fun, to new adventures and meeting new people.

Even when she was kind of sad the person turned out to be gay because damn, that man had been fine.

They might be able to be friends. Maybe Hale would turn out to be the first friend she'd made in a long time. Hopefully his partner was nice and weird. She'd learned weird people tended to not mind when she was weird, too.

But before she tried to make new friends, she needed to put in some time looking for the elusive Mel Hughes, who might or might not know Luthor Hughes. She'd asked a couple of people and gotten strange looks before they practically ran away from her. One woman with red hair and a baby in her arms had looked like she was ready to answer but then her husband...or brother-in-law...had whispered something to her and she'd clammed up.

If no one would talk to her, she might have her answer. If she couldn't find anything, she would look for another place to spend Christmas with her sister.

Though she thought Sabrina would love it here.

She glanced around, trying to decide who to talk to next. Was it the classified nature of her bio dad's work that had everyone closing their mouths and practically running from her? She'd even told a couple of people she was looking for her dad.

To her left she could see the woman she'd asked previously was talking to one of the men who could be her husband, but she thought it was the other one, the one who hadn't told her not to talk.

His eyes widened and he blurted out, "Are you kidding me?"

The woman sent the cowboy a look that was far colder than the snow falling.

That was none of her business. She saw a familiar name on one of the vendor booths. Trio. That was where she was meeting Hale and his boyfriend tonight. She strode across the snowy expanse. It was a good place to start, and she could use a drink.

She walked up to the booth and the man who was running it, and for the second time that day her heart seemed to skip a beat. The men in this town were all gorgeous. This one was tall, with broad shoulders and dark hair that curled around his ears. He was wearing a jacket and a T-shirt with the name of the restaurant he worked for on it. Trio. That word was playing around in her brain a lot today. His eyes were a steely blue that likely should have seemed cold but weren't. He stared at her like he hadn't seen a woman before.

Maybe she was about to get lucky.

"Could I get the boozy hot chocolate?" She was supposed to chase joy. Joy had turned into potential friendship this morning, but here was another shot.

"Absolutely." A smile creased his handsome face, and she wondered if he was too young for her. "How are you doing today?"

Why did it matter? It wasn't like she was staying for too long. He couldn't be more than a couple of years younger, and she was probably overestimating her charms. The man worked for tips and was likely used to making the tourists feel special.

He went to work, making her hot chocolate in a small carafe. He moved with a masculine grace, pushing up the sleeves of his jacket and showing off muscular forearms.

She needed to focus on why she was really here. To look for her biological father and find out if he was as awful as her mom had been. "I'm good. Are you from around here? I'm looking for a man named Mel Hughes. Do you know him?"

He stopped what he was doing, and for a moment she expected his demeanor to change, to go from friendly to cold as some others had done. He stood there, his hand on the carafe as it made a frothing sound, and then it was as though he'd committed to a path. His eyes lit up as he turned her way. "Sure do."

She was surprised at how relieved she was at his answer. "Really? Because I got the feeling this was a very small town. The kind where everyone knows everyone else, and you are the first person to know him."

He waved that off. "Oh, they're all lying because Mel's a little on the crazy-as-fuck side and it's easier to lie than to have to tranq him. It's okay. I've been told Doc Burke is excellent at putting him down with the first shot. He's had a lot of practice."

The guy talked pretty fast. Had she missed something? "I'm sorry, what?"

"Do you want whipped cream?" he asked. "I'm putting in an extra shot of Bailey's because you're going to need it if you're looking for Mel. Are you from the government?"

She was finally getting somewhere. "No. Why would you think I'm from the government?"

"Because Mel came by and said someone from the government was looking for him. Military, in particular."

"I used to be in the military," she explained. "I've been a civilian for the last two years. Why would the government be looking for Mr. Hughes?"

One big shoulder shrugged as he passed her the mug. Even through the gloves on her hands, she could feel the warmth of the hot chocolate. "No idea. I'm fairly new to town, but Mel is known as something of a character around these parts."

"Everyone's acting like they don't know him." It kind of hurt. She knew it wasn't, but it felt like rejection. That redhead had seemed pretty nice, but she'd lied to her. "Does he not come into town often?"

"Oh, he's always around. He was here earlier to place the alien tree."

"The alien tree?" Maybe this guy was fucking with her.

"Yeah. It's the one with the beets. I didn't hear all of it. Something about the Reticulan Greys using the holidays as a mating season. Or it was some other alien. I don't know. I was setting up at the time. You were a soldier?"

He was confusing her a bit. "Yes. I was. What is a… What did you call it?"

The handsome man crossed his arms over his chest. "Reticulan Grey. It's a type of alien. Think little green men except taller, scarier, grayer. It's what most people think of when they think about alien abduction, which is a big thing with Mel. He's very much against it, if you know what I mean."

"I do not." She was fairly certain she didn't know what anything meant right now.

"I only know about it because I spent half a year in a commune in Arizona that was dedicated to helping survivors of alien abductions renormalize to the human world," he explained. "My dad was absolutely certain he had an alien encounter, but he finally figured out he'd mistakenly taken some peyote. According to him he thought it was an herbal blend for anxiety, but let me tell you it did not work. Once he figured out it was the peyote and we were probably alone in the universe, we moved on to California. I had an interesting childhood."

It seemed he had. She was still confused. "Why would everyone tell me they haven't seen him?"

"I told you about the tranquilizer darts, right?"

She nodded.

"There you go." He looked up and gestured at someone behind her. "Max, come here." He sighed. "Please. I don't think she's here to take the old guy in. She's not from the government."

50

"Which is what she would say if she was from the government," a deep voice said.

One of the two men she'd seen with the redhead was suddenly beside her. He was a very attractive man with brown hair threaded through with red and gold. He was slightly taller than she was and had a well-kept beard. Just like the other one. She glanced back and the man's twin was playing in the snow with the girl she'd seen him with earlier. One wore a dark coat, and the man beside her was in a khaki-colored coat. She wondered which one was the father of the kids.

"I'm not from the government, though I'm starting to get worried that so many government people want to talk to this guy." She decided to go for honesty again, even though it hadn't gotten her far. This guy's twin had definitely not wanted to talk, but she was going to try again anyway. "A long time ago, my mother had an affair with a guy she worked with. That man's name was Luthor M. Hughes. His last known address was in Del Norte, Colorado, but it turns out the actual cabin was owned by a woman named Cassidy Meyer. I was told she's in Dallas and that the neighbors don't know a man named Luthor Hughes."

The cowboy snorted. "Luthor?" He turned. "Hey, Rye, did you know Mel's real first name is Luthor? That's terrible. I thought Melvin was bad. His momma must have hated him."

"Max!" The redhead shouted, and the girl stood up taller as though she understood that tone in her momma's voice.

"Daddy!" The girl's hands went to her hips, and she looked an awful lot like her mom.

The man named Max frowned back at them. "Well, it doesn't look like she's going away, and I think Van here likes her and told her everything. Don't yell at me. Yell at his di...male private parts that are obviously doing the thinking instead of his brain."

The twin who'd been called Rye stepped up, making quick work of the snowy distance between them. "You know he doesn't want us telling her anything. Did he not talk to you before he left?"

She turned to Van, who had gone a nice shade of pink.

"Uhm, he might have said something, but I don't think she's government," Van explained. "She seems nice. I suspect if she was working, she wouldn't be drinking a boozy hot chocolate. I don't think feds are supposed to drink on the job. Also, wouldn't she have a partner? They always have partners on TV."

She needed to stop this. "I am absolutely not with any government. I'm looking for my biological father, and according to my mother his name is Luthor Hughes. He was in the Army thirty plus years ago and he had an affair with my mom."

"Yeah, I already heard this rumor," Rye said and then stopped, his head cocking slowly as he stared at her. "You know you kind of look like him."

"She does not. She's gorgeous," Van said quickly. "He didn't mean that."

Max had gone to stand beside his brother, an identical expression on his face. "She has his eyes."

"And his chin." The woman had joined them, a baby on her hip and the little girl at her side. "Wow. Actually, she kind of holds herself the way he does."

Now she was definitely getting somewhere. And she wasn't falling into the whole she's gorgeous thing. She wasn't. The hot bartender who seemed like he might be into her was definitely a background thing that wasn't going to affect the main mission. Which was finding her father and not her joy. Joy would have to wait because apparently her bio dad knew she was here and had a mistaken impression of her. "I only want to talk to him. Do you know him?"

The redhead nodded. "Yes. We know him quite well. But I'm not sure about the timing. I know he was in the military, but thirty years ago he would have been here. He was very active in my husbands' childhood."

So she was definitely married to one of the twins. She couldn't tell which, but it was good to put the relationships together.

It might be the one named Rye because he took the baby from her, hauling the boy high against his chest. Though the girl had called Max *Daddy*, so maybe he was a helpful uncle. "Not so fast, Rach. He was definitely in the Army, but even when I was a kid and he was around most of the time, he would go on these long trips."

Max nodded. "Someone would come and pick him up and he would be gone for weeks at a time. He said he was alien hunting. You know there were rumors when those Texans came through that they knew about Mel's service and that it was highly classified."

That was the thread she needed to pull. "My mother worked intelligence. According to her journals, she worked with Hughes on classified projects. He went by an Army rank, but she thought he was actually working with the CIA."

Rye and his wife laughed but Max stayed serious.

"I can assure you our Mel was not some CIA agent," Rye said.

"That's what you said about Henry." Max turned to his twin. "You know there was a rumor when Jax and his friends first came to town."

"That was that Taggart fellow messing with us." But Rye had gone solemn, too, and looked at her again. "She does remind me of him. A little. Do you think it could be true? Could the old man actually have a kid?"

"She's a fully grown woman," Van added helpfully.

Rach sighed. "Not to him she won't be. They're always your babies. Hi, I'm Rachel Harper. These are my husbands, Max and Rye, and the kiddos are Paige and Ethan. I take it you haven't been able to even get close to Mel?"

What had she said? She wanted to follow up on the *s* part of the word *husbands*, but she didn't want to stop down the dialogue now that it was going. "I went to a house in Del Norte and then I went to a cabin here in town but there was a note that said they were at some place called the bunker."

"Yes, the minute the word got out that someone was looking for him, Mel would have taken Cassidy and hunkered down," Rye explained.

Things were starting to come together. "Cassidy Meyer? That was the name of the woman who owned the place in Del Norte. Is she involved with him? Do they have a kid named Ripley?"

Max snorted. "Ripley is a hound who Noah Bennett managed to convince Mel can sniff out alien life. Noah's the town vet and he's an ass...a very nice man who is concerned with all animals and does not mind misrepresenting them in order to find each one a forever home."

"The animal doc found my kitty," Paige said with an adorable grin.

"Yep, found your kitty who was supposed to solve our mouse problem in the barn," Max explained. "Because she was described as a fierce feline warrior."

"She's pretty much a dog in a cat's body," Rachel added. "I've never seen a cat who loves everything she sees. I caught her licking a mouse, and not in a I'm-about-to-eat-you way. I'm pretty sure she thought it was her baby. I bet that poor mouse was scared to death."

"No, she wasn't because the fucker lived and probably had a thousand more babies," Max complained.

Paige's head tilted up. "Daddy said a bad word."

"Well, Daddy has to deal with those rodents, so I'm giving him a pass on this one," Rachel said to her mini me. She turned back to Elisa. "Look, Mel is touchy about certain things, likely thanks to his time in the military. Why don't you let Max and Rye go out and talk to him?"

"You would do that?" She might have finally caught a break.

"Of course." Rye patted his son's back. "Hell, I'll do it just to see the look on his face."

"If we can convince him." Max didn't sound sure. "He thinks she's government."

"My mom's name was Nora Leal, and she was a first lieutenant at the time," she explained. "From what I've been able to put together, they worked on a few jobs. At least one of them was in Germany. Mom was stationed at Panzer Kaserne outside of Stuttgart. If he doesn't want to meet me, I'll understand. But I would like for him to tell me himself. I'll give you my email and my phone number if he would rather contact me that way. I would just like to be able to say I tried to connect with him. I need the closure of him saying he doesn't want to know me."

"Oh, that won't be the problem," Rye said.

"Nope," Max agreed. "I think you're going to find that Mel will definitely want to know you. I hope you like beets. Come on, Rye. If we go now, we should be able to catch him before he goes into lockdown."

She gave Rachel her phone number and the family went off to find Mel Hughes.

"So, it looks like you might be hanging out for a while."

She turned and Van had a bright smile on his face. She felt more hopeful than before. Or maybe not since it seemed her biological father was on the complex side. Still, she'd promised Sabrina and her therapist she would give this a shot.

No. She'd promised *herself* she would give this a shot. None of this worked if she didn't do it for herself. If she didn't value herself and acknowledge she was worthy of the work she was putting in. "Yes, it seems so."

She wouldn't mind getting to know this man. He was genuinely beautiful, and she liked his energy. And he was weird. She liked the weird ones, as she'd shown earlier when she'd completely misread the vibe between her and Hale. She felt some of that now with Van. She couldn't be wrong twice in a day, could she?

"If you want a guide around town, I've been here a couple of months. I know that doesn't sound like long, but I think it's the perfect amount of time to be a good tour guide. I know where everything is, but I can't bore you with a crazy amount of history," he said with a heart-stopping grin.

Nope. She wasn't wrong about this one. They had chemistry. "I would like that."

"Good. How about we start tonight? I'm not working tonight so I can take you out to dinner. There's a great restaurant up at the lodge. It's got gorgeous views of the pass," he offered.

It had been a long time since she had enough of a social life that she had two competing events. The idea of spending the evening with a guy who might want to do more than talk to her was tempting, but she was giving friendship a try, too. "I'm sorry. I'm meeting a friend and his boyfriend tonight. I can go tomorrow night. Or if you're working we could grab some lunch."

"I'm off all day tomorrow," he said with a smooth smile. "I would love to see you. I'm going to give you my number and we can meet up whenever you like."

She handed him her phone.

Her day was looking up.

* * * *

Hale stepped into Trio, an odd anxiety coursing through his veins.

Anxiety itself wasn't odd. He'd dealt with that all of his life. Since he'd been a kid left on his aunt's doorstep, his mom choosing to walk away and leave him behind. He'd had the ground beneath him shake more than once since that particular aunt had done the same thing two years later when she'd gotten married and her husband hadn't wanted a kid with disciplinary issues. Then it was off to the next aunt who'd ended up dying on him and leaving him in the foster care system.

He knew anxiety on many levels, but this was different. This anxiety wasn't entirely unpleasant.

Maybe he should give it a different name. Wasn't that what Elisa had said? Life was easier when every emotion was called by its proper name.

Maybe what he was feeling was anticipation.

He glanced around the small bar. He'd been in a hundred bars like this one. Every small town had some version of Trio—a meeting spot with everyday sports bar food where everyone gathered. But there was something special about Trio, and he'd known it from the day he'd walked in.

He belonged here. He—the unique person he was and not simply a paying customer—was welcome here.

"Hey, Hale." Alexei Markov greeted him. The big Russian ran the bar portion of the bar and grill, but not for long. He was finishing up his degree at Adams State. He'd had a few classes with Van.

Callie Hollister-Wright was apparently working the evening shift. She had a bunch of menus in her hand as she walked to the hostess station. "Hello, Hale. How are things going for you today?"

It might be the easy way he fit in with these people that had made this place special. In other places he felt like either the guy who blended in with the background or the guy who stuck out like a sore thumb. The latter tended to get him in trouble. The former chipped away at his soul. But here, he was seen, and not in a bad way.

"Good. I ran into Alamosa to get the bathroom shipment. You should see the tub I'm installing." He reached into his pocket and pulled out a small bag. "And I picked up the heating element for the bread oven. I can head back and fix it if you've got time."

Callie's eyes closed in obvious relief. "Thank you so much. We're having to bake in Stella's extra oven, and running between here and the café in the snow is dangerous. Zane is going to break his neck. You're a lifesaver. And I totally want to see that bathtub. I know I probably can't afford one, but it might give me some inspiration for the add-on this spring."

The Hollister-Wright family was adding on to their small cabin. "You know there are a lot of cabins for sale in this area. You could probably find one without having to go through a reno."

She shook her head. "Absolutely not. I love that cabin. All it needs is an extra bathroom and some more space. We'll stay up at Stef's while you're working. I can't wait."

Neither could he. He loved working here, and it looked like he wouldn't be hurting for a job anytime soon. It was more fun to work for a community he belonged to. "I'm excited about working with the guys who hand chink the logs. I'm going to learn a lot."

He'd worked on many different types of buildings. Wherever he and Van went, Van found a bartending job and he got on some sort of construction crew. He'd been building things since he was sixteen and he was still fascinated with the business, but especially with the artistry of working on something unique.

She gestured toward the kitchen. "Feel free to grab a plate back there if you're hungry. Zane made some amazing chili."

"That sounds great, but I'm going to need a table out here in the dining room."

Callie's eyes narrowed as she looked him over. "You are wearing a collared shirt. And you shaved. Holy crap, Hale. You have a date. Did you meet a woman? Or a man? Does Van know?"

It just went to prove he and Van had been going through a real dry spell. He kind of liked that Callie didn't assume. "She's a woman and she's in town for a few weeks. Van doesn't know but I'm about to tell him."

"You made a date for the two of you without letting him meet her? You are a brave man," Callie said.

"No, he is smart man," Alexei corrected as he walked by. "Woman will slip through his fingers if he does not act quickly. Look what happens with Lucy. Van was interested. He waits too long and now she is somewhere else. I blame him."

They hadn't replaced Lucy yet, and Alexei was obviously bitter about it. "I'm pretty sure Van could have asked her out and she still would have ended up with Michael and Ty. They just needed to get their shit together. The good news is Van and I already have it together. We've been doing this ménage thing for years."

Short term. They'd only had one girlfriend they'd shared for more than a couple of nights, and it had been fairly casual. She'd been a "free spirit," and when she'd found a spirit she liked more than the two of them, she'd been gone.

Somehow he didn't think Elisa would be the same. They'd only had one conversation, but he could already tell she was solid.

He moved through the bar area to the kitchen, and there was Van coming in the back door, hauling a tray of dirty dishes.

"Hey," Van said with a smile. "I thought you'd be at the cabin working on the bathroom. Did you manage to get into town today?"

Hale moved to the broken oven. "I did and I picked up this baby so you and Zane won't have to run in between here and Stella's."

There was a visible look of relief on Van's face. "Thanks, man. You have no idea how crabby Zane gets when that bread isn't warm. I told him it's impossible to walk two blocks in the snow and keep the bread at butter meltable temps." Van dropped off the dishes at the big sinks where Micky Lang was busy scrubbing down before the dinner crowd.

Hale pulled the bad element. "This should get the oven working tonight." He glanced over at his partner, taking in Van's Trio shirt and jeans as he shed his coat and put it on the rack by the back door. "Do you have extra clothes in your locker?"

"Yes, why?" Van asked, one brow going up.

"Because we have a date tonight," he announced. "I met this amazing woman this morning. She's from North Carolina. She's in town for the festival."

A tiny lie, but he wanted Van to meet her before he dropped the whole ex-military-looking-for-her-father thing on him. All Van needed to know right now was she was completely fascinating and gorgeous, and they were going to have a great time getting to know her.

Van frowned. "But I met a woman today, too. I would rather

we saw her. We have a date with her tomorrow night."

Naturally it was feast or famine, but he only wanted to feast on one woman. He quickly slipped the new heating element in and turned the oven on to test it. "And I would rather we saw mine. This woman is special."

"I think mine is special." Van frowned his way. "Since when do you find our women?"

It was true. He normally didn't talk much, was perfectly happy to allow Van to lead the way. But she'd been easy to talk to. He'd felt a connection with her right away. It rankled that Van was pushing him. Did it matter that he didn't usually make the first move? "Since when am I not allowed to find our women?"

"I didn't say that," Van returned.

"He kind of did," a deep voice whispered.

Hale turned and noticed the two big guys standing outside of the office. Zane Hollister and Nathan Wright had obviously been inside and come out at an inopportune time. Or maybe it was opportune since he knew at least Zane totally viewed the entire population of Bliss as his entertainment. The former DEA agent turned restaurant owner lived for gossip.

Hale had never been gossip before. He wasn't sure how he felt about it.

"I did not, and you should stay out of it, boss. I'm off the clock. Pilar is taking the evening shift in that shack you call a booth," Van announced. "I hope she doesn't freeze, and just so you know lots of people want coffee without booze."

"Then they can buy it from Stella's booth. That coffee is paired perfectly with the whiskey. They complement each other," Zane replied. "And Pilar was smart enough to turn on the space heater I had built into the booth. It's in the ceiling and has a fan that keeps it toasty warm."

"What? I've been freezing my ass off for three days," Van complained.

"All you had to do was ask," Zane countered. "Or look up. Or press the *on* button next to the register. Now go back to fighting. I'm more interested in that. You both found a tourist to tempt back to your lair, but you can't decide which one."

"Why should they have to decide?" Nate was still wearing his uniform. "They're young. They could date both. Are they both tourists?"

"I think mine will be here for a couple of weeks." At least Hale hoped she would.

"I'm pretty sure mine will leave in a day or two," Van hedged. "She's going to find out this place is weirder than she imagined. She seems cool, but sometimes Bliss can be a lot. Especially some of the wilder citizens."

Excellent. Van was making his point. "So we should see mine. You can call yours and tell her you're busy. She'll be gone as soon as the festival is over."

"I'm afraid she might not make it through the whole festival, so I would like to see her before she leaves," Van argued.

"Or—to reiterate—you could see them both," Zane pointed out.

Hale stepped away from the oven, which seemed to be heating up nicely. "I don't want to see anyone else. I'm interested in her. I have always followed Van when his heart or brain or dick decided to chase after a woman. I think this once he can follow me."

"My heart, dick, and brain are concentrating on the woman I met." Van proved he was a stubborn asshole.

Was he really not going to give him this one ask? He'd never asked before. "I'm not going to cancel my date. She's going to be here soon. I don't want to cancel on her. I want to see her."

Van got a stubborn look on his face, his arms crossing over his chest. "Then I guess we should each date on our own."

"Is Van Halen breaking up again?" The sheriff was excellent with sarcasm. "This is an eighties nightmare."

Zane groaned. "That was cold, man. I thought you two were a solid pair."

"I did, too." Van stepped away and started toward the employee locker room.

Hale was left feeling like the world had violently turned on him.

He'd never dated a woman on his own. Never. He'd had sex. In some of the group homes he'd lived in, there had been young women who'd invited him to their beds. And a young man. He'd tested the waters and decided he was wired one way, though he'd enjoyed the intimacy of being with the man. He'd enjoyed how close they'd been, how much of themselves they could share.

Then he'd met Van, and while they never got sexual with each other, they had the deepest relationship of Hale's life. He didn't have a brother who bailed him out. He didn't even have siblings he couldn't count on but who might at least give him some sympathy.

He had Van, and now he was starting to wonder how much longer his best friend would be around. Was it worth losing Van for a woman who would walk away in a few weeks? Was he pushing this because internally he wanted to get to the moment when he had to choose between Bliss and his best friend? Just so he could get it over with?

Nate pointed a finger his way. "Don't."

"Okay." He wasn't sure what he wasn't supposed to do, but it seemed better to agree with the sheriff.

Nate's eyes narrowed. "Tell me you're not thinking about calling the woman you're interested in and telling her you can't see her."

It wasn't like she would be around forever. She was here to do one thing and then she would go back to her home.

On the other hand, it seemed like Van was getting tired of the life they shared here, and he might be ready to move on, too. Hale couldn't be sure he would even get an invite to go to Dallas.

He definitely wasn't sure he wanted to leave Bliss.

This was the moment when he would normally retreat and go back to his quiet place somewhere at Van's side.

But something was changing. He was changing. He could walk away or he could test these new relationships. One path was fairly safe and put off the conflict. One made him vulnerable, but maybe that was okay here.

"Yeah, that was going through my head." Hale chose his path. Maybe before Dallas he would have receded, but after spending all those months watching how a chosen family could work, he wanted more for himself. Being here in Bliss around multiple families like the one he wanted had helped too. "Am I making a mistake?"

"No, Van is," Zane said with a frown. "I'm not sure what's going through his head."

"Of course you do," Nate replied, sending his partner a

knowing look.

Zane's eyes rolled but it looked more self-deprecating than anything. "Of course I do." His expression cleared, and he sent his focus Hale's way. "I would bet you don't advocate for yourself, Hale. It's easy to let your partner call all the shots because deep down there's a part of you that doesn't trust yourself to do it."

That was a fair assumption. "Van's kind of been the leader."

"Yeah, that only works for so long," Zane began. "Almost every friendship or partnership or any relationship starts like that. One person tends to take the lead, but the problem is people grow and change and if the relationship can't do the same, it tends to die."

It hurt his heart but Zane was right. "You think even if I give in, our friendship is toast because I want to make some decisions?"

"No," Nate said with a shake of his head. "Absolutely not. I think you and Van are in a place every partnership gets to sooner or later. You've shaken him up a bit. He needs some time. He'll probably think about this for a while and come to the conclusion he doesn't want to wear a condom either and he'll have this big revelation, and I hope it happens in private and not in the middle of a town hall session."

"I actually think we should all wear condoms." Hale was a bit confused.

Nate's head shook and there was a soft look in his eyes. "That's an inside joke. What you should understand is that Zane and I have been where you and Van are. One of us was ready to go all in and the other was kind of an asshole who needed his ass kicked."

Zane grinned. "Him. He was the asshole, but we worked it out. Go on your date, man. Let Van go on his and you can both see what happens without your other half. Maybe it works out. Maybe it's what you need. Or maybe it's terrible and you both figure out once and for all you're better together than apart."

"And what if I find out we're better together and he figures out I drag him down?" He said the quiet part out loud.

"I don't think that's going to happen." Zane put a hand on his shoulder. "If Nate understands Van, then I get you, man. I've been right where you are. It took seeing Callie again to make me understand I deserved to be a full partner in this relationship. And it wasn't Nate who made me feel that way. It was me. I went through some shit in my childhood that made me hesitate, made me more confident in Nate's abilities to guide us through whatever we came up against. It might surprise you but no one was happier for me stepping up and making some decisions than Nate."

"It was good to finally have some balance between us, but it was also a challenge because I had made those decisions for years," Nate admitted. "We had to find a new way to work together, but if we hadn't I believe Zane and Callie would be married and I would be miserable somewhere in a big city with a job I thought I wanted."

It was pretty close to where he and Van were right now. "How did you solve it?"

"I got my head out of my ass and Zane and Callie gave me the space to figure it out," Nate explained. "Look, he's not going anywhere soon. He's got another whole semester to figure this out. Date this woman and see where it leads, and he'll do the same. Be his friend. Listen to him and make him listen to you. If he doesn't, then you'll know. And hey, there's always some sad-sack single dude who comes into town and says no way am I sharing a woman with someone else and a couple of years later they end up in bed with Ty Davis."

That made Hale snort. Because Michael Novack had probably said those words and now he shared a bed with a man he'd claimed to dislike. Of course there was a woman between them.

He hated the thought of going into this without Van, but Nate was right. He had a decision to make, and he wasn't willing to float through life any longer. He could build something here, something he couldn't in Dallas.

It might be time to choose himself.

It was definitely time to choose her.

"Thanks," he said, moving toward the dining room again. "I'll think about everything you've said. Elisa should be here soon. Tell Van I'll see him at home."

He walked away because it was almost time for his date.

Chapter Three

Van slammed into the locker room and wondered when the fuck his day had gone to hell.

And then he stopped because he was way more angry than he should be. It was right there, the need to go and have this out with Hale.

Why?

He didn't get angry often. Never with Hale.

He was pissed because he was excited about seeing Elisa. More excited than he wanted to admit, and the idea that Hale was going to fuck this up for him caused this weird rage he was feeling.

His cell phone buzzed, and he was happy for the distraction.

Until he saw who it was. Jake. His brother who had everything and never once fucked up the world.

His brother who had shown him such kindness and opened his home to him and offered him a future he'd never thought he could have. Yeah, that brother. He was on the edge and hated the nasty jealousy he was feeling. He shoved it down deep and answered the phone. "Hey, Jake."

"Hey," Jake answered, and there was something going on in the background. Music was playing somewhere behind Jake. "I'm sorry to bother you but I haven't gotten your tuition bill in and I thought it was due soon."

Yep. That brother who wanted to make sure he didn't miss paying for a grown-ass man's tuition because he'd promised to help out. "I don't actually register until January. I think I'm going to be able to pay for this semester. I've got some money saved up, and we don't have to worry about rent for a couple of months."

Because Hale had worked out a deal with the Taggarts that allowed them to live in the cabin while Hale was renovating it, and when he was done they would move straight into the Hollister-Wright's cabin. Callie and her family would be staying at the Talbot estate until the new addition was ready for move-in.

It was a job that could last longer than the spring, long into the summer, and he would have a decision to make.

"I would rather you saved," Jake said. "Dallas real estate isn't cheap, and even rent can be expensive. I'm looking around trying to find a good starter place for the two of you. Luckily I found some fixer uppers since Hale's so good with renovations. By the way, I've already got a list of clients lined up for him. He won't have trouble finding work."

He wasn't having any trouble here. Hale had a long list of people waiting for his services, and he'd caught Hale more than once looking longingly at real estate listings in the area.

"That's great. I'll let you know when I'm going to register," Van conceded. "But you have to know I intend to pay you back."

"You can pay me back by taking over the marketing team one day. I'm not joking, brother. This guy is killing me. Adam hired him, and he thinks we're some kind of happy-ass, 'we'll track down the family dog if you pay us enough' company. He wants us to do commercials. I'm not doing commercials."

But commercials sold, and he wasn't actually opposed to that for Miles-Dean, Weston, and Murdoch Investigations. They wouldn't be happy family dog commercials since what the company specialized in was missing persons. Actually, what he thought they should do was work with some cold case television shows or podcasts. They could build their name in a viral way. Still, he wasn't going to argue with Jake. The way to sell an idea like that was to work on Adam first. If he could get Adam on board with that form of marketing, Jake would follow.

Of course if he could figure out a way to make Hale slightly more talkative, he could try to sell a renovation show. Hale was brilliant when it came to fixing things and coming up with ways to make things work on a small budget. Given the cabin they were working on now, it would be a renovation/ghost hunters crossover show. *Flip or Haunt. Love It or Sage It.* The possibilities were endless.

"I don't think you should hand over your entire marketing team to a kid who recently graduated from college," Van began and then winced. "I should amend that. I'm not exactly a kid. How about to a dude just getting his shit together at almost thirty."

"Stop," Jake said, his tone going deep. It was times like this it was easy to remember his brother had been in the military, and he hadn't been doing simple jobs. His brother had been Special Forces and damn good at his job. "Don't talk about yourself like that or you're going to end up meeting with my friend Kai."

Kai was a therapist. "You know I've been to therapy before."

Jake chuckled over the line. "You've been to a shaman and had your palm read many times. I'm joking about sending you to Kai, but it's not such a terrible thing to do. It can be good to talk things out."

"Hale wants to date a woman he met today but I met a woman, too, and now we're fighting over who to date." The words came out before he could stop them. He sounded like a five-year-old fighting over a toy with his brother.

Jake was quiet for a moment.

"I'm sorry." This was why he didn't talk things out. Because most of his problems were stupid and caused by himself.

"No," Jake said over the line. "Don't be sorry. So Hale changed the rules on you and you're having a problem with it. Did you fight with him?"

There was one problem with that question. "We don't have rules."

Jake chuckled. "Of course you do. Every relationship has rules, especially ones like ours. We have to. We have to have rules and roles, and even when we don't think they're there we have boundaries we don't want our partner to cross."

"But I don't," Van argued. "Or at least I didn't think I did. I haven't consciously made decisions for us. It just happened."

"Hale has always been okay with deferring to you. I'm going to admit that I did this a lot with Adam. He had more opinions than I did, stronger opinions about things I didn't care about," Jake admitted. "It was easy to let Adam make a lot of the decisions because it didn't matter to me. The big stuff, I would put my foot down and Adam understood."

"So you were always a D/s couple, and you were the indulgent top." This was a fun thing to tease his brother about.

"You spent too much time with Big Tag." Jake's tone had gone distinctly disgruntled. "But there is some truth in what you're saying, and turn it around on yourself, little bro, because you and Hale are so much like me and Adam. And when I say that I don't mean you're me. Hale is very much like me and you're Adam. Hale's foot came down for the first time, and you need to figure out why and if you can handle it."

"I'm not the submissive one." He hadn't even thought in those terms until he'd spent time with his brother. He didn't do the whole lifestyle thing like Jake and Adam and their wife, Serena, but he'd learned a few things. There were aspects of D/s that worked and explained non-sexual relationships, too. He couldn't use the word *normal*. He wasn't sure normal was a thing.

"Neither am I. Honestly, neither is Adam. He floats in a middle ground that works for all of us. Hale's the same. He doesn't have to be in control twenty-four seven. He doesn't mind giving you the right to make decisions he feels are more important to you than to him. But now he's found something he does care about, and you fight him on it."

Put like that it made him sound like an asshole. "I've always found our women. I wish he would give this a try. I think he'll be crazy about her."

"And he's actually into someone else. Why should he give up the woman he wants to date?" Jake asked. "Why not let him have this one?"

How could he explain this to his brother? He barely understood it himself. "Because I think she's special. Because I felt some connection I've never felt before, and I want to explore that before she leaves."

"So she's a tourist?" Jake asked.

Van had an excellent counterpoint. "Yes, but so is his woman."

"All right. Let me see if I have this right. You are both willing to have a major conflict over two women who won't be around a couple of weeks from now," Jake said. "Have you met his woman?"

"No, and he hasn't met mine."

"Maybe you should," Jake offered. "Why don't you meet her, let him meet yours, and then talk about it. Or spend the next week seeing the woman you want and letting Hale do the same. You'll figure out quickly if you're at a breaking point. I'm worried because it sounds like you are, and you need to get ready for that if it's going to happen. You've been with Hale for a long time."

He didn't want to be at a breaking point. He didn't want to imagine his life without Hale. "If I give in, do you think we'll be okay? You're right. She's only here for a little while. I don't want to lose my friend over what will inevitably be a short fling."

"It doesn't have to be."

He didn't see how. "I'm going to Dallas sometime this year. She's in North Carolina."

"And there are planes. There are opportunities there and Dallas. If you like this woman, see what happens," Jake said. "Or like I said. Meet Hale's woman. Hell, if you haven't met her, how do you know it's not the same woman? You're in Bliss. I joke about the weirdness of the locals, but that place attracts strange events. That would be funny if you're both fighting and she's the same woman."

"That's not possible. We both met her today. And mine is looking for her bio dad, who happens to probably be Mel the Alien Hunter. Hale spent the day in Alamosa. Except for..." He remembered what Hale had done this morning. Was it possible? "He got called in by Gene at the motel who said the shower had gone out in one of the rooms."

There was a knock on the door, and Zane poked his head through. "Hey, man, I know you're all about making a stand and shit, but Hale's meeting Elisa right now if you want to try to save this."

The familiar name stopped him cold. "Elisa?"

"That's what he said her name was," Zane replied. "And she's pretty, though she reminds me of someone. I can't place it."

Van knew. "Mel Hughes."

"Huh." Zane seemed to think about that for a moment. "That's weird, but she does look a bit like him."

"Holy shit," Jake breathed over the line. "Is your girl's name Elisa?"

"Weird Bliss forces win again." He remembered what Elisa had told him earlier today. "And she thinks she's meeting with a friend and his partner, and Hale took that in a Bliss definition of partner."

"What other definition is there?" Zane seemed genuinely confused.

Jake laughed, the sound booming over the cell phone.

He hung up on his brother because Hale was meeting with the most intriguing woman Van had ever met, and she thought they were a couple—he and Hale.

Did she like Hale? Or did she think he would make a fun friend, and a gay couple would be easy to hang out with?

"Oh, she thinks you're gay." Zane nodded like he'd figured out something really hard to understand.

"No, she knows I'm not." This was a serious problem. "She thinks Hale is, and he's totally into her. He thinks this is a date. She thinks this is a fun hangout, and Hale's going to get hurt if I don't turn this around."

And he was going to have to do it in his Trio T-shirt because all he had in his locker was a clean work shirt and a pair of jeans. It wasn't the kind of job where he had slacks and a nice shirt sitting around in case he needed them. He wore a T-shirt and jeans every day. He didn't keep date clothes hanging around, and now that seemed like something he shouldn't have overlooked.

It didn't matter. He raced out of the locker room because he wasn't about to leave his best friend alone.

* * * *

Elisa only briefly paused outside of Trio, and it had nothing to do with being worried about the man she was meeting inside. She'd asked about Hale and gotten nothing but praise from the man who ran the Movie Motel. Gene thought the world of him, and apparently he served as the go-to guy for most of the town's handyman needs.

Her sister had reminded her that people thought Ted Bundy was a nice guy, but Sabrina watched way too much murder TV. Elisa was sure she was following all of the rules for single women who didn't want to end up on *Dateline*. She was meeting him in a public place, and she'd parked in front of the building. The bar was on the main street and well lit.

No. She wasn't worried about meeting with Hale and his partner.

She was annoyed that her biological father still hadn't called her. No text. Nothing. Either the Harper twins had told him and he didn't care, or they'd lied to her and he probably still didn't care.

She was searching for something here, and she wasn't going to find it. If it hadn't been for tomorrow night's date with the attractive man from the festival, she might pack it up and head home in the morning.

A big SUV pulled up next to her car, and she watched as a tall man stepped out and opened the back door. A blonde woman came around from the passenger side after another big guy opened her door.

"Tell me she didn't fall asleep, Cam," the blonde was saying. "She's a bear when she wakes up before she's ready."

The man named Cam came back out with a toddler against his shoulders. "I can hold her while you and Rafe eat, and then we'll switch off."

"And if she wakes up and is a crabby baby girl, I'll take her on the dance floor and get her giggling," the man named Rafe promised. He leaned over and kissed the blonde. "Stop worrying. She's fine. It was an ear infection, and Caleb took care of it. Relax and let her fathers take care of her. You were up most of the night. I expect you to drink a couple of glasses of wine, and then Cam and I can carry both our girls out of here."

The blonde's lips curled up. "You two are the best. Have I mentioned how happy I am that I married you?"

They were chatting as they walked into the restaurant.

She was hearing things wrong because it almost sounded like the blonde had been talking about marrying both of the men. Maybe she was the one who needed a nap.

70

Maybe this was a terrible mistake and she should have stayed in North Carolina and taken the first job she was offered and been happy she'd survived. Why had she gone looking for more rejection? Her mom had been cold as ice most of the time. Any man involved with her likely had been, too.

Sometimes it was best to leave the past alone.

She rapidly made a couple of decisions. Earlier today chasing joy had seemed like a good choice, but she was tired again now, the weight of her past pressing down on her. Grief was an odd thing, and grief wasn't confined to people. She could feel grief for the parts of her life that were done, for the trauma she'd been through.

She would go inside and have dinner with Hale and his boyfriend because it would be rude to not show up. And she was hungry. Then she would text Van and let him know she was heading home tomorrow and would have to cancel.

She'd thought having a fling while she waited for her bio dad to make up his mind would be fun, but now she worried it would be one more mistake. She was good at making them.

You need to walk into every situation with the expectation that it will go poorly. That way you'll be prepared for the worst, and it will be a nice surprise if good things happen.

Her mom had not believed in the power of positive thinking.

Or she could give this the smallest amount of time and spend this evening making friends. Tomorrow there was a whole bunch of fun to be had at the festival, and tomorrow night she could find out if Van was a man she could trust enough to go to bed with once or twice. She could test the waters, find out how this new body of hers worked.

If it worked. She hoped it worked.

She pushed through Trio's doors and warmth flooded her system. It was toasty inside the bar and grill, and there was a lovely, welcoming ambiance to the place.

A pretty woman with brown hair was returning to the hostess stand and gave her the biggest smile. "Hi. Welcome to Trio. One tonight, or are you meeting someone?"

"I'm meeting some friends." She hoped they would be friends. "His name is Hale. I'm meeting him and his boyfriend. He's got dark…"

The woman was staring at her. "His boyfriend?"

There was suddenly a big man with a cowboy hat on beside her. "Yep. She's here to meet Hale and his partner. Or boyfriend. Whatever you want to call him. They're not married, you know. I'm not sure why. I think Hale's holding out on Van."

The dark-haired woman's jaw dropped as she looked up at the man who had a shiny star on his khaki button-down that marked him as the sheriff of Bliss County. "I'm confused."

The sheriff simply grinned. "Me, too. Isn't it exciting? I already called Teeny and asked if she could watch the boys for another hour or two. I promised her we would give her lots of updates."

"Okay, then." The woman turned back to her. "I'm Callie and I'm happy to take you over to Hale. His boyfriend isn't back yet, though."

"He is." The sheriff seemed to not have any crime to deal with. He stood right beside the hostess as though he wasn't going anywhere. "He got back from his shift a couple of minutes ago, and they've already had a talk about tonight's…meet-up. He was surprised, to say the least, because he also met a…friend today who he has a meet-up planned with for tomorrow."

"Is there a problem?" Elisa got the feeling there was a whole subtext she wasn't understanding.

"Not at all. Zane's going back to talk to him, but I already figured out that there has been a slight misunderstanding between the two of them," the sheriff said. "I believe this is Ms. Elisa Leal of North Carolina. Or do you prefer Lieutenant Leal?"

She was unaware she'd done anything that should have caught the sheriff's attention. "I'm no longer in the military, Sheriff. I'll ask again. Is there a problem?"

"Not at all, but your father is a careful man and running a background check before Max and Rye go out to meet with him is the least I can do. Mel trusts me and if he knows I've cleared you, he'll be more willing to meet with you." The sheriff seemed to have gone serious. "He's a good man. Just quirky and a little on the paranoid side."

Which was understandable if he'd worked in intelligence. Her mother was always cautious and suspicious of anyone new. Anyone at all, when she thought about it. "So they haven't talked to him yet?"

"They're going out there this evening," the sheriff said. "Once they explain things, Mel will want to get to know you. You're sure he's your father?"

"No, but my mom was. She wasn't one to lie. I don't know why she would have lied in a journal no one was supposed to have read." She was glad the twins hadn't blown her off, and there was still a chance to get some of her questions answered. "I'm not here to ask him for money or anything. I want to meet him because we have a connection. I'm not here to upend his life, though I understand this could come as a surprise."

"To all of us," Callie agreed. "I honestly didn't think Mel had a serious relationship until he met Cassidy. I mean I'd heard about him and the alien queen. Your mom…"

This place was weird. "Was completely human, and I don't know how serious I would say it was. At least from her end. The way she explained it in her journals their relationship was pretty casual. She saw him when he came through town. I didn't know he existed until recently. She never talked about him at all, but she wasn't one to have heart to hearts with either me or my sister. I'm glad everyone seems to think he'll be willing to meet with me. I'll keep it public if he's worried about letting me into his house."

Her father seemed as odd as the place she found herself in. Though there was something comforting about the tiny town with its mountains and snow. She doubted she would find the same comfort in this military man who was her biological father.

"Hey, I'm back here." Hale walked up behind Callie and the sheriff, one hand up in greeting. He'd changed his shirt and looked like he'd gone through a careful grooming routine because his previously slightly ruffled hair was now tamed, and he'd lost his five-o'clock shadow.

That man was hot. And weird. And the slightest bit nerdy over fixing things, and she would never have expected that would work for her. His awkward social skills combined with his utter confidence when it came to home improvement made for the strangest attraction.

Van she understood. He was classically attractive and seemed fairly smooth, but Hale was a revelation.

And a completely safe one since he had a boyfriend. She gave him a smile. "I was just telling them I was meeting you and your guy."

He seemed to consider that for a moment but waved something off. "Yeah, I think I'm alone tonight, but I'd still very much like to have dinner with you. If that's okay. I know it's kind of weird here, but I don't care. I want to spend time with you."

Yes, there was his awkwardness. Those odd words were said with such determination it made her wonder if the boyfriend had been adamant against hanging with a random chick tonight. "If you don't think it will cause you trouble."

"What if I've decided you might be worth some trouble?"

And there was the certainty that he knew what to do, that sexy confidence she was almost sure usually came off as gruff and stubborn. It might put off a lot of women, but it felt familiar to her. Probably because she was a little similar in her life. He was a lot like the town around her—strange and yet oddly like home, unsettling but she felt welcome. Still, she didn't want to cause trouble. "I don't want to come between the two of you."

"Why not?" Hale asked and then frowned and shook his head. "I mean I certainly didn't mean for you...you know...not tonight. That's obviously really quick, but somewhere down the line..."

"You expected me to break you and your boyfriend up?" She was confused.

"Boyfriend?" Hale asked.

"No." Van was suddenly moving in behind Hale, coming from the back of the restaurant. He looked exactly like he had earlier this afternoon. He still wore his Trio T-shirt, and she should have thought about the fact that she'd met him because he worked the bar's booth at the festival. It wasn't surprising he was here. "He didn't think you would break up anything but a long dry spell. He's not gay. He's from Bliss. When he says he doesn't mind you coming between him and his partner it's because that's how his relationships work. One woman. Two relatively heterosexual men."

"Relatively?" the sheriff asked, one brow raised.

"Dude, you see an awful lot of Zane's junk," Van pointed out. "You might not touch it, but it's there. I would bet you are not nearly as careful as Max and Rye."

The sheriff shrugged. "Truth, brother. Also, it's hard to be careful because Zane's dick is unnaturally large. How is it not supposed to get in the way?"

"What the hell is going on?" Now the weirdness was getting to be a bit much.

"You're confused. When Hale told you he wanted you to meet his partner, he meant it would be a date. Between all three of you," Van said as though it was perfectly normal.

"That's exactly what I said," Hale argued.

It was so not what he'd said.

"It's what she heard," Van pointed out. "It's what I should have said."

"What?" Was she being played? Or maybe the town wasn't as nice as it seemed. Maybe this was their way to get her to leave.

A big, gorgeous dark-haired man walked up behind Callie, grinning the sheriff's way. "Did the new girl figure out Hale's looking for a threesome? Dummies hadn't mentioned they were both crazy about the same woman."

"I knew that five minutes ago, Zane," the sheriff said with a snort.

Normally a guy looking for a threesome would mean he wanted two women to service him.

She was pretty sure that wasn't what was happening here in Bliss.

Callie turned her face up and let the dude—who apparently had a very large unavoidable dick—kiss her right before the sheriff leaned over and did the same.

That was the moment she caught sight of the three people she'd seen earlier.

The threesome she'd seen earlier.

Like the Harpers were a threesome.

So much suddenly made sense.

"Hey, I did want you to meet my partner," Hale was saying.

"That would be me." Van held up a hand and looked so adorable in a sexy sweet way. "I didn't mention him because I thought it would be a little much, but I totally planned on sneaking him in there."

"They were fighting over which woman to date," Zane said

with a big grin. "Except it was the same woman. You."

"So three menus?" Callie asked. "Would you like a table or a booth?"

"We're at a table right now, but maybe a booth would be cozier," Hale offered. He looked to Van. "If you're done being an asshole."

"I'm totally done being an asshole." Van gave her a smile, the kind almost guaranteed to get any woman's heart racing. "Especially since—when you think about it—I won the battle. We're seeing the woman I wanted to see."

Hale's eyes rolled. "We're seeing the woman I wanted to see. Also, I'm pretty sure I saw her first."

"But she thought I was straight," Van argued.

"Or you could get something to go," Callie offered. "Sometimes it's nice to be alone."

It might be when a woman had two gorgeous men who wanted her. Elisa hadn't experienced that.

"The booth will be fine."

Maybe there was still some joy to be chased right here in Bliss.

Chapter Four

"Is it a cult?" Elisa asked.

She looked awfully pretty as she glanced around the crowded dining room. There were plenty of perfectly normal tourists hanging out, but there were definitely more than a few of the regulars, and by regulars he meant people who slept three to a bed. Elisa was studying Trio as though trying to figure the place out.

Hale could promise her Bliss was extremely easy. Live and let live and love and battle aliens. Still, he could see where she would be concerned. "I don't think so. There is a church, but the pastor isn't actually in a threesome. Unless you count God. He talks a lot about keeping God close, so technically, maybe."

Van's jaw had actually dropped open, and that was how he knew he was a dumbass who should stop talking. "No. It is not a cult."

"He should know. He's been involved in at least two." Hale couldn't seem to do what he needed to do. This was the time when he should fade into the background and let Van handle the whole charm offensive part of the seduction. It was what they did. The actual sex was his time to shine.

He didn't want that with her.

"Really?" Van shook his head. "That is where you go? First, I did not belong to the People of Heaven. I was five. Mom liked their produce, and we were stuck in that town until we managed to fix the RV. And I only went to that weird one where they believed humans were rapidly evolving into cloud creatures because there was a cute girl there."

"I was only saying you would know what a cult looked like." He snapped his fingers as a thought hit his brain. "Hey, Hope Glen was actually involved in a cult." Or maybe that wasn't a helpful fact. "Do you think that means she's more or less likely to join another one? I mean when you think about it, there are a lot of meetings in this town and we have all kinds of community events. And there's some kind of secret room out at the Talbot estate that a lot of the throuples of this town visit."

Elisa's eyes had gone wide as her gaze moved from one of them to the other. Like she was watching the weirdest tennis match ever.

"Are we still in some odd competition I don't understand since we just figured out we were always talking about the same woman?" Van asked.

"No. I was answering her question. I don't think it's a cult." He was sticking with that answer. It was better than admitting that maybe it was. But a cool one. One he kind of wanted to be a part of. Technically there would have to be a leader to a cult, and he was pointing Talbot's way. Everyone tended to do what Talbot wanted them to. Except for Nell and Henry. Well, and Max. And the doc. And Mel and Cassidy, if they thought aliens might be involved.

When he thought about it, it was actually pretty tough to be Talbot.

Not a cult.

"I'm sorry. I don't understand what's going on. So you both thought you'd found a date and you were fighting?" Elisa asked. She'd shrugged out of her coat and wore an emerald green sweater that contrasted beautifully with her skin.

Van seemed way more comfortable with that question. "Yes. We hadn't talked all day until a couple of minutes ago, and neither one of us mentioned your name."

"But I was up front about the date. She knew she was meeting you, too." He thought he should get credit for his honesty. "Van was counting on the fact that I'm not hideously unattractive, and you wouldn't notice when he slipped me in."

Her lips pursed as though she was holding in whatever she was going to say. Or maybe a laugh. It was good if he amused her. "I would definitely have noticed." She paused as Callie dropped off their drinks. Two beers for them and a glass of Cab for her. "I'm sorry I misunderstood, Hale."

"Don't be sorry," Van interjected smoothly. "He didn't exactly lay it all out for you. Now in my defense, I understand that the idea of dating two guys can be intimidating for a woman, so I was taking a softer approach."

"The one where I wake up asking who the extra guy is?" A brow had risen over those pretty eyes of hers, and he could see the military officer was still in there.

Van winced. "I was going to introduce you. I was."

"I was absolutely going to introduce you to Van." Hale liked being the good one. He got the feeling she was not as irritated with him as she was with Van. It was not a position he was normally in.

Her lips curled up in the sweetest smile. "Yes, you did mention that. You could have mentioned his name. If you had, I would have gotten clued in when I met him. There couldn't be too many Vans around."

"You didn't mention my name?" Van huffed. "I was some random dude who hangs around with you?"

Hypocrite. "Uh, I didn't exist in your scenario."

Van sighed and turned to Elisa. "I wanted you to meet him because I've found when I blurt out that I come with a friend, the woman I'm interested in usually walks away."

He was wrong about the timing, and Hale didn't want to set unrealistic expectations. "We don't come at exactly the same time. It's not like it's coordinated or anything."

Van's jaw dropped again, and Hale realized he'd taken that way too literally. He was pretty overstimulated and sometimes missed cues when he was anxious.

He might have fucked this up.

Except Elisa's head dropped back and she laughed, a truly magical sound because he was almost certain she hadn't had a lot of laughter in her life lately. When her head came back up, she was smiling and had to reach up to brush a tear away. She took a long breath. "Oh, you are going to be fun, Hale." She sobered. "Is the awkward thing a bit? Or is there something I should know? I ask because it's better to put everything out there. Like the cancer thing."

"Are you asking if I'm on the spectrum?" Hale thought that was what she was interested in.

"I guess what I'm asking is if this is the genuine you. You take things very literally and you don't mince words. You seem to say what you mean, but it wouldn't be the first time a guy had an act," she said quietly.

"Oh, he's not smart enough to have an act," Van shot back. "That is one hundred percent Hale. And now you know why I sometimes try to sneak him in."

"He is smart." Elisa was now giving Van a death stare.

Oh, he could lose her if he didn't put this on the right footing. "He's joking. It's payback for all the times I blurt out something he would rather I kept to myself. We're guys. We call each other dumbasses all the time. Trust me. He knows how smart I can be when I want to. He's the one who built me up enough to get me to try to do the things I've always wanted to do."

"Sorry. He's my best friend in the world." Van was entirely serious now. "We've basically been together our entire adult lives. I can be pretty sarcastic around him. As for whether or not this is the genuine Hale, he wouldn't know how to be anything else. He's probably on the spectrum but he doesn't have a diagnosis, and all that means is his brain works a little differently and he can struggle with being incredibly literal. But he's actually quite good at processing emotions. He doesn't fight them the way some of us do. He's an amazing guy, and I think I should bow out of this and let you two talk."

He started to slide out of the booth, and there was the panic again. He wasn't ready to lose Van. He was supposed to have another whole semester to fix the problem, and he suddenly knew if he pursued Elisa on his own, they would go their separate ways. This was a fork in the road, and they might not be moving in the same direction after the next few moments.

They would be friendly, but they wouldn't have the deep friendship that almost made Van half of Hale.

Elisa reached out and put a hand over Van's. "Please stay. I was surprised, but I can't say I'm not open to the experience. Especially now that I know Hale's not a player."

"What would I be playing?" Hale asked. They hadn't talked about any games. He was good at games, especially the ones with the complicated rules.

Van grinned at Elisa. "See what I mean? And I'm sorry. You are absolutely the most gorgeous woman to come through town since we've gotten here, and I didn't want to lose the chance to spend some time with you."

So that was not about game playing, or rather not the kind he'd been thinking of. It was the nasty kind of games, the one a man could play with a woman that hurt her. It was good she didn't think he was a player.

She sat back and picked up the menu, seeming to relax. "Excellent. Then we'll put all our cards on the table and be up front and honest. Hale, I'm glad you're attracted to women because I'm attracted to you. But you should understand I thought you were interesting enough to be friends with, too. So, just to get it all out there, I'm divorced. I've been divorced for two years. I haven't dated at all since then, so you will be my first flirtation since. I used to be in the military. Now I am unemployed, but I'm ready for a new challenge. I recently recovered from breast cancer, and I'm nervous about whether or not I'm still attractive."

He could clear that up for her. "You are."

She smiled again. "Thank you, but you haven't seen the part I'm worried about. I guess what I'm trying to warn you about is I'm damaged and I'm working on it. I don't know how long I'll be in town, but if my dad has any interest in getting to know me, I might hang around for a while. So if you are looking for a quick lay with a tourist who you never have to see again, I might not be your girl."

"I'm not looking for a quick hookup. I'd like to get to know you. I'm glad you might stay in town," Hale replied without thinking about how eager he might look. He *was* eager. There was something about this woman that pulled at him. She didn't seem bothered by how weird he could be.

"Then I have to be honest and let you know that while I'm not looking for a quick hookup, I also don't know that I'm a good bet if you're in the market for a boyfriend." Van sat back and seemed a bit grim. "I'm about to start a new semester of college, and it's my last. When the time comes, there's a job waiting for me in Dallas. I have to concentrate on work."

"We're just having dinner tonight." Hale didn't like the way this was going. "Nothing more."

"Yes, we are," Elisa agreed. "But I appreciate the honesty. I don't see why we can't go with the flow for a while. I simply didn't want you to think I'll be gone in the morning."

Wait. That sounded like a good thing. "I don't want you gone in the morning."

"I don't think I'll want you gone in the morning, either," Van agreed. "So, we're going to enjoy dinner and if you feel comfortable, we would like to invite you back to our place for a drink or whatever we choose. I have a ton of crazy stories about growing up in a motor home. Hale can do some weird things and entertain the hell out of you. You might find us charming enough to stay the night."

"I think I will accept that invitation." Elisa's eyes went back to the menu. "What's good here?"

Awesome. They'd gotten through the dangerous part. Well, hopefully. It was Bliss and there was no guarantee there wouldn't be a mob war or a serial killer. He should probably wait to tell her about that. "Most of the menu is organic. Even the beef is from a local ranch and the cows are grass fed and no growth hormones were used."

"I think she meant what's tasty," Van corrected.

Ah, but he had a good reason to have made that mistake. "She's had cancer. Sometimes a healthy diet and avoiding processed foods is part of the recovery plan."

Van nodded. "Oh, well, the chicken salad is actually quite good. Totally organic, and the chickens are raised a couple of miles from here. And I don't believe that the spirits of angry chickens will tear up my gut. Nell makes that shit up."

"I do try to eat well," Elisa replied, her eyes warm on him. "But I can have a couple of fun meals, too. How is the chili?"

He loved Zane's chili. "It's excellent, and he makes the most delicious cornbread that he can now cook because I fixed the bread oven. They do this weird thing here and slather it in butter and molasses. I love it."

"Then that sounds like a meal to me." She waved over Callie.

Hale sat back, finally comfortable that this could work out.

* * * *

Van watched as Hale…was that dancing? Technically he might meet the definition of dancing. There was music and Hale's body was moving, but he managed to make it pretty awkward.

"Do you think he's having a seizure? Should we call the doc?" Cameron Briggs's head tilted slightly as he watched Hale moving on the dance floor.

Elisa was faring much better, but the truth was she was on the awkward side as well. Like there hadn't been much dancing in her life. They'd had a lovely dinner, but he'd barely noticed the food. She was feminine but in a different way. She was upfront and honest and didn't hold back. She took charge when she decided to, and that did something for him.

This wasn't a woman who would float through life for long. If she decided she wanted them, she would want a commitment and… He was getting way ahead of himself.

"He is showing off his moves." He wasn't about to tell Cam that he agreed that Hale looked like he might be having a stroke. The big deputy wasn't a close friend, though he seemed nice enough.

"Well, I'm glad your lady seems to not mind." Cam chuckled as Elisa sort of ducked to avoid Hale's water sprinkler move.

It was kind of a workout. "She's very open minded."

She would fall into bed with them. Maybe tonight. His whole body hummed with anticipation, but there was some piece of him that was already bracing because he rather thought this might be more complicated than it looked.

"I'm glad to hear that." Cam stood beside him at the edge of the dance floor, a beer in his hand. It was getting late and the crowd inside the pub had thinned out, many hitting the dance floor or playing pool in the back room. "Is she really Mel's daughter?"

"She seems to think so."

Cam shook his head. "Wow. I never thought Mel would do anything so normal as have a child. It's weird to think of him as having a life before Bliss."

"According to Max it was during Bliss. He was already living here but he did some work for the military as an intelligence officer." Just because the dude was whacky now didn't mean he hadn't been a serious force in the world once. People changed, grew. Grew apart.

"It's hard to think of Mel leaving town. He barely travels anymore," Cam remarked. "Says he's happier here. You know now that I think about it, he told me once he'd seen the world and didn't need to ever leave Bliss again. I guess I thought he was talking about Creede or Del Norte. It's weird to think of Mel in Europe or Asia."

Van could understand that. He'd seen a lot of the world. At least the parts of it his parents' RV could get to. They'd once gone as far south as Panama, where they'd discovered they would have to ship the RV across the Darian Gap if they wanted to get to Brazil. It had been cost prohibitive, and they'd spent the winter on an organic commune in Costa Rica. "He would definitely have had to travel if he was in the military. My brother was a Green Beret. He's been all over the world. But he still likes to travel."

"Well, Mel does not, so I hope your friend out there doesn't mind spending some time here," Cam remarked. "Mel is going to want to get to know her. I hope she doesn't think he's too weird. I would hate for her to take one look at him and run the other way."

Well, she was still out there dancing with the dude who did look like he could use some medical intervention. "I think she'll be cool. She told me she was thinking about hanging around for a while. She's in between jobs. She might try to find some temp work and see how things go with her dad."

"You don't say." Cam nodded as though he approved. "Well, that's good news. I'll have to think about that. Now, I came over here to talk to you about something else."

Elisa might stay for a while, but where the hell would he be a year from now? There was nothing for him professionally in Bliss. He hadn't gone back to college so he could work at a bar. It would be a complete waste of his degree and his brother's money and faith in him. There wasn't a lot of need for a marketing specialist here in Bliss. It wasn't like there were offices here. Every business was a small business, and they tended to do all their own work.

"Van?"

Had he missed something? "Yeah?"

"I lost you for a minute. I wanted to tell you that I went out to the lodge today and it turns out someone was looking for you. Someone went in a couple of days back and asked about you and Hale," Cameron said. "Lucy remembered a woman coming in and asking the front desk about you, but she didn't remember who. She's going to find out and hopefully get back to me tomorrow. I'd like to talk to whoever met with the woman who asked about you."

Damn it. He'd managed to forget about what the sheriff had said. "So you think someone came looking for me, the lodge gave them my forwarding address, and then they trashed the place when they couldn't find me?"

"I don't know," the deputy admitted. "But I don't like the coincidence. It's been quiet around here for a while."

So the deputy was bored. "The murder at the lodge a couple of weeks ago wasn't enough for the season?"

Cameron's lips quirked up. "That didn't even involve a citizen. It was only coincidence that Lucy got pulled in the middle of that mess. This feels more like it's directly attached to you or Hale."

"Well, if it's a woman angry at me for something, I don't know who it could be." It wasn't like his sex life had been going crazy while he was here. "I've had my head down, man. I've been either working or going to class. Hale's spent pretty much every minute fixing something. We had a couple of hookups at the lodge, but they weren't serious, and any woman from there would know exactly where to find us so she wouldn't need to ask."

"And if she works there, the front desk would know her," Cam pointed out. "Anyone in the last couple of years who seemed like they might be unstable?"

Van smiled because the only unstable one here was Hale on his feet. He jerked to the music and kind of stumbled but then unsuccessfully tried to make that shit look cool.

He might fall in love with Elisa simply for the fact that she brought out another side of Hale.

Cam had asked him a question. "Uhm, are you asking if I ever slept with a crazy chick?"

"No, you are absolutely the dude who sleeps with crazy chicks. I'm asking if any one of them stands out," Cam corrected.

It was sad when the question had to be asked that way. "Hale and I had a relationship with a woman in Dallas who was upset when we left, but I don't think she was violent. She just didn't believe we would actually leave. It wasn't love or anything, but she liked being able to say she had two boyfriends. There's probably more over the years, but I can't imagine anyone actually being angry enough with me to tear up a place where I used to live."

"And Hale?" Cam asked as the music started to fade and a slower beat took its place.

Out on the dance floor, Rafe took the wife he shared with the deputy in his arms and started to dance with her.

No one thought a thing about it. When Jake went out with Adam and Serena, they always got looks. There might be some from tourists here, but for the most part, Bliss seemed like a haven for the kind of relationship he wanted.

"Hale doesn't ever piss anyone off. He doesn't honestly connect with a lot of people. He sticks to himself." Except here in Bliss, Hale had actually made friends. He had the weirdest relationship with Max Harper, who seemed to think of himself as Hale's mentor.

Hale didn't need a mentor. Hale had him. Hale had always had him.

"Well, I'll let you know what we find out from the lodge." Cam straightened up as he looked back at the dining room. "It looks like Sierra is up. Gemma was watching her, but she'll want some dinner now. It's been a rough couple of nights, man. Kids are hard and there are three of us. I have no idea how two people handle it."

The idea of kids… He didn't even know what he thought about that. He didn't think about it at all because that was something that felt so far in the future he didn't have to. He lived in the moment.

But if he always lived in the moment, he wouldn't have much of a future.

Cam walked back to take care of his daughter as Hale and Elisa came off the dance floor. Holding hands.

Hale was holding her hand. Hale wasn't particularly affectionate but there he was, clutching this woman like she meant something.

Could she mean something?

"I think you should take the slow dance." Hale brought her hand up, offering it to Van. "I should practice more before I try. I do not have any rhythm, and I'm worried I'll step all over her toes."

Elisa grinned his way. "You do have rhythm. It's just a different rhythm from the music." She turned that high-wattage smile on Van. "What do you say? Wanna dance?"

That seemed like way too much temptation, but he'd never been a guy who was good at walking away from something he wanted. He was the guy who was excellent at getting his stupid heart broken, and he didn't even hesitate because he never learned.

He took her hand and led her out to the dance floor where other couples were swaying to the music.

He eased his arm around her waist and gently brought her close, very much enjoying how good she felt in his arms. He liked that she could look him in the eyes. "You're lucky. The floor is full of couples tonight. Usually there's at least one weird threesome trying to figure out how to dance together."

He always found it amusing. The woman in the middle would have to twist and turn to try to keep in contact with both her partners. Often one of the dudes couldn't dance and made it all look weird. And yet they always made it look like none of that weirdness mattered. To them it wasn't weird at all. It was everything they wanted. They were connected and happy, and dancing was simply another way to be together.

She glanced around as though confirming what he was saying. "I hadn't noticed. I was having too much fun with Hale."

His conversation with Cam was completely forgotten, along with all the reasons why this was a terrible idea. All that mattered now was being here with her. "He doesn't dance much. Actually not at all. I don't think I've ever seen him dance, and now I know why."

"He's not that bad," she retorted and then shook her head. "He's sweet."

He'd never once thought of Hale being sweet. "You seem to bring out that side of him. He's usually quite taciturn. He's talked more tonight than I've heard in a long time. You and Hale seem very connected. But I'm glad you're willing to let me dance with you, too."

A soft look came over her face. "I don't dance much, either.

I'm afraid I might be as bad as Hale. I guess that's what kind of makes it okay. I'm not worried about embarrassing myself in front of him."

"You dance fine." Even the little awkwardness in her movements called to him. They made him wonder how she would move when she was comfortable, when she trusted the hands on her. Would that charming awkwardness fall away, replaced with pure sensuality?

She felt so fucking good in his arms. He wasn't sure if it had simply been a long dry spell or if it was all about her.

"Well, it's been a long time," she said. "Not much dancing in the military. Well, there is. We have parties and everything, but I usually didn't go to them. I make it sound like it was all dreary responsibility, but I think it was more about me than the actual Army. Now that I look back, I can see where people tried to engage me and I didn't know how to connect."

"Didn't know how?" She seemed so open but she talked about how disconnected she was.

"My family wasn't outwardly affectionate. Not inwardly affectionate either. My mom taught me to tamp down most of my emotions from an early age," she admitted. "She didn't have an easy life, and she kind of bred her pessimism into me and my sister. It's taken a while to realize that the impulse to suspect everything and everyone doesn't actually come from me."

He knew exactly where she'd gotten that from. "Ah, so you went to therapy."

She winced slightly. "It's still weird to say that because it's the last thing my mother would have wanted, but yes. It's made a big difference in my life and my sister's. It's absolutely why I'm here tonight. If you'd met me years ago, I wouldn't have given either of you the time of day, and not because I wouldn't have found you attractive. I would have thought it was ridiculous to even entertain the idea that you or Hale might want me."

He could prove her wrong and hoped he had the chance to do that tonight. "You don't understand men then. We're pretty simple creatures. If we tell you we think you're hot and want to get to know you, we probably do."

"Well, I believe you. I'm not so sure about all men. Hale is…

Well, I've never met anyone quite like him before. I like him a lot. I like you, too. I've definitely never met a man with your background."

"Oh, there aren't many of us out there. Even the ones who start out going nomad tend to give up after the kids come. Not my parents." He brought her a bit closer. "Sometimes I wonder if we're doomed to repeat our parents' mistakes."

"My therapist swears the answer to that question is no," she promised and then let her head drop down to his shoulder. "Is this okay?"

"It's perfect." He swayed with her, enjoying how easily she moved with him, following his steps.

"It does feel that way," she said quietly. "I am going to try very hard to trust that it's okay to feel this way for a little while."

"It is." Even though he'd been worried earlier, he knew what he was saying was correct. It was okay to live in this particular moment. In this tiny slice of his life, he still had a best friend who was waiting for him, and he had this place and he had her. He probably wouldn't have any of those things later. Time moved and stole and never seemed to give back, so all a person had at the end of their days were the memories they made. He intended to make a few right now. "Do you think you want to come back to our place for the night?"

Her head came back up. "I would be with both of you?"

He wasn't sure why she was asking, but he intended to be honest with her. "Yes. Have you decided you only want one of us? If it's Hale, I can back away."

He wanted her badly, but he wasn't sure he could hurt Hale that way. If he was the one she wanted, he might have to choose his friend.

"No, I want you both. I'm just wrapping my head around the idea," she replied. "I'm trying to picture it, to think about how it would work."

He reached up and cupped her cheek. "Don't. Let it happen. Understand that if you decide you don't want it, we'll stop. No questions. No trying to change your mind. You're in charge of this. But give us the chance to show you how good this can be. Give us the chance to learn what gives you pleasure. That's what will give us the greatest pleasure—knowing we've given it to you."

Her skin flushed a pretty pink. "Okay. Then I think I would like to go home with you and Hale."

His whole body felt alive suddenly. "Then let's get Hale. I'll grab a bottle of wine and some beer from the bar and we can go home and get comfy. We'll go at your pace, Elisa. If all you want to do tonight is talk and cuddle, then we'll be happy for it."

She stared at him for a long moment. "I'm pretty sure I'll be up for a little more than that, but I don't mind the idea of talking. I'd love to know how you and Hale met. I'd really love to know about the first time one of you suggested 'hey, let's share a girl.'"

"Now see, that's a fun story because Hale didn't get what I meant and…" He was about to go into how that night had gone when he realized this one had gone straight to hell.

The music was still playing, but everyone else on the floor had gone perfectly still, all eyes on something—or someone—behind him.

It was Bliss. It could be anything. It could be a deranged biker gang coming into town to start WWIII and he wouldn't be surprised.

He moved to get in front of Elisa when he realized they weren't in danger. Though his plans for the night definitely were.

"Who is that?" Elisa asked as she caught sight of the man standing at the edge of the dance floor.

"That's your dad."

Chapter Five

Elisa wondered what had gone wrong. One minute she'd been kind of floating along and perfectly comfortable with the decision to sleep with two hot guys and the next, the world seemed to shift. Van stepped in front of her like she needed a shield. The music was still playing but it was obvious something had gone very wrong.

Or not. She didn't actually feel a threatening presence. She'd been in the military long enough to have developed pretty good instincts as to when danger had entered the building, and she didn't feel that. No. Van was wrong. This was more an air of anticipation.

Though it was sweet that he thought he needed to shield her. She could kill a man in ten different ways and absolutely had more combat and close-quarter fighting training than most of the people in this bar combined. Though she would bet the sheriff and the big guy who owned the place could give her a run for her money.

And then she wasn't thinking about the possibilities of having to fight her way out of the situation—next to none—because she caught sight of the man standing at the edge of the dance floor.

He was tall, topping out at least six foot three, but there was a slight hunch to his shoulders that made him seem smaller. The hunch didn't feel like some mark of age. No, it was almost a readiness, as though the man was constantly on edge and prepared for battle. She couldn't tell the color of his hair because he was wearing a trucker hat, but his eyes were so familiar to her. "Who is that man?"

Van seemed to relax. "That's your dad."

Elisa had to take a deep breath because the world seemed to oddly slow down as she took in the man who wore overalls and had a big dog at his side. And a woman with long gray braids who was grinning like this was the best day ever.

The music suddenly changed from the sexy R&B song that had served as the soundtrack to her saying yes to kinky ménage sex to the opening song of *Lion King*.

Someone was an asshole.

It made for a deeply surreal moment.

The man who might be her dad was frowning as he stared at her.

Was he going to publicly denounce her? Tell her to go away? That he wanted nothing to do with her?

He took a step toward her, and his eyes narrowed. "The Harper boys tell me you're looking for me. You from the government?"

She moved around Van and noticed Hale had made his way to her side, too. Well, it was good to know at least she wouldn't be alone in her humiliation. "I'm not from the government. My name is Elisa Leal. My mom was…"

"Nora." He stopped a mere foot from her, and his gaze softened. "Nora Leal. You look so much like your momma. She was… Well, she was a good partner. She was smart and brave, and I wish she could have accepted love the way she deserved."

Tears pierced her eyes because that did not sound like a man who was about to throw her out of town. It sounded like a man who'd really known her mom. "I do, too. I'm a lot like her, but I'm trying to do better for myself."

"Is it true?" The man asked. "What the boys said… They told me you think you might be my daughter. They said you look like me, but I don't see it. You're far too pretty for anyone to say that."

"I see it." The woman with braids had joined him, and there had never been anything cold about her. She was a warm presence. "She has your eyes. I don't think she's the alien one." She turned her attention to Elisa. "See, we've always known Mel probably has a kid because the alien queen stole his sperm years ago, but you look very human."

Oh, there was a scenario she hadn't considered. That they were loony toons.

She was going to go with it. "I'm a hundred percent human."

"Of course you are. Ripley likes you," the man who was probably her dad said.

Apparently the dog was an important part of her dad's life. The good news was she liked dogs. She held a hand out, palm down, and let the dog sniff her before she offered her head up for a pat. Elisa got to one knee because this she could definitely deal with. Dogs didn't hesitate to ask for the affection they needed. "Hey, girl. You're a good girl, aren't you?"

Big doggy eyes looked up at her. She'd never had a dog as a child or an adult, but she'd been around them in the military.

"She is a good girl," the woman assured her. "I'm Cassidy. I'm your father's wife, though you should know we're technically not married because that would create a paper trail for the Reticulans to follow. But I love him and intend to spend the rest of my life with him, and that means I'm going to love you, too."

Yes, the crazy was strong with that one. Elisa straightened up and held out a hand. "Good to meet you."

A weird gasp went through the bar as someone finally unplugged the obnoxious soundtrack. They still had an audience, but she felt like the chances of Luthor Hughes lifting her up like he was showing her off to the savannah had decreased significantly.

Cassidy stared at her hand for a moment as though trying to make a decision.

Was she not a hand shaker?

Before she had the chance to take back the super-awkward offer, Cassidy was invading her space, opening her arms and pulling her into a hug.

There was a collective breath of relief.

Okay, so she had a weird woman in her arms, and she was going to go with the flow. That was what she did now. It wasn't that she didn't like hugs. She just hadn't had that many of them. So she didn't know if she liked them. Her sister hugged her. With her ex-husband, a hug usually was actually a request for sex.

So what did this hug mean?

"I'm so happy to meet you, sweetheart. I'm so happy to have you in my family."

This woman didn't know her at all. Elisa slowly moved her arms, hugging her stepmother. "Well, I hope you feel that way after you get to know me."

Her stepmom leaned back. "I'm sure I will. Why don't we sit down and have a nice talk? I'm so happy we don't have to stay in the bunker. I didn't want to miss the festival."

Her brand-new stepmom started to lead her away, and she glanced back to where Hale and Van stood.

Her crazy sex life was going to have to wait.

Thirty minutes later Elisa sat back and wondered exactly what was going on.

Her father had greeted her with seeming kindness, but then he'd let his wife take over completely.

Cassidy was beyond welcoming. She'd led Elisa over to the corner booth where they'd been joined by Max and Rye Harper, who'd come into town with Mel. From what she could tell they lived close to her father and had since they were kids.

She was glad the brothers had joined them because they were turning out to be excellent translators.

"Now, I have two sons," Cassidy Meyer was saying. "And I don't want you to be afraid of them."

"Why would I be afraid?" Sometimes she didn't completely understand what Cassidy was saying. Or her dad. When he did talk, it was usually to add something to whatever Cassidy had said. They seemed to have their own language.

"Because Leo's a therapist in Dallas, and he works with all kinds of weirdos," Max explained.

Rye's eyes rolled. "I think she's talking about the fact that she believes Leo and Wolf are the product of her time spent with aliens."

"Well, I think the fact that Leo is writing a book about all my mental health issues is way scarier than him having alien DNA," Max pointed out.

"That book is going to set a record for length," Rye said under his breath.

"They're good boys." Her father did what he seemed to do and brought it back to the topic of aliens. "Nothing to be afraid of at all, and their wife turned out to be completely human, too. All that fretting and she's just a nice human lady."

Cassidy frowned. "Well, she wouldn't take the beet."

Rye was sitting next to Elisa and leaned in as he had many times over the course of the last half an hour. "Aliens can't process whatever is in beets. So a way to tell if a person is or isn't one is to take a shot of beet juice. It's fine. If you do it quick, you don't even taste it."

Yep, this was what she was dealing with.

Max shook his head. "She was getting married, Cassidy. I know the beet shows us many miracles, but it's also hell on your teeth."

Cassidy grinned. "I like to think of it as my version of hair dye, but for my teeth. And it's good for you. Not only does it keep the aliens away, my blood pressure is perfect. Doc says I'm in peak condition for a woman my age."

She wasn't sure if they were being serious. Was this some weird version of punk the new chick? Her father hadn't said much. If he was her father.

Was this some way to get her to leave?

There it was. Suspicion.

Suspect everyone. Everything. It's the only way to keep yourself safe.

But lately she'd been wondering if her mother's version of safe was more about locking the world away and not having to ever risk her heart for anything or anyone. She wondered if her mother's version of safety would inevitably lead to loneliness and despair. "So let me see if I understand. You had some kind of relationship with an alien and you had a couple of kids by... Do aliens have genders?"

"Yes," her father said. And that was all. He was back to staring at her as if she might turn into one of the aliens he apparently hunted.

This wasn't going the way she'd planned. For a moment out there on the dance floor, it had felt like he wanted to know her. Now she was starting to wonder. He'd let his wife do all the talking. She knew what Cassidy wanted her to know, and it was mostly alien stuff and the fact that the bunker wasn't as comfortable as the cabin they shared.

Ripley had slept through all the talking, turning over on her back and sleep running from time to time. She did not seem like the alien-chasing warrior they'd named her after.

She was unsure of what she should do in this case. If all they wanted to talk about was aliens, then she should probably step away and think about heading home.

It might be for the best.

In the moment it had seemed like such a great idea to get to know Van and Hale and maybe spend a couple of wild nights with them, but she would probably make a fool of herself. What had she been thinking?

"Oh, but some of them have more than one gender. I've found aliens can be very fluid," Cassidy said with a shake of her head.

She wasn't sure what she'd really hoped for, but it definitely wasn't this.

How much longer did she have to sit here and listen to a list of aliens and their attributes? What was the polite amount of time to spend on it? Cancer. She could play the cancer card. She was so tired from fighting the cancer and needed to get to bed early. It was one thing everyone respected, and she'd talked to other survivors and they'd all decided that for at least a year after her last chemo it was a perfectly acceptable card to play. She'd earned it.

"Cassidy, my dear, could you go and ask Zane if he could make a sandwich for me? I'm a little hungry." Her father patted his wife's hand.

Cassidy seemed thrilled to do it. She scooted out of the booth. "Of course. And I'll get us some of the ice cream I keep for our special occasions."

She moved off toward the kitchen while Max and Rye seemed to pick up on some silent order Mel Hughes gave them.

They gave the excuse of going to grab another beer. Though the service had been excellent, and Elisa didn't understand why they needed to do it themselves when that Callie lady came by to check on them often. Very often.

The man who'd probably delivered half of her DNA looked

grave as he stared at her across the table. "I was worried about this. You have to forgive my wife. She doesn't understand that most people think we're crazy for the things we believe."

She hadn't expected that. "I certainly don't think that."

"But you do. It's there in the way you pulled back. I'm sorry about that, too. She's a hugger and doesn't always understand other people's boundaries." His eyes looked older than they had before. "She's the love of my life, and I have to protect her. I would like to know if you can be kind to her."

"I haven't been kind?" She was surprised at the accusation since she'd sat here and listened to everything the crazy lady had to say. She shook her head because stupid therapy made her look at things differently. Her father was right to ask the question. "I've been polite. Not kind. In my defense I haven't had much of a chance to be kind yet."

"No, but you think she's weird, and I can tell you're wondering how long you have to stay," he replied, though there wasn't bitterness to his tone. "The answer is you don't. I understand that we can be a lot. I'm sure I wasn't what you were expecting."

"I didn't know what to expect, but no, you certainly aren't what I would call my mom's type." She wasn't sure her mother had a real type beyond the dude who would always leave her.

"I wasn't, and she wasn't mine. But we worked together quite a bit over a couple of years, and we got to be what I would call friendly. Intelligence can be lonely work. It's long hours stuck together, mostly waiting for something that might or might not happen. If you want to know about my relationship with Nora, well, we spent time together when we were working but when we weren't, we didn't talk. I'm not sure she even liked me."

"She did." She'd gone over and over her mom's journals, looking for anything that would give her a piece of the story. "She thought you were excellent at your job. I'm not sure what that was though. Even in her journals she was vague about the nature of her work at that point in time. She left intelligence after I was born. I think she wanted something with more stable hours. She said she didn't contact you after she found out she was pregnant because she didn't think you would be compatible as parents. She thought it would be easier to do it by herself. She was in Europe, and you were here."

"I like to think I would have moved, but it's hard to know what we would have done in the past," her dad mused. "I know I would have wanted a relationship with you, but I also worry that I wasn't in the best place back then. I could be what your mother would have seen as erratic. I did work for the government. She provided me with logistical support, and more importantly cover because my work was classified."

"The alien stuff?"

His lips curled in a bittersweet smile. "Something like that. Nothing you would believe, darlin'. But I do want you to understand that I wouldn't have left you alone. I would have tried my hardest to be a father to you."

"It seems like you kind of were to the Harpers." The men had deferred to him the way they would have a father. They'd been careful with him, helping both he and Cassidy navigate the situation.

"I think a lot of us were father figures to Max and Rye and their sister, Brooke, after their daddy left," he admitted. "I taught them what I knew, watched out for them. I liked being around those kids. All of them, really. Elisa, I'm not sure if I can give you what you want. I'll answer all your questions to the best of my ability."

"But you don't think a relationship between us could work out." It was funny because she'd come to the same conclusion, but it hurt now that he was suggesting it. Rejection sucked even when one was prepared for it.

"I know I seem crazy, and I can try my hardest to tone that down for you. I can talk to Cass about letting you lead the discussions more. But if you're uncomfortable, I can't fix that. I see the world the way I see it."

A little bitterness flared to life. "So I'm supposed to pretend I believe in aliens if I want to hang out with you."

"No. Just be okay with the fact that Cass and I might understand a different reality than you do. This...the things we've seen and lived through, I wouldn't wish on anyone. I'm glad you don't believe because it means you've had a normal life, and maybe that was a good enough reason for the universe to deny me something I always wanted."

She pushed down the nasty feeling because something was

happening between them. He was being honest with her. "You wanted a kid."

"More than anything, but my life was complex and I didn't find a woman who was willing to be my real partner until I was far too old to be a daddy." His gaze held hers as he went grave. "I guess what I'm saying is I would rather you weren't ashamed of me."

Her heart threatened to seize. Had she been giving off that vibe? She'd had some thoughts about how weird the situation was, but she hadn't wanted him to feel this way.

What the hell was normal? She'd come into this town hoping he wasn't cold and unwelcoming, and he wasn't. He was weird and not at all like she expected and maybe a little on the outside of... He had some problems. Was she willing to push him aside so she didn't have to deal with them? The people of the town seemed to love this man. The people of this town also seemed outside the norm.

The norm sucked as much as rejection did.

"Don't cry, honey. I didn't mean to make you cry. That's the last thing I want to do." Her father reached out and put a hand on hers.

Her mother would have told her to suck it up, that this kind of emotion in public wasn't becoming. She wouldn't have reached out a hand. Elisa stared at that hand on hers. It was a strong hand, the skin worn and weathered, but there was such warmth to it.

If she'd been raised by him, would she understand how to hold a hand? Accept a hug? Defeat aliens?

Would she be comfortable with the idea of real love?

He started to pull away but she turned her hand over, stopping him and curling her fingers around his.

"I'm not good at affection, but I want to be," she admitted. "And I'm so sorry if I made you think I was feeling any kind of shame. I'm not good with emotions either, but I'm working on it. My mom wasn't physically affectionate, and I've been through some things in the last couple of years that made me pull into myself. I came here because I wanted to meet you. I'm awkward with meeting new people. Please forgive me. I don't want to stop talking, and I think Cassidy is perfectly lovely. Can we start over again?"

His hand squeezed hers. "Of course. Elisa, you should understand I'm probably not going to be good at saying no to you.

Except about…well…"

She could guess. "You can tell me what to do in case an alien comes calling. I will follow your every order and the good news is, I like beets. I like them quite a bit."

"Oh, well, I have some great recipes." Cassidy was back. She was smiling one moment, and then her face fell. "Is everything all right? I didn't mess anything up, did I?"

Her heart ached for the rejection this woman must have been through. Elisa didn't know where this was going but she wanted to go a few steps further down the road, and that meant starting to be the person she wanted to be. She let go of her father's hand and reached out for Cassidy's. "We're just having a nice talk. Come here and tell me about my stepbrothers."

Cassidy's face lit up, and she began to talk.

Elisa listened, hope filling her in a way it hadn't in a long time.

Her family had just gotten weirder, and that suddenly seemed perfect.

* * * *

Hale glanced over and Elisa was laughing at something Cassidy was saying.

"Hey, she's doing okay now." Max Harper slid onto the barstool next to him. "I think it was touch and go at first, but Mel had a talk with her and she seems much more at ease now."

"She does look happier." Van had hopped behind the bar when it became evident that Elisa wasn't going to be done any time soon. The bar back had needed to leave early, so Van was helping out.

It had given Hale a whole bunch of time to sit and nurse his second beer and think about exactly what he was doing.

She was here to spend time with her father, and she would leave at some point. Was it worth getting his heart ripped out of his chest? Because he was pretty sure if anyone could do it, it was Elisa Leal.

"I'm glad to hear it."

Max frowned. "No, you're not. We need to work on that. See,

when you want to lie and make it sound like you're not, your expression has to match your words."

"I wasn't even looking at you." He'd been staring at his beer.

"Didn't have to. I can see half your face, and it was obvious that you are not glad to hear it."

He was bad with lying, and it wasn't really true. "I am. I'm happy she's getting along with her dad. It's why she's here."

"Yeah, but she seemed to be getting along with you pretty well, too."

He simply nodded because he was fairly sure he wasn't supposed to say all the things he kind of wanted to say. He had some thoughts on how the evening had gone now that the rush of actually being with her was over. He knew exactly what Van would say if he expressed those doubts. Van would tell him he was being a morose Eeyore and he should look at the positive side of life. Even if Elisa thought he was a weirdo and wouldn't ever introduce him to any of her friends or consider having an actual relationship with him, she was obviously down for sex, and that should be all that mattered.

He wanted her to like him.

"What is that look for?" Rye was sitting on the other side of his brother. He pointed Hale's way. "I don't think he agrees with you, Max."

Rye looked like he'd found some clue in a mystery.

Max frowned his brother's way. "Well, of course he doesn't believe it. He's not confident like me. Yet. I told you he's a puppy who got kicked a whole bunch, and he'll never be a whole and happy dog if we don't fix him."

"Wait," Hale began.

Max ignored him. "What makes you think she didn't like you?"

"He doesn't think that." Van was suddenly in front of him, a frown on his face.

Damn it. "I didn't say anything."

"You didn't have to. I can read your expressions," Max replied.

"I don't have expressions." He was pretty sure he didn't.

"You have two," Van countered. "You have your working expression and then there's the one that lets everyone know you've mentally checked out. It's those two. Except tonight the fucker actually smiled. Three times. I didn't know his face worked that way."

"Ah, see, now we're getting somewhere." Max looked pleased with himself. "So you really like this woman."

"I think everyone knows I like her." That might be part of the problem. He'd realized how many sets of eyes he had on him this evening.

"So?" Max asked.

"He's not used to having a lot of friends," Van offered.

That made him sound like a loser. "I'm not used to staying in one place for long, so I often don't make friends. It's only been tonight that I realized how nosy people are here. I've had three people ask me where I'm taking Elisa for a date. I took her here. This was the date."

Now he was thinking it might be their only date.

"I think they were wondering if we were going to ask her out again," Van pointed out.

Max held out a hand as though he was about to impart great wisdom. "Who asked?"

"Stella, Polly, and the lady who keeps all the bees," he replied. "And the pastor asked if she believed in Jesus. I did not get into her religious beliefs. I just met her."

Max nodded as though he'd expected that answer. "They were all looking for business. Stella is subtly telling you the café would be a better place for a date. It's not. It's way louder, and the lights are real bright in there. And there's no booze. Polly wants to know if she's going to get a shot at doing the woman's nails and hair. Recently she's had some stiff competition from a lady in Del Norte who does your nails while giving you a psychic reading. She claims she can tell your future based on the strength of your cuticles. Not that I know what those are."

"He does," Rye interjected. "Look at those nails. He's Polly's best customer."

Max curled his hands and brought them to his chest as though protecting them. "Some of us believe in self-care, asshole. And it feels nice. And I get a lot of gossip. That's how I know the bee lady has started putting together picnic baskets and those shark board things, and she's looking to see if you need one for a date."

"Shark board? I don't think I want a shark board." Hale was confused, but that seemed to be his state tonight.

"He means charcuterie," Van corrected. "It's a meat and cheese tray. And if we invite Elisa to our place, it would be a good idea to grab one of those. I can make some pasta and a salad, but the charcuterie board could make us look like we know what we're doing."

"See, that's why she asked," Max pointed out. "Don't view them as nosy. View them as shrewd businesspeople. Now tell me why you're morose, and it better not be because she's spending time with Mel and Cassidy and not you because that would make you an asshole. I'm supposed to be turning you from an awkward dude into a functioning member of our society. I can't do that if you're an asshole."

"I don't see why." Rye smirked as he ordered another beer. "You're the biggest asshole in the county. Don't deny it. He's won the trophy twenty years in a row. He's trying to protect his place."

"Don't mind him. He's jealous." Max turned Hale's way. "Seriously, are you upset she's spending time with her dad?"

"I think he's..." Van started.

Max stopped him with a wave of his hand. "Nope. Hale needs to use his words. He's a fully grown weirdo who can express himself without a translator."

Could he? He needed to start trying. He wasn't sure where he would be a year from now, but he needed to get a handle on this part of his life. Honesty. It was shitty. "I'm worried that there was a particular zone I was in tonight that I might not be able to find again."

"Ah." Max nodded. "That makes sense."

"I was going to say that," Van muttered under his breath. "He does this thing where he replays everything that happened in an encounter and puts the worst spin on all of it."

"And you never see that things can go wrong." Hale felt the need to defend himself.

"Look, you two are doing a lot of the things Max and I did for a long time." Rye seemed to have gotten serious. "I've been teasing Max and you about this mentorship thing, but now I can see you actually could use some advice from a couple of idiots who've been there. You two are in trouble, and you need to figure it out if you want your friendship to be a good thing in your life."

"What the hell is that supposed to mean?" Van asked before Hale could.

Because he definitely wanted the answer to that question.

"It means you've fallen into the trap of letting each other sink into your distinct personalities so heavily you don't access the other sides of yourself. It's not healthy," Max explained.

"That is very astute of you." Rye looked impressed. "And self-aware."

"I can be smart. And I also read a bunch of the notes Cassidy's son made for that book he's writing," Max admitted. "Now before you accuse me of breaking into the dude's room, I did and I would do it again because he was writing about me. Now, as to the pained looks of incomprehension on your faces, first I find them funny."

"Max," Van began.

"All right, so here's what I've observed. You two have gotten to a place in your partnership where Van handles all the joy and Hale takes on all the anxiety," Max announced. "It's not sustainable because Hale can never be happy, and Van can't have deep relationships because he's coasting on the surface."

"I assure you I feel anxiety." Van was frowning like someone had insulted him.

"But do you talk about it?" Max asked. "Or do you smile and put on a front because that's his world? Hale, do you talk about the shit that makes you happy?" Max stopped, seeming to think about something. "Does anything make you happy?"

He could be an ass. "Yes, but I do get your point. I'm not looking at the positive side of tonight. I was sitting here doing what I always do. I go through all the ways this thing could go wrong and wait for Van to point out that it's not so bad."

Van shrugged like he didn't understand why *that* was so bad. "It's what we've always done. And he's still here. I'm proud of him for not deciding to go home to brood. This whole public brooding thing is a big step for him."

"All right. I will admit that the minute she walked away I was already writing the whole thing off." He had to be honest if any of this was going to work. "It's easier to move on than to put myself out there again, but I don't want to move on. I want to sit here and wait until she's done and then make sure she gets back to the motel okay. It's snowing pretty hard outside, and she's not used to mountain driving."

"Excellent. That's a real fine excuse to see if you can still get an invite inside." Rye nodded approvingly. "That is some nice, positive thinking."

"Uh, that was my idea the whole time," Van pointed out.

"It needs to be Hale's idea sometimes," Max countered. "Look, I know this sounds weird coming from a set of twins who often can read each other's minds, but you have to be two whole-ass human beings, and that means you can't constantly take opposing positions where you try to convince the other you're right."

He didn't think that was… Except was that how their lives ran now? Hadn't they spent a good portion of the beginning of the evening arguing over which woman they would date without taking the time to actually discuss the situation? Had they become so grounded in their own positions that it was becoming increasingly difficult to build anything good? He'd been sitting here but he'd also been planning on giving Van all of his reasons why they should leave and spare themselves the embarrassment.

He wanted her. If she didn't want him that was one thing, but if he didn't take the chance that was totally fucking on him.

Hale pushed off the barstool. This was why he put up with Max's sarcasm. Sometimes the man was right. He did let Van do all the positive thinking, and that wasn't fair. He could imagine Van needed lifting up from time to time, too. Maybe that was why things had changed when Van's brother had come back into his life. Jake provided Van with something Hale hadn't offered, and that needed to change. He'd allowed the past to drag on him, and if he didn't try to change his mindset, he might not have a future.

Hale put a hand on the bar, his attention on Van. "I'm going to go and tell her that we're staying here for her. We're going to follow her and make sure she gets back to the motel okay, and we'll firm up plans for tomorrow night's date. Then I'll go and see if we can get a shark board. Don't correct me. I like shark board. Those things are shark boards from now on."

Van gave him a salute. "Shark board it is."

Max said something about not rewarding the bee lady for her aggressive marketing tactics, but Hale was laser focused on Elisa. He marched right over to the table where she was sitting with her dad, who was known for being a little out of whack and needing to be tranquilized from time to time, marched past the surprisingly full dining room for this time of night, well aware those eyes were still on him.

"Oh, he's making a move," Callie said into her cell phone before pretending like she wasn't watching him.

Small town. He liked Bliss. He would have to get used to the fact that everyone knew everyone else's business and felt like they could comment on it. In this case, he could use his ability to deflect like a shield. He walked right past all of them and found himself at her table, staring at her like an idiot because she was awfully pretty.

Mel looked up first and cocked a brow his way. At least he thought that's what he was doing because that trucker hat of his rode low on his head and he'd done a halfway decent job of hiding the fact that it was lined with tin foil. It still poked out. "Is there something I can help you with, Hale? Your name is Hale, right?"

"Yes, sir. I'm Hale Galloway, and I just wanted a moment with Elisa." Hopefully no one would have to tranq Mel tonight. It might not help his case, but he was going to be upfront and honest.

Elisa slid out of the booth. "Of course. I'll be right back."

She took his hand, and he was almost immediately back in that place he'd been before, the one where he didn't care if he looked like a fool as long as she was okay with it. She led him away from the dining room back to where the hallway started to lead to the office and the bathrooms. She stopped. "I'm sorry. I didn't think about talking to you when my father showed up. It was kind of crazy. I didn't mean to walk away."

He didn't want her to feel bad about that. "I'm happy he's here. This is what you came here for. Is it going okay?"

"Better than I expected," she replied. "I think I'm going to stay around for a couple of months. At least through the holidays. I'd like to get to know him better. Since my mom died, it's just me and Sabrina. Mom didn't have much family, so we're kind of alone in the world. It would be good if I had a connection to my father."

"It is. I wasn't coming over to complain. I wanted to let you know that Van and I are going to wait for you. Not because we're trying to continue what we started. There's plenty of time for that. We want to wait because it's snowing pretty hard, and we'll worry about you driving home."

"Ah, my dad already told me he thought I shouldn't drive back tonight. He offered."

He squeezed her hand. "I understand, but I hope you'll let Van and me take you out tomorrow like we talked about."

"Or you could wait and take me back to my place and maybe stay the night with me."

He felt the flush go through him, arousal lighting his skin. "Okay."

She was blushing, like she was surprised she'd said what she said, but she didn't back down. "Okay. Give me another half an hour and I'll be ready to go. Unless you changed your mind and you want to take things slower. I'm okay with that, too."

He was going to be bold for once in his damn life. Playing things safe had never gotten him anywhere. Max was right. It was time to change things up. He moved in and put a hand on her hip. "I've changed my mind about absolutely nothing."

Her head tilted back slightly and he leaned over, pressing his lips to hers. It didn't matter who was watching, didn't matter that it hadn't been a part of his plan. All that mattered was she was here with him, and he had a chance with her.

He pulled away because he wasn't going to make out with her here. It would be disrespectful to Van when they'd made their intentions plain. But that brushing of lips had shown him everything he needed to know. He was excited again. Excited about her, about where the night could take them. "I'll be at the bar, but you should know I'm not getting drunk. I'm just waiting on a lady."

He walked away, secure that he was on the right path now.

When he returned to the bar, Max and Rye were watching him with wide eyes while Van grinned his way.

"So will we be following the lady home this evening?" Van asked.

"We will be driving Elisa back to her place, and she's asked if we might want to come in for a while." Hale intended for a while to be all night.

Max held his arms up in victory. "I am better than any therapist. I should charge for this."

He was not paying Max. Though he might buy the guy another beer.

* * * *

"Your dad can be intimidating." Van parked the Jeep in the space in front of Elisa's motel room. It was lucky he'd found one. The place was full this evening, likely because of the festival going on. It was late enough that the movies that played nightly were done. He'd noticed the marquee out front despite the fact that Gene had turned out the lights. The Movie Motel was proudly showing a Christmas double feature of *Elf* and *It's a Wonderful Life*.

He wondered if Elisa had sat in her room and watched the films the night before. It might be fun to get some popcorn and watch with her and Hale. He wasn't sure why they hadn't been out here before. Hale often worked at the motel, but they'd never come by for fun. His life had been devoid of fun lately.

He was going to change that tonight.

"Really?" Elisa slid out of the passenger seat and closed the door behind her, stepping out into the snow.

"He gave me a very pointed stare." He held out a hand and helped her up the curb so they were standing in front of her room.

Hale was going to have to walk. He'd driven Elisa's rental, and they'd agreed that since he'd kissed her in front of the entire dining room at Trio, that it was only fair she ride with Van. He'd made sure everyone saw him helping her into the Jeep.

He was not going to be left behind. It was what he'd been thinking about since Elisa had moved to the table to talk to Mel and Cassidy. He'd decided to help behind the bar, and Hale had sat there brooding until Max and Rye had some weird therapy session with him and he'd become Mr. Take Charge.

Hale was making connections. His best friend was changing, and what the hell was he going to do if Hale didn't need him anymore?

He wanted to forget about that for the night and concentrate on the most intriguing woman he'd met in forever.

"Oh, I don't think he meant it to be intimidating." She looked incredibly pretty in her puffy coat, a wool hat on her head. He couldn't see a single curve, but he still thought she was sexy as hell. "He seems to be a nice man. Odd, but nice, and his wife is lovely."

She hadn't been there when Mel had stared him down and told him he would be watching. Cassidy had frowned at him, reminding him they'd had a run-in once. One he'd thought he'd won, but circumstances had changed.

"You think that because Cassidy has never decided you were an alien life-form. I mean, damn, mention you don't like beets once and she never forgets." He'd had to explain that he'd worked at a beet farm over a summer when he was sixteen, and he'd never recovered. Sometimes he was sure his fingertips were still purple.

He looked out over the parking lot, but Hale had turned down another aisle searching for a space.

"I don't understand the whole alien thing," Elisa admitted. "But I liked them anyway. Once we got Cassidy off aliens and she started talking about what it was like to be raised around here, it was a lovely conversation. My dad didn't get here until he was older. It's weird. I'm calling him my dad and we're not even sure it's true."

He had no doubt that man was her father. He'd watched her, and even some of their expressions were the same. "Why would your mom lie in a journal she never expected anyone to find?"

Elisa seemed to think about that. "I know. The truth is my mom was a lot of things, but she never lied. Even when it would have been far kinder than telling the truth."

He got the feeling her mom hadn't been the greatest. He'd had problems with his parents, too, but his mom would never have knowingly said something that would hurt him. If anything he could have used a bit more discipline.

Was Max right about he and Hale sinking into roles that put them both in corners? If Hale was the broody, moody asshole, then did that make him the always smiling clown?

"I'm sorry I messed up our date tonight."

He frowned, turning back to her. He needed to get his head in the game. Because this didn't actually feel like a game. He was interested in her, and now they had some time to explore the connection between the three of them. "I'm glad you got to spend time with him. It's okay. If I'd met my long-lost dad, I would have wanted some time with him, too. So you think you're going to hang out for a while?"

"I'm in a weird place. Like in my life. I don't know what I want to do next, but I also know I want some change. My sister keeps pointing out that I have a chance a lot of people don't ever get. I don't have anything holding me back. Not family. Not money. I can take some time and figure out what comes next," she said. "I know that sounds amazing, but it also feels a little sad."

He understood. "Because the things that would hold you back are all the things that make life worthwhile?"

"Yeah. I thought I would have a kid by now." She winced. "I shouldn't talk about that with the guy I'm about to hook up with. That would be a rookie mistake."

He needed to make a few things plain to her. "I thought we settled this. One quick night isn't what I want. I know it's not what Hale wants."

That seemed to throw her a bit. "That feels like pressure."

"It's the opposite. I don't want you to feel any pressure at all. Not for sex. Not to have a relationship with us. All I want to know is that you're open to seeing where it leads."

"And if all I want is to blow off some steam tonight?"

"Then I'm going to bow out because I want something more. Or at least the possibility of something more. I've been a good time for a lot of women. It gets old. Very, very old. All the things you feel about not having ties that would keep you in one place? I feel the same way and I'm sick of it. So while I know society tells you that men like me and Hale should take any sex we can get and shrug and walk away in the morning, I don't think we're those guys anymore. You're a couple of years too late."

Hale turned the corner and started walking up at the absolute worst time. "I don't think she's too late."

Elisa's expression had gone blank as she turned to Hale. "He was telling me he wasn't interested in being my personal stress relief for the evening."

Hale stopped, and Van could see his brain working, trying to figure out what had gone wrong because it had seemed to be going right mere moments before. Had he read her wrong? He'd thought they were on the same page, but she seemed to be pulling back now.

"Is that all you said you wanted?" Hale seemed to find the problem. Likely because they knew each other so well.

"I asked if that was all I did want, would he still want to come in." She hadn't put it exactly like that, but Van didn't need her to say the exact words.

"And he said no." Hale took a deep breath and slid his hands into his pockets as though he needed them there so he wouldn't reach out for her. "Elisa, it was so good to meet you. If you change your mind, well, we're always around."

Elisa groaned. "Damn it, I said something weird and I got self-conscious and I'm not good at this. I don't even know why I'm arguing."

"It's okay if you're not ready." His dick would curse him, but some things were more important than his dick. "We'll back off and if you find that you are ready, you can call us because we'll be waiting."

She moved in, her body bumping against his. "I felt vulnerable and I threw up a wall. It's something I always do. It's something I'm done with. I was vulnerable because I'm worried you'll look at my scars and you won't want me."

He reached up, putting a hand on either side of her face. "I will want you. He'll want you. We might want you more than is comfortable for you."

"Comfort is overrated," she said quietly. "Would you kiss me? When Hale kissed me I didn't feel like it was all going to go wrong."

That he could do. He lowered his mouth to hers, bringing them together with a tenderness he hadn't felt in a long time. Even with the snow falling all around him, he felt warm, and it wasn't all about his dick. Something infinitely warm seemed to flow through his veins.

This. This was what he'd wanted to explore.

She pulled back slightly, her face flushed and lips curling up. "Okay. I kissed two guys tonight and it felt good, and I don't feel dirty about it."

"You shouldn't." Hale was behind her, getting her in between them for the first time. "There's nothing dirty about it. Not on an emotional level. Sex is inherently…"

He did not need a lecture on hygiene. "Amazing, and that's all it's going to be between us."

Her eyes lit with obvious amusement. "Was he going to talk about how dirty sex could be on a sexy level? Or a cleanliness level?"

"Sexy level," Hale insisted. "Totally sexy level."

Liar, but he was Van's partner, and he was supposed to back him up. "I'm absolutely certain he wasn't going to talk about bodily fluids. He was going to talk about how good we want to make you feel. He was talking about how gloriously filthy all the things we want to do to you are."

"I was talking about how you're going to be surrounded by us." Hale picked up on the vibe. "There's not going to be an inch of you we don't touch and stroke and kiss." Hale's hands were on her hips as he leaned in, whispering in her ear. "And we'll love every part of you. There's nothing to worry about or feel self-conscious about. Your scars will be every bit as lovely as you are."

"Let that worry float away. I want you to think only about whether you like what we're doing or not," Van continued. "If something doesn't feel good, tell us. I'm going to tell you some of the things I like. I like kissing, but I'm also going to want to get my mouth on your pussy at some point."

Her breath caught, and that was when he realized Hale's hands had moved up and were right under her breasts.

"Do you want Van to eat your pussy, baby?" Hale whispered the question. "He won't stop until you come all over his tongue, and then I'll do the same damn thing. This will not be some quick lay where we get off and run out the door. You let us in and we'll be all over you for hours."

"And when you're too tired to take another second, we'll hold you until you fall asleep and be there in the morning," Van promised.

"Unless you ask us to leave," Hale added.

Van frowned his partner's way. "We're going to make sure she doesn't want us to leave."

"Consent is important," Hale insisted.

Her body shuddered as she laughed. "I consent." She grinned up at him, looking so much happier than she had before. She seemed to genuinely appreciate their differences and the way they often got off course.

He needed to get them back on. "Then let's go inside."

She fumbled to get the key out but managed to open the door to her room. She held it for them as they walked in. It was time to get serious about her pleasure because he got the feeling there would be more awkwardness between them until they got her comfortable with them. Elisa didn't seem like a woman who'd had a bunch of generous lovers in her past. He knew she was divorced, but she hadn't talked much about her ex. Still, he would bet her sex life had been lacking. Most divorced couples didn't have great sex. And then when she should have been out in the world sowing some wild oats, she'd been fighting cancer.

He stepped in front of her. She was tall but he still had an inch or two on her. He tugged the hat off her head, letting those dark curls free. He studied her face for a moment while he stroked her hair. "You are so fucking beautiful."

"You make me feel that way," she admitted. "I don't know anyone who has ever made me feel that way before. Not really. It's not like I've never been told I was pretty, but I didn't feel it until Hale walked in and I looked like a drowned rat and he kind of ate me up with his eyes. And then I thought he was gay so I decided I was fantasizing."

"Oh, I would have eaten you up with more than my eyes." Hale pressed his lips to the nape of her neck. He was doing what he always did when his sex drive took over. All the gruffness fell away, and he was in his element. "Let me do what I wanted to do the minute I saw you. Let me touch you."

"You're already touching me," Elisa replied, her eyes closing and head tipping back toward Hale.

"You know what I mean. I would touch you anywhere else, but I want permission to cup your breasts. I want you to tell me it's okay because I know how they've felt like the cursed center of your universe," Hale whispered.

Sometimes the man really did connect. "Give us permission to show you how happy we are you're here."

Her eyes were suspiciously bright as she stepped away, her chest moving as she took a deep breath. "Take off your shirts. I'll feel better if I'm not the only one."

He shrugged out of his coat as she started to do the same. Hale hung all three on the coat rack. He was the one who kept them organized.

They each had their jobs, as though they were part of a single being. Van pushed them along. Hale made sure they were comfortable.

Max's words had gotten into his brain, but he pushed them away. He would examine them later, taking each out and weighing them for their truth. But tonight he wanted to do what he'd promised Elisa. Tonight there was nothing else in the world except her and nothing more important than her pleasure.

He pulled the Trio T-shirt over his head and laid it out over the chair. It was quickly joined by Hale's button-down.

He turned to Elisa, watching as her hands started to work on the buttons of her shirt, and knew that no matter what, tonight would change his whole world.

Chapter Six

Her hands were trembling, but she wasn't going to stop. She hated the fact that she'd nearly run them off because she'd said something too personal and gotten embarrassed. The old Elisa was looking for a way out. She'd likely been overly stimulated and needed to hide.

But she wanted to deal with that emotional overload in a different way this time. She wanted to jump into the deep end and see if there was any way she could learn to swim.

She looked up and the guys had taken her request seriously. There were two big, gorgeous chests on display. Hale was the tiniest bit shorter than Van, but he was broader, his muscles bigger. Van was lean, his body perfectly defined.

They were gorgeous, glorious specimens of masculinity at the height of their desirability.

And she had eighteen-year-old tits. She'd worked for those tits. Suffered for them. They were perky and round and yes, they were mainly made of silicone, but they were hers. The anchor and lollipop scars had faded to a glossy pink, and they were more like lines than the raised scars she'd feared. Like someone had taken a pink marker to her chest.

The doctor had done an excellent job and her nipples hadn't even died and she took care of them, so it was okay to have sex again.

It was okay to enjoy them again. It was okay to find something good out of all that fear and pain.

It was okay to find some joy.

Why was it so hard for her to reach out and take something for herself?

She shrugged out of the shirt and wrestled with her bra. Despite the many months since that initial surgery, she sometimes still felt like she'd woken up in a body she didn't belong in. She hoped tonight helped change that. It had been a long time since she'd had sex. The last year of her marriage had been mostly a dry spell, and she hadn't dated since. Until Hale had shown up on her doorstep, she hadn't given sex much of a thought.

Now it seemed like an excellent idea. Now it seemed like the start of something.

She tossed the bra aside and shivered because it was still a little chilly in the room.

Van moved quickly, getting in her space and wrapping her up in a hug that brought their skin together, sending immediate heat through her. "I knew you would be gorgeous. Can I touch you?"

Hale was behind her, covering her back with that beautiful chest of his. His big hands skimmed her skin from the curve of her hips to just under her breasts.

Something eased inside her, some place that had been tight and knotted up before. She felt her body loosen as though their acceptance of her had given each muscle permission to relax. "Please touch me."

No one had touched her in so long. Not in this way. She'd been poked and prodded and sliced open and sewn back together, but no one had stroked hands across her skin, warming her with their own body heat.

She gasped as Hale caught her arms, hooking them with his own and drawing them back so her breasts thrust out.

Van was staring at her breasts, studying them carefully.

"Why would you think for a second that anyone would reject you for those absolutely gorgeous tits?" His voice had gone deeper than she'd heard it before. He moved in and let his fingertips trace over her scars. "Even this is pretty. It's soft. It doesn't look like any scar I've ever seen."

"The doc was pretty good with the surgical glue, and I was careful." She'd been told not to sweat. In the middle of summer in North Carolina. "I had to wear a surgical bra for eight weeks, and I had to sleep in a chair because I couldn't roll over." She shouldn't be talking so much. They didn't want to hear about her surgeries, but he was touching her and Hale was holding her back. Restraining her. It should be annoying but it kind of did something for her. Her body was heating up in ways it never had before. "One of them is smaller than the other. It tightened up during radiation and that's why it's firmer, too."

Van reached out and cupped them both, sending a thrill of arousal through her. She could still feel them. Not the way she had before, but she could still enjoy hands on her breasts.

"I think they're both perfect." Van's head was down, watching as he ran his thumbs over her nipples. He dropped down to his knees and leaned over, licking her.

She was sure she'd had far more sensitivity before, but in the moment it didn't matter because the warmth of his tongue alone made arousal shoot through her and suddenly her pussy was softening, getting wet and ready.

He played with her nipples, gently at first, as though testing her limits.

"Do you like how that feels, Elisa?" Hale asked, his mouth against her ear.

"Yes. I'm not very sensitive, but I like the warmth." She liked how the rest of the world was falling away and all that mattered was being with the two of them.

Hale's tongue traced the shell of her ear, making her bite back a groan.

She'd thought she would have to get through this initial encounter, hoped she could find a little pleasure in it. This would be a test of sorts to see how far she could go.

All of that flew out of her brain as arousal took over, and she wasn't self-conscious anymore. She wasn't overthinking every single thing. No. She was going on instinct, and instinct told her to let these men do anything they liked.

She let her head fall back against Hale's strong shoulder, and somehow his mouth found hers. This wasn't the soft kiss he'd given her before. This kiss was dominating and overwhelming. He released one of her arms so he could cup her cheek and gain more access. His tongue moved over her lips and she opened for him, giving him exactly what he wanted. He surged inside, stroking against her tongue and reminding her how good it could feel to give over to the needs of her body.

Van stood up and his hands went to the button of her jeans, undoing it and letting his fingers tease inside. "Look at me, Elisa. It's my turn."

Hale shifted and she found herself being offered up to Van, who looked so much taller and bigger than he had before. His fun, charming persona had fled, and she was left with a man who knew exactly what he wanted and it was her and he was going to devour her. She was going to love it.

Van put a hand on either side of her face and lowered his mouth to hers. "You'll find we're good at taking turns, but we need to have a talk about how this is going to work if we keep doing it." He ran his tongue over her bottom lip, and she felt that in her pussy. "I suspect you don't have a lot of experience with double penetration."

She'd known what they would want, and she'd decided she was open to the experience. Life was short and she needed to live it for once. She was throwing caution to the wind. "I can handle it."

"Not yet, you can't." Hale tugged at her jeans, pulling them down around her thighs. "If you don't have experience with anal sex, we'll have to make sure you're ready. It'll be fun. We can take our time and do it right."

Van leaned over and picked her up, carrying her to the bed.

She was tall and not slight by any definition. Years of military work had given her muscle, and she'd put back on most of the weight she'd lost during chemo and radiation. No one had ever picked her up and carried her before. At least not since she was a child.

Van set her on top of the bed and then they were stripping her down, pulling off her boots and socks, easing her jeans off. She was quickly down to nothing but her cotton undies, and she was pretty sure those were already soaked with arousal.

When she was naked, with their gorgeous faces staring down at her, she let go of any thought that there wasn't a place for sex in her life anymore. She realized that was what had been in the back of her mind. She'd tried and failed and had been ready to put that part of her life behind a door and lock it away. Between the divorce and cancer, she'd dismissed her body as one more part of her life that had failed her. But she'd been the one who'd failed. Failed to try again. Failed to have some faith. Failed to appreciate the wonderous instrument her body was.

It didn't matter that this wouldn't last forever. She'd gone into every relationship she'd ever been in with the thought that she would make it work or die trying. Not everything had to be forever. Life wasn't the zero-sum game her mother had made it out to be. It could be made of experiences, and she was ready for this one.

Van moved to the foot of the bed, taking her ankles and dragging her down so her ass was on the edge of the bed. "Put your feet on my shoulders."

Her heart rate tripled as she realized what he was about to do. It had been so long since she'd felt worshipped and adored in a physical way. She shoved aside any thought of being embarrassed about how awkward it was to place her feet on his broad shoulders and open herself fully to him. That emotion had zero place in the here and now. He'd asked her to do it. He wanted to see her pussy, to get his mouth on her.

Hale moved in behind his partner, his eyes going straight to that part of her that was now fully on display. "Damn, she's pretty."

"There's a reason we were fighting over her," Van said with a chuckle.

They hadn't been fighting over who got to date her. They'd been fighting for the right to see her together. It made a girl feel pretty fucking special.

Then Van leaned over, and she couldn't feel anything but the velvet swipe of his tongue.

She let out a shuddering breath and her eyes closed as she concentrated on the feeling of his mouth on her pussy. She let herself float as Van went to work, licking and sucking and sending her to crazy heights.

She felt the bed dip and then there was warmth on her left breast. Hale. He was on the bed with her, his lips closing over her nipple and filling her with warmth. He played with her right breast, palming it before giving her nipple a tweak that had her gasping.

Van eased a finger inside her pussy, stroking her in exactly the right place. The sensation built and built. Layers of pleasure that lifted her higher and higher. It was like nothing she'd experienced before. All the sex she'd had seemed bland and boring compared to what these two men were doing to her.

She reached out, putting a hand on Hale's neck and holding onto him as the orgasm sparked through her body.

Then Hale moved up, kissing her, stroking his tongue against hers before pushing off the bed and getting to his feet. There was a look of dark desire on his face, and she loved the fact that she'd put it there. He shoved out of his jeans, taking the boxers he'd been wearing with them and leaving him naked. She wasn't sure why this god of a man had decided he wanted her but she was so grateful to be here with him.

"You are not so bad yourself, Hale." She felt energized as Van gave her pussy one last kiss and helped her sit up.

"Baby, I want you to take care of me while Hale takes care of you. Do you understand? You're going to kneel on the bed and he's going to move in behind you." Van's voice had gone deeper than normal and his usual happy-go-lucky expression had been replaced with a seriousness she hadn't seen in his eyes before.

One in her pussy and one in her mouth. She would be between them, surrounded by them. It would be the single kinkiest thing she'd ever done, and she wasn't even hesitating.

She could get addicted to this feeling.

She got on her hands and knees, ready for whatever came next.

* * * *

Hale prayed he could last because his cock was ready to go off simply watching that woman move. She had an athletic grace that made her every move sensual. She climbed on the bed and moved into the position Van had requested, her round, sexy ass pointed his way.

He'd nearly lost it when he'd felt her come. Her body had gone stiff under his hands and then every muscle seemed to relax, and she was so fucking soft and warm.

Van shoved out of his jeans, but not before tossing him a condom. Hale managed to catch it but only barely. It would be exactly like him to end up having to crawl naked under the bed to retrieve a condom. He needed to make this good for Elisa. So good they had a shot at keeping her around long enough that they could figure out if a relationship could work. There would be time for him to be his weirdo self later, after he'd shown her how good it could be between the three of them.

So far she'd responded beautifully. Once she'd realized how hot they thought she was, all of her unease seemed to melt away and she'd opened herself up to the pleasure they could give her.

Van stood at the end of the bed stroking his cock as he stared down at her. "You know what I want."

"Yes."

"Say it." Van could get bossy during sex. Those tendencies had gotten stronger when they'd spent time at the BDSM club his brother had been a founding member of. "I want to hear you say what you're going to do to me."

"I'm going to suck your cock, Van." The words came out on a husky chuckle that went straight to his dick.

"And I'm going to get inside you." Hale discovered he wanted to hear the words, too. He was normally quiet. Sex was a bodily function that seemed to require no words, but he needed them tonight. "I'm going to fuck you, Elisa. It's what I've wanted from the moment I saw you."

"Me, too," she promised.

"Go on then." Hale wanted to watch her another few minutes.

This was straight out of their normal playbook. Van handled the oral and Hale got the pussy. They'd done it a hundred times. Oh, if they stuck with a woman for a while they would change things up, but in every casual encounter they'd ever had it had played out this way.

He didn't want to fuck her from behind. It didn't seem as sweet as he wanted this to be.

He was looking for more than an orgasm with this woman. He was looking for real connection, and he didn't think he would get it doing her from behind.

Fuck. He was using the wrong words again because the words he should use scared him. He wanted to make love with her.

He watched as Elisa leaned forward and licked the head of Van's cock. Van hissed and his hand found the back of her head, sinking into her silky curls. She used her tongue to trace Van's cockhead before it disappeared behind her lips. She settled in and moved up and down on his dick, whirling her tongue over him.

Van's eyes opened and he looked Hale's way. He sent him a questioning look.

Hale knew what answer his partner was requesting. Why wasn't he fucking their plaything for the night?

Because she wasn't a plaything and he wanted more than a night. "I want to watch for a minute. I like seeing her suck your cock. Do you know how hot you look, baby? I'm thinking about how it's going to feel when it's my cock you're sucking on like it's the best lollipop you've ever had."

She responded to the praise by upping her game. She reached out with one hand, stroking Van's balls.

"Fuck," Van gritted between clenched teeth. His eyes closed again, and he seemed to settle in, his hips moving in time with Elisa.

"More, baby." Hale got close, putting a hand on her back. "Take more of him. You can take all of him. Take his cock all the way to the back of your throat. Just breathe and you'll take all of him."

He let his fingers trace her spine from the nape of her neck all the way to the place where those gorgeous cheeks split and rounded into the most perfect ass he'd ever seen. He couldn't wait to start preparing her. He would have so much fun playing with her little asshole, fucking her with the plug that would get her used to having sex there.

"Elisa, slow down," Van said, but his tone had gone breathy and soft. "I'm going to come, and Hale isn't even ready yet."

He was ready. He was so hard he could barely breathe, but he wanted something more. This wasn't a game where they tried to see if they could come at the same time.

So he gave her cheek a squeeze. "Don't slow down now. Take him all the way. I want to watch you and then I'll roll you over and I'll make love to you for as long as I can. But first take care of Van, and then it's all about you for the rest of the night."

"That was not the plan," Van managed, but it was easy to see he was getting close.

"Plans change," Hale replied quietly. "Don't stop, baby. He's almost there."

She worked his cock over and over until she'd managed to take all of him, and Hale watched as she gently stroked his balls, and that sent Van right over the edge.

When she sat up, there was the sexiest curl to her lips, and she ran her tongue over them.

She was going to kill him.

He wasn't willing to wait a second longer. "Come here, baby."

He moved in, cupping her face and kissing her until he was breathless. He felt like he could devour this woman whole and still want more of her. He kissed her again, dragging her in close so he could feel her skin against his. Those breasts she'd been worried about nestled against his chest perfectly. Their tongues tangled and the rest of the world seemed to fall away.

He eased her down on the bed, spreading her legs and making a place for himself there. Her hands moved over his chest as she looked up at him with those big brown eyes.

He needed to make this good for her. She'd chosen them, and that made him feel like the fucking king of the world.

He kissed her again, tasting his partner on her tongue. He knew some men would find it distasteful, but he shared everything with Van. He loved the fact that Van was still with them.

He was actually surprised Van wasn't on the bed by now, but his focus was on Elisa and the thought floated away. He kissed his way down her body, her hands moving across him, exploring. When he made it to her pussy, he found her wet and so aroused he knew he couldn't wait another minute.

He went to his knees, ripping open the condom wrapper and somehow managing to roll it over his cock. He stared down at her for a moment, taking in how pretty she was all flushed and ready for him. He wanted that image imprinted on his brain for all of time.

Hell, he just wanted her.

He let his instincts lead him, spreading her legs wide and

pressing his cock inside. Heat suffused him, filling his whole body with warmth. Liquid desire seemed to course through his veins, and he pressed in and pulled out, gradually gaining ground. Her hands found his forearms as she pressed up against him, her impatience pushing him. He wanted to make this last, but he didn't think it would. This first time would be fast and furious, but he could still make it sweet, too.

He laid his body over hers, holding his cock deep inside as he kissed her. He wrapped his arms around her and felt her do the same as their tongues stroked each other. This was what all the other sex had been missing. This wild connection he felt, this tenderness that did nothing to quench the fire between them.

The only thing that could make it better was Van being with them. He wasn't sure why Van hadn't joined them, but he wasn't going to stop for a therapy session. He kissed her again and started moving his hips, dragging his cock in and out, twisting his hips so he ground down on her clitoris. He found a rhythm that worked, feeling her tighten around him. Her nails bit into his shoulders, a minor pain that he enjoyed mightily. It made him growl and thrust in harder as her legs wrapped around his waist, tightening.

Her back bowed, and she was calling out his name as she came.

He felt his balls draw up and then he lost all control. He thrust into her, giving her everything he had.

When he dropped on top of her, her hands smoothed over his back and he let his head find the crook of her neck.

This was the moment when they would normally switch positions and start everything over again, but she needed more than to be passed between them.

He kissed her cheek and let his body slide to her side. "You okay?"

She looked at him with sleepy, satisfied eyes. "So much more than okay. I'm perfect. I actually think I might sleep. I never sleep."

He loved that they'd put that happy look on her face. His whole body was humming and he could probably run a marathon, but all he was going to do was deal with the condom and hop back in bed with her. "You stay here and let Van keep you warm. I'll be right back."

He rolled out of bed and Van was standing at the end of it. He'd put his boxers back on and there was a blank expression to his face that changed the minute he realized Elisa was looking up at him. Then he slid into bed beside her, giving her a smile that didn't seem quite right.

"Come here. I barely got to kiss you." Van settled her in his arms.

And Hale hoped he was wrong, but he could feel trouble coming.

Chapter Seven

Van laid in bed, waiting for the moment when he could slip out. He'd manage to sleep for a couple of hours, and now he was pretty sure it was almost dawn. There was enough light from the crack in the curtains that he could see Elisa wrapped in Hale's arms. Her head lay against his chest, and she looked so peaceful.

So did Hale.

He was not needed here.

That had been apparent since the moment Hale decided to change up the game plan and go completely rogue. They were supposed to get her between them, to show her how good it could be to have two men pleasure her.

They were not supposed to show her how good it could be to get Van off real fast and then let Hale take over and have the two of them so wrapped up in each other there was no place for him.

By the time he'd gotten his hands on her, she'd been sleepy. He'd kissed her and cuddled her and she'd fallen asleep in his arms, but the minute Hale had come back she'd shifted and wrapped herself around him.

Would they even notice if he left? He thought not. They'd barely noticed when he'd climbed into bed next to Elisa after Hale had finished fucking her.

Ah, but he hadn't fucked her, and that's what's bothering you. He made love to her. He's so invested in this woman and you're still not sure if you're even going to be here in a couple of months. Hale is changing, and that's what's bugging you.

He did not want to be reasonable tonight.

He eased out of bed and then stopped as Elisa turned over in her sleep and seemed to reach for something. She found the pillow he'd been using and sighed as she cuddled it close.

He needed to get out of here. He would sit down and reassess and decide if he could move forward with the understanding that he was the outsider in this relationship. If it was a relationship.

If it's not a relationship, then why the fuck are you panicking?

Yeah, he needed to figure that out. He found his jeans and shirt and quickly got dressed.

He could text her later and explain he had an emergency…bartending event. Yeah, that would work. He didn't want to hurt her feelings, but he also didn't think she needed a big emotional discussion with a dude she barely knew who already had the feels for her and worried she liked his best friend more and he was going to get cut out.

That would definitely scare her off.

Emergency bartending was back in play. He could take a shift. Someone always needed to take off this time of the year.

He was being a coward, but he wasn't sure how to deal with this tight feeling in his chest. He definitely wasn't sure he could handle sitting down at breakfast with them, feeling like the third wheel.

He put on his boots and coat and made sure he had his keys in hand when he slipped out of the room. The sun was coming up, and he glanced behind him.

Was he making a mistake? Should he go back in and hope this antsy feeling left when she woke up and they inevitably had some hot morning sex?

Damn, it was cold out here.

The snow came down in a light shower, dusting the world a lovely white. It would be a beautiful day at the festival.

He started for his SUV, and that was the moment when Hale came out wearing nothing but the slacks he'd had on the night before and his shoes. "What the hell are you doing?"

This was what he'd wanted to avoid. He needed some time to process. He needed to think and feel all his crappy feelings so he wouldn't say bad shit. "I'm going back to the cabin. I got a text from Zane. He needs help opening."

It was a lie but a necessary one.

"Trio doesn't open for hours," Hale pointed out. "Come back inside. You said you'd spend the day with her. I can't. I've got to work on the bathroom today or I'm going to get behind on the project. I can't let those dominoes start to fall or we won't be ready to start Callie's cabin on time. Also, I don't want to be the one who tells that Taggart guy he can't bring his family on vacation this spring. I think he could be cranky."

Did Hale think he was the only one with responsibilities? "And I need to study. I've got a final coming up in accounting. So I'm going to be working all day. I think you should take the day off and show Elisa around. I'll help you with the bathroom install tomorrow."

Hale stared at him for a moment. "What the hell is going on?"

"Nothing. I told you I need to study and work." He didn't want to have a fight in the middle of the Movie Motel parking lot.

Hale's arms came up around his chest, the big guy finally showing a sign that the temperature was getting to him. "You know the accounting stuff backward and forward, and that test isn't for another two weeks. You've got plenty of time."

He liked his accounting class way more than he'd expected he would. He was taking a tax course next semester just for fun, and wasn't that sad. "I have to take this seriously, Hale. I graduate in another semester, and I have to be ready. I owe my brother."

Hale's jaw went tight. "You know you can pay him back in cash, right? Like you don't have to sacrifice the rest of your life because Jake paid for the last year of your degree. Hell, he won't even miss the money. I'm sure he would be open to a payment plan."

Hale didn't understand a damn thing. "I think I'll handle my relationship with my brother. You can stay out of it. You have no idea what it's like."

Hale's teeth were starting to chatter, but there was still no way to mistake the look of hurt on his face. "Yeah, I guess your family is your business."

This was exactly what he'd been trying to avoid. "I'm only saying I have to think about it. I wasn't trying to say anything else."

"No, you were pointing out that I don't understand what it means to have a family." Hale got straight to the point. "And you're right. I don't have a brother who cares about me."

He was taking this to the worst possible place. "Of course you do. You have me."

"No, I've got a friend, and that's what I am. We can call each other brothers all day but when it comes down to it, we're not. We're two guys who've enjoyed spending time together. We needed each other when we first started out, but no matter how much I want it to be different, your family—your real family—is always going to come first." He backed up, his body physically shaking at this point. "I'll spend time with her. I'll make some excuse for why you're gone."

"You don't need an excuse. I already gave it to you." He wasn't sure how to convince Hale he wasn't leaving him behind when he graduated. He wasn't sure Hale was the one being left behind at all.

"I thought you liked her."

"I do. Maybe I can meet you for dinner." By then he might have figured out how to handle the whole third-wheel thing. By then he might calm down and be ready to see what happened last night in a different light.

Hale nodded. "All right."

He turned and Van felt the weight of guilt hit him. It wasn't like he was telling Hale the whole story, but he didn't want to fight. "Tell her I'm sorry I had to leave early. I would do it myself but I didn't charge my phone last night. It's probably dead."

"Sure." Hale turned and then stopped again. "Fuck. The door locked."

"Knock on it." He couldn't stay out here for long.

"I don't want to wake her up. I don't want her morning to begin with me having to tell her you suck," Hale admitted.

Frustration welled inside Van. "Maybe you wouldn't have to if you'd minded your own business."

Hale's arms went tight around his chest. "My own business? Somehow this isn't my own business?"

"I just… Damn it, Hale. Will you get in here? You're going to get frost bite." He pulled his keys out. It was obvious Hale wasn't about to let this go. They were going to have this out and they would have to do it in the car or his best friend would get frost bite.

"Is it because of her scars?" Hale asked.

He thought they knew each other. "No."

Hale studied him as though there was some way for him to see the truth on his face. "It is, isn't it? They're not that bad."

"It's not about the scars." Why wouldn't Hale give him some fucking space?

"Then what? Because I enjoyed the hell out of last night, and I think we should pursue this," Hale insisted.

"And I want to think about it."

Hale stared at him like he'd kicked a puppy or something.

"Do I not have the right to take some time to think about whether or not I want to get involved with a woman we barely know?" Somehow that was an easier explanation than putting the blame in the real place. He was afraid he would get close to her and he would lose both of them.

This kind of relationship had been easy when there weren't wild emotions floating around. It struck Van that they were all at a crossroads. He and Hale and Elisa were all at a point in their lives where change was happening. "Shouldn't we all take some time to think about this?"

"Absolutely," a soft voice said.

That was the moment he realized they weren't alone. Elisa stood in the doorway, her robe around her and Hale's coat in her hand.

"Hey." Van felt his whole body flush. "I was heading into work. I got called in."

"Sure." She passed Hale his coat. "You should keep it down though. I think everyone else is trying to sleep."

Hale nearly fell over trying to get that coat on. "Elisa, he didn't mean anything by it."

"By what?" Elisa asked. She disappeared briefly and showed back up with Hale's cell phone. She was careful to keep the door open so she didn't get locked out. "He said he needed time. So you should give it to him. You shouldn't push a person who doesn't want to be someplace."

"I didn't say I didn't want you." He couldn't let her think that.

Her expression had gone blank. "It was fun but it was also casual. We don't have to repeat the experience. It's fine. I wasn't expecting anything but a good time, and I got it. Do I get a T-shirt? *I came to Bliss and all I got was a threesome and this T-shirt.* I would buy that shirt."

Hale managed to get into his coat, shoving the phone in his pocket. "Elisa, you have misunderstood this. I don't know what's going on in Van's head, but I know what I want. I'm going to take the day off and show you around town."

"I don't think that's a good idea." She stepped back. "Like I said, it was fun, but I think we should leave it here."

That was not how the morning was going to go before he'd gotten out of bed. She'd cuddled with Hale all night long. She'd been so into him. She hadn't meant to break things off with them this morning.

This was all his fault. She wouldn't be shoving Hale away if they hadn't been fighting in the parking lot. "Hey, Hale is not the one with the problem. It's me. I need some time. Things got intense last night. I don't know if I'm ready for that."

"It's okay." Her expression had softened. "I appreciate that, though I wish you'd left a note or something. But I do understand."

"Good." Hale looked like a man who'd been told he wasn't about to be executed. "I'll take a shower and then we can go to Stella's for breakfast."

"They're not that bad?" She asked the question on a soft sigh. "I knew it would be hard to get comfortable with my body again, but you two managed it. Now I wonder how bad it was for you."

Hale's skin had gone from pale to pink. "I think you are gorgeous. Whatever you think I meant by that I didn't. I didn't."

"You always say what you mean," she replied. "That's one thing I did learn about you. Good-bye, guys. I hope we can be friendly if we see each other again."

"He didn't mean it like that," Van insisted. He knew exactly why Hale had said what he'd said. "He thought I needed convincing, and he's learned that sometimes he's gotta shift my point of view. It wasn't about your body. God, Elisa, I think you're the single most beautiful woman I've ever seen."

"That's a nice thing to say. You two have a good day," she said before firmly closing the door between them.

"What the hell just happened?" Hale asked.

"Well, I think you said something that made her worry she's not pretty enough. I don't think women like the phrase *it's not so bad* when it comes to their various body parts." Gene turned the corner. He was an elderly man with a friendly face and a balding head. He carried a box of what had to contain the cinnamon rolls he always offered guests in the lobby along with fresh coffee. He picked them up from Stella's, where Hale would no longer be taking Elisa for breakfast. "I thought you two would be smoother. You've been together for a long time. You should know how to handle a woman."

"I didn't mean it like that." The angry expression on Hale's face had been replaced with pure confusion. "I think she's beautiful. How do I make her understand?"

"Maybe some flowers," Gene offered. "I think Teeny's got some pretty roses in."

He didn't think flowers were going to solve this problem.

Hale stared at the door. "No. I'm pretty sure she wouldn't take them from me." He turned away and started for the SUV they shared. "We should go."

"I think you should talk to her." He hated the defeated look on Hale's face.

"You heard her. She said she didn't want to be pushed into something she didn't want, and it appears that she doesn't want me now." He stood at the passenger side door. "Drop me off at the cabin. I won't need the car today."

This was not what he'd wanted. How had it gone so fucking wrong so fucking fast? But he recognized the blank look on Hale's face. It was how he dealt with rejection. He closed himself off. He would brood for days or weeks.

He'd fucked this up, and he had no idea how to fix it.

It was the longest ride home.

* * * *

She hated this feeling. Vulnerable. Fragile.

Figuring out Van was leaving hadn't broken her. It was okay that he hadn't enjoyed the night before the way she had. Or that he needed time to think. She kind of did, too, because it had been more intense than she'd expected, and it hadn't been all about the sex. The real deep intimacy had come from sleeping between them, from feeling warm and adored.

Like so many things in life, that feeling had been false.

She sat in the booth at Stella's and wondered if she would ever try again.

This was not how she'd thought her morning would go.

She'd thought she would be here with both of them, enjoying the morning and refueling after a night of physical activity. She'd thought she would walk around the festival with them, spend the next few weeks seeing if anything could come out of it.

Now she was right back to thinking she should go home.

Was it home? Had it ever been home? Or had it always been the place where she slept and waited for something better to happen? Something that never seemed to come along.

"Hi, honey. I'm so glad to see you here." Cassidy stood at the end of the booth. She wore denim overalls and a big puffy jacket. "I was going to come looking for you."

She would have to look for her since neither Cassidy nor her father carried a cell phone because…there were a lot of reasons. Still, it was nice to see a friendly face. "Here I am. Are you here for breakfast?"

Cassidy slipped out of her coat and slid into the booth across from her. "I came into town to run a couple of errands and to see if I could convince you to come to dinner tonight. I've got some stew in the slow cooker and found some old picture albums I'd like to share with you. If you're not busy."

She wasn't busy. She was here for a reason, and it hadn't been to hook up with two ridiculously hot guys.

Who'd seemed to like her. Hale hadn't hesitated when she'd gotten naked. There had been no momentary horror in his eyes. Had he hidden it that well? She wouldn't have thought he could.

"I would love to have dinner with you." She had to admit she was curious to see her dad's place. She was definitely interested in learning more about her father. He seemed like a genuinely kind man, and he had some interesting stories.

Cassidy reached out and put a hand over hers. "Are you okay, honey? You have a sadness in your aura today."

Auras were another thing Cassidy believed in, and apparently she was right. "I'm okay."

"No, you're not," Cassidy said, her voice quiet. "What happened?"

"Nothing important."

"Was it those boys? Did they make you feel bad? I heard something about it, but I was hoping it was only gossip."

There was gossip? "What did you hear?"

"Well, I heard that the boy who fixes things and the boy who pours drinks had a fistfight in the parking lot of the Movie Motel."

Elisa shook her head. "They did not."

"I heard that you kicked them out of bed and they were naked in the parking lot, and Hale might have frozen his willy off." Stella put a mug of coffee in front of her.

"How did you hear anything at all?" She was sure she'd gone a nice shade of pink.

Cassidy waved off that worry. "Everyone knows what happens in a small town."

"Everyone knows something happened, but usually by the time it gets out to Mel and Cassidy's it's morphed into something else." Stella leaned over to speak to the person in the booth behind her. "Beth, did you hear about anything happening at the Movie Motel this morning?"

A pretty woman with brown hair turned slightly and smiled. She'd been in the middle of spooning oatmeal into her baby girl's mouth as she sat in a high chair. "Oh, I heard there was a sasquatch sighting and Van and Hale tried to fight him off and that's why they were half naked in the parking lot."

Gossip really moved fast in this town. "There was no sasquatch involved."

"Are you sure? This is not their mating time, but they do sometimes come out when it snows," Cassidy said. "I blame Gene. It's the cinnamon rolls. Sasquatches are attracted to the scent of cinnamon, and he parades Stella's rolls by every day. It was only a matter of time."

"My cinnamon rolls do not attract sasquatches, Cassidy," Stella argued. "Well, except during Woo Woo Fest when I do sell a sasquatch special twelve pack to help draw them out. It does work then. But only for the tourists."

"You are playing with fire, Stella. They will come for you one day and then you'll be serving a bunch of sasquatches right here in this diner," Cassidy pointed out.

"You know my policy. If they've got money, they're welcome. Hell, I've served Max Harper all these years. The sasquatch should be simple," Stella announced. "Now would you like the usual?"

"Yes, that would be wonderful." All of Cassidy's sternness had disappeared. Apparently that was only around for sasquatch advice. "Elisa, honey, have you ordered? Hal makes the most wonderful pancakes. He infuses them with beets."

"That's the Cassidy special," Stella explained. "We also have beet-free pancakes."

"I just want some bacon and eggs and toast." She handed over her menu. "Thanks. And sorry about the gossip. They needed to leave early this morning. They had work to do. Nothing more."

Stella nodded and then strode back to the kitchen to put in their orders.

"I really am sorry I seemed to have made a scene." That was the last thing she'd wanted. "I didn't mean to embarrass anyone."

"Why would you embarrass someone?" Cassidy asked. "Are you talking about me and your dad?"

"I'm sure he didn't think he would meet his adult daughter and she'd immediately spend the night with two men."

Cassidy seemed to think about that for a moment, as though processing the words and trying to find their real meaning. "You think I would be ashamed of you for doing something normal like dating? Like having a nice night with some handsome men? Why would I be ashamed of that?"

"Because most parental figures would be."

"I'm not most people," Cassidy replied. "I know people see me as weird and they think I have mental problems, but you should know that I see things in a different way than the rest of the world. I don't understand the concept of shame. I guess I might feel it if I did something bad, something that hurt someone else. But I would never feel it over someone I love, and certainly not when they do normal things like trying to find connections with the people around them."

She wished they hadn't gotten into this because now she was getting emotional again. "I did more than find a connection. Or rather the connection that felt real turned out to be entirely physical."

"Did they hurt you?"

She shook her head. "Just my feelings. It didn't end the way I hoped it would."

"And you feel shame?"

Elisa thought about that word for a moment. "I feel...sad. I guess I don't feel shame. I was worried I would embarrass you and my dad. It would have embarrassed my mom. She would have been upset with me."

She'd been hearing her mother in her head all morning long. Since the moment she'd realized she was alone in bed, she'd heard a long lecture about how stupid she'd been to think it could work. Every bit of self-doubt came out in her mom's voice.

"But why?" Cassidy seemed to genuinely not understand.

"In our world it would be considered slutty behavior to sleep with one man the same day you met him, much less two."

"But you liked them and they liked you. Women have needs, too. That's nothing to be ashamed of." Cassidy's eyes narrowed. "Unless they did not meet your needs, and then I will have a talk with those boys."

The thought of Cassidy lecturing Van and Hale on how to pleasure a woman made her smile, and something eased inside her.

She didn't have to live her mother's life. She didn't have to run away and hide because this morning hadn't worked out. Things didn't even have to be weird between her and the guys. She would take some time and think about it because she might be too sensitive. Or instead of sitting on it, she could talk about it with the weirdest, kindest, coolest woman she'd met in a long time. "I was worried about how I would feel being naked because radiation left me with some skin discoloration, and I have scars."

Now Cassidy was sitting up straight. "Did they say something to you?"

If her mom had been the one sitting across from her, she would have taken this time to point out that she was a fool to think a man would accept her imperfections. She wouldn't have had a retaliatory gleam in her eyes. Elisa wouldn't have had a little worry that her mother might try to fuck with Van or Hale's auras. "Not really. Hale said something about it not being so bad, and I worry I might have been overly sensitive about it."

"You have every right to be sensitive after everything you've gone through," Cassidy insisted. "I want to make it plain to you that I am so happy you're here and proud that I get to be your stepmom. I know it's an odd situation to be in, but I'm so excited to get to know you. And your dad is, too. He would have come into town with me but he had some work to do."

There was something deeply soothing about being around this woman. "It's okay. I don't want to disrupt his life, but I would like to spend time with him. I've been thinking about hanging around for a while. I don't have much to go home to. I have my sister, but she works a lot. Neither of us is happy where we are. I want to see if I can find a place for us. Something new."

"You want to see if you like it here?" Cassidy had the biggest smile on her face.

"You and Dad...you are my only family besides Sabrina. I don't have a big group of friends. I think if I like it here my sister might come with me." She wasn't giving up on this. There was no amount of embarrassment that would make her walk away from getting to know her dad. And her stepmom. "Would that be okay? I could maybe stay through the winter."

Cassidy practically beamed. "I would love it so much. Your sister can come out for the holidays, and we'll have such a lovely time. Oh, it's beautiful here at Christmastime. There is nothing I would love more than you staying here. I know we just met, but I already love you, honey."

Maybe she'd been looking for the wrong connection the night before. Maybe this was what she needed. "I hope I can be worthy. I don't know that my mom taught me how to be a good daughter."

"All you have to do is show up. That's the secret to most things in life. Just be present and we'll find our way. You know you could stay in our guest room. Right now it's dedicated to our network communications, but we can move all that equipment to the bunker."

Oh, she was starting to love this woman, but she was also realistic. "I think I need my own space, but I promise to let you feed me as often as possible. I would like to find a cabin or maybe an apartment in Del Norte. It's close enough. I need to find a job though. I'm not good at sitting around."

Cassidy lifted a hand and started to speak.

"No alien hunting, bonus mom." Elisa was already figuring her new family out. "Something that pays a little."

"Oh, it pays. It's just sometimes the money isn't accepted here on Earth," Cassidy conceded. "Well, we'll have to find something for you. How about I show you around town and we can see if anyone's hiring."

"That sounds perfect."

The day had started off bad, but it looked like she was going to make some real progress.

When breakfast came, she even tried the beet pancake. It was delicious.

Chapter Eight

"You are more morose than usual, my friend."

Hale didn't look up from his work, simply continued inspecting the water lines. He should have locked the door. Or checked to make sure Van locked the door when he'd slammed out of it. "What do you need, Max?"

It was early afternoon, and he couldn't get the morning out of his head. He was a roiling ball of emotions he didn't like to feel, and the last thing he needed was a Max lecture.

He hadn't talked to Van since the moment he'd closed the door to the passenger side of the SUV. Van had tried to talk but Hale couldn't handle it. They were in this situation because Van was an asshole. He was a fucking asshole who had ruined the only chance he might have had to have a relationship with a woman he cared about. He was an asshole who was going to leave and then Hale would be alone and none of it mattered. Nothing fucking mattered except the look on her face when she'd told him to leave.

"Well, I wanted to see if you survived your sasquatch encounter."

That was weird enough to get his attention. "What?"

Max was wearing his usual uniform of jeans and a dark T-shirt, boots on his feet and a hat on his head. He'd probably taken off his coat when he'd let himself into the cabin without even knocking, which was presumptuous of the man. He leaned against the door that led from the primary bedroom into the ensuite. "There is a wide-spread rumor making the rounds that the new girl was attacked early this morning by sasquatches looking for cinnamon rolls, and the only reason she wasn't carried off was you and Van's quick thinking. Although there was a lesser rumor that you and Van were involved in ritual combat, with the new girl as the prize for whoever won. Now Nell's gotten hold of that one, so you should expect a protest."

There had been absolutely no quick thinking at all. "What?"

"Yeah, you already asked that, buddy," Max pointed out. "You know how the Bliss rumor mill goes. I take it whatever happened this morning is the reason for that scowl on your face and it involved neither cryptids nor medieval mating rituals. It's why I decided to come over and check on you. If you—the quietest dude I know—is being talked about, something went wrong."

"It was nothing like that. Although Van and I did get into an argument. How did that story get around?" He asked the question but the answer was clear. "Gene. He was there. He probably called Stella, who called Callie, and so on and so on."

If he needed to get the word out quickly, all he had to do was whisper something to one of those three and everyone in town would know in an hour. Of course, they wouldn't know what he wanted them to know because after the rumor had filtered through a couple of layers, it would evolve into something outrageous.

He loved the Bliss rumor mill right up until the moment he was trapped in it.

"I suspect so." Max glanced around the bathroom. "Do not let my wife see this. She'll want a tub like that. I would never get her out."

The tub truly was a thing of beauty. "It's not as expensive as you think it would be."

"Only because you don't charge as much as you should."

He shrugged. It was probably true. He could charge two or three times what he did if he was in an urban area. "I charge enough to get by. I don't need much."

He never had. Since he'd gone into foster care, everything he'd owned had fit into a backpack. Well, and a tool kit. Lately he'd been thinking about how nice it would be to have a permanent shop where he could make custom furniture. Right now if he needed to do some woodwork, he used Henry Flanders's shop. It would be nice to have something like that. Henry could work in peace and still be close enough for his wife to call him in for dinner. He would make the short walk to the cabin and be immediately greeted with his baby girl's smiling face.

Hale was never going to have that.

"Or you don't know your own value." Max waved that off. "So things didn't go well? They looked like they were going well last night."

"Did you come by to get more gossip?" He wasn't sure how he felt about people knowing how poorly this morning had gone.

"I came by because we're friends and if you and Van are fighting, then you likely need some advice. I don't know if you've figured this out, but you don't always make the best decisions when it comes to interpersonal relationships." Max's lips tugged up. "I sound real smart, don't I. I listen to a lot of what Alexei says."

Yep. Max was here for a session. Max thought he could help Hale fit in, but Hale knew he pretty much didn't fit in anywhere. "It didn't work out."

"So the sex went wrong? Come on, man. I love a good sex-gone-wrong story. Once Rach and I were at the Feed Store Church setting up the Easter displays. So we start going at it in the Feed Store part, not the church part. Rach was real explicit that we not move into any space where God could see us. I did not go into the all-seeing, all-knowing philosophy of the Almighty because I was really horny. But I was about to start the real action when I tripped and fell against a display of pitchforks—why would anyone do that—and that started a line of dominoes that ended with me flooding the aisle we were on with a thousand pounds of wild bird seed. Now the problem was I had already gotten Rach out of her clothes, and those were lost in the bird feed, but I was a quick thinker and found a couple of aprons that I fashioned into a nice dress, if I do say so myself. Yeah, I paid for that in more ways than one. That kind of sex-gone-wrong story?"

"The sex was fine." The sex had been more than fine. It had been spectacular. It had been the best sex of his life because it had been about more than sex. "And it's not any of your…"

Damn it. That was exactly what Van had said. *Not any of your business.* The words still hurt, and he'd turned right around and given them to Max.

Was Max his friend? Max felt like his friend, but sometimes it could be hard for Hale to tell. He'd been kicked so many times, with Van being the only exception. But now it looked like Van was going to join that long line of people he couldn't trust anymore. Van had reconnected with his real family, and while they'd tried for a little while, real family would always win out.

"Am I supposed to guess what you were going to say next?" Max asked.

He had a decision to make. Was he going to shut down entirely or was he going to keep trying? "No. I'm sorry. This morning fucked me up, and I'm being an asshole."

"I'm glad you can acknowledge that, but I understand if you don't want to talk about it. I came by to check on you because it can be hard the first time a sasquatch tries to eat your cinnamon rolls."

"I didn't..." Ah, euphemism. Max wanted to clear up the whole rumor thing. "It's okay. People talk. I don't think they mean anything by it. In some ways, it feels like people at least give a damn."

Trying meant not allowing himself to go to the absolute worst place. It meant opening himself up to the positive. Optimism was an act of bravery, and it might be time to find some real courage.

"I was hoping you would get that. There's not a lot of scandals around here," Max explained. "People genuinely want their neighbors to be happy. Hell, the fact Mel has a daughter is pretty much the biggest thing this town has seen in a long time. Being involved with her was going to bring some scrutiny."

His optimism took an immediate hit. "Well, I'm not involved with her anymore, so I can fade into the background again."

Max's blue eyes rolled. "I know you don't want to talk about it. I wouldn't want to talk about it. But it does help sometimes. Did she do something that set you off her?"

He didn't want to talk but not talking had gotten him nowhere. "No. She was perfect. I fucked up."

"Ah, then you have come to the right place, my man." Max sat down on the tub, settling in like he would be here for a while. "I have fucked up in every way possible."

He doubted it. "Did you ever make a woman who survived breast cancer feel like shit about her body?"

Max's eyes went wide. "You did that?"

Hale sighed and sat down across from Max. Guilt and anger had been burning in his gut, but below all of it was a deep sense of weariness. A base layer of disappointment he wasn't sure how to deal with. "I didn't mean to. I said something when I thought she wasn't there, and she took it to the worst place."

Max seemed to think about that for a moment. "Probably because she was afraid that was exactly how you would react. Before or after sex?"

"After."

A low whistle came from Max's lips. "You are lucky she is not from Bliss because a Bliss woman would be joining the *I Shot a Son of a Bitch* club this morning. They have a ceremony and everything. Or so I've heard. Men are not allowed, and that is one secret society I try to stay far away from."

"It wasn't what I meant." He still wasn't completely sure what had gone wrong. "Van was trying to leave, and I was trying to figure out why. I asked if it was about her scars. I said they weren't so bad. I didn't mean it like that. I think she's beautiful. I wish I was still in bed with her. But I don't know how to fix it."

"What was wrong with Van?" Max asked. "Why was he trying to leave? I take it she wasn't awake at this point. He was trying to sneak out?"

"Yes. And that's what I was upset about. I don't know. I guess he didn't feel the same way about her that I did." Maybe it was time to say the problem out loud. Again, not talking about it had gotten him nowhere. "Once he graduates, he's leaving Bliss. He's going back to Dallas to work for his brother's company. I don't think he wants to get too involved."

"But you do?"

"I don't think I'm going to go with him. I think I want to stay here." That wasn't right. He needed to stop hedging. "I am going to stay here in the area. I have enough work lined up for at least a year, and if I widen my range, I can probably work steadily for a long time."

"Good. I think you belong here, and I know we can use your skills. It can be damn hard to find a truly skilled contractor who's willing to come all the way out here." Max studied him for a moment. "But you've been with Van for a long time. You sure you want to break up the band?"

The idea of not having Van around hurt, but he had to be realistic about this part of his life. "I think if I go to Dallas, it won't be long before I find myself getting left behind. Van has a real family there."

"Real family? As opposed to his fake one?"

"You know what I mean." Or maybe Max didn't. He'd grown up here in Bliss. He was still close to his childhood friends, and he'd never gone a day without his twin. He might not have any experience with being alone in the world. "When one friend doesn't have a family, the other friend says you're my brother now or something and he means it, but it's not the same as his real brother. I liked his family, but I did not fit in there. I fit in here."

Max nodded as though he finally understood. "And if he's got to pick between you and his blood relation, you think he'll pick his brother."

He'd thought a lot about this, and there was no bitterness when it came to Van's family. "I don't blame him. I've never had a real family so I don't know how I would feel. Everyone I was close to growing up as a kid is dead or lost to me. I've come to the conclusion that relationships, even friendships, are not forever. Inevitably you grow apart, and friendship isn't enough to keep you close. You have to have something else to bind you. A business, a shared home, something you build together, and we don't have that so it was only a matter of time. I wish he hadn't wrecked my chances with Elisa on his way out."

"It sounds like you did that, buddy," Max corrected.

And that was why he'd come back here to work. "Yeah, I know. She made it clear that she understood why Van needed time. I'm the bad guy here."

"You were trying to make things perfect, and that is always a mistake. I know you've been surrounded by a bunch of relationships where it looks like two guys found a girl they liked and easily settled into a happy life together, but it was tough, man. I had to convince

Rach to give Rye a shot. That woman walked in and took one look at me and knew what she wanted. I had to be clever to ensure I didn't leave my brother behind."

Somehow Hale didn't think it had gone exactly that way. He'd heard some of the Harper family history, but at the heart of the story Max was telling him lay a very important question. "What would you have done if she hadn't accepted Rye? What if Rye hadn't loved Rachel?"

Max blew out a hard breath. "Well, that would never have happened because my Rach is the most lovable woman in the world. But if she hadn't been able to tolerate Rye's eccentricities, then I would have picked her. You have to pick your wife. If you love her, really love her, you pick her every single time."

He wasn't going to have the chance. "Well, I don't think I'll be doing any picking at all."

"You are going to be stubborn," Max said with a shake of his head. As if he'd known it all along.

"I'm not being stubborn. She told me to go away."

"Did she tell you to stay away?"

Well, she hadn't said that exactly. "She said she changed her mind."

"Then change it back," Max advised as though that was the simplest thing in the world. "Go after her, and this time do it without Van. If he wants time to think, give it to him. See how long he likes that."

He'd been willing to go it alone when Van said he wouldn't date her. Of course he'd been talking about her at the time. They just hadn't known it. When he'd woken up this morning, he'd thought Van was being his scaredy-cat self. Nothing more. Things had gotten deep the night before.

It was hard for Van to get close to people, especially women. His family had moved so much when he was a kid—sometimes four or five times a year. He'd never been taught how to make long-term relationships work. Not that Hale had either, but he was willing to give it a shot.

"I am not good with women." He wasn't good with people period, but he'd felt comfortable with Elisa.

"You looked like you were doing okay last night. You

145

managed to convince that gorgeous woman who obviously has not led a wild life to go to bed with you on your first date, and to let your best friend join you. That's some pretty smooth talking. And from what I heard she's even seen you dance, so…"

Was he going about this the wrong way? Should he have stayed in bed with Elisa and let Van figure his shit out on his own? He'd panicked at the thought of losing his best friend, but sometimes when a man held what he cared about too tight, he strangled the very thing he loved.

He would never have said he was capable of smothering anyone, but hadn't he been doing that to Van this morning? "I've never dated anyone without Van around."

"Then it is time, brother. I'm going to be honest, I rarely dated without Rye. Not until I met Rachel and knew that whether my brother was with me or not, she was the right one. Guys like you and me, we're not players. We're not smart enough to play games. Guys like you and me are going to fall once and never again. You willing to let that go because you might make a fool of yourself?"

"No." The answer was super easy. "And she felt it, too. I screwed it up because I followed Van thinking I could have everything I wanted, when I wanted it, the way I wanted it. I did this and I have to fix it. Between me and Van, and definitely between me and Elisa. But Max, I'm terrible at starting relationships. I don't even know how to make amends for being a dumbass."

A light sparked in Max's eyes. "Oh, but I do. You have come to the master of amends. See, the key is you gotta get the woman to think that the way you make up for doing something stupid is to give her a whole lot of sex. Do not fall into the 'I'll clean the house, baby' trap. You just gotta do that. No amends required. It is going to come as a surprise to you—I know it did to me—but when you live with a woman, she wants you to do a healthy part of the chores, and dear god, when you have kids with her she definitely wants you to be a part of that. Something about you living in the house, too, so you should help keep it up. And do not say you'll babysit because that will start a whole other fight. It's not babysitting when you provided half the DNA. Even if you can't prove which of you actually provided the DNA. She will not listen. So the key is to start groveling in a way that makes her think of oral sex."

That wasn't a terrible idea. Could he turn this thing around? The thought of dating without Van made him ache, but he would ache more if he didn't try with Elisa. It might still all go to hell, but he had to give it a real shot, and that meant changing his mindset. "All right. How do I make this work?"

"I have a few thoughts on that." Max leaned in and began to talk. "See, I think you can make this awkward thing work in your favor. And you might have to let that grudge of yours go."

* * * *

Van looked up from the textbook as the door to Trio came open and a bit of sunshine walked in to chase away the gloom of the afternoon. The afternoon had brought dark clouds and cold winds and a general sense that the world was complete shit.

Elisa smiled as Micky Lang greeted her.

Damn, she was pretty, and he totally hadn't planned on seeing her again so soon. The weight of what had happened this morning hit him hard. He hated that he was fighting with Hale, but he hated that he'd hurt her even more.

Could he disappear into the floor or maybe sneak away? He wasn't sure he was going to be welcome at home tonight. He was pretty damn sure she wouldn't want to see him again. And Cassidy was with her. The older woman stepped inside, waving to someone through the window.

Micky put away the menu he'd been holding and gave her a nod before turning and starting for the back of house.

That was the moment she glanced around the dining room and spotted him sitting at one of the back tables, a couple of books in front of him along with his laptop.

He wished the morning had gone differently. He held a hand up, hoping she would take it for the friendly gesture he intended.

He expected her to wave back and dismiss him or turn away entirely as though he wasn't worth seeing. He would have accepted either reaction as normal and deserved. Instead she said something to her stepmom and started walking his way.

Damn. He wanted to run away, but he was a whole-ass grown man who owed her an explanation or to sit here and let her tell him what a dick he was.

Because he was. He was stupid for getting out of that bed. He should have sucked it up and stayed. It wasn't like he hadn't had his heart broken before, and it would be better to have a broken heart than to be the one who'd done the hurting.

"Hey. Accounting, huh?" She looked down at his books.

"I've got a final next week. Right before the break," he explained. "Then I'm supposed to head to Texas for the holidays."

Her eyes lit up. "Then they'll need a bartender for a couple of weeks."

She was looking for a job? "I think Zane just works more. But maybe. I'm sorry about the way this morning went. I didn't mean to make a scene."

She chuckled as if the whole thing was nothing more than a funny incident. "I know. You meant to sneak away quietly. Hale meant to make a scene."

Van knew what it looked like to bluster through a painful incident. She wasn't unfeeling. She felt too much, and this was her way of handling it. "I don't think he meant to make one either. Hale is unused to dealing with emotional situations, and he mishandled it. He never meant to hurt you."

That seemed to throw her. Her face lost its pleasant expression and went blank in a way he was starting to associate with her being emotional. "Are you two okay?"

She hadn't expected him to apologize. Van assessed the situation quickly. Elisa had walked over because she was the kind of person who wanted to rip that bandage off no matter how much it hurt. She'd wanted to get the awkward first encounter out of the way. She was still hurt, and he could potentially make some headway with her if he was open and honest. "No. I don't know that we're going to be okay. He's upset with me. I know you think you heard something bad this morning, but he didn't mean it the way you think he did. I think he's willing to blow up ten years of friendship over what happened this morning."

"I hope that's not true." Her hands went into the pockets of her jacket as though she didn't trust herself not to reach out to him. "And maybe I was a little sensitive. I know I look super confident, but I was trained to not show weakness. This morning hurt like hell, but I'm coming to the conclusion that it was my fault. I made too much of the situation. I went into last night telling myself I would live in the moment and I utterly failed to do that. It's cool. I came over to show my stepmom that we're good. I think I need to because she's going to report back to my dad, and I think he could prove to be overprotective."

He wasn't sure he wanted Mel Hughes to come after him. "You think he's going to sic some aliens on me?"

Her head shook, those dark curls caressing her cheeks. "No. He would never do that. It goes against some protocols he follows. He mentioned like a United Nations but for a whole bunch of planets or planes. I don't know. I'm still confused by how all that works. I do know that using a non-alliance approved contractor for any kind of work here on Earth is strictly forbidden, and my father follows his contract to the letter," she said with absolutely no hint that she was joking. "So if he comes after you, it's pretty much him. I know that sounds like it's not a big…"

He held up a hand. "There is a reason your dad sometimes gets tranqed. I would not tangle with that old man. I've also heard he's good with poison."

"He is not," she said with a frown. "It's whiskey. He makes it himself."

"It's moonshine, and I've heard many a man has found himself waking up in the woods after partaking." He'd been told to avoid Mel's whiskey at all costs. He stared at her for a moment, remembering how good it had felt to kiss her. "I'm sorry how I left hurt you. It was the last thing I wanted to do. It was why I left."

"Was it?"

"I don't know. I think maybe it was because I don't want to get hurt, and I think you could tear me up. I don't think you would mean to, but it became apparent to me that last night wasn't casual. It wasn't to me, and it definitely wasn't to Hale. We don't fight or argue." He could still see the desolate look on Hale's face. But more than that, he could remember how different Hale had been the night before, and that was the real problem. "Last night was not how most of our encounters go, and it threw me."

"How do most of your encounters go?" She flushed. "That wasn't a question I should have asked."

"Why not? It's one of the great things about Bliss. We get to ask all those uncomfortable questions because no one gets upset. They might not answer but they don't get offended. I hear a lot about the ley lines around Bliss and all the mystical properties of the area, but I'm pretty sure the real magic of Bliss is that this is a no-fucks-given zone. I think there might be like a dome that keeps them out." It was one of the things he loved about the place. When he got back to Dallas he would have to think about how to act all the time. There would be spaces where he could be himself, but nothing like the freedom he had here in Bliss. "As to your question, we've found it's easier to have a game plan going in."

"Going into intimate situations?"

"Yes. It's easy to go with the flow when there are only two of you. Throwing that third body in can be tricky. Like all things in life, you get into patterns, and that pattern was broken last night," Van admitted. "Hale usually follows my lead, but I don't think he wanted to do that with you. You were special to him. It felt like change I wasn't ready for. I got scared and ran away. It wasn't fair to you. It wasn't fair to him."

"Thank you for that. I appreciate the honesty. I'll give you some of my own. The way I reacted to what Hale said… Maybe I'm not ready for this either." She gave him a half smile. "It felt serious. I was ready for all the good stuff, but that's not the whole of any relationship. There's bad stuff, too, and you have to be ready for all of it."

"I'm not staying, Elisa." Even saying the words made his gut clench. "I have to go to Dallas after I graduate. There's a job waiting for me. My future's there, and I think getting involved right now would only cause a whole lot of heart ache."

"The funny thing is, I'm starting to think about staying. I know it's too soon, but I like my dad," Elisa admitted. "I really like my stepmom. I like the idea of having family around me, and there's nothing for me back in North Carolina. If I can convince my sister to at least move a little closer, I might stay."

"Yeah, I think Hale's leaning that way, too. Last night made me face that fact."

A brow rose over her eyes. "Are you telling me this is as much about Hale as it is me?"

Yeah, honesty hurt. "I think it's about change that I'm not ready for."

"I kind of got the feeling the two of you were a package deal. Mostly because everyone said you were. You two have been together for a long time. Why would you break up now?"

He didn't argue over her terminology. Maybe he would have had they been in Dallas, but here in Bliss, he let it be. Hale was the longest relationship of his life, and the idea of it changing had him reeling. A "breakup" with Hale would likely hurt worse than any he'd ever gone through with a girlfriend. "I didn't think we would. I guess I thought he would come with me like he always has. Hale kind of floats along. I mean he did. He pretty much went along with whatever I wanted, and that sounds worse than it truly is."

"You made the decisions," she confirmed. "I get that. I did that with my husband until he found someone else. From what I understand their relationship is very different than ours was. He cares enough to make an effort with her."

She didn't understand, and suddenly it was important that she did. "That wasn't Hale's problem. I think his childhood was so crappy, he doesn't ask for what he wants because he never learned to. His mom left early. He didn't know his dad. He got passed around a lot. The only mother figure who actually cared about him died, and then he went into foster care. Hale has learned to accept what he's given and not ask for more. But I think he wants more now, and you were a part of that. He would never have argued with me about who to date before he met you."

"Well, maybe if we both stay here in Bliss, we can revisit the idea somewhere down the line," she offered. "Friends, then?" She held out a hand.

He wished he could be more. He took her hand in his, feeling the warmth she always brought him. "Friends. And could you please think about giving Hale another chance? Seriously, he's not talking to me, and I don't handle silence as well as he does."

She squeezed his hand and then stepped back, her answer obvious before she even spoke a word. "I think we should all be friends." She glanced over her shoulder at the hostess station where Micky was back, a form in his hand. "Could you stand to work with me? If I can get a job here. I've already applied at Stella's and the

Trading Post."

It would be absolute torture being around her and not being able to touch her. "I think it would be great. I'll put in a good word for you. I don't know if there's anything full time though."

In the background he heard the door open again, but he was focused on Elisa.

"I'm good with part time for now while I look around. My only real plan is to spend some time figuring out my future. I was in the military for so long, I don't know a lot else," she explained. "I might figure out I need to do the school thing again."

He knew all about that. "It can be weird to be the oldest person in class, but the good thing about a college like Adams State is you can always find the actual working adults who are trying to better themselves. We share a lot of notes."

"I would honestly rather avoid it," she admitted. "I didn't love school, though I like learning new things. I tend to prefer to do it hands on. It's another reason I'm pretty committed to staying. I've been told I can learn all kinds of things here in Bliss. My dad apparently can teach me how to make pottery. And fight aliens, of course, but the pottery thing sounds like fun."

"Hey," a familiar voice said.

Van looked up and Hale was standing there, his hat in his hand. "Hey."

Elisa turned, her face flushing a pretty pink. "Hey."

The circle of *hey* was complete. "I thought you were working at the cabin all day. I'm sorry. I would have left you the car if I'd known you were coming into town."

"Max gave me a ride." Hale turned to Elisa. "I was hoping I could talk to you. Not like for a long time or anything. I know that… Well, I lost that chance this morning when I screwed up. I need to make a few things clear though. I loved last night. It was one of the best nights of my life. Probably the best night."

What the hell was Hale doing? He was reaching for Elisa's hand, taking it into his own. He covered hers with both of his, surrounding her.

"But I wrecked that this morning with thoughtless words," Hale continued before glancing his way. "To both of you. Van, I'm sorry. I should honor your boundaries the way I would hers."

"I have boundaries?" He had no idea what was happening.

Hale ignored him. "I need you to understand that I think you're the most beautiful woman I've ever met."

Elisa's lips turned down but she didn't pull her hand back. "That's laying it on a bit thick."

"It's simple truth. Sometimes you meet a person who seems brighter than the others, and maybe then you see them with something other than your eyes," Hale said. His thumb moved over Elisa's wrist. "I hope you stay around and that we can be friendly because I would hate to be the person who ran you off."

Her eyes rolled and she sighed. Now she did take a step back, but her hand came up to her chest. "I'm not leaving. I was telling Van I'm looking for a job. I was also telling him that I might have been overly sensitive this morning, but it's probably for the best. I'm not ready for a serious relationship."

Hale looked like a kicked puppy for a second, but then seemed to rally. "Well, it's not the first time I've heard that. I understand. I can be a lot."

"It's not about you. I like you." She seemed to stumble in her efforts to reassure him.

"I thought it went well, but I can misread situations," Hale admitted. "I get caught up in how I feel, and I forget that you don't feel the same things."

She looked confused for a moment.

Sometimes he had to translate for Hale. "He thinks the sex wasn't good for you."

Her skin went an even deeper pink, and she glanced around as though trying to see if anyone was watching them.

Everyone was watching them, of course. And he was pretty sure his boss could read lips.

"It wasn't bad." Her hand flew up to cover her mouth. "I can't believe I said that. I didn't mean that. I was good. It was amazing."

"So are your breasts," Hale said somberly.

Had Hale meant to do that? Holy crap. He'd never seen Hale navigate a situation with any real dexterity, but he was handling this one beautifully.

"I think what he's trying to say..." Van began out of habit more than any real need.

"He's made his point." Elisa nodded. "Sometimes we say things that don't fully express how we feel. All right. All is forgiven, but I do think I'm right about the whole serious-relationship thing. I need to concentrate on building a relationship with my dad and finding my place here."

Hale gave her a soulful look. "I understand."

"It's not about you." Elisa looked like she did not believe him in any way when he said he understood. "If I thought we could hang out and it wouldn't be too serious…"

"Like I said, I understand. I think if we were to be alone together, it would be hard for me to keep my hands off you. I've done nothing but think about last night all day. If we were alone, I would be tempted to show you it can be better," Hale said, his voice going low.

"It was pretty perfect, and that was the problem," she muttered. She looked back as though she needed a distraction. "I should go. I need to get some more applications in. Uhm, I'll see you guys around."

She practically ran away.

Hale frowned after her. "I don't think that worked the way I hoped it would."

Van wasn't so sure. Elisa joined her stepmom, but she looked back at the two of them before she walked out of the tavern. "What did you hope it would do?"

Hale shrugged. "I wanted her to remember that it was good because it was. She wasn't faking anything. I know women can, but she wasn't. She was right there with us…with me."

"I think she remembered. That's why she ran away." Van hated the adjustment he'd made, but it was probably a good thing. "The good news is she's sticking around. I agree with you. She was right there with you. If I hadn't…"

Hale shook his head. "No. I made the mistake of going after you. It was your choice, and I didn't let you make it. I apologize."

"Hale, you don't have to apologize." He hated the queasy feeling in his gut. "You thought you were helping me."

"I thought I could fool myself and that if I convinced you to stay with us, nothing would have to change." Hale slid his coat off and hung it over the back of the chair across from Van. "But time's not going to stop, and you're going to leave for Dallas in May. I'm almost certain I'm going to stay here. In fact, I think I'm staying here for the holidays."

So that apology was complete bullshit. "You're punishing me."

"I'm not. I like your brother and his family, but this place is starting to feel like home," Hale explained. "I worry if I follow you to Dallas, I'll be living your life, not mine. I have to stop running at some point, and I think this is where I try to build something. I'm going after that woman. If she's staying, then I can take my time with her."

Hale had found what he wanted, and he was going after it.

Van didn't even know if he wanted to live in Dallas.

"Do we have to make decisions right this second?" Van didn't want to think about this. He needed time to figure it out. "Who knows. I could flunk out. Jake could find someone he likes more. We could all die in an alien invasion and then we'll have spent our last days in emotional turmoil for no reason."

Hale stared at him for a moment like he wanted to argue but then sat back and sighed. "Sure. We don't have to make any decisions right now." He picked up the menu. "What's the special today?"

"I could stay, you know." He felt like they should talk more even if Hale had given him exactly what he wanted. He was obviously putting it all aside and moving on.

So why did that feel like the wrong thing to do? The trouble was, Van wasn't sure what the right thing was.

"For Christmas?"

Van shrugged. "I could tell Jake I have to work. I've spent every Christmas with you since we were like nineteen or something. It would be weird to not have you around. Besides, I've heard Serena has some friends coming in and they're taking the guest house, so if I go alone, I'll end up bunking with Tristan. I love that kid, but why does his room always smell like feet?"

"Because he's a boy." Hale sat back. "I don't want to be the reason you don't see your family for Christmas."

But Hale was his family. "I'll see them next year since I'll be there." And Hale would be here with Elisa, if he could convince her.

"Besides, I haven't gotten a ticket yet so I'd end up flying out of Alamosa on Rocky Mountain Scare Ways, and you know how that goes."

Flying small planes over the mountains could be a true experience. He would fly from Alamosa to some small city airport and from there to Dallas, and he would be alone the whole way.

If he stayed, he could see where things were going with Hale and Elisa.

"You okay, guys?" Pilar stopped at their table. It was obvious she was about to head out to the festival. She had her parka on and carried some extras for the booth. "Van, I thought you were taking the day off. Was it… I heard…"

Yep. Everyone had. Absolutely everyone. "I'm great. Sasquatch was a kind and gentle lover."

Hale shrugged. "I wouldn't know. He rejected me. He has a type."

She snorted. "Okay. I had to ask. You get the wildest rumors around here. I also heard there was a meteor shower coming next week and it's a cover for an alien invasion. I hope they're gentle lovers, too. Also, there was someone asking about you last night. She looked super serious."

Huh. "She asked about me?"

"She asked if I knew you or Hale. She said she's a lawyer," Pilar replied. "That seemed a little scary to me."

It was the second time he'd heard someone was looking for him, and he had zero idea why a lawyer would be interested in him. Or Hale. "Let me know if she comes back. I don't think I'm in any trouble."

"Okay. I wanted to ask you first. If I see her again, I'll let her know you work here." Pilar gave him a wave before heading for the back door.

He watched as Elisa walked by the window, carrying a bag from the store next door. It was new and sold mostly the honey from the bee farm on the other side of the mountain. It had been owned by an elderly gentleman who didn't have a lot of contact with the town, but his daughters had recently taken it over, and they seemed determined to build a business out of it.

How would he work with Elisa if she got a job here? How

would he be able to be around her and not get his hands on her? Hale would hate him if he did.

Or maybe he could gently work her back to Hale, and he would suck it up and be the bigger man and get his heart broken when he had to leave.

Maybe the best thing he could do for Hale was to make sure he didn't leave him alone. What if the best gift he could give Hale was to replace himself. It would hurt like hell to watch them be happy, but Hale was worth the sacrifice.

"I wonder what that's about." Hale sat back. "I don't know why a lawyer would be looking for one of us. Do you think it's about the car accident we witnessed?"

It had been a minor thing, nothing more than a fender bender on the highway on the way to Pagosa Springs. No one had been hurt. Or at least it seemed that way at the time. They'd stopped and both men seemed fine. Still, Van had given the police his number in case they needed a witness. "That could be it. But why wouldn't they call?"

"No idea." Hale went back to studying the menu. "Maybe the officer got the number wrong. Who knows? Or it could be they've got the wrong people and they're looking for someone else. They'll figure it out. Maybe a burger."

Hale started talking about lunch, but Van couldn't stop thinking about the fact that his time was running out.

Chapter Nine

Elisa came awake to the sound of a knock at her door and wanted to curse whoever was on the other side.

She'd been having the sweetest dream. It was five days after that night she'd spent with Van and Hale and every single night since, she'd found herself dreaming about being with them again.

Most likely because Hale showed up wherever she was and suddenly all she could think about was sex. It was horrible. It was hot. It was very, very frustrating.

The man had eaten an ice cream cone in the middle of winter. They'd been at the festival two nights before and he'd been talking to her dad about the upcoming meteor shower, which she'd been assured would not bring an actual invasion. When Hale had become so interested in astronomical events she had no idea, but the man knew how to use his tongue. It wasn't like he'd been doing anything weird. He'd been eating an ice cream cone and he was a licker, and all she'd been able to think about was his tongue. She'd stood there watching him, almost in a trance, and realized she was a complete pervert.

Is everything okay, Elisa? He'd looked up and found her staring.

She'd had to think fast. *Just wondering what flavor that was.*

And then his lips had curled up in the sexiest smirk. *Peach. I know it's a summer flavor, but I really like peach. I've just been craving it lately.*

She hadn't needed her damn coat anymore. She sometimes got hot flashes from the meds she was on. That was what had happened. Except this heat had come from a very specific place.

But in her dream she hadn't had to worry about Hale thinking she was a complete weirdo. He'd been way too busy eating her peach while Van had cheered him on. Van had been behind her, his big hands cupping her breasts while his legs spread hers wide so Hale could get to her pussy.

She groaned in sheer frustration. She'd thought she could avoid them, but she'd underestimated how small the town was. When she went into Stella's, usually one of them was in there either getting a coffee to go or having lunch. They would look at her with soulful eyes, and she would think she'd made a terrible mistake.

The knocking started again, this time louder.

"I know you're in there, Ms. Leal. Gene told me you haven't left yet." The voice coming through the door unmistakably belonged to a woman, and a no nonsense one at that. "If you think you can wait me out, you're wrong. I am a rock, and I don't move. Ask anyone."

Elisa shook her head and forced herself to get out of bed. Who the hell was at her door at… She glanced over at the clock. Damn it. It was past ten. It was a perfectly reasonable time to expect someone to be up and about. Especially when someone didn't have a job yet. It was the weirdest thing. All of her interviews got canceled because of strange occurrences. She'd missed the one at the Trading Post because the road had been closed even though it had looked perfectly fine. Stella had told her she'd lost at poker and had to forgo hiring anyone at this time. She was scheduled for an interview up at the lodge tomorrow and hoped she managed to make it.

She wasn't sure if she could stay as long as she wanted to without a job.

And the one her dad had offered her with the Galactic Security Council didn't count.

She didn't bother with her robe, throwing open the door and frowning at whoever was behind it.

Which turned out to be a blonde chick in nice heels and a chic coat. She had a Chanel bag on one arm and held a garment bag in the other. "Hello, I'm Gemma Wells. I work for the sheriff's department, and now you do, too. I brought your uniforms and your work schedule. I told Nate that you were not working Christmas or New Year's this year because you're doing him a favor. You're welcome."

She strode into the motel room like she owned the place.

"Excuse me?"

"I know it seems like a lot, and I should have called you, but I'm more of a hands-on girl. See, we've been down a deputy for a long time, and we're about to be down two because Cam is going part time. He does way more than you would think he does." The woman seemed to make herself at home.

"I don't know him, so I don't think about him at all."

"You will once you meet him. He's a very attractive man," Gemma assured her. "That's one of the perks. The guys around here are phenomenal and also trainable. That's part of the problem. I'm used to dudes from Bliss. I'm sick of the rotating clowns Nate brings in from all over Southern Colorado. They get all excited about the extra pay and then they whine because they don't know how to deal with the Detector 6000 or what to do when two moose decide to take a nap on someone's porch, and yeah, there wasn't a lot of sleeping going on, but that's the circle of life. Maurice has decided to join it. And don't live in Colorado if you can't handle a couple of bears. So you're my solution."

"I did not apply at the sheriff's office." She hadn't thought to ask. Actually, when she thought about it, she was pretty qualified. She'd even done some time with military police. On the other hand, it felt like jumping in with both feet. Also, who was Maurice? She should probably hold that question until the end of this weird session. "I was thinking a couple of hours a week selling honey or waiting tables would be a good start."

The blonde shook her head. "There are no other jobs for you. You'll find I've cut you off from all other employers in the area. I am the one who shut down the road into town just as you were trying to come in for the interview with Teeny. You'll discover she's no longer hiring. She wasn't really. She's trying to get Marie to slow down, but they do this every year. She asks Marie to rest more and Marie then drives her up the wall and Marie goes back to work where she's happy and then whoever they've hired quits because Marie can be a lot to handle. So you're welcome."

She was fascinated by how fast this woman could talk. And she seemed slightly evil. It would be better to kick her out, but she kind of wanted to know where all of this was going. "And Stella's? I take it you set up some kind of poker game."

"Oh, I didn't have to set it up. The girls play out at the palace once a month. Luckily the game was last week and all I had to do was get Stella to go deep. Do you have any idea how long I've had those boots worn by Dolly Parton herself when she was inducted into the Grand Ole Opry in 1969? I tracked those suckers down two years ago when I realized someday I might need a real favor from Stella, and she cannot be bought by normal means. Now they were far too expensive for me, so I had to strong-arm a rich dude who likes to pretend like he's not rich into buying them, but the doc and I now have an understanding. I talked his nurse into staying around even though he's a weirdo and this place can be difficult on the medical professional."

"Okay, so you traded the nurse to the doctor for Dolly Parton's old boots and the boots to Stella for not hiring me?" It was kind of nice to be wanted, even though she still hadn't figured out why the woman named Gemma Wells wanted her.

A satisfied smile crossed Gemma's face. "Oh, that's the brilliant part. I still have the boots. I caught an ace on the river, and that's how I won you."

She had so many questions. It was odd since she never questioned shit back at home because she didn't care enough to. It felt like she was waking up out here. "And the Bee Bliss Store?"

"Oh, I told her I had looked up your record and that you're a scam artist who hires on at businesses to rob them," Gemma admitted. "And Zane owed me. Also, it turned out he wasn't down an employee for the holidays. Van is staying in town. I wonder why that is."

He was? She'd seen Van a couple of times, too, but he was more standoffish. Not unfriendly. She'd caught him looking at her the last night of the festival, but he hadn't come over to talk the way Hale had. "He probably decided he needed to work."

"Sure he did." Gemma held up the garment bag. "Do you want me to put these in your closet? I had them pressed and everything. I run the office. I also ensure the uniforms are clean, so

I'm going to need your dirties every Monday by noon or you'll be stinky all week, and that makes people nervous. No one likes a stinky deputy."

Oh, but there was one person Gemma Wells hadn't bribed yet. And it was an important person. It struck Elisa that she found herself in a position of power. A place she so rarely was. She was wearing flannel PJ bottoms and a sweatshirt that proclaimed she was a Boss Babe her sister had given her that one time she'd thought of opening her own gym. She'd then realized she preferred to work out alone and tossed that idea right out the door. But the sweatshirt was warm as she sat back on the bed and regarded her opponent. "I don't know that I like the idea of being a deputy. They have terrible hours, you know."

Gemma's blue eyes narrowed as though she'd realized there was a challenge to be met. "That's why I made sure you had Christmas and New Year's off, and you don't have to work night shifts for the first month. You'll work with Nate so he can bring you up to speed, but at some point you would be his number one. Cam going part time means we need a deputy to be in charge of the other deputies. I'm offering you an almost immediate promotion."

"To a job I never said I wanted," Elisa pointed out.

A little humph came out of the blonde. "Look, Leal, you're perfect for this job. You spent a lot of time in the military."

"So maybe I want some time off from being the authority figure."

"I promise you it's different out here. It's not going to be some rigid organization. It's super chill."

"Except for all the murders." She'd done her research. For a town so small they had a healthy murder rate.

Gemma waved that thought off. "That is mostly tourists and criminals. I make zero apologies for killing the dude who tried to off me. I cannot help it if Bliss manages to attract a surprising number of people who other people want to kill. It's not Jen Talbot's fault she worked for an art forger who ran afoul of the Russian mob. It wasn't Rachel Harper's fault that she picked up a stalker. Now I do blame Hope Glen. She should be able to recognize a cult when she sees one."

"All of that seems interesting, but it still makes me think I'll get shot at a lot. More than when I was in the military. Also, who is Maurice?" She was settling into the fact that she was probably going to take this job. When she thought about it, it was far more stable than waitressing, and maybe way more interesting.

"Maurice is the town moose. Lately he's been frisky," Gemma admitted. "It freaked out some people who were renting a cabin, and they called the sheriff because when you're a rural department you deal with everything. Including oncoming alien invasions."

She said the last like it totally made her point, like it was now Elisa's obligation to take the job because the department often had to deal with her father. "Dad has promised me he can handle any upcoming invasions."

"I think it would be helpful to have someone your dad knows on the team." Gemma laid the garment bag over the chair at the small desk that was the only other furniture in the room. "The older he gets, the more he can be triggered by certain things. I worry that the never-ending rotation of new guys is making him worse."

That was a low blow. "He's okay. I know he has some eccentricities, but he's not dangerous."

"He can be dangerous to himself," Gemma said quietly. "We had to get him out of a tree two weeks ago. He'd climbed up because he thought he saw evidence of the Greys nesting, but he couldn't get back down. One of the temps was on duty, and he wasn't exactly kind."

She hated the idea of her dad being dealt with by someone who didn't care to understand him. A sheriff's department in a town like this would be different. It wouldn't be like big-city police work. She would have to get to know everyone and let everyone know her. She wouldn't be anonymous. There would be no place to hide the way there would if she worked at Stella's, where she would deal mostly with tourists, and only for brief periods of time. Still…it was presumptuous of Gemma, and they needed to start out on a proper footing. "Fine. I'll agree that it would be best if someone from town dealt with my dad when he's…working. You seem to have some knowledge about alien life."

She'd mentioned Greys. In the short amount of time she'd spent with her father, she'd learned a couple of different alien species concerned him, and one of those were the Reticulan Greys.

"When I took the job at the sheriff's department, I realized the best way to deal with Mel was to speak his language. He's a nice guy. He deserves to be treated with respect, and hell, I've seen a lot of weird shit in my time. Who knows. He could be right. I'm a hedge my bets kind of girl. Now let's talk about getting you a county vehicle."

Oh, she needed so much more than that. "I don't think I can handle a full-time job while I'm living here in this motel."

It was another thing she hadn't managed to sort out yet. She needed some space if Sabrina was coming into town. Cassidy had offered up the bunker, but that would not work. Elisa knew there were plenty of cabins for rent in the valley. Most of them were short-term rentals, but that would work for now. She'd been told that some of the cabins were used as summer homes, and the owners rented them out most of the rest of the year, so they would come furnished and everything. By the time she would need to move out, she would know if she was staying for the long term. But finding a place took time and knowledge, and Gemma seemed like a chick who knew everything.

Gemma sighed. "If I find you a rental, will you take the job?"

So her negotiating skills worked here. "Yes."

"Done. You start tomorrow morning at seven. Don't touch my coffeemaker. It's my baby and I'll murder anyone who hurts her. Leave me your coffee preferences and I'll handle it," Gemma said briskly as she moved to the door. "And be ready to move. I'll have that deal done in a couple of hours."

That got her on her feet. "Seriously?"

"Things move fast in Bliss," Gemma announced. "Except when they move real slow. I'll have your county vehicle ready in the morning, so you can turn your rental in this afternoon. You can use it for personal driving unless you're leaving the state."

The door closed behind the whirlwind that was Gemma Wells.

And Elisa thought about the fact that her life here in Bliss might have just begun. She found her cell phone and called her sister. It was time to get started.

* * * *

Hale wasn't sure if any of his plans were working. Not that they were his plans. It had been Max Harper's idea to tempt Elisa back into bed and then give her so much pleasure she couldn't think straight and oops, how did that ring get on her finger? Van wasn't so sure that would work—or that Max was a brilliant mentor. Given that Max was pretty much living what Hale considered to be the perfect life, he disagreed.

"Did someone rent my brother's cabin?" Van came in from the porch, shrugging out of his coat and hanging it on the hook by the door. It was a sunny day but still cold, with a light snowfall that clung to Van's dark hair.

Hale looked up from the list he'd been working on. The bathtub was installed, and now it was time to work on the kitchen. That meant a long trip into Alamosa, and he didn't want to forget anything. There was a hundred miles between him and the nearest real supply store. He could get a lot of basics at the Trading Post, but anything beyond that required the drive. "No idea. Did you ask him?"

Van shrugged. "Nah. I don't want to bother him. He's getting ready for the holidays. They're having a big party at the office this afternoon."

"You could be there."

"I want to be here," Van insisted, though he'd stopped arguing about it. "Marie's truck is parked in my brother's driveway. I wonder what that's about."

Hale moved to the big front windows, looking out over the only recently paved road. The Taggart cabin was nestled in a curve, with an acre of land on either side that went all the way down to the river. This was the last cabin on the road. To the east sat national forest land. The closest full-time neighbor in this part of the valley was Caleb, Holly, and Alexei's big place. There was a smaller cabin across the street that Van's brother had bought even before Taggart had purchased his place. It was a two bedroom with spectacular views of the Sangre de Cristo Mountains. But Jake tended to only come up during the summers. He would bring the kids for a month or two at a time, and Adam and Serena would join them for a week here and there. Jake spent the whole time with his son and daughter fishing and decompressing in a way Adam and Serena didn't seem to need to.

That was part of the beauty of their relationship. They could be themselves. If they needed alone time or time away from the city and the other didn't enjoy that, they weren't alone. There wasn't pressure on Jake to do what Serena or Adam wanted to do because Serena and Adam simply did it. And Adam always had someone to watch baseball with. Serena could take writer retreats with her friends knowing Adam and Jake had the homestead locked down.

Sure enough, Marie's truck was parked on the gravel drive that led up from the street. She stood on the porch, a key in her hand.

That was the moment he realized another car was coming down the road. A familiar car.

He knew because he'd driven that car before. The sedan moved slowly across the road and turned into the driveway, parking beside Marie's truck.

"Holy shit. It's Elisa." She'd said she was looking for a place, but he'd never thought it would be so close. He'd expected her to stay at her dad's.

Van moved in beside him. "Are you serious? She's moving into Jake's?" Now Van had his cell phone out, and he didn't seem to care about Jake's office party. He punched a number in and put the phone to his ear. "Hey, did you rent the cabin to Elisa Leal?"

Hale watched as the woman of his dreams slid out and waved Marie's way.

There was zero chance that she knew he and Van were right across the street. She would have picked a different place, but if she'd signed a lease there would be nothing she could do about it. Damn it. He wished it was summer. He could walk around without a shirt on if it was summer. He would look like an idiot if he did that now. A blue, frostbitten idiot.

Firewood.

He could chop firewood. That was manly. Women liked it when men chopped firewood. There were whole romance novels dedicated to lumberjacks.

"That's the girl. Woman. That's the woman Hale and I were seeing," Van said before pausing. "Well, yeah, it didn't go as well as we'd hoped. It was totally my fault."

Hale had come to the conclusion that wasn't true, but he wasn't going to argue with Van. They had so little time left, and he wanted to spend it in friendly ways.

"How long is the lease?" Van asked as he moved toward the back of the cabin.

Hale watched as Elisa made it to the porch and took the keys from Marie. She opened the door and disappeared inside.

He happened to know that Jake's place was due for maintenance in a couple of weeks, and who was scheduled to do the work? Yup. That was him.

If he thought for a second he was annoying her, he would back off, but the couple of times they'd talked, she'd been the one to initiate it and the one to keep the conversation going. She'd also been the one to watch him like she was ready to pounce. He could have told her he was available for any pouncing she would like to do, but he had to play it cool.

It might be time to heat things up.

"She signed a lease through the end of May. She's there until Jake comes up in June. According to what Jake knows, she's planning on staying there alone with the exception of her sister coming to visit her." Van had slid his cell phone into his pocket and joined Hale again. "I think she's planning on making a real go of it here."

That was right about the time Van would be leaving. "Yeah. I heard she's taking a job with the sheriff's department."

Van sighed. "Then she'll probably get a look at my arrest record. So it's for the best."

Hale thought she was made of sterner stuff than that, but he wasn't going to push it. "She'll need help maintaining the place. She's never lived outside a city. I know she was military, but that doesn't mean she knows how to properly heat a cabin."

"Oh, you should chop wood." Van nodded beside him. "Women love it when dudes chop wood."

It was good they were on the same page, but he couldn't help looking at the dark side of things. It was kind of what he did. "Do you think she'll be upset when she figures out we're here?"

"How do you know Marie didn't tell her?"

Hale pointed toward the cabin. "Because she's obviously

moving in."

"We all decided we could get along. I'm not sure what the problem would be. I don't know why she would refuse a place she wants to live in because there are two men she's friendly with living across the street. I would think in this case it would be a plus. I know she's competent and independent, but it's the dead of winter in a climate she's not used to. It'll help to have two dudes who'll pretty much move heaven and earth to help her."

"Would you?"

Van went quiet, his eyes on the cabin in front of them. "I never said I didn't like her. I said I didn't want to get my heart ripped up when I have to leave. That's all. I know you don't believe me, but I was thinking about her, too. Now that I know you're not coming with me, I think you should do everything you can to pursue her. Especially if she's planning on living here."

The words were said with a stiffness that made Hale wonder if Van had rehearsed them. He could point out that it was Van's choice to leave, but that would start another fight. Instead, he would focus on what he could do. "Should we get the bad part out of the way? Or should we let her move all her stuff in before she catches sight of us?"

Marie was back on the porch, Elisa following behind. There was a big smile on her face as she spoke with Marie. She liked the cabin. She was excited to be here.

That was when Marie said something and pointed toward the cabin Hale was standing in, and Elisa's eyes widened.

The urge to drop down and hide was strong, but he managed to resist. Elisa probably couldn't see his face, but she was definitely going to be able to make out two dudes standing in front of the window looking out at her. And she didn't look happy.

"You need to go out there right now and assure her you're not going to bother her," Van advised. "Just walk out like you're going to the shed. Wave and look surprised she's here and then promise to be a super quiet neighbor and hey, if she needs something, let us know. Otherwise we both look like creepy stalkers who keep staring at her."

That was some sound advice right there. He grabbed a jacket off the hooks by the door and zipped it up as he walked out.

He was not good at acting. He was well aware he was

probably awkward as hell as he walked on the porch and held up a hand. "Hey, Marie, Elisa. How are you doing?"

Elisa bit her bottom lip as she obviously decided how she was going to handle things. "Well, I'm thinking about renting this cabin for a while."

"She's already signed a lease," Marie assured him. "I made sure to get that signature on the line before I brought her out here."

"Why would you..." Elisa began. "You knew I wouldn't...would think about it if I knew they were across the street. That seems pretty rude."

"Or smart. The guy who owns this place gave me a bonus for a longer-term rental." Marie looked wholly satisfied with herself as she moved back to her truck. "And honestly, this is the best open cabin in the area. I could have put you in the old Klein place, but it's falling apart, or the one on River Bend that's haunted. I could still get you in there. Some people think it's a bunch of chipmunks living in the walls."

"I think that might be worse," Elisa replied.

"Then you've never been in a real haunted house. Let me tell you those chipmunks have nothing on an angry poltergeist," Marie said with surety. "I've recently gotten really into paranormal investigations. If you hear anything weird in there, let me know. There's a woman who comes in for Woo Woo Fest who can clean it right out. You all have fun. Rent's due the first of the month."

And Marie was off.

Elisa made her way down the steps and toward the road.

"What is Woo Woo Fest? And is she serious?"

At least she wasn't running away. "It's actually called the Festival of Spiritual Renewal, and it's held in the fall. We have a lot of festivals and big town parties. And what part was she being serious about? The lack of good rentals or the paranormal stuff?"

Elisa frowned before answering. "Both?"

"Most of the cabins get rented this time of year by skiers who don't want to stay in one of the lodges," he explained. "They rent out early in the year so even if a cabin was open for a week or two, it wouldn't be available for long-term rental. The cabin you're in is owned by Van's brother. He only takes long-term rentals, and never during the summer. He doesn't want people partying in his sacred space or something. I don't know. He fishes a lot. Look, I don't want you to freak out. I'm not going to bug you. I was surprised to find out you were here. That's why I was staring. And we'll be moving in a couple of months anyway."

"You're going with Van?" She asked the question with a gasp.

Oh, she didn't like the idea of him leaving. Maybe it wasn't going as poorly as he thought. "No. I'm pretty sure I'm staying. I should be finished with the reno on this one in about six weeks, and then we'll stay in the cabin the sheriff and his family own while I'm working on it. It's a pretty big job. We're adding an extra room and bathroom and redoing the primary bath. It's cool because I get to learn how to properly chink a cabin from a master, and this is probably not all that cool to you."

Her shoulders had relaxed, and she seemed much more comfortable. She looked gorgeous in her cuddly coat, the snow falling around her. "I think it's interesting. You like learning new things. I do, too. And I'm not upset about you being across the street. I was surprised, and I think that Marie person knew exactly what she was doing. However, I desperately need to get out of the Movie Motel. It's fun for a while, but I'm pretty sure all my clothes smell like popcorn, and I've seen *Elf* five times in the last week. I hear the phrase 'you sit on a throne of lies' in my dreams now. It's disconcerting."

He loved how funny she was. "Well, you will not hear Will Ferrell out here, but you may hear a wolf pack. They come down off the mountain this time of year. Do you have a shotgun? Not that you should shoot the wolves. You should stay out of their way, but if you need to defend yourself, you should probably have a shotgun at hand."

She glanced back at the forest to the east as though looking for said wolves to appear. "I'm getting some kind of gun tomorrow when I go through orientation. I'm apparently the new deputy. I was informed this morning, though I have to tell you that Gemma Wells works fast. I thought it would take days to find a place, but here I am." She stared at him for a moment as though trying to decide how to proceed. "I'm glad you're close by. I'll find my feet, but it will be nice to have someone who's lived out here close while I'm figuring things out."

He breathed a sigh of pure relief. She wasn't running. "I'm right across the street if you need anything at all. And I'm going into Alamosa this afternoon if you need supplies. You can give me a list."

"You would do that for me?"

"Of course." He would do it for anyone, but he would do it with a smile for her. "We're neighbors. You'll find we have to rely on each other out here. Especially in winter."

"Well, neighbor, if you're going into Alamosa, can I follow you and catch a ride back? I need to turn in my rental. I'm getting a county vehicle tomorrow, and they'll let me drive it around town until I get a personal car. But I need someone to drive out with. I was going to ask my dad, but he's got a meeting this afternoon."

"I would love to help you." He was about to tell her about the errand he would need to run when a crack split the air, and he felt something hit his left arm.

Pain flared and then he was tackled by Elisa, who sent him right into the snow as she covered her body with his. "Don't move. Someone's shooting."

And it looked like he'd been hit.

Chapter Ten

"Hey, can I get you some coffee? The doc should be done in a minute or two, and he'll let you know how things are going." A beautiful woman in scrubs walked into the small waiting room. She'd been the one to greet them when they'd come into the clinic.

Elisa shook her head. "I'm fine. I think the last thing I need is coffee. My heart's still racing."

"You couldn't tell." Van sat across from her. "You were amazing out there." He looked to the nurse. "She was cool as a cucumber. She didn't even think about it, just jumped right on Hale and protected him and then got them out of the line of fire. Meanwhile I'm freaking out. I'm sorry about that. It probably made things harder for you."

He was exaggerating, but she appreciated the fact that he'd likely never taken fire before, and it could throw a person off balance. "You were fine. You did everything I asked you to do."

After the shot, she'd managed to carefully roll them to cover behind a tree, and she'd had Van drive the SUV around. She'd been fairly sure whoever had taken the shot was gone, but she hadn't wanted to take the chance so she'd used the car as cover and had Van get in the back with Hale. Then she'd driven them here to the clinic.

Her gut had been in a knot, but panicking solved nothing.

Her first thought when he'd been shot was that she didn't want him to die, and not in an "I care for all people" kind of way. In an "I want another chance with him" way.

"Well, I felt like I panicked." Van's head dropped back. "I hope he's okay. I can't…"

"Honey, he's going to be fine," Nurse Naomi assured them both. "I saw him a few minutes ago. It clipped his tricep. Doc is stitching him up, and then he can go home. I'm sure he'll need some pain meds for a day or two, but he'll be fine. Now the hunter who did this better be sure he's never found, or we won't be able to say the same for him."

"You think it was a hunter?" Van asked.

Naomi put a hand on his shoulder. "I think it was an accident. Unless we've got another assassin in town and they're after Hale. I don't suppose he's on the run from the mob? Secretly a CIA operative?" She gave Elisa a grin. "It happens a lot here."

"Hale's never been in trouble with anyone that I know of," Van replied.

"Then it was probably a hunter," Naomi assured them. "I've already called the park rangers and the sheriff. I have to call in any gunshot wounds."

The door opened as though Nate Wright knew exactly when to make his entrance. Her new boss nodded her way. "Hey, Deputy Leal. Hale okay?"

She stood, the long habit of respecting her CO ingrained in her. "He's going to be fine, sir. The bullet clipped him but there was a lot of blood, so I wasn't sure until we brought him in. I probably should have administered first aid in the field, but I couldn't be certain it was an accident. If someone was targeting him, I needed to get him out of the line of fire."

"You did exactly what I would have had you do," the sheriff replied. "If you're worried your performance this morning makes me rethink your position, you're wrong. I'm absolutely certain we've lucked into you, Deputy. Has Van brought you up to date on the situation he and Hale are in?"

"We're in a situation?" Van asked.

She was not aware of any danger they were in. "Not at all. What's happening?"

"Some lawyer is looking for us. Or me, I think," Van explained.

A brow rose over the sheriff's eyes. "Lawyer?"

"Yeah, apparently she came into Trio and talked to Pilar, but Pilar sent her away." Van sat back, his expression worried. "But she was clear that she was a lawyer. I don't think she would have trashed a cabin."

"Trashed a cabin?" It seemed like a lot was going on in the background.

"A couple of days back there was a break-in at one of the rental cabins up the highway that leads toward Creede," the sheriff explained. "It was one Hale worked on for a couple of weeks. They stayed there right after they left the lodge. Around the same time, a woman went looking for them at the lodge, but the person she spoke to didn't realize they'd moved on. That would have been their forwarding address."

"We didn't tell HR at the lodge when we left that cabin." Van waved that off. "I guess it didn't occur to me that we should do it. Lucy runs the place, and she knows where we are. Also, if Lucy had talked to that woman, she would have known better than to even mention she knew who we were. I mean, if you can't hide out in Bliss, where can you hide?" He frowned, obviously realizing what he'd said. "I don't have anything to hide out from."

But there was something off. Lawyers didn't run around small towns hoping for clients. She turned to the sheriff because Van was not going to be helpful. She wasn't sure Hale would be either. In this case, they needed someone far more pragmatic than they were. "You thinking a scorned lover?"

"I haven't scorned anyone," Van argued.

The sheriff ignored him. "At first. Now I'm not so sure. I don't see him dating a lawyer. If anything, the lawyer might be looking for him because of an incident that happened in Oklahoma City a while back. He was involved in a bar fight last year."

Ah, that made sense. "And the statute of limitations on civil suits is two years after the injury. So any complaint would have to be filed fairly soon."

Van had paled. "Seriously? You think that asshole is trying to sue me?"

"I'll have Gemma check to see if anything's been filed in Oklahoma. This might be a process server," the sheriff concluded.

"But that wouldn't explain the break-in." She didn't like the situation. Something wasn't right, but she knew what the sheriff would say next. It was the logical road to go down.

"We've had a couple of break-ins. We do every year, especially outside of the valley," the sheriff conceded. "I'm probably hearing hoofbeats and thinking zebras instead of horses. It's been quiet for a couple of weeks, so I'm looking for the next crazy event to happen. I also don't see why a lawyer would want to shoot Hale."

"No one wants to shoot Hale, but he was wearing my jacket, and from a distance, we look a bit alike." Van glanced over at the exam room door. "He picked up the closest jacket and it was mine. Do you think he got shot because of me?"

"I think you live right next to national forest land, and sometimes hunters are idiots. Most of our hunters know exactly what they're doing, but every now and then we'll get a group that pays more attention to their beer than the deer they're hunting. Or a shot went wild. I'm going to check with the rangers. They should know who's out there."

"Only if they came in legally. There are plenty of ways to enter that forest without the rangers knowing." It wasn't like there was a fence up.

The door to the exam room came open, and a man in a white coat strode out. Dr. Caleb Burke was an attractive man with curly red hair he kept close cropped. He wore blue scrubs under his coat and stretched one arm over his chest as he moved into the waiting room. "Hale's fine. Sheriff, you have got to do something about those hunters. This is the second time this month I've dealt with a gunshot wound. A hunter mistakenly shot his buddy in the leg a couple of weeks ago. Hale's going to easily recover, but I want him to rest here for a couple of hours. I've got him on an antibiotic drip just in case."

"You think it was hunters?" Van asked.

"Unless there's a sniper trying to take out handymen." The doc looked around, suspicion playing on his handsome face. "Tell me we're not turning this into a crazy conspiracy."

"Well, there was this lawyer," Van began.

"Although there was only the one shot, right?" the sheriff asked.

She nodded in the affirmative. "And he had time to take

another."

The doc shook his head. "Then drop the conspiracies. Hale got clipped with a rifle, and the hunter either didn't realize what happened or he freaked out and ran. Talk to the rangers. Or simply be happy he's okay and when this happens to one of the Taggart kids, let him handle it. I assure you then it won't be a problem after that."

The sheriff sighed. "I'll go out and talk to them. I don't need that big bastard running around looking for revenge. You don't like to do autopsies."

"See that you do," Dr. Burke said and then turned to his nurse. "Check on him in twenty minutes. I'm going to go call in his prescriptions and see if I can get someone to drive them out."

"I'll check around and see if anyone's already in town," Naomi offered.

"I could go." Elisa wanted to help. She was torn though because she also wanted to sit with him and keep him company.

"Could you please stay and help me get him back home?" Van asked quietly. "He can be a bear when he's sick, and I think he'll behave around you. Unless you don't…"

"I want to," she assured him.

"You can fill out a report in the morning when you come into the office." The sheriff held out a hand. "I'm glad you agreed to take the job. You're absolutely the most qualified candidate I've seen, and we could use a woman on the team."

"Did I have a choice?" She couldn't help but needle him a little, but she shook his hand. "And it's not like you interviewed me."

"Didn't have to. I know quality when I see it, and I talked to your old CO. I knew you would stay the minute you walked into town," he said, stepping back and tipping his hat. "That old man is going to love the hell out of you, you know that, right? He's been a dad to a lot of kids in this town, but he practically glows when he talks about you. He's so proud of you."

That damn near made her cry. It was so odd to have a parent who was proud of her. She'd spent her whole life trying to impress her mom. All she'd had to do to impress Mel Hughes was show up and not be an asshole. "I already love him. I didn't think I would, but I do. He and Cassidy are already family."

"I'm glad to hear that." The sheriff walked to the door. "I've sent Cam out to see if he can find the bullet that shot Hale, and he'll try to figure out where the shooter was. All you need to worry about is getting Hale home and making him comfortable. I need that man healthy. My cabin is too small."

The sheriff strode away, and before she knew it she was left with Van.

"Should we go see him?" She didn't like the dark look in Van's eyes.

"Do you think it was an accident?"

She wasn't willing to lie to him. "I don't know. I don't like coincidences, but they do occur. I'll look into it. And we should be able to figure out the situation with the lawyer fairly easily. I can track her down."

He nodded and stood, seeming to force a smile on his face. It wasn't the one that lit up a room. "Then we should go and see how he's doing."

She followed him into the room, but she didn't like the look on his face.

When she'd been in the military, she'd been known for her incredible instincts when it came to things that were about to go wrong.

Trouble was coming. She could feel it.

The smart play would be to walk away. She could do it. She could leave right now having done her duty, and no one would think less of her for it. Hale would be disappointed, but he would understand.

When she'd seen the blood bloom on his shoulder, she'd felt her heart crack.

She was being a coward again, the lessons from her mother leading her away from heartache, but she knew where that road would end. Her mother's existence had been lonely. She'd put up wall after wall, building them higher and higher until not even her children could breach them. She'd died alone because even in illness she hadn't let Elisa or Sabrina in.

These men would leave, but nothing was forever.

Trouble was coming and they might need her.

Trouble was coming, and she had a choice to make.

* * * *

Van watched as Elisa closed the door to the room Hale was in. Normally they slept in the smaller rooms, the ones he was sure the kids used because it felt weird staying in the primary bedroom with its massive bed. Hale was in there now because Van had convinced him he needed the bigger bed to rest and recover in.

"He's asleep." Elisa wore a V-neck sweater that showed off the way her skin glowed and the gentle curve of her breasts. She looked fucking delicious, and everything about her made him a bit mad right now.

It wasn't her fault. She was practically perfect. She'd handled everything brilliantly, including getting Hale to eat some dinner and take his pain meds. Hale hated anything that made him feel out of control. Van was sure something awful had happened to him in foster care or during the time he'd spent on the streets. But he was sleeping peacefully now, and all because of her, and Van wasn't going to get to be any part of this.

He could see it now. They would find a cozy cabin and get married and be fucking happy, and he would be that guy they knew once, the kind of pathetic one who could never get his shit together.

He turned and stared out the window of the beautiful cabin that would never be his, looking at that place where the shooter had to have been standing.

The shooter who'd been aiming at him.

"You okay?" Elisa moved in beside him.

"Sure." He knew he sounded surly, but he wasn't capable of acting right now. He'd managed to get through it with the sheriff, and he didn't think Hale had picked up on his shitty mood, but he was reaching the end of his rope.

His past was coming back to haunt them all.

He had no idea how he would have gone on living if that bullet had been true.

"You didn't eat anything," she pointed out.

No. He hadn't wanted to try the soup she'd managed to make out of the crap they had in the house. It was probably delicious, like everything else about her. "Sorry. I'm not hungry. I might go to Trio for a while if you think he'll sleep."

"You're going to a bar while your best friend is laid up with a gunshot wound?"

There had been no small amount of judgment in the question. Well, at least she was starting to figure out who he was. "Sure. Can't let a little thing like that stop me from drinking. Maybe I can pick up a woman."

He heard her sigh behind him. "You think this is about you."

He turned. Maybe it would be good to lay it all out to her before he had to do this with Hale in the morning. "You heard the sheriff. If there's a lawyer looking for me it's probably because someone wants to sue me. That particular incident happened in a bar in Oklahoma City where I separated a dude's shoulder, but it's one of a dozen incidents over the years. It could be any one of them."

"Yes, it's obvious you're a very bad boy," she replied with a chuckle. "What did you get into the fight over? Oh, a better question—during these numerous fights, how often were you working versus drinking?"

"I actually don't drink all that much," he admitted. "I was almost always working, and I had to deal with some asshole who thought it was okay to harass the waitstaff. The worst fight I ever got in was over a waiter. Nice guy, but it was hard to be out and proud in that particular town. Drunk guy gave him hell, and I ended up breaking drunk guy's arm. Spent a night in jail over that, too."

"You have anger issues and maybe a savior complex." Her hands came up, smoothing his shirt over his chest. "That is in the past, and you shouldn't borrow trouble. I'm going to look into this, but until I find out otherwise, I think we should trust the doc and the sheriff and view these things as two separate incidents. Now, I would like to talk to you about something."

What on earth did she want to talk to him about? He felt anxious, and he hated it. It was like his skin was too tight. He'd been taught to live in the now. The past didn't matter. But it did and it would. "I think I should go."

"Go where? To Trio? Getting wasted isn't going to fix the situation. Tell me what's going through your head." It was obvious Elisa wasn't ready to give up on him.

He needed to give her a reason to. "What's going through my head is I fuck everything up. I fucked up Hale's relationship with

179

you, and now I almost killed him."

"That's hyperbole, but I understand the sentiment. First of all, you didn't upset my relationship with Hale. If he'd stayed in bed, I would have shrugged your leaving off and happily spent the day with him. My own insecurities got in the way, but I think I'm over that. He says he didn't mean it, and I believe him. I assume you didn't run away because the thought of seeing me in daylight was far too much to bear."

"I told you why I left." He wasn't sure why he wasn't walking out the door right now. He didn't want to argue with her. She was everything he wanted and absolutely nothing he could have.

"Because you're going to have to move to Dallas as some sacrificial offering to your brother."

Although she could poke him in the worst way. How could she not understand? She had a sister. "I owe him."

"Have you told him you want to stay?" Elisa asked as though she knew the answer. "You should because this feels like a simple conversation."

"We had a deal." He couldn't let Jake down. The family always let Jake down. He couldn't be one more sibling who walked away. "He paid for school, and I come to work for him."

"Is he a selfish jerk?"

He found himself frowning at the thought. His brother was practically a saint. "Did you forget the part where he paid for everything? I'm here because my brother moved heaven and earth to get me here. I would be rotting in a jail if it wasn't for him."

"What if he did that because he loves you and wants you to be happy, but you wouldn't take the money if you thought he wasn't getting something out of it? Sometimes it's hard to accept a gift that feels like charity, even from our loved ones. If my sister was in your position, I would tell her to be happy."

Nice words, but she was forgetting their current situation. Even if he was willing to disappoint his brother, there were other things to consider. "It doesn't matter because if I hang around here, I'm going to get us all in trouble. Have you thought about the fact that you could have been shot today, too? There's more than one person in the world with reason to come after me."

"I wasn't shot." She looked so pretty in the glow from the

fire. It made every inch of her skin look warm and inviting. Like just touching her would ease the chill he felt in his soul. "And Hale's okay. So what I am hearing is you're not simply going to Trio. You're walking away because you think it's dangerous for us to be around you."

"Well, I wasn't aware there was an *us* at all," Van pointed out. "Not anymore. Hale's made it plain he's staying here, and you don't want a relationship."

She shrugged. "Maybe I changed my mind. Maybe I've decided that I want time with the two of you more than I want to ensure that I don't end up with a broken heart. Maybe I just want sex. Maybe I hope that I can change your mind. You can't know what's truly in my heart. I could tell you, but you can't be sure. If I take you at your word and it's not all bullshit to get yourself out of an awkward situation, then I'm going to ask you to reconsider. I like Hale. A lot. I like you. You're here until the end of May, and I'm now living across the street from you. Hale is very honest when he's on meds. He's planning on chopping a lot of firewood in the hopes that I will see his lumberjack side and give him another chance. I don't need to see his lumberjack side. I'm half in love with his authentic self. It's inevitable that I'm going to fall into bed with him at some point, so why fight it?"

She was already giving Hale another chance. That was good. It was excellent since the right move at this point would be to walk away, and at least Hale wouldn't be alone. "I'm glad."

"So what do you say? Want to join us until you have to submit to your brother's will?"

"I didn't say that."

"You are very dramatic," she said with a sweet twist of her lips. "You're two halves of a whole. That's what I've figured out. You're all emotion and he's logic and reason, but you're not in balance because you need someone who can see both sides. I think that might be me."

"Have you listened to a word I've said?"

"Listened to and dismissed," she admitted with a wave of her hand. "You're jumping to conclusions. We don't know this thing was about you. It's a puzzle, and we can't be sure how the pieces fit together yet. We can't know the pieces fit together at all. According to Pilar, the woman who came in asked about both of you. Not only you."

"How would you know that?"

"Because I called Trio and got Pilar's number and I talked to her. I've got a basic description of the woman, and I'll start looking for her tomorrow. I'll get to the bottom of this. It's apparently what I do now. I think I'll make a good detective. I've always been good at figuring out a mystery."

"I'm not a mystery to solve."

She laughed at that thought. "You're not a mystery at all, Van. You wear your pain like a sweater you wrapped around your soul at a young age, and you can't figure out how to take it off. All of this, all the fights and anxiety and moving from place to place, it's because you haven't planted a flag in the ground and said this is my home. This is the place I can't be moved from. You were taught that in childhood by your parents."

"My parents, who are actually pretty happy."

"Because they take their home with them always. Because they're each other's home. I know how you feel. I grew up on various bases, though we did have one place to go back to. I had a traditional home in a sense, but what I didn't have was a mother who invited me in. I never knew her in the way I should have because she wouldn't allow it. I've been looking for a place to plant my flag for a long time now, but what I've figured out is I can plant it but if I don't feel it, it means nothing. I married a man because I thought it was time and he was the next logical step. There are no steps. Moving here could be the most foolish thing I've ever done, but I'm doing it because it feels right and for the first time in my life, I'm going to chase that feeling. I'm going to let the instinct I tried to kill off lead me, and if it all falls apart, I'm going to give myself the grace to know that at least I tried." She moved into his space. "And I'm going to try with you. You are too young for me. You are way too damaged for me. I'm still going to do this."

She tilted her head up and brushed her lips over his.

His whole body went taut, desire flooding his system. This was a terrible idea. Hale was in the other room. He was hurt and it was Van's fault, and he couldn't possibly think about kissing Hale's girl.

But she could be more if you let her. She could be your woman. She could be the woman who completes us.

The kiss turned into wildfire, his tongue surging into her mouth, dominating hers as she went soft under him. This was such a mistake, but it was one he was helpless not to make. The minute her lips had met his, all the reasons he wasn't good for her had flown out of his head. All that mattered now was getting her naked, getting her under him and showing her what he was good at.

He dragged her sweater over her head and tossed it to the side. He should take her to one of the bedrooms, but there was no time. He unhooked her bra and it joined the sweater, and she was bathed in the warm light from the fire. He stared down at her. "You are so fucking gorgeous."

"You make me feel that way. You and Hale. I've never felt like this before. I'm worried I'll be chasing this feeling for the rest of my life."

Or he could stay around and ensure she didn't have to. He shoved the thought out of his head because he wasn't worried about the future tonight. He would have to deal with a lot of things in the morning, but not tonight. She was giving him refuge, a sanctuary where he could find some comfort, and he was going to take it. He turned her around so her back was to his chest, and he cupped her breasts.

"I love how these feel in my hands." He weighed them against his palm, trying to memorize the shape and feel of them.

Then he let one hand trail down her body, seeking her heat. He teased his fingers under the waistband of her pants and found the edge of her panties. "I definitely love how this feels."

He let his fingertip glide over her clitoris and felt a deep satisfaction when she gasped and shuddered in his arms. Her pelvis thrust gently against his hand, begging him for more.

He gave it to her. His thumb worked her clit while he let his fingers find the wet heat of her pussy. She responded so quickly. Already her pussy was coated with arousal, warming his fingers and making his cock hard as a rock. He rubbed himself against her ass, trapping her between his hand and cock and holding her there.

She was right where he wanted her.

"You are so fucking hot. I need you to understand that in the past I might have had a problem with the law, but I'm going to follow every one of your orders, Deputy. I'm going to be a very good citizen indeed."

"I'd love to see that, Van. I bet you'll give me hell at some point." Her head fell back on his chest as she moved her pelvis against him, shuddering when his fingers dove deep. "I'll be honest, I think I'm in over my head with this job, but I'm going to try."

Because she was brave. Because she was a woman who knew what she wanted. Could he trust that he would be what she wanted for the rest of her life? He nipped her ear. "If you get stressed, you know where to come. And I don't think it will be so bad. Hale's mentor loves getting arrested. Says it's restful."

"I don't even want to think about having to deal with Max. I've already heard stories," she admitted. "Oh, that feels so good. How do you do this to me?"

He rotated his thumb, and she was panting in his arms, her body shaking as she rode out the orgasm.

Then it was his turn. He withdrew his hand and picked her up, moving her now relaxed body over to the big couch. He laid her out and shoved his jeans down, freeing his dick.

She stared up at him, a dreamy look in her eyes. "You make me feel so good."

He was going to make her feel even better. He found a condom and rolled it on before joining her on the couch. It was awkward, but he was going to make it work. She hooked a leg around his waist as he thrust inside her, satisfying the urge to connect.

She felt so perfect around him. He should have gotten out of his clothes, but the moment had been too hot, too intense. He would get naked with her later. For now he felt the burning drive to imprint himself on her. He let his cock lead the way, thrusting in and pulling out. He fused their mouths together as he fucked her hard, his tongue mimicking the rhythm of his dick.

She held on to him, wrapping around him in the best way he could think of.

Her whole body went tight, her pussy seeming to clamp down around him in a way that sent him right over the edge. The orgasm shot through him, energizing him in a way he hadn't felt in forever. He fucked her over and over, not wanting to give up the feeling. He kissed her one last time as he thrust deep, giving her everything he had.

Van slumped down, not holding an ounce of his weight off her.

"Really?" a familiar voice said. "On the couch? There are like six beds in this house and you two chose the couch."

Hale. Fuck. Van jumped off Elisa like a man who'd gotten caught in a crime. Normally he wouldn't feel that way. Not at all. They shared their women, but Elisa was going to be Hale's, not his.

He zipped up his jeans, not bothering with the condom. He had to make Hale understand.

Elisa had gone pale, and he could see the trepidation in her now. She hadn't thought this through either, and she was obviously worried she was going to pay the price.

Hale moved toward the couch and looked down at her, his expression going soft. "Hey, gorgeous."

Elisa breathed an obvious sigh of relief. "Hey."

"He didn't even get out of his pants." Hale held out his good hand. "I'll do better for you, baby. It's cold and lonely in that big bed. Can we move this in there?"

All of Elisa's self-consciousness had fled. She stood, paying no mind to her nudity. She moved to Hale's side. "You recently had stitches. You need rest."

Hale's lips curled up in a grin he'd never seen before. It was something between mischievous and utterly content. "I'll let you do all the work."

She practically glowed. "I bet you will. Lazy man." She glanced back at Van. "I'm taking our guy to bed. You coming?"

His heart ached at her use of the word *our*. That was what he wanted. A relationship between the three of them where jealousy had no place. Where they didn't count the seconds she spent with one of them and weighed it against the other. Where they were just the three of them.

"I'm going to stay up and study a while." He couldn't do it. He was fairly certain he would end up in bed with her again, but he wouldn't sleep with her. She'd said she wanted him for the remainder of his time here, that she would be satisfied with what he could give her.

Hale kissed the top of her head, brushing off Van's announcement. "Did it take a bullet to get you to change your mind?"

"I think it's probably inevitable, and I've decided I'm a 'don't fight fate' girl," she replied.

"Then it was worth it." Hale took her hand. "Van, if you change your mind, you're welcome to join us."

He watched as they walked into the big bedroom and the door closed.

It was the longest time before he got to sleep.

Chapter Eleven

Elisa drove up the mountain, a little worried she was going to fall off the other side, but this was the way she'd been told she had to go if she wanted to get to Elk Creek Lodge. She was on her way to speak to a woman named Chelle McIntyre who worked the information desk. It was Chelle's first day back at work after a vacation and Elisa's first chance to try to get more information on the lawyer looking for her guys.

This was her first real investigation as a Bliss County Deputy, and she was not going to screw it up. She was going to be a professional and prove Gemma hadn't been wrong about her.

"Now if you take that road right there, you can get up to Mountain and Valley."

She was a professional who was taking her dad with her on her first case.

"Mountain and Valley has a great telescope," her dad explained. "Can see all the way to the Nebular's home system. Can't see the planet, of course. They keep that locked down real tight. Got excellent shields, and they use their sun to hide, too. Smart fellas those ones."

She knew too much about aliens, but it was fun to have her dad around. He could talk forever about the aliens he'd hunted, but he could talk about other things, too. He was smart and she enjoyed his company, and when Sabrina got here she would fall madly in love with him and Cassidy and she would want to stay and they would be a family and...

She had to stop with the unreasonable expectations. Like the one where Van didn't put up wall after wall.

"Of course you don't need a telescope to see the rest of what Mountain and Valley has to offer, but I say live and let live," her dad continued. "I'm not much one for the nekkid lifestyle, but it doesn't hurt anyone. Well, except when they go on those nature walks and end up covered in poison ivy. Why anyone would want to walk through the woods nekkid, I have no idea, but then I've had to do it myself a time or two when I got dropped off. See, the transporters don't always pick up on things like clothes."

"Mountain and Valley is the nudist resort, right?" If she let him, he would go into a long discussion of the various teleportation rays used around the galaxy. She'd already learned how to gently ease her father back to earth.

It was odd because she would have told anyone who asked that she wasn't a person who dealt with nonsense. What she'd come to learn was nonsense was relative. She likely wouldn't put up with it if she thought he was trying to be funny or play a joke on her, but this was serious to her dad. She'd had some time to think about it. He could be processing trauma in a different way than others, but he was kind and seemed to very much enjoy his life, so who was she to push him?

He was so unlike her mother.

"Yes, it's a real nice place, and they have some fun parties," her dad replied. "You don't even have to take off your clothes if you don't want to, but you do have to be respectful. I'm sure Nate went over all that with you."

She snorted at the thought. "The sheriff passed me a handbook it looked like he wrote himself and then told me he was going fishing. I've been mostly working with Cam or by myself with Gemma. They still have some temp guys taking night shifts. Gemma was right. They need a larger staff."

The handbook had helpful hints on surviving Bliss as a law enforcement officer. It included a map of the town and coupons for free drinks at Trio.

What had she gotten herself into?

"You okay, honey?" her dad asked.

"I'm fine. Why?"

"Because when you're nervous, your hands tighten around the wheel. Up until now I thought it was because you're not used to mountain driving. You're doing an excellent job, by the way. In a couple of months you'll be an expert, and this won't bother you at all." Her father sat in the passenger seat of the big county vehicle, though when she'd picked him up, he'd tried to climb in the back. He'd told her the back was comfy, but she wasn't going to ride with her dad where she would normally put people she arrested.

She'd only been on the job for three days and she'd already arrested Nell Flanders twice. The woman liked to protest, and she didn't mind chaining herself to property that was not hers. She even announced it wasn't hers. The problem was she fully believed that tree the county was trying to cut down should belong only to the earth that it would surely scorch if it got hit by lightning again.

Luckily she'd learned the jail had vegan options, and Nell's husband was quick to bail her out. She had the cutest baby girl who'd looked up at Elisa with wide eyes as though to ask *why did you arrest my mommy?* She could have told the kiddo that wouldn't work on her. But it kind of did.

She was totally getting soft.

"But see, now I'm wondering if this is about more than the drive," her father was saying.

She'd picked up her dad because he had a meeting at the lodge and his truck was currently at someplace called Long-Haired Roger's. According to him, he'd gotten in a tussle with something called a Plejaren and his windshield had cracked. Her dad, that was. As far as she knew, Long-Haired Roger didn't regularly take down extraterrestrials.

"I'm okay." Mountain driving made her anxious, but she would get used to it.

"Is this about those boys?"

Sometimes it was weird how normal it felt to be around this man. Like they fit together in a way that had to do with more than DNA. She'd wondered a lot lately how different her childhood would have been if he'd been in it. The fact that he called them *those boys* like she was in high school and they were dating made her heart squeeze tight.

They were. Kind of. She was definitely dating Hale. They'd been out to dinner twice, and she'd hung out at his place the other night. They'd watched TV and generally just chilled. It had been lovely.

Van was another problem altogether. He was a broody asshole, and he wasn't giving up on the whole "I'm bad news" attitude of his. He was willing to join them for sex, and he seemed to enjoy hanging out with them, but he wouldn't go on planned dates and he wouldn't sleep with them.

Her dad had been around a lot of threesomes. He might have some wisdom when it came to this. Again, it was weird talking to her dad about her threesome, but something about it felt okay. "Hale and I are doing well, but Van is holding back. I think it's because he's worried he's going to get hurt when he leaves, and now he thinks someone might be coming after him."

"Oh, that kid's not leaving. I know a Bliss citizen when I see one. He's not going anywhere. Even if he does go back to Dallas, I give him six months. Once Bliss is in your blood, you can't ever live somewhere else. Baby girl, I've been across the galaxy and there's no place like Bliss."

She rather agreed with him. "He's sure he's leaving when he graduates. He thinks he owes his brother. Hale has decided to stay here, but I have to wonder if he can be happy without Van. And where does that leave me if he isn't? I know the relationship is new, but it feels like the right place to be, the right guys to be with. I can't help but wonder about the future. I know I shouldn't."

"Why? If you don't plan for the future, you might not like it when it gets here. I know a lot of people will tell you to live in the present, that the past and the future don't matter, but we're a product of all three," her dad said somberly. "Our past is the ground we stand on, whether it's solid or shaky. Our future is where we put all our hard work. All our dreams and hopes and wishes."

Sometimes in between all the alien stuff, her dad proved he understood the world. "That's profound, Dad."

"It's true. You can do a lot of thinking on a star ship long-haul freight vehicle. I thought a lot about how we view our lives when I was stuck on that thing. It was right after the last time I saw your mother."

They'd gone over the logistics of the affair, but not how he'd felt. "Did you think you had a future with her?"

His head shook. "No. She was clear that what we had wasn't permanent. I'll be honest. I'm not even sure she liked me all that much, but I was a young man. She was beautiful."

"Mom didn't like anyone." She didn't want her dad to feel too bad. "She wasn't a people person. But you're wrong. She wrote warmly about you in her journals. She said you were friends, and she didn't call many people that. Growing up I didn't think she had friends."

"You told me she got married, though. Who did she marry?"

Sabrina's dad was a peach of a guy. "A man from her hometown. A guy named Phil."

Her dad snapped his fingers. "I knew I recognized the last name. She talked about Philip Leal. I think she was in love with him, but in high school he didn't give her the time of day."

"Well, like I've told you, it didn't go well. He ditched us after Sabrina was born and didn't look back. Mom was always a negative person, but after Phil left, she was a black hole. I was raised to not expect good things to happen. My mom's philosophy was if you anticipate the worst, you're ready for it, and if the worst doesn't happen then it's a pleasant surprise. The problem is when you have that philosophy even when the best happens, you're always waiting for it to go bad again. You can't trust the good things."

"Good things happen, Elisa," her father assured her. "They happen all the time. They happen in the strangest places and when you least expect them to. The problem is your mom thought good things only ever happen when you deserve them, and she had very specific thoughts about what deserving meant."

"You have summed up my childhood. There was a lot of talk about getting what I deserved," she admitted as she made the turn. The hairpin turn that if she got wrong would send them both over the edge and down the mountain way faster than they'd gone up.

It didn't seem to freak her dad out at all. He sat back, glancing her way. "There's a problem with centering your life around that philosophy. If good things only happen because a person deserves it, then they deserve the bad things that happen, too. When you really think that way, when it's the basis for your whole life philosophy, deep down you don't see the difference between something you earned and something that happened. Deep down, when something real bad happens, you blame yourself. There's a difference between working hard and earning success and getting a disease, but I don't know that your mom would have been able to see that. I hope you can see the difference. Why don't you pull in? Right up there is the highest point here. You should see it and take it in. It can be distracting."

She needed the distraction because this talk was starting to get to her. Tears had formed, pooling in her eyes as she tried to stop them from falling.

Who the hell was this person she was becoming?

Elisa Leal was tough. Elisa Leal survived everything without shedding a tear. Elisa Leal was lonely and tired of shutting off her every emotion.

She turned into the parking lot that led to what was described as the scenic overlook.

"If you take in the sight, you'll get used to it and it won't distract you," her father advised. He opened his door and slid out of his seat. "Come on. I'll show you. It's the best view in the Sangre de Cristos."

She didn't want to see the view but also didn't think she should drive until she got her damn emotions under control.

She wiped her eyes when her dad wasn't looking and took in a deep breath, forcing herself to move.

There were times when her body still didn't feel like her own, when she would look in a mirror expecting to see the woman she'd been before. Or when she would move a certain way and muscles would tense that hadn't before.

She felt different. So different, and not always in a good way.

She followed her father up the path. There were only a couple of cars at this time of day, and up ahead she could see an observation deck had been built on the side of the mountain.

Would she have guessed even last year that she would be walking a mountain path, following behind her father? That she would be in a town where she'd met two men and no one shamed her for it.

Her father moved to the deck and turned to offer her a hand up the last step. "Come on, honey. Let me show you something amazing."

She took his hand, and he led her out.

She stared for a moment because it seemed she stood in the middle of giants. The mountains rose all around her, and she could see down to the highway below. From here she could see the road stretching toward Pagosa Springs, and when she turned she could see the valley where she lived, a gorgeous blanket of white dotted with cabins, the glow of life and warmth coming from inside. It was like standing at the top of the world and seeing it from a perspective she couldn't have before.

It was more than beautiful, more than picturesque.

It was life in all its outstanding glory. The mountains had developed over millions of years. They'd begun flat and gradually rose from the earth. The clouds dipped down from the skies above as though caressing the tops, a gentle hand that stroked them. The valley had hollowed out and formed a home for the humans who came so much later, but they were here. They had sacrificed and built these homes.

"I will never get used to this, Dad."

He stood beside her, his hands on the railing. "No. No, you won't. Elisa, I know I can be a bit much to take, and most people don't believe me about the stories I tell. That's okay. I still love every one of them. This is my home and I'll always protect it whether or not its citizens ever understand the danger. But I want you to take what I'm about to say seriously. You did not deserve to get cancer. You didn't get it because you should have exercised more or taken more vitamins. The universe did not punish you. It was something that happened. Not something you earned. People like your momma, they need to feel like they're in control, but the truth is there's so much we can't control. Things happen. Sometimes good. Sometimes bad. How we handle the outcome is what makes us who we are. You are handling it with grace, daughter. You are building a new life and you are opening yourself up to new people. If Van leaves, you didn't deserve that either. Make a home with Hale if you fall in love with him. But always know that I love you and will stand by you through everything. I think once we accept that we can't know what the future will bring, the next more important thing is to not let that fact stop us from trying."

Now she couldn't stop the tears from falling.

It felt like things were changing so fast, but hadn't it taken years to get here?

What if she'd never gotten cancer? Would she have gone to the therapy that led her to accept this amazing, kooky, wonderful man as her dad? Or would she have written him off as a mistake her mother had made?

Maybe he was right and the past was the ground they stood on, the one from which they made each choice that brought them to the future. Her ground had shaken eighteen months before, but when it had settled, she'd found herself in a new place, with a new perspective she might never have considered before. She'd been forced to change—careers, her body, her thought processes.

What if what her mother considered tough was nothing more than stubborn? Was nothing more than fear?

What if she wasn't getting soft here in Bliss? What if what she called softness, what her mother would have scoffed at, was actually resilience. Was the ability to be hurt and still try again, still get up from the ground and open her heart again?

Her dad slipped an arm around her shoulder. "It's good to cry sometimes, honey. I do it myself. We can just stand here for a bit. Work can wait."

She stood there with her father, looking out over the paradise she'd found. She let the tears fall.

And for a moment was completely content.

* * * *

Hale walked into the Elk Creek Lodge with his toolbox in hand.

He might have left his job as handyman here, but they still called him when the task seemed too much for the new guy.

"Hey, thanks for coming up." Lucy Carson stood outside the door to the back entrance of the lodge. The front was a magnificent lobby decorated in what he'd heard called rustic elegance. The back was purely functional. "The water heater for the third floor is giving Hank hell again. I know you showed him how to do it, but he's not getting it right. Surprisingly enough when you pay for an expensive hotel room, you tend to want hot showers."

"No problem. It's tricky." He'd gone many a round with that water heater. "How are you doing?"

Lucy stopped, staring at him like he'd grown an extra head.

"Did I say something wrong?"

"No," she insisted. "It's just you've never asked that question before. You are all business. But I'm great. I love working here at the lodge. Ty and Michael are doing well. Moving in together hasn't been as weird as I thought it would be. How are you? I heard you and Van are seeing someone new. Is it true she's Mel's daughter by an alien queen and she was dropped off via spaceship?"

He hadn't heard that one. "No. No spaceship. I think she took a plane and then rented a car. We took it back a couple of days ago. And I'm sorry for not asking. I forget. Also, her mom was definitely not an alien queen. She was in the Army. Max has been telling me I need to ask more questions. Apparently people like it when you ask them questions about themselves. I'm glad you're doing all right."

"I don't know that you should be taking advice from Max Harper."

He got that a lot. "Yeah, everyone says that but since I started talking to Max, I got a job I love and I'm really into this woman. I talk to people more, and it's not as terrible as I thought it would be. It can be nice to talk."

"That is the most words I think I've ever heard you say." Lucy nodded, looking him up and down. "Well, Max for the win, then. Come on inside."

"Yeah, I was happy you called. I've been meaning to ask about that woman who came looking for Van." He'd been thinking about this for days.

Lucy closed the door behind him and started down the hallway toward the service elevator. "I'm so sorry about that. I've already had a talk with Chelle. She's not allowed to give out any information. She's new and I would have fired her, but there was crying and I didn't have the heart. She won't do it again."

"I didn't want you to fire her. I only wanted to get some

information. Did the woman who was looking for Van say she was a lawyer?"

Lucy seemed to think. "I don't recall hearing anything about that. You know Chelle's talking to the new deputy this afternoon, right?"

Elisa was here? She hadn't mentioned it this morning, but then she'd had to leave in a hurry. He'd hopped in the shower with her and made her almost late for her brand-new job.

Luckily his was more laid back. "No, I hadn't heard that."

"She should be meeting with the deputy very soon." Her face suddenly lit up as the elevator doors opened and Michael Novack walked out. He was dressed in slacks and a Western shirt, a dark suitcoat covering his broad shoulders and a Stetson on his head. He was a US marshal who worked an area that included Colorado, New Mexico, and Arizona. He was often sent to help local law enforcement track down the most dangerous of criminals, but he didn't look like a rough-and-tumble law enforcement guy as he caught sight of his girlfriend.

The man's whole face lit up, and a wide smile appeared. "Hey, you. I thought you would be in the conference hall making sure everything runs smoothly." He tipped his hat Hale's way. "Hale, good to see you."

This was where Max said he should say something back, even if he wasn't happy to see a person. He wasn't happy to see Michael, but he also didn't mind. "Michael."

Lucy went on her toes to kiss her boyfriend. "I've got plenty of people to cover the conference. What I don't have is a working water heater on the third floor."

Michael groaned. "Damn, they need to replace that thing. Hey, did you notice someone dug out circles in the snow last night? I looked out over the east field and it's the damnedest thing. Pretty, but I can't figure out why someone would do that. Did you have the grounds crew do it?"

Lucy sighed, a tired sound. "Oh, no. I was warned this could happen. Apparently there's someone in town who plays pranks on us. It's been going on for years. Every now and then we get crop circles. Except without the crops. Snow circles. Once every winter and once sometime during the summer. I would love to figure out how they're doing it. I would bet Mel is on his way as we speak."

"Why would anyone take the time to make snow circles?" He understood the principle behind it, but the whys eluded him.

"No idea, and the lodge tries to keep it quiet. The last thing we need is a convention of alien hunters. We have enough with the squatchers and covens and that group that swears there are werewolves in town." Lucy pulled out her cell. "I'm going to let maintenance know we need to plow over it. The last thing I need is the local media to whip up a story about aliens landing here. Be right back."

"Hey, you doing okay?" Michael watched as Lucy stepped away for a moment. "I heard you had some trouble out at Hiram's old place."

"It was an accident. Nothing more. Hunters mistook me for a deer or something. I'm all healed up."

And not pissed about it since it had led Elisa right back into his bed. If Elisa and Van hadn't been all stressed about what had happened, they might still be in separate cabins pretending they were nothing more than friends, so it had been worth the shot in the arm. It was only a little sore now.

Of course Van was being an ass, but he supposed one of them had to be. He'd listened to a lot of tales of how Bliss throuples came to be, and usually one of the guys was an ass.

He was pretty sure Michael had been the ass in that threesome.

"Hunters?" Michael asked. "Did Nate check the hunting licenses? Because I think the only thing you can hunt with a rifle right now is white tail."

He'd been over this with the sheriff. He'd gotten far too familiar with Colorado's hunting license process. It was done online. "There were only three permits that day, and Nate checked with all of them. Two of the men were together and in another part of the forest. The third wasn't close. He was up near Bear Creek, but he claims he saw another man hiking with a rifle. Nate had him look at the pictures of the guys who had licenses, but he didn't recognize them."

"So you had an unlicensed hunter," Michael surmised. "I mean, we all know it happens. I'll let Nate know I'm free to do some digging if he needs help. I'm pretty good at finding people. If the rangers didn't have a record of him, then he likely walked in or used a snowmobile to bypass the official entrances."

"It was probably a guy out hunting who didn't want to pay the fee. It's fine."

"I don't know. I don't like coincidences, and the fact that someone was looking for you makes me wonder. I would feel better if I was Nate if I could track this person down."

Hale wanted the whole thing to go away. "I think that's a lot of manpower for what was clearly an accident. I don't see why someone would come looking for Van one day and then shoot at us the next. Also, the person looking for us is a woman."

"A woman can shoot a rifle," Michael pointed out.

"But there's no record of a woman being on the land that day, and I have to ask why she would walk in here and boldly ask where we are if she intended to kill Van. It doesn't make sense to me." He wasn't sure why Elisa was so determined to track the woman down, but he was hoping once they did, Van might have some answers. But he didn't think the two incidents were connected. "Besides, Nate didn't find any evidence of a lawsuit filed against either me or Van. He had Gemma calling and searching through records for days, and she found nothing in the civil court system."

"Which makes me think the woman who asked about you might have been lying about her profession. After all, from what Chelle said she didn't mention she was an attorney when she was here at the lodge. She didn't become an attorney until she showed up at Trio," Michael mused. "I don't know. I need to think about it some more. Something doesn't feel right to me."

He'd heard a lot about instincts lately. Elisa talked about this situation not feeling right, too. He did not have any of those alarm bells. "Well, let me know if you need anything, and I thank you for thinking about it. I'm worried about Van. This whole thing is making him anxious. Tell Lucy I'll be up on three looking at that heater."

Michael nodded, and Hale made his way to the elevator. The doors closed when his cell buzzed.

He glanced down and then slid his finger across the screen to accept the call. "Hey, what's up?"

He played it cool with Van. He was trying to be laid back. No deep discussions about where the relationship with Elisa was heading. No pressure on him to stay. He was going to be chill and let Van figure this out.

"Where are you? I've been waiting for ten minutes." Van, on the other hand, was not chill. He sounded irritated and unamused.

"What are you talking about?" Hale asked.

"You called up to Trio and told me to get here as fast as I could. It was an emergency. I nearly had a heart attack and you're not here."

Hale had no idea what was going on. "Where is here? I'm out at the lodge. I didn't call you."

"I'm in the lobby. You called and told Micky you needed help right away and I should get here ASAP. I left a shift for this," Van complained.

"I didn't call anyone." He pressed the button that would take him to the lobby. "Lucy called me an hour ago and asked me to come look at the heater on three. Why would I call Trio when you have a cell phone?"

That seemed to stop Van. "I guess I thought it had something to do with the emergency. I don't know. All I know is I was worried. I thought maybe…"

The doors opened, and Hale strode through the hall that took him into the luxurious lobby. He knew exactly what Van wasn't saying. "I'm fine. I've been fine for days."

No one had tried to shoot him or take out his truck or even looked sideways at him. Everything was fine. Everything was perfect, with the singular exception of his scaredy-cat best friend who couldn't sleep with their woman. Oh, he could do all kinds of other things to her, but he ran away at the end of the sex, and that needed to stop.

But he was playing it cool. Yep. That was what he was doing.

"Then who the hell called?" Van was pacing in front of the big wooden doors that led out to the front lot of the Lodge. He looked up and caught sight of Hale. He slid his cell into his pocket and started walking his way.

Hale put his cell away. "I have no idea. I don't know why anyone would want to get us both here at the same time. Actually, they couldn't have known I would be here. So this must be about you. Do you know anyone here? Do you think it might have been that lawyer?"

"Well, it was a man on the phone. Specifically you, according to Micky. I don't get it. Why bring me to a public place? It's not like someone's going to try to take me out in the middle of the lobby." Van glanced around as though looking for threats.

"Boys, I'm glad you're here," a booming voice said.

Hale looked over as the big doors were closing again after admitting two new visitors to the Elk Creek Lodge. Elisa looked surprisingly hot in her uniform. Not surprising. He thought she looked hot in pretty much everything. That was not the sight that worried him. It was Mel Hughes walking beside her. The man was tall and lanky and even weirder than Hale considered himself. It was a big plus that Elisa seemed to not mind weird, though she did seem surprised at what her father had said.

Elisa strode over to them. "Hey, I didn't know you would be here. I'm interviewing a witness. Is everything okay?"

"Someone impersonating Hale called Trio and told me I needed to get here ASAP." Van couldn't quite hide the way he looked at Elisa. Like he was ready to eat her up, but he held himself back.

Did the uniform trigger something in Van? Or did it remind him of all the ways he thought he wasn't good enough? He shoved that problem aside for the moment since they had other things to worry about. "I'm here to work on the heater on…"

"The third floor," Mel finished. "It goes out every time those damn Neluts show up to use our forests for their mating rituals. I bet they didn't even bother to get a license."

Elisa ignored her father's banter. "Who would want you here at the same time?"

"Me, of course." Mel gave them all a friendly smile as he settled a big bag over his shoulder. "Are there or are there not circles and lines in the snow in the east field that are likely a landing map?"

Hale frowned. "Lucy's pretty sure it's a prank. She's going to have maintenance smooth it all over."

That got Mel moving. "Well, we better hurry then. Come along, boys. We've got some aliens to hunt."

"But the heater…" Lucy had been worried about it. Guests tended to get upset when they didn't have hot water.

"Will just bust again when the Nelut ship flies overhead," Mel insisted.

Van looked to Elisa. "Do I have… Yep. I'm going to go make sure he's okay."

Hale caught a hint of the look Elisa had sent Van. It was intimidating to say the least, and he remembered what Max did when Rachel was obviously irritated. It was simple. He did whatever Rachel wanted and with a smile.

Hale forced a smile on his face. "Let's go. It's going to be fun."

Van's eyes widened. "Seriously?"

"Yes." He must be getting better at this because Van followed right behind him.

Chapter Twelve

The days kept getting weirder.

Van stepped out of the lodge's door. It was at the back of the main building and led to the ski section of the lodge. Cold blasted over his skin even as the sun was almost too bright. He pulled his sunglasses over his eyes as he followed behind Hale, who was still carrying his tool kit.

If the aliens crashed and needed a tune-up, Hale would be there for them.

If Mel didn't kill the fuckers first.

He was going to miss this place so much.

"Why?" He rushed to catch up because Mel might be pushing seventy, but the dude could move. Now that he watched the man, he had to admit there was an oddly predatory grace to his movements. Like an old tiger moving through the snow, looking for prey.

"Well, the atmosphere is right for fertilization. See the Neluts lost their own planet centuries ago. They tried to invade way back in 79 AD. But the Atlanteans defeated them. Had to blow up Pompeii, and from what I've heard they were never the same. Guilt can kill whole cultures," Mel was saying as he left the nicely shoveled path and started walking on the snow. "Anyway, the Neluts became a space-faring people, and now they only leave their ships to mate. Fertilization requires specialized conditions they can't replicate on a ship. Also, they have some fairly detailed religious beliefs that require the touching of Earth for first life."

Hale simply followed along. "Sir, I have questions."

Oh, that was not happening. He was not getting a lecture on the lost continent of Atlantis. "No, I meant why did you call and say you were Hale?"

Mel stopped, putting a hand over his eyes and searching the horizon for something. "Because I didn't think you would come out here if I told you I wanted to have a talk."

Would he? "I don't know we have much to talk about."

"I would have come." Hale was such a kiss ass when it came to parents.

Mel reached over and gave him a pat on the shoulder. "I knew you would be here because of the heater. Something about the wiring in the building. It really does happen every time. You remember when you spent a week installing new pipes because you hoped that would fix the problem?"

"Yes," Hale admitted. "It was down again in a couple of hours."

"Neluts are on a biyearly mating schedule. That was their summertime ritual. The winter ritual is more intense." Mel seemed to find what he was looking for and took off to his left, his long legs moving with ease. "Though I prefer winter because I don't have to worry about the sasquatches trying to get involved. As a race of cryptid, they do not rank high on the discrimination scale, if you know what I mean."

He understood nothing. Absolutely nothing. "Did you bring me out here to talk about fussy sasquatches?"

Hale's head shook as he walked behind Mel. "No, I think he meant the sasquatches *aren't* fussy. I think he was saying they try to like join the party. How would the Neluts handle that?"

Mel stopped, looking at Hale. "Well, you wonder what happened to our bees, right?"

Hale nodded sagely. "Ah."

The asshole was acting like he understood what Mel was telling him. Like it all made sense somehow. "What do you want to talk to me about, Mel? If it's about your daughter, you should understand, we're just friends."

Mel turned again, walking toward the east field. In the summer it was a beautiful carpet of wildflowers, the colors so stunning it looked slightly surreal. Now it was a blanket of perfectly pristine… He had to stare for a moment because something was wrong with that snow.

"Friends who sleep together." Mel's destination was obviously that snow that looked like someone had drawn in it.

Where Van stood, he was slightly elevated and could see the hint of circles and lines. "Is that a crop circle?"

"We call this a snow circle." Mel set down his bag and pulled out what looked like an old-school walkie-talkie. "Cass, sweetheart, you have my location?"

"Sure do," came the tinny reply.

"Send the drone here. Grid pattern twenty-two should do it." Mel put the walkie back down. "Technically you can't call it a crop circle if there aren't any crops. What you are looking at is a visual message to any Nelut ship that they should meet up at whatever spot this says. I can't read it from down here. Hence the drone. Think of it like that tender thing but for alien hookups."

"So it's an emotional experience for them, too?" Hale asked.

Van rolled his eyes. He knew he was being an asshole, but it kind of rankled that Hale was doing such a good job with Mel. "He's talking about the dating app Tinder. Sorry, he's not big into that kind of tech."

"No, he's not. Hale's a real nice fella. Good with your hands. That's what Elisa tells me," Mel said.

Hale went a bright shade of pink. "She said that? To you?"

"Dude, you're a handyman. You fix things," Van pointed out.

Hale breathed a big sigh of relief. "Oh. Yes. I'm a quick learner if you ever need any help."

And Van could help the man do his taxes. Did he make enough from alien hunting to pay taxes? How would he handle write-offs?

"Like I was saying," Mel continued, "I'm not worried about Hale at all, but I am worried about you, son."

"I'm not your son." The words were out of his mouth before

he could really think about them. Damn. "I'm sorry. I didn't mean that to come out so harshly. I know that's just a phrase some men use."

"Is it?" Mel's brow had risen. "I find it interesting you had that reaction. You close to your papa?"

"I call my dad George because he wanted me to understand that he was a person in his own right and not simply a father. He thought it was unfair that bringing children in the world meant he lost his identity, though I think he would put it differently."

"But you were a child and that's what you heard, and now you think you're no one's son. That's a hard thing to be, so...Van."

"I had an odd childhood. So did Hale."

"So did a lot of people. I don't like to use the word *normal*. It's not a very good describer of the world. Normal or average is something you should say when you're talking about blood pressure, not our families. All loving, functional families are normal in their own way. My daddy was a hunter, but see, I didn't want to go into that."

The man wasn't getting to the point, but at least he could understand him now. "You grew up around here? I'm not surprised your dad was a hunter. Lot of that around here, as we recently learned."

"Oh, no. My daddy hunted werewolves," Mel explained. "They're not as bad as they sound. Some real nice fellas, and they can smell an alien from a mile away. Helpful creatures, but my daddy was mean."

And reality was gone. "None of this explains why I am freezing my ass off when I should be warm and toasty back at Trio. Elisa and I are friends. We have a good relationship where I've been open and honest about what I can give her. I know you're her dad and I respect the relationship, but we don't have to do this thing where you warn me off. She's the only one who gets to do that."

"I assure you if I felt the need to warn you off my daughter, I could make it happen, Sylvan," Mel said, that perpetual look of innocence gone from his face. He stared at Van with much older eyes, eyes that had seen a lot of the world. "But I wouldn't do it out in the open. I'll be honest, I wouldn't warn you at all. That's the mistake a lot of people make. When you want to protect someone you love, you don't let the enemy know you're coming. You simply pick a time and take out the threat, and no one ever has to know. So many people go missing these days. They walk away and leave everything behind and are never heard from again."

"Shit, man. I think Mel's planning on killing you," Hale whispered.

Or letting the Neluts take him. "I'm not trying to hurt Elisa."

That dark look left Mel's face. "I know that. Like I said, I wasn't trying to warn you off. You're close to my daughter. That means you're close to me. You don't have any family out here, so you can spend time with mine. Today is our first task, boys. Next week we're manning the aerial watch tower on the alien highway. There's a meteor shower, and lots of those suckers like to sneak in," Mel said with a cheery smile. "Cassidy's going to make us sandwiches."

"Like I was saying, Elisa and I are casual." He could think of nothing less he wanted to do than sit in whatever a watch tower was with Mel.

And it wasn't merely about the fact that the alien thing was weird. That actually could be fun. He'd been around enough people who believed ley lines could heal and crystals attracted wealth and prosperity. He'd spent a whole week camping with a woman who was looking for proof of the Jersey Devil. He'd seen it, but he was pretty sure that had been the secondhand smoke from whatever she'd been smoking.

He was over those adventures. They were wasted time. Spending a night with his future fath…

There it was, the impulse to throw himself right over the emotional edge and jump in with both feet, and where would that lead him?

"You're not, but I get that you're afraid. She's smart and beautiful, and way more intimidating than either of you," Mel pointed out. "You're probably thinking you're not good enough for her, and you are right. Thing is, she gets to decide. Let her. If you fall for her, if you have even an inkling that she might be the right woman for you, don't fight it, Sylvan. Fighting it only wastes time and turns you bitter. Life is too short for that. But even short, it can be so good. Blessings come when you least expect them. I was happy just having

Cassidy's boys in my life. I thought that would be enough family for me and then Elisa walks in and… I spent so much of my life lonely, and the idea that I get these years with her and Leo and Wolf, and she says her sister might come here. Sabrina doesn't have a mom or dad. She'll need a family. Can't you see what a miracle that is?"

Mel had brought him out here to offer him a place in his family? That seemed inconceivable, but here he was, trying to pass on his knowledge. Some potential father-in-laws would take them fishing or want to teach them golf.

He got alien hunting.

The thing was he didn't actually like fishing or golf, and he did like a surreal experience.

The sound of a motor came from overhead. Van looked up, and there was a small drone flying their way.

"Ah, you're going to take video so you can see the whole pattern from above." Hale seemed determined to state the obvious. "Will you be able to decipher it?"

"Sure thing." Mel watched as the drone started flying in a specific pattern. "Though I know most of their mating nests. Normally I wouldn't make a fuss, but there's a lot going on right now what with you two being the target of a rogue sasquatch."

"It wasn't…" There was no arguing with the man. "So what do you do once you figure out the code?"

Was he looking at Jake like the father he wished he'd had, the one who'd let him call him Dad and didn't expect him to get himself out of trouble by the age of eight because he wasn't going to treat him like "some infant"? Had Jake become the father figure he could count on, therefore he could never disappoint him?

He was trying to have the life Jake had, but what if he was starting from the wrong place? He'd viewed the job and the friend as the starting place of Jake's successful life, but what if it had been Serena all along? What if the steady job and nice pay meant far less than sharing a woman he loved with his best friend?

Jake had built a family for himself. He spent his holidays with them. His kids had met their parents, but they barely knew them. They had an Uncle Ian though. And an Aunt Charlotte, and cousins they shared no real blood with.

Was that what Mel was trying to tell him? That there was no

one way to have a family? There was only the willingness to be part of one?

"Well, I'm going to let Lucy's men snow plow the hell out of this because they aren't supposed to be this far south during winter." Mel looked up to the heavens. "You're supposed to go mate in Montana!"

That was the moment a skier seemed to go off track. They were all over the place, but the majority were heading for the ski lifts or going back to the lodge. This swiftly moving barrel of fun was coming down the mountain, and he hadn't stayed on the track. He plowed right through it and seemed unsteady on his skis.

Mel moved closer, waving his arms. "No, go over there. I'm not done with my survey. Go that way."

"Help!" The man was definitely not an expert skier.

He was out of control and could hurt himself.

So naturally Hale stepped right in his way like he could catch the guy himself.

"Give me one end of your scarf." Van quickly moved into place on the other side of their rapidly approaching skier. "You hold the other. Spread it out and try to catch his waist. The snow will break his fall."

The scarf was wide. Teeny Warner had made one for both of them, and Hale had wondered if it was a blanket. Now Van was grateful for it. Trying to stop this guy with their bodies could kill them both, and letting him fall into the deep patterns the Neluts had made seemed dicey, too.

He had not just had that thought.

He tossed it aside because he had a runaway dude to clothesline and hopefully not kill.

Hale seemed to understand and moved into place, drawing the heavy scarf taut.

The skier hit it square in his chest and went flying back, skis up in the air and back on the snow, but it was a far softer landing than the one that had been waiting for him.

Van moved in, dropping to one knee. The man was wearing some kind of designer ski suit, covered in logos. Van did not get that. "You okay, man?"

Already he could hear someone calling for the medics.

The guy lay there in the snow for a moment before pushing up his goggles. He looked to be in his mid-twenties to early thirties, with dark hair and an oddly familiar face, though Van couldn't put a name to it. Had he met this guy before?

"I was going too fast," the guy gasped and then managed to sit up. His shoulders sloped down at an odd angle, but that just seemed to be his body type. It made the suit he was wearing look wrong on him. "I'm fine. I'm okay. Wow. That was quick thinking."

"He's smart like that." Hale had a grin on his face as though the whole day had been one big, long adventure.

Hadn't it?

The man glanced up at Hale and then stopped, his expression going blank. "I should get up." He pulled his goggles back down. "Help me up and I'll be on my way. Thanks."

"I think you should wait for the medics," Hale said. "They'll check you over."

But the guy was insistent. He was up on his feet and skiing away in less than a moment, though it was obvious he was in some pain.

"Well, that was weird." Mel watched the man go.

And that was saying something coming from him.

* * * *

Elisa had to check the urge to leave the conference room and go find her dad. It wasn't that she was worried about her dad. Quite the opposite. Really she would be checking on Van and Hale. Who were with her dad. Who her dad had somewhat sneakily called out here.

Why?

He'd told her he had some work to do up at the lodge, and she'd assumed it was about tracking down aliens or the survivors of aliens. He apparently was considered a great counselor when it came to helping others process their alien abductions. She hadn't thought he would be doing any of that with her boyfriends.

Well, her boyfriend and his friend, who sometimes slept with her and was definitely going to leave them both.

"I told my boss everything that happened. Am I in trouble?"

The woman named Chelle McIntyre looked like a brown doe

trapped in the headlights as she stared at Elisa's badge.

She'd gone over the report Chelle had made about fifty times. "You're not in trouble. You didn't break the law or anything, but you could know something that might help us track this person down."

"What did she do?" Chelle asked.

"We're not sure, but we have reason to suspect she might have broken into one of the cabins down in the valley and committed vandalism."

Chelle's big eyes managed to move into anime territory. "No. That's awful. The valley is so nice. Did you know all the guys are hot down there? Like super hot. At first I thought maybe it was some reality show shooting around town, but no. Some of them were born there. They all actually live there."

"Yes, I was aware that people lived there."

"Hot guys."

"And the women who love them and have a club called 'I Shot a Son of a Bitch,'" Elisa pointed out. She was already getting protective of this town she found herself in. While the lodge was technically in Bliss County, many of the people who worked here for the most part kept to the lodge.

Chelle looked like she was still a teen, though according to her records she was twenty-two and had recently graduated from a community college with a degree in something called hospitality management. She'd moved from Boulder to the lodge, where she now worked the front desk. Her blonde hair was in a high ponytail as she nodded. "Yeah, the women are scary. They're so strange. It makes me wonder if what they say is true."

She should avoid this, but she couldn't. "What do they say?"

"That the women of Bliss are all in a coven and they use the ley lines to enhance their magic and make the men do their bidding. I don't know what a ley line is. Is it about getting laid?" She seemed to consider something and leaned forward. "Do you know? You're a cop. You're supposed to know things. The lodge seems normal, but sometimes weird things happen here. Did you know the east field was taken over by aliens sometime last night?"

Oh, this was what Nate had talked about in his pamphlet. Patience was absolutely required. "Okay, they are not witches. They are perfectly nice women who simply don't like other women planning to steal their men. Ley lines are these things that people made up to describe weird but perfectly normal for the planet we live on phenomena. It has nothing to do with getting laid. Cops don't know everything and if they tell you they do and they're young and male, that is them trying to get laid. Ignore them. And if the east field was taken over by aliens, don't worry. My dad is here, and he will handle it."

"Who is your dad?" Chelle asked around the gum she was chewing.

It was nice to know not everyone had figured that out. She'd been called Mel's daughter more than once as she'd started to get used to Bliss life. "He's the head alien hunter around here, though I've been told he also handles sasquatches. Before you ask, they don't exist either. Probably. I don't know. I'm new here. I need a couple of years to get into the mindset. Now, did she give you her name?"

Chelle sat for a moment and then her brain seemed to turn on again. "Oh, we're back to the lady who almost got me fired. I thought we were talking about the aliens or witches or something. You're sure they're not witches, because some of those women have two hot guys and that doesn't seem right."

It seemed perfectly right to her. When she thought about it, they were truly halves of a whole. Van was outgoing and easy to be with. Hale's waters ran deep. They both struggled to navigate the world sometimes, and that was what she was good at. She didn't mind being assertive.

Had all her struggles brought her here only to lose again?

"No witches, just smart women and a bunch of seriously needy men. I want you to think about this, Chelle. Do you enjoy doing laundry? Because unless you know how to train a man, you'd be doing a whole lot of it. How well can you cook?" Van was a pretty good cook, and Hale had been in her cabin one afternoon and noticed the washer was full of towels. He'd moved them to the dryer.

Her ex-husband wouldn't have touched laundry to save his life. Despite the fact that they both worked, he needed to relax when he got home, so she'd done all the housework. She'd also run most of the errands, kept the books, made all the plans.

Van and Hale didn't seem to mind being given tasks to do.

She got the feeling the three of them could fall into a nice routine if they let themselves. Maybe that was the key. Showing Van how good it could be.

"Eww, I don't do those things. Our uniforms are handled by the laundry here, and I pay to have my personal clothes done. I did not get into hotel management so I could cook," Chelle admitted. "Of course I also thought I would be in Paris by now, but they want you to speak French. How weird is that?"

Yes, Chelle was lucky to be at the lodge. "Did she give you a name?"

Chelle looked down at her manicured nails. "No. I didn't ask for one. She said she knew them and that they used to work here. She was pretty cute. I mean she was like probably thirty-five or so, but the old girl kept it tight."

She was not going to punch Chelle. She was sure somewhere in the new hire manual there was a no punching witnesses rule. "Did she say how she knew them?"

"I guessed it was how most women know most men. Like I thought she was a girlfriend or something. I don't know. It was busy that day, and if I had an ex looking for me, I would want someone to help them out."

"Haven't had a lot of bad exes, have you?"

She shrugged. "You never know when they could make a lot of money. I don't want to turn down a good chance."

"So you didn't ask for her name and you didn't ask why she wanted to find two men who used to work here?"

"Like I said, it was busy. And people talk about those two guys all the time. Apparently they were very popular."

Nope. She shouldn't go there. She should stick to the task. "Popular?"

Chelle's lips turned up in a grin. "Very. Like down in the valley popular, if you know what I mean."

She was pretty sure she knew what the younger woman meant. She definitely knew it wasn't her business and yet… "So they had a lot of girlfriends?"

"From what I've heard girlfriends wouldn't be the term. They were straight up players," Chelle replied. "They were getting notches on those bedposts. But I never met them, so I didn't get to try them out. Marnie from accounting told me they were heavenly. Like really good in bed, but they were very one night and move on."

Players? For a second a question whispered in her brain. *Were they playing her?*

She caught it. This was the whisper in her head that constantly told her she wasn't good enough and everything was going to fail.

She accepted that it would always be there, but she didn't have to listen.

She answered it. No. They weren't playing her, and Chelle had heard some stories that had been through the gossip mill. Her guys were sincere and had given her no indication they didn't truly enjoy spending time with her.

So she let that worry go because it was not required.

"I'm sure they're nice men. I need you to describe this woman to me."

"Okay, but why don't you get a screenshot from the security cameras?" Chelle pointed behind Elisa. "They're everywhere, and they don't like dump the footage for a year or so. It's all digital. Very top of the line stuff."

That was good. An actual face would make things so much easier. She didn't have one from the woman's foray into Bliss. If she could get a shot from here, she could take it to Pilar and make both IDs.

If she didn't...

That was a worry for later. "All right. I can go down to security. I've got a date. I need a rough time."

"Around check-in, which is why it was so busy," Chelle explained. "Between 2:30 and 3:30. There's a camera that faces the front desk. Security will know which one to check. And you know now that I think about it, I don't think she was alone. Or like she was just really friendly because after she walked away, I saw her talking to some guy in the lobby. I think he was a guest. Is a guest. Kind of cute. I didn't check him in, but I did overhear him talking to one of the bartenders about the fact that he's super rich."

He sounded like a big old douchebag, but she would try to make a note of what he looked like and if it appeared they were having a casual conversation or something more.

There was a knock on the door, and Hale popped his head in. "Hey, your dad wanted me to tell you he's going to be a while.

Something about Nelut mating habits, and there might have been the word *apocalypse* thrown around."

"It's fine. It's one of his favorite words." She stood because she'd gotten everything out of Chelle she was going to get.

"Anyway, Cassidy's going to come pick him up if he runs too late. If the world doesn't end, that is."

He was truly adorable. Maybe she could put in her request with security and they could have lunch.

She turned to Chelle. "Thank you for your time. If you think of anything else, give me a call."

Chelle stared Hale's way. "Hey, I think that's one of those guys we were talking about. You know the ones who slept with every woman in the lodge."

"I did not." Hale frowned, his brows furrowing.

"It was more like half." Van was suddenly beside him, as though he'd been waiting so he could make an entrance.

"It was not." Hale's voice went low, and he sent his partner a shut-the-fuck-up look.

Chelle had gotten to her feet, her chest coming out a little. "I'm Chelle. I've heard so much about you guys."

"Wrong things," Hale shot back.

"I thought you guys left. If you're still working here, maybe we could have a drink sometime," Chelle offered.

The need to stake her claim rose fast and hard, but she held back, wanting to see how her guys handled a woman hitting on them. Technically Van wasn't hers. He could have a drink with anyone he wanted to. He was free and easy.

"No." Hale's hand slipped into hers. "I'm with her."

She probably should have mentioned that to Chelle, but it hadn't mattered to the investigation. That hand squeezing hers did though. It mattered a lot.

"I'm totally her adjacent." Van took a position on her other side. "Not looking for anyone else. She's all I can handle."

So at least he was in for now.

Chelle stared at her standing between two gorgeous men and her jaw dropped. "See, its witches. I know it. I need to find a way into that coven."

"Hey," Hale began.

But she didn't mind being called a witch under these circumstances. It truly was magical. "Come on. I'll buy you guys lunch while the security crew finds my footage."

She walked happily out the door.

* * * *

"I thought we were going to the restaurant." Elisa stared back down the hallway they would have been going down had they actually been going to the lobby.

Hale had other plans.

When he'd realized she was still at the lodge and likely would be for most of the afternoon, he'd quickly gotten the heater working again—though oddly it had only worked after Mel had allowed maintenance to flatten out the field. When Lucy had tried to pay him, he'd asked for something other than cash.

"We're going someplace better." Van had picked up some sandwiches, drinks, and cookies from the small café at the front of the lobby.

"What are you planning?" Her eyes narrowed but her lips curled up in the sexiest smile. "You know my father is still here, right?"

"He's busy ensuring no alien mating happens in unsecured zones," Hale explained. Or was it in secured zones? He wasn't sure, but he was certain Mel was busy. And he didn't think Mel would turn out to be one of those "don't touch my daughter, she's so pure" dudes. He was one of those "you better make her smile and make her happy in all ways" type of guys.

He kind of liked Mel.

He pressed the button to call the elevator and gently pulled her inside when the doors opened.

Van joined them, a big smile on his face. "I'm supposed to be at work. I couldn't violate you if I was at work, so what's about to happen is your dad's fault."

"Uhm, I'm actually at work, guys," she pointed out. "I'm in uniform and everything. I'm not sure my new boss would like to think his deputies drop everything for a nooner."

He and Van both laughed at that thought. She hadn't been

here long enough to know Nate Wright's reputation.

"The only thing the sheriff loves more than fishing is sneaking his wife into his office for sex," Van explained. "And sometimes Zane's in there, too, and there's complaining about how small the office is, and then Gemma complains about how thin the office walls are, and there are a lot of conversations about who has to clean what."

"Besides, it's your lunch hour." He wasn't sure she had a lunch hour, but if she didn't, Hale was going to tell Nell Flanders and he would join that protest. "And you're waiting on security, so it's not like you can leave. I've got the big suite for three hours. That's when Lucy told me the housekeeping staff would be in for the weekly cleaning. It's actually the owner's suite, so it's not in use unless they're here."

"If you think about it, Hale exchanged his services for sex," Van pointed out.

Elisa's cheeks went hot pink. "I didn't even think about it that way."

The elevator stopped at the penthouse floor. "That is not true. I exchanged my services for a few hours in a nice suite. Lucy does not know what I'm planning on doing in this suite."

"She does. That's why she told you where the condoms are. Mr. Cole is shockingly open about sex. He wouldn't mind. If they were here, his wife would probably ask if she could watch," Van explained helpfully.

His heart fell when he realized she wasn't getting out of the elevator. He'd thought it was a romantic thing to do, but he hadn't expected that she would be embarrassed. He'd been in Bliss too long. No one cared. Sex was a part of life, and they all joked about it and talked about it, and if someone needed advice, they discussed it without shame.

She hadn't been here long at all.

"You're right. Let's go down to the restaurant," he offered. He didn't want her to associate shame with anything they would do together. Maybe later she would be more comfortable. If she never was, that was okay, too. They could be a very circumspect threesome. Couple. Whatever they would be.

Van was already standing in the elegant foyer, his bag in

hand. He looked like a kid who'd had his toys taken away. "But I figured out where Cole keeps the butt plugs and everything."

"Van," Hale hissed. He looked over at Elisa, praying she wasn't offended.

She was silent for a second, and then a laugh came from deep in her chest. She laughed and made her way out of the elevator and threw her arms around Van. "You are a wicked pervert, and I am some kind of witch."

He hadn't liked it when that young woman had called her that. He stepped out of the elevator, and it closed behind him. "Chelle was rude."

Elisa stepped back and moved into Hale's space. "Sorry about that. For a minute I forgot where I was. I don't have to be worried that people will judge me harshly here. Well, except for the Chelles of the world, and even then she was more jealous than judgmental. She'd heard about how you plowed your way through the women employees of the lodge and wished she could have been one of the many."

"There weren't that many." The last thing he needed was Elisa to think she was some kind of conquest. She wasn't a stop in the road. She was the destination.

"It was a lot." Van seemed intent on playing the happy-go-lucky, good-time guy.

Elisa grinned Van's way. "You're going to make him crazy. And you should both know that I don't care who you slept with before as long as we're all exclusive while we're seeing each other. I know Hale feels that way, but you're…"

"Not interested in seeing anyone else." Van dropped the goofy grin and moved in close, one hand coming up to smooth back her hair. "I know I can't give you a long-term commitment, but I'm not going to sleep with anyone else while we're together. Or have drinks with other women. Unless Marie orders me to. I'm scared of her."

Elisa's gaze softened. "I'm glad to hear that. I'm scared of Marie, too, so let's all do our best to not piss her off. Now let's see this place Hale sold his soul for."

"Uhm, it was a couple of hours of maintenance work. The job I just did and one in the future. Apparently the mating ritual thing throws off the third floor water heater," Hale explained.

She turned his way, leaning in and kissing him briefly. "The Galactic Council thanks you for all you do to keep Earth running."

Okay, even he knew that was a joke. "Maybe I'll get a medal. But for now, I'll take a couple of hours up here. Come on. I'll show you why it's special."

He took her hand and held the key card Lucy had given him in the other. There was a big set of double doors that led into the living area of the massive suite. He swiped the card and the door unlocked.

"This guy doesn't mind his place being rented out?" Elisa asked as he opened the door.

"It's not rented out, per se," he argued. "It's a perk."

"Consider Cole Roberts an honorary member of Bliss." Van walked in behind him. "He lives here part of the year with his wife and husband."

"Oh, he's in a threesome," Elisa said. "But I've only heard you guys refer to yourselves as partners. Even when you're married."

"Cole and Mason love each other romantically as well," he explained.

"Ah," she said as she stopped in the hallway with its marble floors and elegant columns. She caught sight of a picture of what she suspected was the owners of this amazing place. "They look like a lovely family."

"They're also lifestylers," he added. "Cole is the Dom and they are his submissives. In their sexual life. I've heard they were once twenty-four seven hard core, but not anymore."

"They found a good balance. At least that's what my brother says." Van found the tablet that controlled the smart suite. "Mr. Roberts knows my brother from the BDSM scene in Dallas."

"But you're not into that," she murmured.

Van shrugged. "I don't need it the way Jake does, but I don't mind playing a little if you want. I've been in clubs before."

"You've been in one club." Hale also didn't want Elisa to think they were big into the D/s lifestyle. It was fine to play around, but he was never going to be some hard-core top. "His brother is a founding member of this club in Dallas. When we lived there for a couple of months, we went to have the experience, but that's not anything you need to worry about."

"I'm not worried." She slipped out of her jacket. "Just curious. This place is pretty."

Oh, but she hadn't seen the half of it yet. "Van, could you do the honors?"

"Of course." He touched the tablet, and the long curtains began to come apart, revealing the floor-to-ceiling windows that covered over half the room.

Elisa walked to the middle of the living room, looking out over Cole Roberts's version of paradise. It was a winter wonderland, with tall aspens and cedar trees that seem to be trying to find the sky. Everywhere the world looked white and pristine.

"In the summer the fields are full of wildflowers." He moved in behind her, wrapping his arms around her waist. "And you can watch the deer grazing."

"And Maurice trying to get it on with the local moosette," Van added. He'd set his bag down and now sank onto the big leather couch.

He was pretty sure that wasn't what a female moose was called. It was probably called a female moose, when he thought about it. He would have to look that up.

It hadn't even been hard to convince him to skip the rest of work. He'd checked in, and Alexei had already come in to cover for him. No one had said a word when he'd explained Hale was all right and it had been Mel who wanted to bond over alien mating rituals. Zane had simply told him to come in tomorrow and watch out for secretions or something. That part had been a jumble, but the point was, Van was here and he wasn't being an asshole.

"I think the proper term is cow," Elisa said with a smile. She leaned back against Hale. "Maurice would be a bull. Not that I've seen him. I've been told you can't be a proper Bliss resident until you've met Maurice."

"He'll come around," Hale promised.

"He licked me." Van shuddered. "It was horrible. Do you have any idea how huge that tongue is? It was pretty much my whole face."

Hale wanted to lick her.

More than that, he wanted to be happy with them for a while. He wanted to make memories with them. It was precisely why when

Lucy had offered him a check, he'd asked for this instead. He'd wanted to see Elisa standing here in the middle of this magnificent room, the winter wonderland forming the background of an afternoon they would never forget.

He kissed the shell of her ear, loving the way she shuddered.

Van lost his grin.

"We've put this off for a couple of days, but we should think about preparing you," Hale whispered as he let his hands drift up, cupping her breasts through the khaki shirt she wore. He started to unbutton it, revealing her gorgeous skin to his partner.

Her head nestled against his, and she offered herself up to him in a way that made him feel invincible. She trusted him with her precious body. "Is this the plug thing? The one I have to wear for hours at a time?"

He was not about to send her out after potential criminals wearing a butt plug. He wanted her wholly focused on her job and not her anus. "For today we'll play and get you used to it. When you're not working you can wear it."

"I think it would be kind of hot for her to take down the bad guys with a plug in her ass," Van said.

"Not happening," she replied, but she was rubbing against him. "But I agree to the other terms. I do want to do this right. I love what you do to me in bed. Both of you. But I want you at the same time. I want to feel you both inside me."

He could hear what she wasn't saying…even if it's only for a little while.

He would take all the time he could get with both of them and then be happy to be with her. He would find a way to be enough. He would find a way to not always be waiting for Van to come home.

He kissed her neck as he continued to unbutton her blouse. The material she wore was utilitarian, but her skin was softer than any silk. The contrast reminded him of the woman herself. Elisa was solid. He could depend on her. She was stalwart and strong and also fragile. The scars proved that she was both indomitable and vulnerable.

She was everything he wanted.

His whole body felt alive as he undressed her. She moved with him as he eased her uniform off. He tenderly kissed the skin he uncovered, taking his time because he never wanted this to end.

"I'm going to hope that no one can see in here," she murmured but didn't try to stop him.

"The glass is tinted," he promised. "We can see out, but no one can see in."

Van stood, his eyes going hard. "Stop worrying. We've worked hard to make this time special, and part of that is taking care of you. We've thought this through, so you don't have to think about anything but how we can make each other feel. Can you let go for the next hour or so?"

"Yes." Her breasts seemed to swell in his hands as she took a deep breath. "Should I add a *sir* to that?"

Van moved to stand in front of her, his mouth curling up in a grin. "Sorry. I spent a lot of time around that lifestyle. There are some benefits. So we're going to take what works for us and not worry about what doesn't. I don't think you would ever be a high-protocol girl, but when we set up a special time like this I want you to let go of everything else and focus on us."

"I can do that," she promised. "I don't think I'll be able to concentrate on anything else."

That was how he wanted it.

Van leaned over and kissed her briefly. "Good. I'm going to get the plug ready. Lucky for us, Mr. Roberts is a thoughtful host. He keeps new toys for his guests. Apparently most of his friends are in the lifestyle. I like it. Butt plugs are the new party favors." He sobered, sinking a hand into her curls and staring down at her. "I want you to suck Hale's cock. When I walk back into this room, I want you on your knees, your mouth on him. The rest of the afternoon will be all about you, so I want him satisfied. He tends to whine when he's not."

"I do not," Hale replied. He didn't. Did he?

Van stepped away, letting her go, a hint of a smile on his lips. "You definitely do. Be right back. Finish getting her undressed."

He was being extremely bossy, but that was one command he wasn't about to argue with. He had her out of that uniform in no time at all, folding each piece since she'd have to get back into it.

"Damn, but you are gorgeous. I'm not even in your league, woman." She looked every bit as beautiful as he'd imagined her.

She was stunning in the golden daylight, warmth against the frost of winter.

She stepped in close to him, her hands on his chest. "You are in a league of your own, Hale Galloway, and don't ever let anyone tell you otherwise." She leaned in, pressing her lips to his. "Now I think I was given a task."

She bit her bottom lip and then pulled his shirt free of his jeans. The room had been warm before, but now it seemed to go hot because he knew what her task was and he knew how good she was when she focused on her work.

She sank to her knees in front of him, her hands working the buckle of his belt first and then the button and zipper of his jeans, folding the sides down. She worked carefully, methodically, easing his jeans down so she could find his boxers and unleash his cock.

Which was desperate for attention at this point. His dick was long and hard and weeping with arousal. His breath caught in his throat as she took him in hand. Her palm was warm and soft as she gripped him, her thumb swiping across the slit of his dick and coating his cockhead in fluid.

And she brought her thumb to her mouth and her tongue came out, tasting him right then and there.

It took every bit of his concentration to not come. She was the sexiest woman he'd ever laid eyes on, and if he played his cards right, she could be his.

She seemed to respond to Van's authority. Oh, he knew better than to try to be the boss out of the bedroom, but it might work here. He sank his hand into her hair. "You were given a job, Elisa. I expect you to do it right. Lick me. Lick me all over and then you suck me deep."

Her eyes lit with desire and she leaned over, stroking his cock while she swiped her tongue over the head of his dick. Her tongue darted around, a butterfly landing and taking off and making him crazy.

"More," he commanded.

She sucked his cockhead behind her lips.

Pure pleasure curled through him, lighting his body up and making him feel so fucking alive. In the moment nothing else mattered. Nothing but the feel of her mouth on him, the proof that they were together, that he wasn't alone.

Her tongue rolled over his cock as she worked him. She stroked him with her hand as her mouth took him deeper and deeper. Soft velvet encased him, and he recognized when Van walked back into the room, but it didn't matter. Van only enhanced the experience.

"That's a pretty sight," Van said. He pulled his shirt over his head and tossed it aside. "Don't stop what you're doing, but I want you to spread your knees wide."

Oh, Van meant to give her a distraction. He was up for that, but he needed to make a few things plain. "Don't you let up or he'll stop."

Elisa frowned, her eyes wide. "Stop what?"

Van moved behind her, getting on his knees and letting his hand curve around her waist to the apex of her thighs. "This."

Elisa gasped as Van started to play with her clit.

Hale tightened his hold on her hair. "Do not let him distract you or we'll find out if the discipline part of the lifestyle works for us."

There was no mistaking the way her gaze went soft, and then she was back to torturing his dick with her tongue. She rimmed his cockhead, worrying the underside until he was ready to spew and then sitting back and stroking him.

It was maddening. It was glorious. It was so much more than sex.

"Finish him off and then we'll see about this pretty little asshole." Van whispered the words against her ear. "You're so wet, baby. I might not even need lube. I can slide that plug along your pussy and it'll be nice and ready."

She whimpered and then seemed to force herself to focus. She reached up and cupped his balls, giving them a gentle squeeze as she took him deep, tongue whirling. She seemed to be trying to swallow him whole, and it sent him right over the edge. He groaned as the orgasm rushed through his system. Whatever Van was doing to her made her moan, the sound reverberating over his flesh and heightening the sensation.

He gave her everything he had, thrusting into her mouth over and over.

And then a blissful peace settled.

Elisa leaned back against Van's chest as he rubbed her clit and made her come in his arms.

Satisfaction swamped Hale as he watched them.

There would be absolutely no whining from him. The day was pretty perfect.

Chapter Thirteen

Elisa slumped against Van, her head falling back. The orgasm had been what she'd come to think of as a starter orgasm. It was insane she now had classifications for her orgasms. She'd had so few of them before meeting these men, she'd thought she should be happy having one in a blue moon. Now, she knew this was nothing more than an appetizer and they would ensure she had at least a five-course meal.

"That's what I wanted, baby. That's perfect." Van's breath was hot against her ear.

She could still taste Hale in her mouth, the salty richness of him coating her lips, but Van didn't hesitate to kiss her. His tongue dove deep, and it felt both forbidden and perverted and right. They were all connected. There was no need for jealousy or shame. Whatever the three of them wanted was okay because they cared about each other.

She was starting to love these men.

Or maybe she'd loved them from the moment she'd seen them, but she didn't trust the emotion because she'd been taught how capricious it could be.

Love could be stalwart, too. It could be a mountain that couldn't be moved, a shelter that would never crumble.

"Now, we're going to move to the playroom," Van announced. "Hale's gotten to see you as a glorious sun goddess, and it's my turn. I want to see you on a spanking bench, your ass in the air waiting for me."

"What's a playroom?" She'd never heard the term before.

Hale reached out a hand to help her up. "It's a mini dungeon. Though knowing Mr. Roberts, it's probably not so mini."

She got to her feet and found herself immediately scooped up into Hale's arms.

The man liked to pick her up, and while she'd never been one of those petite girls who wanted a man to sweep her off her feet, she had to admit she loved it when one of them cradled her against them and took her where they wanted her to go. She barely looked at the beautiful suite around her as they walked her down the hall. She caught sight of some works of art, but nothing was as lovely as the cut of Hale's jaw or Sylvan's eyes as he walked behind them.

Van was a man on a mission today, and the commanding presence he evoked was doing something for her. It would rankle if he used it all the time, but seeing this side of him made her want him even more.

And that way lay heartache, but she'd already decided it was better to have memories than regrets.

Van moved ahead of them and opened the door, ushering them inside.

The "playroom" as they'd called it, was decorated in lush greens and golds and could have been a baroque salon had it not been filled with furniture that was obviously used for sex. There were two *X*-shaped crosses along one wall and a small cage that contained a luxurious bed and pillows. Whoever was locked in there would be a well-kept pet.

Hale walked her straight to an odd bench where someone had set up a table with… Yup, that was a butt plug.

She was actually doing this. She was going to let them lube up a piece of plastic and shove it up her asshole in preparation for one of them shoving an even bigger item there while the other one fucked her pussy.

It was ridiculous. It was perverse.

She was definitely going to do it.

Van had thoughtfully lined the leather pads of the bench with a soft blanket. "You're going to lie on this face down. This is only to get you into the perfect position. If I was planning on spanking that pretty ass, I would tie you down."

She wasn't sure she would ever truly enjoy that kind of play, but she would never say never to these two men. "We're all about the butt plug today. Got it."

"You would be such a brat." Hale set her down and shook his head. "You would get in so much trouble. Come on. Let's settle you in."

She allowed him to lower her down. The position felt awkward at first. Her ass was elevated slightly and her legs were splayed, each resting on its own padded ledge.

She felt a warm hand on her ass. "Have we told you how pretty you are?"

"Yes, Van. You tell me regularly." So often she was beginning to believe him, beginning to feel confident that it didn't matter what other people thought as long as she was good with these two.

And herself. She counted. She mattered.

"I'll always tell you," Hale promised.

She glanced up, and he was staring down at her. "You're pretty, too, Hale."

He was so masculine and strong, and she was starting to learn exactly how to touch him to get him to relax. He wasn't a particularly affectionate person. Van hugged everyone, but Hale held himself back. Not with her. When she touched him, he practically purred.

"I'm glad you think so." He leaned over and kissed her temple. "Now, don't move. I promise you'll get a treat if you stay still."

She rather thought her treat was going to be a big cock fucking her hard, and she was good with that. Van's fingers had done their job, but she was ready for so much more. She'd loved sucking Hale's cock, but it left an ache inside her that only they could fill.

Hale moved back so she couldn't see either of them. That was the moment she realized the whole wall to the side of her was a mirror.

She watched as Van moved to the table, his naked body

graceful and strong. His cock was already hard, straining up, but he was focused on his task. He took the plug in hand and despite what he'd said earlier, he lubed that sucker up. His hand moved over it, stroking it, warming and readying it.

She'd never had anyone prepare for sex the way they did. They'd thought this out and planned it. They'd talked over what they wanted to do with her like the partners they were.

She could get used to a world where two amazing men put her first.

Her breathing evened out as she watched them in the mirror, a sense of peace floating over her. When she was an old woman, she would pull this memory out and be young again, loved again.

"This is a small plug," Van announced as he moved back between her legs, that big cock of his so close to where it might do her good. "We'll move you up as you get used to it. The last thing we want to do is hurt you, but the sensation can be uncomfortable at first."

"How would you know?" she asked.

"Because my brother's an asshole," he replied, but he was smiling. "Made us take a training class and everything, so consider me somewhat of an expert. And I'm nicer than the Domme who trained us was. I warmed up the lube."

"I think that was her point," Hale countered. "She wanted us to experience what it's like for our partners so we're not thoughtless jerks who shove icicles up their assholes."

There was nothing icy about the sensation of Van parting her cheeks. Her breath felt caught as he poured some of the lube on her. It was warm and slippery.

"You're going to open up for me," he was saying as she felt the tip of the plug rim her.

It didn't hurt, but he was right that there was an odd discomfort to the sensation. Odd and jangly, like different nerves were firing off, ones she hadn't used before. He pressed the plug and then rotated it before pulling back out and lubing it up again.

Hale moved to the side, placing one big hand on the small of her back. "Relax, baby. It's weird at first, but then it's fine. Damn but I can't wait until you're between us."

She couldn't either. She wanted to know what the women of

Bliss knew, wanted to share in their secrets of being loved by two men.

Pressure built as Van manipulated the plug over and over, patiently gaining ground with each turn. All the while Hale's hands stroked her, loving her skin with his and telling her how gorgeous and sexy she was.

When Van pushed the plug all the way in, she didn't even squirm. She let the feeling roll over her, examining it and finding it not unpleasant. She was full in a way she hadn't been before. There was pressure but no pain.

"That is a pretty sight," Van said. "Makes me wish we had a camera in here."

Hale laughed, but she wasn't completely sure Van was joking. "There will be no pictures taken."

Van grinned down at her. "I got a mental picture, baby. That will be enough. Be right back."

He disappeared into a small room off to the side.

"How long do I have to wear it?" she asked, a bit disappointed. She'd rather thought they would have sex.

Hale moved back to the table. "Until we're ready to go. We've got a while. And in the meantime..."

He had something in his hand as he returned to her. She couldn't tell what it was, but the minute she heard the humming noise, she knew her disappointment wouldn't last long. Hale shifted her hips so he had access to her pussy, running the small vibrator over her clit. "I thought I would warm you up. He's washing his hands and getting a condom. How does that feel?"

It felt like heaven. "Perfect."

He stayed there for a moment, letting the vibe do its work until Van was back, and sure enough, he'd already rolled the condom over that hard cock of his. Hale moved out of the way.

"This is a preview of how it's going to feel," Van promised, stepping between her legs.

"It'll be so much better when it's real." Hale knelt down beside her, one big hand sliding over hers. "We'll surround you."

She felt Van's cock slide against her, and it shifted the plug slightly, lighting up nerves in her ass. Her hand tightened around Hale's as Van eased inside her.

"You feel so fucking good," Van said as he pressed his cock home.

She was so tight, filled up by the cock in her pussy and the plug in her ass. What would it be like when that plug was Hale's cock and their arms were all around her, encasing her in pleasure and warmth and love?

Then she wasn't questioning a thing because all she could think about was them. Van drove inside her, hitting all her sweet spots. She'd been so aroused by what they'd done to her before, it didn't take long before her body bowed with pleasure and she held on to Hale's hand as she came.

Van picked up the pace and then he was holding himself hard against her, his head dropping forward as he gave her everything he had.

She breathed in the moment, relishing in the perfection.

"I think we should take a shower and do that all over again," Hale said.

It wasn't like she had a time she was supposed to get back. Nate was probably taking a nap, and he would call her if there was an emergency. She had a radio and everything.

Which was out in the living room. She winced at the thought, but it was important. "I have to go grab my radio. Get that shower going for me."

"I'll get it," Van offered.

She shook her head. "I'd like to see if I can walk with this thing."

She eased up with Hale's help and took a couple of steps. Weird, but she was pretty sure she was so relaxed she could handle it. She slipped into a robe and started for the living room. Her radio was perfectly quiet and she didn't have any texts on her phone, so it was probably safe to hang out here for a while.

A gentle chime went through the place.

Was she supposed to answer the door? Maybe the guys had ordered more food or something special.

She opened the door and there was her dad. Covered in something blue.

"Hey, sweetie. They told me you were up here. Didn't move fast enough when I popped that Nelut nesting balloon. Thought I'd

come here for a shower. You do not want this in your car, I tell you."
If he was surprised she was in a robe in someone else's suite, he did
not show it.

"Boys, you better have some clothes on," he called out as he
shuffled in. He started toward the back of the suite. "I need to use the
big shower. It's got the most water pressure. If you don't get this
stuff off you pretty fast, well, you do not need a sibling."

Her cell phone pinged with a text from security.

Her happy time was over for the afternoon. She needed to get
back to work.

* * * *

Van had never been so happy to need a ride. Most of the time it
sucked to have one car between them, and when he'd had to find a
way to get up to the lodge earlier, it had been shitty. But now, he was
perfectly happy with his state.

He glanced around the lodge's security office and thought
about how horrified Hale had looked when he realized he would be
the one driving Mel home. Mel hadn't wanted Elisa driving back
down the mountain alone, so...here he was, watching their woman
work while Hale was getting an earful about alien mating practices.

Life felt pretty good.

For now.

He wasn't going to think about that. He had months and
months before he had to deal with that particular heartache. He was
going to live in the now and worry about everything else later. The
afternoon had been magnificent, and he wasn't going to ruin it with
anxiety and guilt.

"This is what we were able to find." The head of the security
department was a man named Frank Davidson. Van knew him
vaguely, but he'd never spent much time with him. Luckily he'd been
hired directly by Cole Roberts, so he hadn't gone through the normal
security check which would have involved this big, rough-looking
guy asking him a million questions about his record. Or he would
have taken one look at his record and kicked him out.

Would he ever be able to get a job his brother didn't arrange?

"I think this is your mystery woman. She was definitely not a guest of the hotel. This is the only time she shows up here. I looked a couple of days before and a couple of days after." Unlike the majority of the employees, Frank was older and lived off site with his family in Pagosa Springs. He wasn't the type to party with all the singletons.

And there were a lot of parties. The younger employees worked hard and played even harder. In the beginning it had been a lot of fun. It had made him feel like he was part of the group. And then he slept with most of the group.

He shouldn't have joked about all the sex he and Hale had before meeting Elisa. At the time it had seemed a fun way to needle Hale, but he hoped she hadn't taken him seriously.

There hadn't been that many. They had a fairly low body count. For young guys. Who had a lot of kinky sex. Maybe medium. Not high. Probably. It wasn't like he counted and compared.

The crazy thing was it wasn't hard to think about not ever sleeping with another woman. It didn't bother him at all. Monogamy was a nice idea when that woman was Elisa Leal.

She leaned over, looking at the monitor. She was buttoned up and in her uniform again, her hair neat and expression controlled, but he could remember how hot she'd been, how her ass had wiggled and pushed back against the plug. How tight she'd been when he'd driven his cock deep inside her. How pretty and trusting she'd been when she laid on that bench and let him do all kinds of dirty things to her. When she'd told him yes and looked at him with trusting eyes, he'd felt like he was finally worthy of something good.

"Van?"

He straightened up and crossed one leg over the other so maybe no one noticed his unruly dick. "Yeah?"

"I asked if you can take a look at the security feed and tell me if you recognize this woman." Her lips kicked up in an amused expression, as though she could see right through him. "If you need a minute…"

He kind of loved it when she teased him. She knew exactly what his problem was, and he liked the intimacy of sharing that with her. He stood and was glad his jeans weren't tight. "I'm fine. I was lost in thought. Let's take a look at this lady who seems to want to kill me."

Yeah, that did it. No more dick problems. His inevitable

murder was enough to clear that right up.

He moved around the big desk and leaned over to look at the monitor. It showed the security feed from one of the cameras in the lobby. He recognized the young woman they'd met earlier. She was at the front desk in her uniform, talking to a woman in slacks and a blazer. Her back was to the camera at this point, but he could already see a problem. "How tall would you say she is?"

Elisa's head cocked as she stared at the monitor. "I don't know. The way the camera's placed, it's hard to tell."

Frank pointed to the screen. "Chelle's roughly five seven. This woman is definitely shorter than that. The desk itself is about three and a half feet. Given where it hits her, I would say she's no taller than five four, but I can't estimate precisely."

He didn't need precision. "How did Pilar describe the woman she met?"

Elisa's brow raised. "Tall. Thin. Damn it. It's two different women."

Yep. The woman on the video was short, and while she looked perfectly fit, he wouldn't call her thin. The mystery deepened, and he had zero clues why one woman would be looking for him, much less two.

"She's about to turn around," Frank pointed out. "See, that's Chelle handing her the address we had for Van and Hale. She should have gotten fired for that. Lucy's soft."

Lucy was new to the job, and he was sure firing people during her first few months would be hard for her. They were also deep into the ski season and right before the holidays. Being down even a single worker could make things difficult for the team. "She made a mistake. I don't think she'll do it again."

Frank grimaced and hit a key to stop the video as the woman at the counter turned, her face captured perfectly.

"Do you know her?" Elisa asked.

He had never seen that woman in his life. She was pretty, her light hair up in a ponytail. She looked nothing like the woman Pilar had described. "I do not recognize her. Can we get a printout? I'll show it to Hale, but I'm almost certain he's going to say the same thing."

"Can you play it through, Frank?" Elisa asked. "Chelle told

me she noticed that the woman stopped and talked to a guest after she walked away. I'd like to figure out who that is."

"Sure." Frank touched the keyboard and the video continued. "I pulled some footage from the other lobby cameras. She moved through and left about five minutes later, but she did talk to someone. She was parked far enough away I couldn't get a plate number."

The woman stepped away from the front desk and began walking through the lobby, sliding the contact information into the crossbody bag she wore. When she pulled her hand back, Elisa pointed to the screen.

"Stop it there. Do you see that?" Elisa asked.

Van was pretty sure she wasn't asking him, which was good because he didn't see anything.

Frank frowned, staring at the now stopped frame. "Damn it. She's wearing a holster. I told Cole I thought we should install metal detectors."

"What?" Van leaned in.

Elisa pointed to the place where the woman's blazer tipped open and showed a line of something underneath. "It's a holster. I mean, technically we can't see the gun, but why else would she have a shoulder holster on?"

It was worse than he'd thought. There was someone looking for him and she had a gun. "But that's a handgun. We're pretty sure Hale was shot with a rifle."

"A lot of people have more than one gun," Frank pointed out. "She can't walk through the lobby with a rifle. The handgun is a better bet for daily use. If she knows what she's doing, she'll use the right tool for the job."

"So you think she's a professional?" It wasn't even something he'd considered. He'd thought about a pissed-off ex-lover—though none had come to mind. He'd definitely wondered if one of those assholes he'd gotten into fights with was looking for some revenge. He hadn't considered someone might hire a killer.

Elisa stared for a moment. "I don't know about that. She walks like a cop."

"I caught that, too. She's got an efficiency of movement I would associate with military or police," Frank agreed. "Which means she should be on record somewhere. I don't have the means to do it, but the sheriff's office might be able to put her through some kind of facial recognition and come up with a name."

"I'm not sure we have a way to do that. We have some computers, but nothing powerful enough to run that kind of software," Elisa replied. "It's a small-town operation. I would guess Nate would have to go to the town council to get the budget for us to outsource facial recognition."

Oh, but he had connections. "My brother can do it. I'll call him."

This was exactly what his brother did.

"No, you won't get involved," Elisa countered. "This is official. I'll call him and see if we can afford his services."

Jake would never make Nate Wright pay for a simple search. He might only be up here for parts of the year, but his brother considered himself a member of the community. Besides, they'd worked with Cameron Briggs on several occasions. "You'll find your fellow deputy has an in with my brother and Adam. He's a pretty spectacular coder himself."

"I'll look into it, but I have to be the one to talk to him. You can make the introduction, but then you're out of it. You can't be involved in the investigation as anything but a witness," she murmured, her eyes still on the screen. "Let's get it moving again. I want to see who she talks to. If she knows someone in the area, he might be helpful in finding her."

"You're going to be disappointed because I did not catch his face." Frank started the video up again. "There he is. He was waiting for her at the front of the lobby. I think he's involved in whatever she was doing. You see the way he keeps his head down?"

The man was wearing a ball cap, pulled low over his eyes. The woman joined him, a hand on her bag as though protecting the information. She said something to him, and he pointed her way. She shrugged.

"She's working for him." He could read the body language. He'd spent an entire childhood studying the people around him because his parents thought he could make decisions about people on his own. There had been very little protection from them. The years of bartending hadn't hurt either. "He's the one who wants the information, but she won't give it to him."

"And he is pissed," Elisa agreed. "He's also aware of where that camera is, and he doesn't want to be picked up on it. I would bet they're arguing about payment."

Then the blonde turned and walked off, the man following behind her, still trying to make his point. The man had a heavy jacket on, like he'd come in from the cold. It looked odd on him, like it didn't fit properly over his shoulders.

"No one remembers an argument in the lobby?" Elisa straightened up, a frustrated look on her face.

"We're not supposed to notice things like that." He remembered well all the lectures on how employees were supposed to act. "Unless we feel someone is in danger, we're supposed to look the other way and pretend nothing's happening. Besides, that was nothing. You should see what happens when Rachel Harper finds out Max is cheating on his diet with a bucket of chicken wings. She is serious about his cholesterol. That is a confrontation you can't avoid watching."

But no one would have noted the man and the woman arguing quietly and briefly in the lobby before they both left. If they couldn't pull a plate off the car they'd driven away in, Jake and his group were their best bet.

He wanted to know who that man was. There was something familiar about him, but Van couldn't put his finger on it.

"Thank you for your help, Frank." Elisa nodded the security chief's way. "If you don't mind printing out that good shot we have of her, I would appreciate it. Maybe capture it and send it to me digitally, too."

"And send one of the guy. Even from the back. There's something about him. I know you said I can't be involved, but this is witness stuff," Van argued. "I think I might know him. I don't know why."

Elisa put a hand on his shoulder. "Sure."

Within minutes they were walking out of the lodge, heading toward her big SUV.

"Please sit in the front with me," she said as she opened the driver's side door.

"Well, I don't want to sit in the back." He hadn't thought about the fact that she drove a county vehicle now even though it was parked across the street from them every night. "I know I have a reputation, but I haven't actually been in the back of one of these. I've never been arrested in Bliss. Though I've heard it's nice. Like real nice." He glanced around the luxurious interior. "This is the nicest police car I've ever seen."

Elisa smiled as she settled in and turned the car on. "According to Gemma, these were a gift from one of the town's really rich people."

"Yeah, we've got a couple of people in town who have more money than they know what to do with. I've heard Stef Talbot is building the schoolhouse and plans to gift it to the town." They'd recently broken ground with plans for the small but high-tech school to open in time for the next academic year.

"I would think there wouldn't be enough kids for a school here."

He hadn't paid a ton of attention, but he'd been at the town hall during a planning session. He'd been hired to pass out popcorn. It had been entertaining. "I heard something about mixed-use classrooms and putting grades together. They want to hire at least three teachers, and there would be a bunch of volunteers to do things like work the lunchroom and provide PE and library services. It's always going to be small, but they want it to grow with the kids. I think technically it's going to be considered a private school."

"They need teachers." Elisa seemed pleased with that idea as she eased the car out of the parking lot and onto the road. The snow had started falling again.

"You thinking of changing professions?"

"No, but my sister is a teacher," she replied. "She's taught several different elementary grades."

His heart clenched at the thought. "You're going to stay, aren't you? You're going to make this place your home."

"I think so, but the idea of a school makes me wonder if I'm not moving way too fast with Hale," she admitted.

"Why would you say that? I know things moved fast, but it's not like you're getting married."

"But I hope that's where we're going, and he's told me he hopes that, too."

They'd talked about marriage? His chest suddenly felt too

tight. Not because the thought of marrying Elisa made him anxious. It was the fact that he hadn't been involved in that conversation. They were moving forward without him. Like they said they would because he'd told them he wasn't going to stay.

Had they been doing more than having sex when they cuddled together after he left? Were they planning their futures in those late night/early morning hours when he ran like the scared child he seemed to be?

"Then I don't see what the problem is." He was well aware that had come out harsher than he'd intended.

"I don't see a world in which I can have a child."

Shit. This was a serious talk, and he wasn't sure she should be having it with him. Or maybe she was looking for someone on the outside to give her advice. She'd said *can* not *want*. "I don't think he'll care. I know I wouldn't. He's in love with you, not the idea of you having his baby. I would bet Hale's never really thought about having kids. I know I haven't. But you have."

Her hands tightened on the wheel. "I'm on medication. I can't get pregnant while I'm on the meds, and I need to be on the meds for at least five years, maybe longer. I could get off them…"

He knew why she was on those meds. "Absolutely not. I know exactly what he would say right now. He would tell you that he doesn't want you to risk yourself for the idea of something that might or might not happen. You are precious, Elisa."

She sniffled but kept her eyes steady as she started down the road. "I appreciate that. I always thought I would have a kid and I would do everything different."

"Then be different. If you want a kid, pick one who needs you. Pick one like Hale. He was fourteen when he went into foster care, and he never came out." His heart actually ached at the thought of not being a part of that family. "There's more to being a mom than giving birth to a baby. You don't have to give up on that dream. All you have to do is modify it slightly."

She chuckled, an oddly emotional sound. "That's more than slightly, Van, but you're right. And I am moving way too fast."

He knew he shouldn't argue with her, but he couldn't help himself. "Or you found what you're looking for, and there's no need to wait. I think sometimes life just clicks into place, and there's no reason to fight it or wait around. You take a leap. It was that way for my brother. He met his wife and they married very quickly."

"But it's not that way for you," she said on a sigh, and then she shook her head. "I'm sorry. I shouldn't have said that. I'm not trying to push you."

"You don't have to, baby. Don't you think if there was a way for me to stay, I would? But I've lived my whole life skirting responsibility, and I can't this time. Even if my brother didn't need me, what would I do here? You've got a job. Hale's constantly working. I don't think the Trading Post needs a marketing manager. Trio has more business than it can handle. No one needs me here."

"Is marketing your passion?"

He could turn that around. "Is being a deputy yours?"

"I think it could be," she admitted. "I know I like helping people, and it would be far harder to do that in a city police force. They have other problems. Here, I can stop and help people on the side of the road, and I can volunteer my time because I'm not going to be forced to work overtime. I can work with kids at the new school. I know I could do some of those things in Dallas, but not the way I can here. Now could you answer my question?"

"Fine. No. It is not my passion."

"What is?" She asked the question as a sedan passed them, her hands tightening on the steering wheel because that car was going a little fast for the weather conditions.

He was happy that she didn't try to turn around and chase the guy. "Okay, I'm going to tell you something and it's going to sound like the dumbest thing in the world because I do not look like this person. Accounting. I really like accounting. All my life I've loved numbers and spreadsheets and balancing things. I never had the opportunity to explore it until I went to college because my parents weren't interested in that kind of thing."

"They should have been because you were," she countered. "I know I wish mine had been interested in anything I enjoyed. The only thing we had in common was the military, so I know where you're coming from. Why not pursue accounting? I would bet the Trading Post can use some help at tax time. There are a lot of small businesses who could use at least a part-time accountant. You put them together and you have a full-time job."

"I graduate in May with a degree in marketing. To switch to accounting would be at least another semester, and my brother's company already has a kickass accountant. She used to work forensic accounting for the CIA. She doesn't need an apprentice. She's got a whole team. This is where I'm needed."

She reached out and put a hand on his. "Okay. I'm sorry I brought it up. I won't again. And thank you for indulging me with the talk about kids. I feel better now. I'll talk to Hale when the time feels right."

He couldn't help but feel like he'd disappointed her. And himself. "It's not that I don't want to… What's that?"

Up ahead he saw a familiar truck, crushed against the guardrail.

"That's Hale's truck," Elisa said with a gasp. "And he was with my dad."

The rear lights blinked off and on, looking ghostly in the swirling snow.

And Van prayed they had arrived in time.

Chapter Fourteen

"See, I knew if I could get a look at that code from above I could crack it," Mel Hughes was saying as Hale turned out of the parking lot.

They needed another car.

He was alone in a car with the woman he'd recently fucked so dirtily and gloriously's father, and it was not a position he'd ever been in before. He was the guy who never met the parents. That was Van's job during the few occasions they'd found themselves in a more serious relationship. He was the "friend" who hung around way too much.

This was the most serious relationship of his life, and he couldn't lean on Van when it came to developing a friendship with Elisa's father. He was on his own, and he was deeply worried he was going to fuck it all up.

"They're an arrogant lot. Think no one can figure out their codes." Mel rolled down the window and shoved a fist out into the air as a blast of cold entered the previously warm cab of the SUV. "I can always find you. This town is not your brothel. Take that crap up to Creede."

Hale was pretty sure the town of Creede—which had absolutely once had a brothel in it—didn't want to be the approved mating ground for whatever had covered Mel in the blue goo he'd showered off an hour before. Now he was wearing a set of coveralls the maintenance staff had loaned him. He rolled the window back up and seemed extremely pleased with the way the day had gone.

Hale had no idea what to say to the man. So he kept driving. The snow was coming in harder now, and the sun was starting to go down. It had been warm enough to turn the road into slush, which was far more dangerous than snow. Something felt off.

"So, you used Mr. Roberts's suite to tempt my daughter into sin?"

Shit. "Uhm, I thought she could use a nap."

Mel's lips kicked up in a grin. "I'm teasing you, son. Elisa is a grown woman, and a smart one at that. And there's no sin in loving a person with your body. Sex is a natural thing to do when you love a person. Or when you're merely attracted to a person. Sex without commitment can be all right as long as everyone understands the boundaries."

He needed to make sure Mel understood his intentions. "That is not what's happening. It's the other one."

"Other one?"

"You know, the other one."

"I believe I need to hear you say that," Mel insisted.

"It's the *love* one. It's the commitment one," he said.

Mel nodded as though he'd known it all along. "Then it's all fine and very romantic of you to make a special afternoon for her. You seem like a good fellow, Hale. But your friend is a fool if he leaves you behind. Stop worrying about that. It's out of your control. You need to worry about finding a place for you and Elisa to live."

"Well, I live in the cabins I'm renovating."

"So she'll have to move every couple of months?"

That didn't sound great for her. "It's been the easiest thing to do while I'm working."

"But Elisa will be moving out here," Mel pointed out. "She'll want to bring her furniture and her things. Will she have to put them in storage? Look, it's something to work on for the future. She's going to want a proper home, and that's why I think you should consider moving into the bunker."

"I'm sorry, what?"

"It's real nice. Cassidy put in a hot plate and everything," Mel explained. "If you move some of the supplies around, you'll have room for Elisa's furniture."

"I thought the bunker was for alien invasions."

Mel nodded. "And when the feds come to town. And when I don't want to talk to someone. And there's always the threat of thermonuclear war and the zombie apocalypse. Honestly, that bunker works for any apocalypse. Maybe not one where the giant land worms take over the Earth. I have to think about that, but the good news is we have you around to do renovations when we need them."

His life pretty much passed before his eyes. He would be trapped in a small space with the love of his life—not so bad—and her de facto parents and their CB radio monitoring everything that could go wrong with life itself—super bad. "I think you and Cassidy should keep that… You're fucking with me again, aren't you?"

A laugh filled the cab. "You're fun to tease, Hale. Cassidy told me I had to go easy on you, but I've never had a son to needle before."

Hale felt his hands grip the steering wheel tighter. He hadn't considered the fact that he wasn't merely getting Elisa out of this. He was getting a family. "Well, I've never had a dad who cared enough to tease me, so don't be surprised if I take most of what you say at face value and work my hardest to please you."

Mel reached over and patted his arm. "Like I said, you're a good man, Hale. You need to understand that you have value, and you're part of the community here in a way I don't think you've ever been before. You have friends here. I think you're going to find your family here. Be patient with Van. He's not as smart as you are."

Hale snorted, taking the switchback with the utmost caution. He still had to get down this mountain, drive across town, and then up another mountain, but suddenly that didn't seem so bad. Suddenly it seemed like it might be nice to talk to Mel about something other than aliens. "Van has always been the smart one, and you might have been teasing me, but you make a good point. I don't have the money for my own cabin. I've talked about buying one, but I would be taking out a loan with the purpose of flipping it. We would still be moving around."

"I think you'll find Elisa has done far better than you have financially," Mel said. "I talked to her about moving here, and she's planning on buying a cabin when the right one comes up for sale."

"She mentioned that to me, but I don't want to…"

Mel cut him off. "Do not say you don't want to mooch off her. Women don't like it when you take their efforts for granted and play the wounded male. Her comfort is worth more than your ego."

"I don't have much of an ego. You're right. If she wants to buy something, I'll put in the work to make it perfect for her, and I'm starting to make real money. She can teach me how to handle it. Van's always been the one to handle what little we had. But man could he make a dollar go forever. He's always been good with money."

He glanced down and noticed the tire pressure light had come on.

"I think my girl is pretty frugal, too. I wish I had a big inheritance to promise her, but unless she manages to make it to Leira Seven, I'm afraid that old ramshackle cabin is all I have. Now if she does, she'll find out she's their version of a billionaire," Mel began.

The words kept flowing, but Hale's mind was laser focused on the road now. The tire pressure gauge often went wonky in the winter, but he thought he could feel a slight pull to the passenger side. Like the tire was slowly but steadily deflating.

He'd recently had his tires checked. The SUV had been looked over by Long-Haired Roger and declared ready for the wintertime. It was an older model but solidly built, and the tires were fairly new.

Had someone screwed with his tires in the parking lot at the lodge, knowing he would have to deal with this dangerous road? Had they screwed around with the water heater knowing he would be the one Lucy called out?

What if this was about him and not Van?

"Mel, do you feel like the truck's leaning a little?" He gently pumped the brakes to slow down, as they were on the steepest part of the road. They were almost to the scenic overlook. There would be a safe place to pull over there and check things out. He couldn't do it here. There was no space, and he didn't trust other drivers not to fly around a switchback and hit him or Mel.

Mel stopped, seeming to understand that the situation had

turned serious. "Yes. I think it is leaning. I thought it was the road, but it seems like one of the tires is blown."

But it hadn't blown. That would have been easy. He wouldn't have ever gotten on the mountain pass if someone had simply taken a knife to his tire or he'd hit something in the lot. No. This had been a slow loss of pressure, so he was off balance at the worst possible time, in the most dangerous section of road Bliss had to offer.

How many people had gone straight over the edge? There was a guardrail that had stopped many an accident from proving fatal, but if he hit it just right or got completely out of control, he could flip the vehicle over and they would die on their way down to the bottom.

"The overlook is up ahead. Try slowing down, and we can pull off there," Mel advised. "Go slow on the brakes. You don't want to lock them up. You're doing good, son."

Mel's patient voice calmed him, and he remembered everything he knew about driving in the mountains. One more curve and he would be able to see the overlook.

That was when a sedan came flying around the corner, no thought to safety. It nearly came into his lane and when it flew by, slapped slush all over Hale's windshield. On pure instinct, his foot came down on the brake because he couldn't see.

And that was when the world started spinning, and he heard a crash and everything went dark.

* * * *

Elisa thought her heart was going to pound out of her chest as she realized who was in that truck. She couldn't panic. She had to do her job. That was how she would help her dad and Hale.

Please. Please let them be all right. Don't let me have found them only to lose them. Please.

She wasn't the kind of woman who pleaded with the universe, but it was right there as she eased to a stop behind the still vehicle. Van was out in a shot, but she had to call this in. The road was too dangerous, and there were too many tourists who didn't know how to drive, as proven by that asshole in the sedan. She picked up her radio. "This is Leal calling the Bliss station house. I've got an accident on the third turn going up to the lodge. Will advise on injuries, but the vehicle will definitely need a tow, and the road needs clearing."

Gemma's voice came back over the radio. "Nate's on his way, and I'm dispatching an ambulance. It's close. Keep me updated."

Elisa got out of the SUV as Van managed to get the passenger side door open, helping her dad out. He looked fine, but she wasn't breathing a sigh of relief until she saw Hale.

"Something went wrong with the tires." Her dad looked harried, his eyes darting around as though looking for danger.

Because he'd been in danger before, been put in a position where he'd had to fight for his life. She wasn't sure she believed that it had been aliens, but she absolutely believed her father had PTSD from his time in the military. He'd worked deep cover ops, black ops. His nightmares sometimes came out during the daytime.

"Dad, you're okay. How is Hale?" She needed to ground him, turn his attention from what might have happened to helping the people around him. He was awfully good at that. She reached for his hand, pulling it between hers. "What happened?"

Her dad took a deep breath and squeezed her hand. "Something was wrong with the back tire. Passenger side. We didn't notice it until we were already on the road. We were trying to make it to the overlook so we could park there, but that damn car nearly crashed into us and Hale lost control."

Van was already inside the car. "He's unconscious but breathing. Did you call an ambulance?"

Her heart threatened to stop. "Yes. Check his pulse."

She wanted to climb in herself, but she couldn't get around the other side. The guardrail had held, but it pressed into the driver's side door.

"What the... Stop. I don't think that's how you do CPR." Hale's voice floated out, and the groan that came from his mouth was the sweetest sound she'd ever heard.

"How would you know how to do CPR?" Van complained, and the fact that they were suddenly bickering like an old married couple made her breathe so much easier.

"I know you have to at least let a dude get his seatbelt off," Hale replied. "I think I hit my head on the steering wheel. Damn sedan. Did it hit anyone else? Is Mel okay?"

"I'm fine." Her dad seemed to have calmed a bit. "You did a

246

good job handling the road."

So no one was going to have to tranq her father. That was one bit of good news. Van eased out of the truck, his arms still inside as he helped Hale out.

There was the tiniest bit of blood on his forehead where he'd hit the steering wheel. She moved to him, checking him over. "You need to sit down. The paramedics will be here in a couple of minutes."

"I'm fine. Just woozy," he said, looking back at the SUV. "Damn it. It was paid off."

"The car can be replaced. You can't, and you probably have a concussion." Van stepped in, taking charge. "Sit down like Elisa asked and wait for the paramedics. This is the second time you've nearly given her a heart attack."

She was pretty sure she wasn't the only one who'd nearly lost it.

Hale frowned. "Well, it wasn't like I was trying to."

"But you are now," Mel pointed out as they could hear sirens in the distance. "Let's both sit in the warmth of the patrol car and wait for the EMTs. I can show you where I stash stuff in the back seat."

Wait. What? She shook that off as she saw Nate's SUV coming in from the other side. It looked like the ambulance was coming from the lodge, but Nate had driven up the mountain from Bliss. "Hale, I'm glad you're all right."

That didn't seem like the thing she should say, but she couldn't lose it. The need to cry was right there, but she had to shove it down deep.

Don't you fucking cry. Don't let anyone see how weak you are.

She was the authority figure here, and she couldn't scream and cry that she'd almost lost him.

He moved back, getting into her space. "I am. I'm fine, baby. I'm glad you're here and I'm glad Mel's okay because we're going to be moving into his bunker soon."

"What?" He'd really hit his head. "You definitely have a concussion."

"Also, you're going to inherit a fortune in Leahan gold," Hale promised.

"It's Leira Seven, and it's not gold. It's more like pasta," her dad corrected. "See, their entire financial system is based on this wheat-like substance…"

Hale touched her shoulder. "I'm okay and you can do your job, and we'll do the whole holding each other thing when we get home."

She felt her walls threaten to shake. She couldn't lose it in front of her brand-new boss. "I can't…"

He leaned over and briefly brushed his lips to hers. "You are perfect. Do your job and I'll be a good patient. But we need to talk because I don't think this was an accident."

"Why?" Van was still pale.

"I think someone screwed with my tires in the hopes that this would happen," Hale replied gravelly. "This was never about you. It was always me they were after. Now the only question is why."

"We can't know this was intentional," Van argued. "And I drive that car, too. This absolutely could be about me."

Her dad was leaning over the passenger side back tire. He felt around it, his arm going to the back side. "It feels like someone knocked a nail in. You can't pick that up on the road."

"Tires get damaged by nails all the time," Van replied.

She went to look at what her dad had found. She followed his lead and felt around the back. "He couldn't have picked that up on the road. It's in the side, and it's perpendicular. Someone put that in. Someone back at the lodge."

A big SUV with Bliss County emblazoned on the side came to a stop, and Nate got out, looking over the assembled party with a frown. "Damn it, Hale. Who's trying to kill you?"

Wasn't that the question of the day?

Two hours later Elisa was finally coming down from the adrenaline high and able to think straight. It didn't hurt that Gemma had put a big mug of coffee in her hands the minute she'd walked through the station house doors.

"You've never seen that woman before?" Nate was staring down at the picture of the woman she'd found earlier in the day. He stood over Hale, who was sitting at the conference table where Nate held shift meetings.

The paramedics had cleared him, and the people doc had come by the station moments before to check their work. She couldn't believe she was already calling Caleb Burke the people doc, but here she was. Bliss had a people doc, and Noah Bennett was the animal doc, though he could be used in a pinch. Strangely, it was all starting to make sense to her, and she didn't blink at some of the Bliss weirdness now. Like she was becoming a real citizen.

She was so not moving into the bunker.

"No." Hale glanced back Van's way. "I don't recognize her. Do you?"

Van had been quiet the last few hours. After he was sure Hale was okay, he'd pulled back into himself. It was almost like she could see his defenses coming firmly into place. "No, but I told the deputy that earlier today."

Yep. Those walls were up again.

"Deputy?" Hale's eyes rolled.

"She's at work," Van argued. "What am I supposed to call her?"

Hale looked her way. "Baby, I don't know who this is. I would say I've never seen her before, but we both know I don't notice things the way I should. If she wasn't a project I was working on or a woman I was actively chasing, she could have sat beside me on the bus every day for a year and I wouldn't have a clue who she was."

"Hopefully we'll know something tomorrow," Nate said, stepping back. "I talked to Van's brother, and he's going to work on it. His company is the best in the business. If she's got any kind of a footprint, they'll find it. And Leal, you held it together spectacularly today. Good job. I would have lost my shit if that had been Callie."

"She's a woman," Gemma answered. "She doesn't get to lose her shit. One show of temper and suddenly you're the queen bitch of the world."

"You pulled out that woman's hair," Nate said with a snort.

Gemma shrugged. "She deserved it, and honestly it wasn't great hair to start with. I'm merely pointing out that Elisa's been a woman in a man's world for a long time."

"I'm afraid fifteen years of military service drilled that into me." She looked Hale's way. "But I was freaking out on the inside. A whole lot of my world was in that car."

Her dad had been picked up by Cassidy half an hour before. He'd stayed around to give a statement and make sure Hale was all right and didn't need alien technology to save him. He'd assured her there were some good aliens, and he had contacts.

She loved her dad. She kept waiting for that feeling to pass, for him to do something that annoyed her, but there was a weird joy that seemed to surround her dad and stepmom. They viewed the world in a way she'd never considered before.

"I was also surprised Mel was so calm," Nate said, looking at her. "Good job there, too."

Hale reached for her hand. "I knew what was going on in your head, baby. I didn't think you were being cold." He brought her fingers to his lips. "You were holding it together, and I appreciate that since Van acted like we were in an episode of *Grey's Anatomy*."

"You were very still. Like you were dead." Van stood, his eyes narrowed as he pointed Hale's way. "I was trying to restart your heart. Next time I'll let you die."

Hale moved in and put a hand behind Van's neck, his expression going earnest. "No, you won't, brother. Thank you for trying."

He pulled Van into a manly hug that involved him giving Van's back a slap, but there was a precious intimacy to the embrace, one she hadn't seen between the two of them before.

Van stepped back after a moment. "Try not to almost die again. It's getting obnoxious." He seemed far more centered when he sat back down. "Now let's talk about this. I know my brother will probably have a name and dossier on this woman in a couple of hours, but I want to know who the man is."

"The man? The one she talked to?" Hale asked.

She slid the printout his way. "This was the man she met in the lobby. We think she might have been working for him."

"I watched the cam footage." Nate sat back. "I agree. I would say he sent her in to get that information and she held it back because she wanted payment. One of them trashed the cabin that address sent them to. I would bet it wasn't the woman."

Hale was carefully studying the photo. "He looks familiar. What kind of hat is he wearing? It doesn't look like a sports team hat. Can we get a close-up? It looks like there's a pattern on the hat."

Elisa looked over Hale's shoulder. He was right. At first glance the hat looked like a plain black hat, but when she studied it there were lighter lines that formed a pattern.

"It doesn't look like any sports team I know," Nate conceded. "But then people at the lodge wear some crazy stuff. You know when you stare at it the right way, it looks almost like a bunch of Fs. Is there a sports team with a bunch of Fs?"

Gemma held out a hand. "Let me look at it." Nate handed it to her, and she shook her head. "It's not a sports team. It's designer. That's the Fendi logo. That damn hat probably cost five hundred dollars. This guy is an idiot. He's trying to go unnoticed but he's wearing a designer hat? The only reason it didn't stand out like a sore thumb was the fact that the camera feed is black and white."

"Hey, that guy today," Van said, looking at Hale.

"Guy?" They hadn't mentioned a guy, but then they'd had a lot to talk about because of the alien mating rituals, and then there had been a lot of sex.

Hale nodded and gestured for the photo. Once it was in his hands, he pointed at the guy's shoulders. "We had to help an out-of-control skier. The body type is roughly the same. I noticed how sloped his shoulders were. I can't be sure because he's wearing a coat here, but it could be him."

"He was wearing a ski suit with a bunch of logos on it, though not the Fs," Van pointed out. "It was a weird experience. Normally a person would be grateful they hadn't broken a leg, but he acted like he couldn't wait to get out of there."

"And then a couple of hours later Hale almost dies after someone puts a nail in his tire." Elisa didn't like how the pieces were starting to fit together. "So if this is the same guy, he knew the two of you were at the lodge. He could have gone out in the parking lot and sabotaged the car. He also could have been in the sedan."

"We don't know that," Nate corrected. "I think we can work on the theory that the man Hale and Van encountered today could be the same one who met with the woman on the video, but we don't need to expand it yet. We have a description of the sedan. I'll send

Cam out to see if he can find anything like it in the parking lot or on our traffic cameras. We don't have any up on the mountain, but once you hit the road on either side, there's at least one that might be helpful."

"So we're back to some guy wants to kill me," Van said, and then put up a hand when Hale huffed. "Or you. Sorry, man. I'm not trying to hoard all the fun for myself. But if it's the same guy, then he knows I use that car, too. We can't be sure."

"Have we heard anything on the second woman? The one Pilar spoke to?" Nate asked.

"We think she probably left town," Elisa explained. She'd spent a good portion of her morning trying to track the woman down. "I don't know why she didn't leave her card or something."

"Pilar said she seemed frustrated," Van said. "Maybe she wasn't thinking."

Or maybe they hadn't asked the right questions. "What if she'd already asked people and gotten a bunch of Bliss nonsense?"

Nate sat up straight. "Damn it. You're right. With the festival ending and the holidays coming up, they might not have thought about contacting me. Or they heard Pilar told you. She probably talked to someone else around town. Maybe the reason she didn't pass out a card is that she ran out."

Elisa stood up because she had a job to do.

Chapter Fifteen

Van was still upset as he poured his fortieth beer of the night.

Hale had almost died. Again. He'd seen that truck and known that his best friend in the world was gone and there was nothing he could do about it, and it was probably all his fault.

"You all right, friend?" Alexei Markov was almost too big to fit behind the bar. He'd been working at Trio the whole time he'd been in college, despite the fact his partner was made of money. He'd once told Van that being a bartender was preparing him for work as a therapist.

He didn't want to be therapied tonight. "Fine."

Alexei chuckled and took an order from his stepson, Micky, who was working the dinner rush. "Sure you are. Everyone is talking about the troubles with the car. Also, why are you moving into the bunker? I hear it will be crowded. We have a small guest house if you need a place to stay."

"I am not moving into a bunker." The rumor mill was at it again. "Hale was joking about that. I'm pretty sure Caleb screwed up and missed Hale's concussion because something's wrong with him."

Hale had been so calm. Not that he wasn't always calm. That wasn't the right word. Peaceful. Hale was peaceful, and that wasn't a word he would have used to describe his best friend. It was like something had fallen into place for Hale Galloway and the world suddenly made sense.

Good for Hale because it didn't make a lick of sense to him.

Alexei gestured out to one of the small tables in the bar area. "He seems fine to me."

Hale was hanging around Trio because Elisa had ordered them both to wait here so she could give them a ride home from his shift. Because they no longer had a car, and they didn't have the money for one. Could they afford a car payment?

Elisa and Hale wanted to get married, and he couldn't even buy a car.

Hale laughed at something Max Harper said. Max had shown up five minutes after Hale, as though Hale had called him. Maybe Max was Hale's best friend now.

He was in such a bad place, and he couldn't articulate why. He wanted Elisa and Hale to be happy. He truly did. So why did his gut roll with anger at the thought?

Why was he swept up with anxiety at the idea of them starting a family? What were they thinking? Elisa hadn't even properly moved here, and Hale had the unsteadiest job in the world.

Alexei reached into the fridge and pulled out a bottle of Pinot Gris. "I ask because it's obvious you're still upset. Has Long-Haired Roger given you a quote? You know he's always willing to negotiate if you find yourself in the spot that is tight."

He'd been told Alexei's grip on English vernacular had gotten far better over the years, but he still came up with some funny ways to say things. "The spot is entirely tight. It's so tight we can barely see straight, but does Hale understand that?"

"I think Hale is only seeing world with his heart these days," Alexei replied.

"Well, Hale's heart isn't going to be paying the bills, is it? How can it? It doesn't have a checking account. Oh, wait, neither does Hale." They had one account, and it was in Van's name because he'd lost at rock paper scissors, and how did he consider himself an adult?

"Hale can get all the banking accounts. I think Max can show him," Alexei said, his Russian accent thick. "I never would think Max would be the one to show other person how to adult, but he is doing good job so far. Hale talks more to friends. He is better at not staring off into the spaces. He is more present. This is good. Caleb used to stare at spaces, and it make everyone worry he is bomb waiting to explode. Not now, of course. Now he is normal."

Caleb Burke was not normal and never would be, but he supposed he was Bliss normal. Dear god. That was what was happening. Hale was becoming Bliss normal. He wasn't panicking about nearly dying because that happened all the time in Bliss. He was able to joke about aliens and not even ask Mel where the hell he'd gotten that much blue gelatin. He'd been covered in it this afternoon, and had any of them asked? No. They'd all simply nodded and accepted that Elisa's father was covered in the byproduct of alien reproduction.

"It's not normal to chill out after someone tries to kill you." Van put another beer on the round tray and set it out.

"What else will you be doing?" Alexei shrugged like it was no big deal, but then he'd been in Bliss for years, so it wasn't to him. "Your woman is working the cases, and she and Nate and Cam will take down the bad guys. Unless Gemma gets to them first. She can do much damage with her handbag."

Elisa was out there looking for a killer. Oh, not right this minute. Right now she was going around town asking if anyone had seen the woman Pilar had mentioned because apparently here in Bliss a person could come to town looking for someone and no one would help them. Because of the Bliss rules of engagement. *Thou shalt not give up thine brother or sister to whatever part of their past is trying to catch up to them.*

Well, they could at least give a dude a heads-up.

Alexei passed Callie the wine for table twelve. "I am trying to figure out if you are feeling guilt or jealousy. Or a mixture of both."

"Guilt. I don't have anything to be jealous about," Van retorted. "I do have guilt because I'm still sure this is about me. Hale never did a damn thing wrong in his life."

Alexei's head shook. "I'm sure he has, but you also must be knowing that sometimes it does not matter if you have done wrong. The innocent of this world can be harmed, too. Hale could have offended someone, or perhaps he has something someone wants."

Was Alexei even listening to him? "That's the trouble. He

doesn't have anything. Nothing. He had half a car, and now that's gone. He has his tools and the clothes on his back and that's about it, but this whole town is acting like that's enough to make a life with, and we know it's not."

"It's pretty much what I have when I come for my Holly," Alexei said, his expression turning wistful. "I did not have car though. I did have many peoples wishing to kill me."

"And you thought you could make a life with Holly?"

A smile came over the Russian's face. "I did not think. I merely follow my heart and know I will do everything I can to care for her and Caleb. I always knew Caleb would pull head out of ass and come with us."

And there was the difference. "Yes, you knew the dude with the medical degree and tons of family cash would take care of you."

"I would have been his partner if he'd had none of those things," Alexei insisted. "I love Caleb. I love Holly. I love my stepson. We decided we could be family, and now we have our beautiful Amelia. I am not to be bragging, but these things do not happen if I am not here. I do not believe Holly and Caleb would be the same without me. I think she is still alone, and he is still in cage if I am not here."

He wasn't sure if Alexei was referring to a real cage or a metaphorical one. It could be either, but he understood the point. "We can't live off Elisa's salary, and what Hale and I make together isn't enough."

"Enough for what?"

"Enough for a house and security. Enough so we don't have to sit up at night and worry about how to pay the bills. Enough to support the kids those two are going to eventually want to adopt. Enough to have the kind of life my…"

Fuck. His brain had tiptoed around the idea, skirting it so he didn't have to face it.

"The kind of life your brother has?"

Alexei had studied hard and obviously knew his way around a confused dude's brain, but he was wrong about this. "I am not jealous of my brother."

"Jealousy doesn't have to be a terrible thing," Alexei said. "Everyone feels a bit of it. It's how we choose to handle these feelings that makes them a bad or good thing. And what we're talking about isn't jealousy. It's envy. Jealousy is about possession. Envy is wishing for ourselves what someone else has. It can crush us and make us bitter or it can spur us on to do good things for ourselves. I am envious of Caleb's education. It is something I want for myself. So I go and do this. What about your brother do you envy?"

Some of what Alexei said was making sense. "He and Adam…they're so together. They've built something. They have everything we're supposed to have, and I don't know how he did it. We came from the same place. Our parents never stayed put for more than six months. When they put me in school it was only to pull me out a couple of weeks later because they didn't like being tied to school hours or someone fed me whatever food my mom thought would cause cancer that month. There was no stability. Jake is the very definition of stability. He has a house and kids who adore and respect him. His wife is amazing, and Adam is half of him. Adam would never think about leaving Jake behind."

Alexei nodded encouragingly. "There it is. You think Hale is choosing Elisa over you?"

That wasn't exactly the truth. "I think we might be able to convince Elisa if he worked with me. I think Hale is choosing Bliss over me, and Adam would never have done that to Jake."

"You know this for certain? You have talked about this with them?" Alexei asked. "Because often there is more to the story than what we allow the world to see. Especially outside of Bliss. We are more open here. Your brother is in polite society. I'm sure he hides much. Have you considered how much harder it will be to have this relationship outside of Bliss?"

"It doesn't bother Jake at all."

"Or he does not show it. I find it interesting that he buys a place here as soon as he finds it. His wife's car breaks down here one day and a few weeks later, they have a cabin in the valley. They come up here often."

Jake loved it here. Was it for more than the fishing? Was it because he didn't have to hide anything here? Because here no one would look at them twice when he and Adam kissed their wife?

"I don't know," Van admitted. "I didn't talk to him about that. There wasn't any reason to because Hale and I weren't even close to having a woman we would consider calling our girlfriend, much less our wife."

"But Elisa is such a woman?"

He knew the answer deep down. "She's the right one. But it's at the wrong time. Or maybe she's the right one for me, but what if I'm the wrong one for her? She's been through so much. I can't be the one who brings her more heartache."

"Then don't." Alexei's voice was steady but there was an obvious sympathy to it. "Wake up each morning saying I am the one who will make her life better today because she is my love. And it will be easier because you will have partner. My friend, this envy you feel is something worse. I believe it is shame. I believe what you are feeling is shame that you did not process what happens to you as a child as well as your brother. But he is older than you. He has more time. And he is different person. His reality, while on outside looks like yours, on inside is different. No matter the circumstances we cannot know how things truly feel for other without asking them. And we cannot measure our success by another's life. The question is what does your brother have that you truly want? Deep down inside your heart. Is it the beautiful home? The company he helped build? Is it to live in exciting city with many opportunities? Or is what you want exactly what you are on the cusp of finding. Is it love with amazing woman you can share with the person who is your partner in life? Is it a family he builds around himself? Is it the stable ground one finds when one is truly content?"

Alexei was right. It wasn't jealousy he felt. It was shame, and that was the most useless of emotions. Shame had led him to believe he didn't have a real place here, that the only way to live was to follow exactly in Jake's footsteps.

"That was beautiful." Callie was standing at the bar, tears in her eyes.

"It was, Pops." Micky picked up a napkin and sniffled into it. "You're going to be so good at this."

"I personally liked the way he differentiated between jealousy and envy." Stef Talbot sat at the end of the bar with his wife, Jennifer. They had two glasses of red wine and apparently were enjoying the show. "That's a fine line not everyone understands."

Jennifer wrinkled her nose his way. "We're supposed to

pretend we're not listening."

Talbot shrugged. "Well, everyone else was. For what it's worth, Van, I don't think Hale cares if you build him a grand mansion. I think he's pretty happy where he is."

"Uh, he's living at the Taggart place," Van pointed out. "I think we're going to get kicked out soon."

Talbot frowned. "It's the Hiram Jones Memorial House. It's in all the records."

Jen's eyes rolled, but she ignored her husband. "Talk to Marie. She'll look for something you can afford."

"I don't want to be a bartender for the rest of my life," he said because while he understood the emotional root of the problem, there was more to it.

"Hey, babe, before you leave tonight, could you check the books?" Zane walked in behind his wife, cuddling up close to her. "I've got quarterly taxes due, and my eyes are swimming. I'll be here all night."

"No, she won't," Van announced. It was time to take a damn stand. All these people wanted his ass to stay here, well, they were going to pay for the privilege, and he would make it worth their while because he would bet Zane hadn't kept up with recent tax code changes. "But I will."

Zane frowned his way. "Why would the hippy dude want to check my books?"

Was that how everyone saw him? Wear one tie-dyed shirt a couple of times... "Are you taking advantage of the deduction for all expenses related to training new employees? You can claim it for up to a year. How about the deduction for the new oven? It's got new energy efficient tech, and there's a rebate you can apply for."

"There is?" Zane asked. "I think the salesperson mentioned that, but it got lost in all the paperwork. There's so much paperwork and honestly, I hate math. I didn't go into the DEA because I was a numbers cruncher."

"But I am." A weird sense of optimism bubbled up inside of Van.

"I thought you were studying marketing," Talbot pointed out.

"Not anymore." It wasn't such a stretch. One extra semester and then he would have to hustle his ass off to find clients, but he could also make better use of the money they had. He would likely never have his brother's wealth, but that wasn't the important thing.

He'd been jealous because Adam would never leave Jake. But he was the one who was leaving. He was the one willing to walk away from what Hale needed. And what Van needed was—them.

"I'm changing my major," he announced. "I'm going to disappoint my parents in a way even my brother going into the military couldn't. I'm going to be an accountant."

Alexei slapped a hand on his shoulders. "This is good decision. You will be very nice accountant. It will be good to have someone to put between Bliss and IRS. I fear often that Marie will kill someone when she does her taxes. You can be go between."

"Good luck deducting the new Detector 7000. Mel paid for it himself, and I'm pretty sure he's going to want that off his taxes," Talbot said with a chuckle.

It would be awful. He would have to explain to his perhaps future father-in-law that he couldn't take the cleaning bill from fighting alien invaders off his taxes. Marie would likely want to argue over every penny. Zane would need an explanation of every line of code.

He could make a life here. All he had to do was believe in himself. And get used to Bliss normal.

"What the hell, Hale?" Max shouted.

That was when he noticed Hale. He stood in the middle of the dining room, a fist raised against a man.

Bliss normal apparently started right now.

* * * *

Hale watched Van working the bar, a sense of deep unease permeating his system.

Something was going on in Van's head, and he was pretty sure he wouldn't like it.

Trio was hopping tonight, the whole dining room at capacity and the lobby full of people waiting for a table. Van was working with Alexei, keeping the drinks flowing. Hale had been lucky to get this table. The bar area was as full as the dining room.

"So you think this is about you, and Van thinks this is about him, and you both think some designer-wearing ski douche is the one trying to kill you." Max had a beer in front of him, but he'd foregone the hot wings he sometimes tried to sneak in. He was in town picking up a few things he'd ordered and was planning on heading back home for dinner.

But not until he had the latest gossip.

That wasn't really fair. In Bliss, gossip was also a lot like caring. So far he'd been sent numerous well wishes and several casseroles because he'd been told nothing helped a person recuperate from a murder attempt like a warm homemade casserole. Given that the women and man who'd made them had actually survived attempts on their lives, he was going to give it a shot. If Hope Glen's cheesy chicken and ranch casserole alleviated some of his anxiety, he would happily eat it.

"Given that I'm the one this guy seems to be coming after, I'm pretty sure it's me." He'd thought almost nothing else this afternoon and it pissed him off because he should have been thinking about how hot Elisa looked on a spanking bench, but no some jerk face had to nearly kill him and Mel.

Max's head swiveled as he looked over at Van and then back at him. "I'm going to be honest. You two look a little alike. Some people still aren't sure which is which. Not me, of course. I am excellent at remembering names and faces, but I'm pretty sure there are some people around town who are confused. Maybe this guy is, too. It's unprofessional of him."

Yes, that was the unprofessional part. "I have no idea why anyone would hire an assassin to come after either one of us. It makes zero sense."

"That's because you've only got one piece of the puzzle," Max advised. "I'm sure it makes total sense when you look at it from the outside."

"Like the snow circles." Max was kind of on to something. "Mel had Cassidy send out a drone so he could get the full picture from overhead and figure out where the aliens were meeting."

"Exactly." Max pointed his way like he'd made an excellent argument instead of talking about aliens that didn't exist except in an old man's mind.

Or did they? He wasn't sure it mattered beyond the fact that it mattered to Mel. Mel was happy with his life. Who cared that he believed in numerous alien species?

They would care in Dallas. In Dallas, he would probably be hospitalized and put on meds so he could be normal. Some people needed that. Mel did not.

In Dallas, he and Elisa and Van would be out of the norm, and the gossip wouldn't be as kind as here in Bliss. Why couldn't he get Van to see that?

"There's something we're missing," Max continued. "I've been around this a lot. Are you sure you've never belonged to a cult?"

"Nope."

"Multilevel marketing scam?"

"Do you see me as an effective salesperson? I don't even talk much to the people I do like."

Max nodded but kept moving on. "Biker gang or criminal gang of any kind?"

"I had two friends in high school who regularly stole food from the cafeteria, but I'm almost certain the lunch lady let us get away with that. There's no way she didn't lock that door." It was the extent of his criminal past.

"Dude, that's so fucking sad," Max said with a shake of his head. "You've never been married or had a relationship with a woman who might want to mind erase you and turn you into a super soldier?"

"Now you're just making shit up." Sometimes Max went off on tangents.

"You talk to that Jax fellow River Lee married. Has that dude got some stories. Like he ends up winning shittiest thing to happen to a guy every time we play," Max admitted. "Me getting shot and dragged by my horse should really rank higher. I swear I would win in another town. But I have to compete with Russian mobsters and guys who got tortured by MCs, and Henry alone has me beat by a mile now that he talks about his time in the CIA. What was your life like before you came here? I know you and Van moved around a lot and he got into some trouble, but you rarely talk about yourself."

Hale was planning on being Bliss's boringest citizen. "My mom was a single mom. Never knew my dad. She told me he was some married guy she had an affair with. He sent her money for a while, but I never met the man. When I was seven, she decided she'd had enough and took me to her sister's and left me there. I never saw her again. I shifted through a couple of relatives until I ended up in foster care. It wasn't great, but I don't think I made any enemies who would come after me years later. I aged out at eighteen, lived in a camper for a couple of months, and then I met Van and we hit the road."

"You're like one of those movies where the kid in old timey gear cries and asks for more, please," Max said.

"Well, I'm not now." Though he would accept that his childhood had a modern Dickensian feel to it.

"Now you're in construction," Max mused. "Ever did a real crappy job?"

"Not one I didn't fix." He knew contractors got a bad rap, but he tried to be better. He was pretty much a one-man business, and that meant he had control over every part of the operation. Except the money. What the hell was he going to do without Van?

How could Van even be thinking of leaving them? Jake didn't need him the way he and Elisa did. They all had roles to play, and Van was abandoning his.

"It's here somewhere. Nate and your girl will figure it out, I'm sure." Max leaned over. "Have you thought about hiring some protection until they can find this guy?"

"Max, I don't have the money to pay Long-Haired Roger for our car," he pointed out. "I'm in this tavern waiting for my girlfriend to pick me up because it's too cold to walk back to the valley. I certainly can't afford to hire a bodyguard."

"That Taggart fellow has a lot of them," Max mused. "Hold his bathroom hostage and get him to send you one."

Sometimes Max's advice wasn't the best. "I'll be careful. And hey, he can't get me in a car anymore since I don't have one." The thought settled in his gut like a millstone. "You don't think this person will come after Elisa to get to me, do you?"

The last thing he wanted to do was leave her, but could he put her in the line of fire when he didn't even know why someone was coming after him? Didn't he owe her his protection? For the first time he thought about pulling away.

For the first time he thought about the fact that he might not be good for her.

He had no money. He had no home to offer her beyond the ones he worked on, so she wouldn't have a place of her own. Now he couldn't even say he was mobile. He depended on her for transportation. He would need a loan for a new vehicle. Could he even get one?

This was what Van was talking about. Dallas would give them financial stability, but what would it take from them?

And on top of it all, someone was trying to kill him—had nearly killed him, and he'd brought her newfound dad along for the ride. He'd seen how shaken she'd been. On the outside she'd been entirely professional but when he'd reached for her hand, there had been a tremble there that betrayed the waves of emotion she had inside. She wasn't cold or unfeeling. She felt far too much.

What if next time she was the one in the car with him? What if next time the killer succeeded?

Max leaned over, his expression going serious. "You keep it down. There are people listening, and that is not a line of thought you want getting back to your woman. They do not take kindly to it."

"I'm thinking about her protection."

Max whistled. "Well, think about your own, brother, because that woman knows how to use a gun, and if you do the whole 'I'm dumping your ass to save it' schtick, you'll not only have her coming at you, but all the other women in Bliss, too. Even the little girls, and don't count them out. My Paige can kick a shin, and Nell's baby has a death stare I swear she learned at birth."

"I'm serious, Max. She could get hurt." She could get more than hurt if today was any indicator. He'd been driving those mountain passes for months now and had in other states before. She was new to them. If it had been her vehicle, she might have gone over the edge.

Max looked around as though trying to make sure no one was listening in. "And I'm serious, Hale. If I have taught you nothing else, I need you to learn this. What did I teach you was the first rule of Bliss?"

He remembered this one. "Don't tell Rachel when you eat hot wings."

Max frowned. "The real one."

"Don't piss off the women." It seemed to be Max's mantra. "But I'm not trying to piss anyone off. I'm trying to keep the woman I love alive. How do I live with myself if I'm the reason she dies?"

"You won't have to if you keep talking like that." Max frowned, his brow furrowing. "Okay, I'm going to get serious with you. How would you feel if Elisa had someone after her and she broke up with you to protect you, and before you say it's different, I need you to think about it because this is where that baby's death stare comes in. I'm not joking. It's like a laser Nell can point at your soul."

He wanted to tell Max to cut it out, but he had a point. Was it different? In this case, Elisa was far more capable of dealing with the situation than he was. She was trained. She was careful. What would he do for Elisa beyond stepping in front of a bullet to save her?

He would be pissed if he didn't get that chance. He understood Max, but how could he reconcile the risk?

Maybe he could reconcile it by putting himself in her shoes. How would he genuinely feel if she broke up with him to protect him? "I would wonder why she didn't trust me enough to let me stand beside her. I would wonder why we weren't strong enough to face the problems together."

"And that is how you get out of Baby Flanders cutting you in half with laser eyes." Max nodded approvingly. "Relax. Everyone in town knows to watch out for you. The festival's over and the tourists are heading home for the holidays. It's quiet here from Christmas to New Year's. We all come together and have a big party, but it's townspeople only. In a day or two, a stranger will stand out like a sore thumb, and it will be easy to keep an eye on them. Let the sheriff's office do its thing, and we'll figure it out before too long. We always do. Say, how do you feel about a couple of days in Mel's bunker?"

Why was everyone trying to get him in the bunker? "No."

But a lot of what Max had said made sense. The tourist season would slow down at Christmas. Despite the fact that they could probably make a lot of money, the lodge closed for ten days between Christmas and New Year's so the workers could go home to their families. Bliss would become a safe, happy bubble. It would be a good time.

It would be the last time with Van. Their holidays weren't all that great. They usually consisted of getting a rotisserie chicken and some sides and a store-bought pie, and then they watched a movie. He'd thought this year would be different for them. This year they'd start understanding why the time was sacred to so many people.

"Don't discount the bunker. Mel's managed to get Netflix down in that thing. He claims someone from another plane of existence sends him intel through the recommendations," Max continued. "And the whiskey he makes does the trick. He's gotten better at it. No one's gone missing in years."

"I'm not moving into the bunker." He was standing firm on that. He glanced over Van's way, and it seemed like the staff was having a meeting at the bar or something. Callie and Zane and Micky were huddled together at the end where the bartenders set the drinks waiting to be picked up, and they all looked serious. "But maybe it would help if I wasn't alone. I'll trade you a couple of days work on your barn for helping me install bathroom tile."

"Seriously?" Max looked excited at the prospect. "I would love that. I've got a whole door I need to replace, and Rye struggles with a hammer. I mean it. He always tries to take off his damn thumb."

A man moved across Hale's line of sight, heading toward the bathrooms. It wasn't a surprising occurrence in a crowded restaurant, but Hale caught the sight of his back as he headed in. The man's shoulders had that familiar slump to them. Was that the same man they'd saved this afternoon? The one he was almost sure was also on the security footage?

Hale stood. He couldn't let the opportunity pass. "I'll be right back."

Max simply shrugged as Hale headed off to follow the man.

When he pressed through the door, the guy was there, finishing up at the urinal.

Hale stepped over to wash his hands, watching the guy in the mirror. He couldn't be absolutely sure it was him. He turned and walked over to the sinks, and Hale noticed the logo on his belt. He wasn't sure what LV stood for, but it was probably expensive.

This was the part where he should have talked to Van because

Van would have walked in and tried to engage this man in friendly talk meant to soften him up before he asked the big questions.

"Are you trying to kill me?" Hale had no game.

The man's head turned, and he looked startled to see him. "What the fuck kind of question is that? I don't know who you are."

"We met earlier today when you nearly died on the bunny slope of the lodge," Hale pointed out.

The man touched his chest, rubbing it as though it ached. "Yeah, I'm not going to thank you for that. I think you bruised a rib, you moron. You're lucky I don't sue you. Now I'm leaving because you obviously have problems. I have no idea who you are except that you're incompetent."

But he did. It was plain to see. Hale's every instinct was firing off that this was the man who was after him. "It's me. You're after me. You sent that woman to look for me. Did she trash the cabin or did you do it?"

A fine flush crossed the man's face, and he stepped back, his hands still wet. "You've mistaken me for someone else. I don't know you. I don't want to know you. You're nothing to me."

The words were said with far too much emotion for them to be true. This man hated him. He wasn't usually good at judging a person, but the loathing came off this man in waves. "What did I do to you? I don't remember you at all. If you tell me what I did, I might be able to clear things up."

The man simply turned and started walking away.

Hale couldn't let that happen. "You took a shot at me a couple of days ago, and you sabotaged my car so I had an accident. I know what you're doing."

The man turned slightly. "Fuck you. You know nothing."

He slammed out of the bathroom and into the hallway. Hale followed. He needed to figure out who this guy was. "I want to know why you're coming after me. I deserve to know. The police want some information out of you, too. We have footage of you talking to the woman who asked for my address at the lodge."

"I don't know what you're talking about." He moved into the dining room. "I'm staying at the lodge, but I assure you there's no woman in my life. My ex-wife taught me to stay as far away from women as possible. Gold diggers every single one of them. I'm not making the same mistakes my father made." He stopped in front of the steps that led up to the bar section of the restaurant. "And as for whatever yokels make up the police force here, I sadly doubt they can ask me anything of value. So you can tell them to fuck off. They can talk to my lawyer."

Now Hale was getting somewhere. "She's been here, too, hasn't she?"

The man had obviously been about to dismiss him again, but he stopped. "A lawyer's been here?"

Oh, he hadn't known that. "Yes, and I'm talking to her tomorrow. I've got a meeting set up and everything. You want to tell me what this is about?"

The man seemed to think about that for a moment, and then a nasty sneer came over his face. "I don't know what you're talking about." He leaned in, his voice going low. "I would watch myself if I was you. I'm a powerful, wealthy man. You fuck with me and I'll be tempted to fuck with you. Or maybe that whore cop you're fucking. Do you want me to fuck with her? You want me to show her what a real man can do?"

He wasn't sure why, but he saw red. Words were words. They could hurt, but he didn't care what anyone called him.

Oh, but he cared about her.

He heard Max yell something and then gave in to his rage.

* * * *

Elisa was still fuming hours later. She'd shown up at Trio just as Hale was being led out in handcuffs by Cameron Briggs. As if that wasn't enough of a shock, Van followed after him, along with Max Harper, both being led to county patrol cars by the sheriff himself.

She'd been ready to pick them both up, maybe have some dinner and then a good long session in bed because the day had been rough, and now she had to deal with bailing them out of jail, which was also her workplace.

"That is a huge mistake, my friend," Max was saying from behind the bars of one of the two cells they had at the Bliss County Sheriff's Office. "Don't skip dinner. It's free. Even if you gotta shove it down your throat, order it. It's the only way we have to stick it to

268

the man."

"I'm not hungry, and the men here are not the ones I want to stick it to." Hale sat beside him on the bench, his expression blank.

"It's too late. You missed dinner," Nate said, frowning as he looked the sad trio over.

That had Max sitting up and fast. "That's not fair. It's barely nine o'clock."

"Yep, and Stella's closes at nine today," Nate replied. "You know we have a strict treaty when it comes to who gets to feed the inmates of Bliss County. Tonight is Stella's turn. The good news is Gemma's got protein bars for everyone."

Gemma looked up from her desk. "They're barely expired."

Everyone had come back in to work for this debacle. "I want to know what happened."

"Hale tried to kill a tourist," Cam explained. "Or at least that's what we were told by the bystanders. I know this is going to surprise you, but he hasn't been very talkative."

Yes, from what she could tell Hale hadn't been cooperative at all, and that was strange for him. She needed to get her embarrassment and anger under control because this was not at all like him.

"I think that guy might have done something to Hale while he was on the potty," Max said. "One minute the guy was fine, and the next he was throwing punches."

"And you decided to help him?" Nate asked.

Max shrugged. "I'm his mentor. One of the things he needs to learn is that when your friend does something real dumb, you pretty much have to do it with him. Now if I had known Van here was going to throw his own body into the fray, I would have taken a more laid-back approach."

"All the good it did me." Van cupped his jaw. "He punched me. I was trying to help him and he decked me. Also, I think this was a false arrest. I was trying to break up the fight. I didn't hit anyone, but I get hauled out? This is profiling."

"No." Cam Briggs looked entirely amused at the scene. "It's not what that means at all. Now who was the other guy because when we walked in, it looked like it was the three of you fighting."

"He got away." Hale's jaw tightened. "I didn't even get his

name."

Max pointed Hale's way. "See, I told you. That fellow did something nasty to him."

She'd been going about this all wrong. When she'd seen they were being arrested, she'd closed herself off and gone cold. She'd heard that Hale and Van had been fighting and gone to the worst place she could. "Nate, can we let them out? It was a bar fight, and apparently the person who they were fighting isn't here. Is Zane pressing charges on destruction of property?"

"It was one table. Hale can build a new one," the sheriff said. "I'm far more interested in why we're here. I thought this was some pissing contest between the two of them."

"Only because no one ever listens to me," Max complained. "I told you what was going on. Hale went all raging bull on that guy. Now he did appear to be an asshole tourist. I can understand that, but as his mentor, I think we're going to have to work on how to handle them without resorting to this kind of violence. See, man, you gotta find another kind of violence. One the cops can't see."

"You need a new mentor." She was pretty sure Max was a terrible influence.

Hale stood up and came to the bars, looking at her through them. "I'm sorry, baby. I didn't mean to lose it like that, but he said something and that's pretty much the last thing I remember until Van was yelling at me and Cam was putting me in cuffs."

"He had that vacant look in his eyes," Van explained. "Like he wasn't really there."

"I didn't mean to hurt you." Hale looked back at Van. "I didn't know it was you. I thought it was him."

"Who is him?" They were finally getting to the questions that should have been asked. She understood that Nate and Cam had to get them out of Trio, but if they'd known these two men better, they would have known something was wrong.

"Asshole tourist fellow," Max insisted. "He looked like one of those lodge people. I bet he can't ski for crap, though. None of them can really. They like to sip their craft beer and take their pictures for social media. Hey, you got any beer, Nate? Has someone called my wife? Because I was supposed to be home for dinner, and she can get antsy."

"She told me to hold you overnight," Nate retorted with a grin.

"Nate?" She wasn't going to get to the bottom of this with Max around. "Come on."

Nate sighed and then he was opening the cell door. "Fine. The new deputy is intent on getting down to business, so be on your way, Max. You two, though, need to go to the conference room. If this wasn't a throw down between the two of you, we need to talk."

Max stepped out of the cell, straightening his shirt. "This has been the worst experience here yet, Sheriff. No food. No beer, and the padding on that bench has gone flat. This will be reflected in my review. Also, I will take the protein bars, Gemma, as a parting gift."

Gemma snorted and grabbed her purse. "I'll give him a ride back to his car and then head home, unless you need me. The temp guy is out patrolling and should be back in the office in an hour, so you have some time to talk privately." She looked at Van and Hale. "Get your shit together, you two. She's pretty cool, and there are other men around here who will snap her up."

"My shit is perfectly together," Van said with a frown. "That's what sucks. I have this great revelation and then Hale's punching me in the face."

Hale stayed back in the cell as though he didn't want to come out.

"What did he say?" She moved toward him, softening her expression. She wasn't the only one who'd had a hell of a day. He wasn't the type of man to get into a barroom brawl. If he was angry enough to lose his cool, then there was a reason. "Was it about me?"

Van huffed and was suddenly beside his best friend. "Shit. What did he say about Elisa? That's the only reason he would have lost it like that. He doesn't care what anyone says about him."

"It doesn't matter." Hale looked to Nate. "You didn't even get his name?"

Nate sat back on the corner of one of the desks. "I didn't realize there was another party. By the time we got there I saw Max trying to pull Hale off Van."

"If you knew I was innocent, why the hell did you arrest me?" Max had made it to the door, following after Gemma.

"Because it's been a while, old friend. I missed your face,"

Nate said with a smirk.

Max shot him the finger and made his exit.

"I'm sorry I didn't understand what was going on." Nate was back to being entirely professional. "I know you two have had some trouble lately and that even the best of partnerships can explode at times. I know Zane and I had some doozy fights when we were younger."

"It was him." Hale said the words with grim resolve. "It was the guy from the lobby cam footage. I realized it when I saw him walking to the bathroom, and I followed him. I would bet he's back at the lodge now. He's a guest there. Van and I saved him from breaking a leg earlier today."

"Shit. It was the same guy?" Van asked. "I didn't see him at Trio, but the guy we met at the lodge today did have the same body type."

If he was right, then he'd taken a dangerous risk. "Hale, why would you confront him? Why not call in the sheriff? You confronted the man you suspect of trying to kill you? What did you say to him?"

Hale shrugged. "I asked him why he was trying to kill me."

Van groaned. "Not the way I would have gone."

Elisa turned to Cam. "Can you call the lodge and see if we can figure out who this man is?"

Cam grabbed his coat. "I'll do one better. I'll go up there myself. Hopefully we can find him and his sedan, too. We're trying to clear up the footage we have from the traffic cameras. We've got a blue sedan that came down around the right time, but the weather was crappy so I don't know that we're going to get the plate number. I'll look around the lot."

"Thanks, Cam." He was supposed to be home with his wife and partner and kid.

Nate grabbed his coat. "I'm going to go with him. I don't like this one bit. You two are free to go. No charges." He stopped as he started to walk by her, leaning in, his voice going low. "Go easy on Hale. He figured out how serious this is and he's scared, and I don't think he's scared for himself. If I was a betting man, I would say you're the first woman he's fallen in love with, and he's not sure how to handle it."

She nodded, grateful for the advice. Nate and Cam left, and

they were alone. "Do you want to go home and talk this out?"

"I don't know if that's a good idea," Hale said slowly.

"Where else are we going to go?" Van asked.

Van didn't understand. "He's not saying he doesn't want to go home. He's saying he doesn't want me to come with him."

"That is not what he's saying," Van corrected, his gaze going between the two of them. "Because that would be ridiculous."

"Why?" Hale asked. "I think the more ridiculous thing would be for me to put her in the line of fire. Look, this is actually what I was talking to Max about when all of this happened, and I know it doesn't seem fair but damn it, I love her and I don't want her to get hurt."

She knew she should rail against him pushing her away, but he'd said he loved her. "I love you, too."

Hale's eyes softened. "Then respect the fact that I need some time to sort this out. I think Van and I should go to Dallas in the morning. We can meet with his brother's friends. This is the kind of thing they handle all the time."

"You're going to Dallas? For how long?" Were they both going to leave her?

"Just until we clear this up," Hale promised.

There was one problem with that scenario. "But that could be a while, and what is the definition of clearing things up? What if this guy isn't the right one? Do you intend to stay away until this guy is caught? What if that takes years?"

Hale's jaw firmed to a stubborn line. "It won't."

"You can't know that." A case like this could last a long time. They still didn't know the guy's name.

"I know that he'll come after you," Hale insisted. "He said as much tonight."

"So that was what set you off." She wished he would tell her what the asshole said.

Hale shook his head. "It doesn't matter."

"It does." She needed to make a few things plain. "I'm working this case whether you go to Dallas or not, so I'm going to be involved."

Hale seemed to think about that for a moment. "And I'm going to ask Nate to move you off it. It can be a favor to the guy

273

who's renovating his house for half what anyone else would charge."

"Then I'll quit and become a private investigator and work the case anyway," she said with resolve. "You don't get to dictate what I do in life, Hale. We might be in love, but you don't own me. You don't get to change who I am because it would be more comfortable for you."

"He hates me." Hale shook his head, his gaze going inward. "I don't know why, but that man hates me, and he's not going to stop until I'm gone."

"And you expect me to stay out of his way? Maybe you shouldn't say you love me because you obviously have no idea who I am." She understood why he was doing this, but she couldn't step away and let it happen.

"I know who I am, and I'm not the man who can watch you get hurt," Hale said.

"Awesome. So she'll get hurt and you won't be watching?" Van asked, sarcasm dripping. "Because why do you think this guy will back away from her? You think he'll be like *oh, that dude I want to wreck went to Dallas. He must not love that woman he nearly killed me over. I'll leave her alone.* Or he could say *thank god that dude went to Dallas and left her all alone. Time to play.*"

Van *was* thinking straight. "He's right. I'm in this, and there's no way around it at this point."

"There has to be a way." Hale seemed to be trying to outthink the problem. "You could go home. You could go back to North Carolina."

She rolled her eyes. It was obvious he needed some space. Fighting about this wasn't going to solve the problem. "I am home, and I'm not letting some asshole push me out. And don't even think about asking me to stay in the bunker. I'm going home. Are you coming with me or should I arrange another ride for you?"

"Maybe I should talk to your dad," Hale said, his tone turning challenging.

"Go do it." She could handle her father.

Van stepped in between them. "Hale, stop being an asshole. You know she can take care of herself."

"She shouldn't have to." Hale didn't seem to be backing down. "She should have someone who loves her enough to know when he's bad for her. Maybe you were right. Maybe we aren't enough for her and she can't see it. Hell, I don't even know how to be in a relationship. You're leaving and you're right to do it. We're going to bring her nothing but pain."

It took everything she had not to groan. Eeyore was back. This was the way Hale saw the world at times, and she couldn't blame the man since up until recently his world had kind of been a black pit of despair.

He wanted to leave her.

Van was going to leave her. He'd already said it. Here they were at their first real hurdle, and they were both going to dump her and walk away. Shouldn't she have known...

Nope. She wasn't going there. She was playing catch and release with her demons today. Maybe later there would be time for her to wallow, but it obviously wasn't going to be today.

"But I just decided to stay." Van moved to her side. "I figured out that I was ashamed I couldn't give her what my brother gave Serena, although when I really think about it Serena had all the money in the beginning, so maybe I am following in his footsteps."

"There's not a lot of money here, babe. It's like thirty K and a decent investment portfolio," she admitted, that darkness she seemed to always have inside her pushed away by Van's words. He was going to stay? "We're still pretty blue collar."

"Well, I'm going to be an accountant, so I'll make sure we're smart with our money." Van turned her way, his hands going to her hips. He stared down at her, his gaze turning hot. "I'll be very smart when it comes to you. I'm going to stay right by your side and when the bad guys come, I'll heroically step out of the way and let you shoot them."

She felt a smile cross her face. "Thanks, babe."

"This is serious," Hale insisted.

It was for him. It was for all of them, but especially for Hale. She held out a hand. "I know, and we're going to get through it. I promise. But we can't do it by being apart. I've been told that's not the way we do things here in Bliss. It's in the pamphlet and everything."

Van leaned over and brushed a kiss to her temple. "Did you find anything out today?"

They hadn't even gotten to her news. "I did. The lawyer talked to Gene out at the Movie Motel. He took her card. I called her but her office was closed. She's with a family practice firm in Spring, TX."

"My mom lived there for a while." Hale was back to his deep-thought face. It was slightly softer than his the-world-is-after-me face but with squintier eyes than his what-should-I-eat-for-lunch face.

"We'll know something in the morning. I'll call her again," she promised, feeling like they were almost past the dangerous part of this conversation. "So can we head home and sleep on this? I promise it will all be okay."

Hale sighed and took her hand. "All right."

She heard the door to the station house open and then a handsome man with dark hair and brown eyes strode in. He wore a winter coat over jeans and boots. "Can I help you?"

"Jake?" Van stepped away. "What are you doing here?"

Jacob Dean held up an envelope. "I found her, and I came up here because the situation is worse than you think."

Nope. The dangerous part started now.

Chapter Sixteen

Van stared across the conference table at his brother. Who should be in Dallas. "You hopped on a plane? You know we have phones here. You could have called."

Jake shrugged out of his jacket, hanging it on the back of the chair before he sat down. "It was an impulse. I don't like this. There's something going on that we don't understand, and I came up here because you're my brother and I'm not going to leave you alone. Also, you should know we're staying through the holidays because again, you're my brother. I remember what it's like to have no one willing to change their schedules to see me. Adam and I spent many a holiday alone."

"Adam's here?" The idea of spending the holidays with Jake's kids, introducing Elisa to his family—it wasn't anything he'd ever thought he would have. It made him feel more guilty about what he was going to have to tell his brother. But he was still going to do it. He loved Jake but he had to put Elisa and Hale first.

Jake nodded. "He took Serena and the kids to the cabin. I had them drop me off here because I wanted to talk to you."

"How did you know he was here?" Elisa asked.

"I track his phone, of course. I think one person in the world should know where he is," Jake replied like that was a perfectly reasonable thing to do to a grown man. "I would have put a tracer in his shoulder but he whined."

He was not going to walk around with a tracker buried in his body, but he did let Jake track him. For his brother it was a sign of his love, and it comforted him knowing where Van was in the world. So Van allowed it. There was nothing controlling about the gesture.

"Fair," Elisa replied with a nod. It was obvious she and Jake were going to get along. Actually, now that he thought about it, she and Jake had a lot in common. "But you do remember I rented your cabin, right? Am I now expected to share it with a whole family?"

"You spend next to no time in it. I check the security logs. You haven't spent a single night there since you rented it," Jake countered. "I figured you could save some money by simply staying where you're actually staying. Please tell me you've done it in every room of that cabin because I want Ian to know. Don't be embarrassed. He deserves it. I'm pretty sure he and Charlotte sneak into Adam's office a couple of times a year and do it on his desk."

"Could you tell us what you've found?" Hale's entire mood was grim, his focus on the envelope Jake had put on the table.

Jake ignored the question, looking at Van's face. "Are you okay? It looks like your jaw is starting to bruise. What happened?"

"Hale tried to take down the dude we think is trying to kill him and got Van instead," Elisa explained. "They were both arrested and brought down here, hence the reason they're at the station house."

"I thought you were in to see her. I'd heard you were seeing the new deputy." Jake had introduced himself to Elisa before they'd entered the conference room.

"Well, I got to see them in jail this evening," Elisa quipped. "It's fine. No charges are being brought, but we do think Hale's right and the guy he fought with is the same one in the security cam footage we sent you. You got here fast. It's only been a couple of hours since we talked to you."

"Private jet," Jake replied. "We bought it for use between our company and McKay-Taggart. It comes in handy when you want to move quickly. We're going to install a security system on Ian's cabin tomorrow afternoon. He was always going to do it, but you guys being in trouble moved up the timeline. And Adam and I will be close in case you need us."

"No." Hale put his hands flat on the table like he was trying to be careful with them. "You can't bring the kids into this. I don't want any of you involved. This guy nearly killed Mel this afternoon, and the other day when he tried to shoot me, he could have hit Elisa instead of me. And now Jake shows up with the kids for a family Christmas party? What the hell were you thinking?"

"I was thinking my family needed me." Jake seemed unbothered by Hale's outburst.

"Then take Van back to Dallas with you and bring Elisa along for the ride. This isn't about him. It's about me, so your family isn't involved," Hale insisted.

Jake sent Van a confused look. "Who does he think he is?"

"He's in a spiral." Van wasn't sure how to bring him out. He'd never seen Hale so dark before. Hale had resting grim face, but he usually didn't go to the worst-case scenario. He rode whatever wave they were on and took what came their way.

And he couldn't anymore because this was a serious relationship, and he had no guidelines. Hale loved rules and boundaries. He thrived on routine and clear expectations, and here he was without any because they hadn't sat down and talked. Van had been far too invested in his own emotions to remember that Hale had no idea how to handle his. Whatever Van's parents had done, they'd acknowledged his emotions and validated his feelings. Hale had lived with none of that.

"I'm not in a spiral," Hale argued.

"You're totally in a spiral." Elisa was handling the entire evening with her usual aplomb.

"I don't even know what you mean by that." Hale's words were peppered with exasperation.

It was better than the dead look on his face he'd had the last few hours. "It just means you're not thinking straight because you're scared. You're panicking, and it could hurt all of us. Let's listen to what Jake has to say and then we'll come up with a reasonable plan to keep everyone safe while Jake's team looks for this guy."

"We don't..." Hale took a deep breath. "I don't have the

money to hire any team at all."

Jake's brow furrowed. "Why would we charge him? What's happening between the two of you?"

"Let me explain since Van will give you a detailed psychological analysis you don't need," Elisa began. "The three of us got together, did some sex stuff, and it got emotional. Van freaked out."

"I did not freak out," he complained.

She ignored him. "So Hale and I played it cool while Van got his shit together, and now he's staying here in Bliss with us so Hale felt the need to bring in more drama by deciding to martyr himself because I could get hurt."

Jake huffed. "Did anybody tell him about all that time you spent in the military?"

"She can still die," Hale insisted.

"Sex stuff?" Van was caught on that.

"He doesn't need a play by play," she replied. "So they've been out of synch for a while now, and it's annoying the hell out of Hale, who is way overstimulated and needs a nap where more sex stuff happens, if you know what I mean."

"I am not a child." Hale's jaw tightened into a stubborn line.

If it bothered Elisa, she didn't show it. "That's why I included the sex stuff, babe. It's been a rough, emotional day and we're at the beginning of what I hope is the last relationship of my life. We need to hold on to each other and bond, and the best way to do that is sex."

There was a reason he was so fucking in love with her. He wanted to move this along so they could get to the good stuff. Van turned back to his brother. "What did you find out that sent you running here so quickly?"

Jake looked like he wanted to talk more, but he pulled open the envelope he'd brought. "I found out the identity of your mystery woman. Her name is Helena Atwell. She was a private investigator in the Houston area. She specialized in missing persons. She did a lot of work for bail bond companies."

"So she wasn't a lawyer," Elisa mused. "We know the other woman who was in town looking for Hale works for a law firm. I've got a call in to her. I'm hoping to hear from her in the morning.

Have you tried contacting Ms. Atwell?"

"That would be hard. She was found dead in a Denver hotel room two days ago," Jake said flatly. "Gunshot wound to the chest. She was scheduled to fly back to Houston the next day. The police do not have any suspects at this time. I'm trying to get a list of her clients."

Hale had paled visibly. "He killed her because she wouldn't give him that address. Or maybe he killed her after she did so she couldn't tell anyone."

He might have to start considering a short stay in the bunker. It looked like he wasn't going to be able to comfort Hale with what Jake had discovered. He'd hoped it would calm Hale down that they were starting to get some traction in the investigation. He needed to put a positive spin on this. "So we hang tight and wait for the client list. Until then we stick close to the cabin, put in the security system, and be as careful as we can. Now our other option is…"

Elisa pointed his way. "No bunker."

"Our other option is for you two to go to Dallas," Hale argued.

"Why would we go to Dallas?" Elisa turned her chair so she was facing Hale. "That makes no sense. I get that you're scared and you're worried you're going to cause pain for the two people who mean the most to you in the world, but your plans to save us have to make logical sense. Can we start there?"

"How about we go back to the cabin and get some rest?" It was getting late and they weren't going to solve anything tonight. "Nate and Cam are looking for him. Jake and his team will look into the PI, and Elisa should hear from the lawyer tomorrow. There's nothing else we can do, so let's go home."

"I don't think that's a good idea." But Hale sounded tired even as he said the words.

"Come up with another one." Elisa stood. "But understand I'm not splitting us up tonight. I'm going to grab my things. I'll see you at the car. Mr. Dean, it was nice to meet you."

"Jake, please," he insisted. "I have a feeling we're going to be family soon."

She seemed to think about that for a moment, a slow smile crossing her face. "I would like that very much, Jake."

Hale followed her out, and he was left alone with his brother. Who'd put his whole world on hold for him.

"I can't thank you enough for helping us." He moved to stand in front of his brother. He was actually an inch taller than Jake, but there was no denying who the big brother was. "But I need to talk to you about something."

Jake put a hand on his shoulder. "You're staying in Bliss. You're not coming to work for me."

He hated disappointing his brother. "I love her. She wants to stay here. So does Hale. He's being overly emotional right now, but he wants what I want. We want to start our family here in Bliss. And I'm switching majors. I don't like marketing. I like accounting. You already have an accountant. I promise I will…"

Jake cut him off, hauling him close for a brotherly hug. "You'll pay me back by being happy. That's all I ever wanted for you. Now give me a ride back to the cabin and then deal with Hale because damn, that morose motherfucker is not handling this well. Has he read none of Serena's books? This kind of shit ends poorly."

A huge weight lifted off his chest. His brother wasn't upset. He seemed perfectly thrilled for him. "I'm going to make this right. I need to get the three of us alone, and we'll hash this out."

He would prove to Hale that they all belonged together. One way or another.

* * * *

Hale stood on the porch as Van opened the door to the cabin. He stared across the way at Van's brother's place. It looked perfectly quiet inside, the only real evidence it was occupied being the warm glow from the light in the living room. They'd given Jake a ride back and he'd disappeared behind the door, walking into the arms of his wife, who'd waited up for him. Somewhere in that cabin was Jake's best friend, who had helped her put the children to bed and settled her in after the long travel. Jake had been able to do what he needed without worry because Adam and Serena had handled everything else. It was everything he wanted, and he was so afraid he would be the reason they never got the chance.

The SUV they'd driven in was parked on the other side of

the cabin. If he wanted to pretend he was alone out here, it would be easy.

But he wasn't. He was surrounded by people who could get hurt in the crossfire. It wouldn't even be crossfire since he didn't own a gun.

It was all so fucked up, and no one would let him try to mitigate the damage.

Maybe it was time to simply walk away.

He would have to literally walk since he didn't have a fucking car anymore.

Elisa moved in beside him, threading her arm through his and resting her head against his shoulder. "It's a beautiful night out."

"I didn't notice. I was far too busy worrying about the guy who wants to kill me." He could still remember the look of utter loathing in his eyes. Like Hale was beneath him and it was rankly offensive to be forced to even notice him. He'd had a lot of people look through him like he wasn't there, but this was a completely different thing. This felt beyond personal, and he didn't even understand what he'd done. That man could hurt him, could hurt the people he loved.

"Even in the midst of pain, you have to stop and find something beautiful about the world," she said quietly. "I learned that during my cancer treatments. When you're going through a hard time like that you have to find something worth fighting for. I think for most people it's their spouses or their kids, their families. I didn't have that. I had just gotten divorced and watched my mom die. It was far too easy for me to think about not fighting at all."

Her quiet words brought him out of his sullen anger. They shocked him because she was so vibrant to him. "What is that supposed to mean?"

"It means I wasn't sure life was worth the pain I had to take," she explained. "I could have made the choice to have the surgery and forgo the rest of it. It was a huge risk that the cancer would come back, but that was an option I considered. I knew what Mom had gone through. I saw it happen to her, saw that it didn't work for her. But my sister talked me into it. I was sick for so long. Every day was agony, and I looked in the mirror and I didn't know who I was anymore. I looked back at my life and realized if that was all there was, why was I fighting at all?"

"Elisa," he began but he wasn't sure what to say. He could tell her how precious she was to him. He could explain how lonely he would be without her. But that wouldn't help keep her alive.

"I did it because I couldn't leave my sister alone in the world," she revealed. "I fought for her. Not for me. I think if it happened again, it would be different."

"The cancer isn't going to come back." He would will that truth into existence.

"It could. Or it could be an entirely different illness, but it would be different because this time I wouldn't walk into that infusion room because my sister needed me to. I would walk in there because I'm worth it. I'm worth the fight. My life is worth the pain and suffering I have to endure to keep living it. It's worth it because I get to stand on a porch in the middle of winter with two men I love and watch the stars."

Tears pierced his eyes at the sweetness of her statement. He knew what she was trying to do, and he couldn't let her. "I need you to be reasonable about this. Don't make me push you away."

He didn't want to hurt her. It was everything he was trying to avoid. He wasn't even sure he could force himself to say words that would cut through her.

"Let me make something clear, Hale. You can't push me away," Elisa countered. "You can walk away, but you can't make me leave you. If you want to say some nasty stuff to rip my heart up, go ahead. I can take it because I won't believe you. I'll know exactly why you're saying it, and I'll still be by your side if he comes for you."

"And I'll have your back," Van promised. He moved to Hale's other side so he was surrounded by them. "Elisa is right. We're worth fighting for. We can't crumple and split up every time something dangerous happens. Not if we're going to stay here in Bliss. Look, man, we are guaranteed nothing in life. Any one of us could die tomorrow. The truth is sometime in the future one of us will be the last one standing, but if it's me, I'll take the pain of losing you because I had the joy of loving you. There is no danger you can face that I wouldn't walk into with you. I need you to understand something. You are worth fighting for, too. You, Hale Galloway, are worthy of love, and you have mine."

"You have mine," Elisa said quietly.

His chest suddenly felt far too tight. Worth. He wasn't even sure what the word meant, but the way they held him, protected him, made him feel something he'd never felt before. Precious. Beloved.

Was he so afraid of losing them he was willing to push them away?

He wouldn't let them push him away if the situation was reversed.

If he wanted to be part of a family, he had to be brave enough to accept everything about them. Including the fact that he could lose them. He had to be brave enough to take that risk.

Emotion welled inside him, hard and fast, and suddenly the world seemed more vivid than it had before. It was brighter and louder and more beautiful as he dumped any idea of trying to deal with this situation alone. He turned and hauled her close. "You have to promise me you'll be careful."

Relief was plain on that gorgeous face of hers. "I will."

He twisted so he could see Van. "And you."

"I will hide anytime I see a douchebag in designer wear," Van promised, a smile on his face. "And I think you'll find the whole town will be on the lookout. They made sure the lawyer lady couldn't find us. I can't wait to see what they'll do to a tourist who's trying to kill one of us. You aren't alone. Not even close."

It struck him how fragile it all was, how odd that all the events of his life and theirs had brought them here.

If he'd had a different childhood, he'd likely be living in Texas, working some meaningless job.

If he hadn't been homeless, he wouldn't have met Van.

If Van hadn't gotten into that bar fight, they wouldn't have found Bliss.

If Elisa hadn't gotten cancer…

If Mel Hughes hadn't had an affair while he was in the military…

So many ifs. So many ways this thing between the three of them might not have happened, but they were here. They were together. Maybe it was time to stop thinking of what they had as fragile and put his full trust and faith in it.

Maybe that was what having a family meant, and maybe he was worthy of belonging to this one.

He leaned over, kissing her. This wasn't a tentative kiss, exploring the possibility of intimacy. He was too far gone for that. He blew past opening kisses and simply devoured her mouth, letting his tongue plunge deep. He felt Van move around, getting behind Elisa so they had her wrapped up between them.

Where she was meant to be.

Maybe it wasn't coincidence that led them all to stand on the porch in the snow beneath a blanket of stars.

Maybe it was fate, and the best kind.

He pressed her against Van and let his hands find her waist, tugging at the shirt she had on.

"Inside," she whispered against his mouth. "Come summer I'll take that risk with you, but I'm not into frostbite, babe."

He loved it when she called him *babe*. He picked her up and carried her inside, Van holding the door for them.

He walked past the living room and made for the primary bedroom with a bed that was big enough for sharing. She was right. This was exactly what they needed after a day like today. They needed to remind each other they were here and whole and together. He loved them both. She was the physical conduit of the love he and Van shared, too. It was a neat circle, and he was so happy to have a part in it.

He needed to remind her exactly how happy he was she'd made the decision to fight.

He set her on her feet in the middle of the room and made quick work of her shirt and bra, getting his hands on her breasts and showing her how much he appreciated them. He loved every scar because they meant she was alive. He got to his knees, kissing them and rolling his tongue over her nipples.

Van was behind her, his big hands cupping her breasts and holding them. Offering them out to Hale.

He nipped at one. "You are the most beautiful woman I've ever seen. Ever will see."

"You can't know that," she teased with a smile, her hand

coming out to smooth back his hair.

"I can." She didn't understand that he wouldn't ever look at another woman the way he did her. There was something different about her, something that had changed him for the better.

"I can, too." Van was right there with him. "I won't ever find a woman as gorgeous as you. I don't even want to look. I'm happy right here."

"I love you both," she vowed.

He was going to show her how loved she was.

Starting now.

Chapter Seventeen

The relief she'd felt when she'd realized Hale was with them again had fled, completely annihilated by the wave of lust that had crashed over her when he'd kissed her. He'd been so overwhelming that she'd known something had changed inside Hale.

There had been such emotion in that kiss. Love and passion and the promise of the future.

It was a future she wanted so desperately—to build a life here with these two men. She had no idea what would happen, if they would have kids of any kind, if she would be successful in this new job. None of that mattered if she was with them. They would be the solid foundation for the rest of her life. Her love for them, the strong ground she stood on.

Hale played with her breasts. They weren't very sensitive, but it didn't matter. She was already wet, her pussy slick with arousal, but he kept pushing her higher and higher.

Van was at her back, warming her and cupping her breasts. He treated them like they were a gift, a toy he loved above all other. "Elisa, I know we said we would take this slow."

She knew exactly what he was talking about, and she was having none of that. Tonight wasn't about careful planning. She hadn't expected any of this. All of her life had been run on routine and schedule. She'd only found her joy when she'd let herself go a little wild. "I want you both. You'll be careful, but I want both of my men tonight."

They needed this. They needed to be together, all three of them, needed the physical reminder that they'd chosen each other, and nothing could break them if they didn't allow it to. If they clung to each other, they could get through anything. This relationship was their sanctuary.

She felt the hard press of Van's cock against her ass.

"Yes. Absolutely yes," he agreed.

"And I haven't said it yet," Hale began, his eyes going to Van, "but I'm so happy you're staying. This is the right place for us. I know you feel like you owe your brother…"

She'd liked Van's brother. He seemed smart and caring, and the fact that he'd upended all his holiday plans so his brother wouldn't be alone made her think everything would be fine between them.

"I already told him." A peace seemed to have come over Van, banishing the restless energy that always surrounded him. He was here with them, and he would stay. He kissed the back of her neck, pressing his lips along her spine. "He said all he wanted was for me to be happy."

Hale nodded, his hands still playing with her breasts. "That sounds like the Jake I know. But we should talk about the accounting thing. That feels boring to me."

"I like numbers." Van kissed along her shoulder. "I think I've been a nerd all my life, and now I'm going to revel in it. I think my good looks held me back in this case. I'm too pretty to be an accountant."

Hale groaned. "You are so not."

If she let them, they would argue like an old married couple and lose focus. "No making fun of Van. He is pretty, and he's going to be an excellent accountant. Now you should pay attention to what you're supposed to be doing. I've had a rough day corralling the two of you."

Van chuckled, the sensation rolling over her skin. "You have done that, baby. It's like herding cats. Once you get one of us in line the other is running off."

"No more running. From either of us," Hale promised.

Hale's hands went to the buckle of her belt, unbuckling and

pulling it free. She toed out of her boots so he could pull her slacks off. The white cotton undies she wore were already slick with arousal.

Hale leaned over, breathing her in. "You smell so fucking good."

He put his nose right against her pussy and rubbed, stroking her clit. She could feel the heat of his breath through the thin material. Even that was too much. She wanted his tongue on her tender flesh with nothing between them.

Her heart rate ticked up as arousal poured through her veins. Van's arms wrapped around her, holding her still while Hale began dragging the panties off her hips. She was naked in front of them, and it felt good and right. She'd felt so far from her body for so long— like she was a foreigner in her own skin. But with their hands on her, feeling the warmth of their breath on her flesh, she felt whole again. She still had a long way to go, but this was the right path. This was the way home.

"Spread her legs for me." Hale's voice was even deeper than normal, the rumble an insanely sexy sound.

Van's feet were suddenly between hers, forcing her to spread her legs wide, making her lean against him for balance. He was holding her up, his strength bolstering her.

And she needed the help because when Hale leaned in and put his mouth on her pussy, she had to fight to breathe. His hand moved around her hips, cupping the globes of her ass as his tongue swiped over her pussy. Fire licked through her system, and she was caught between the silky stroke of Hale's tongue and Van's teeth nipping her ear, his hands still molding her breasts. She let her head fall back against Van's shoulder, utterly surrendering to them.

Hale tortured her in the sweetest way, his tongue caressing her over and over again, hands holding her hard. His tongue lashed at her and then, just as she was on the edge of something magnificent, he sat back on his heels.

Frustration screamed through her. She'd been so close.

Hale stood up. "Not so fast, baby. That pussy of yours is about as soaked as it can be. It's time to settle you onto that bed. One orgasm to start, and then you're all ours."

Hale tossed off his clothes, revealing that gorgeous, muscular body of his. She loved how rough his hands were. He would stroke them over her skin, the friction waking up every cell in her body. His waist tapered down to lean hips, and his cock jutted from his core, long and hard. He stroked himself before reaching for a condom and lying back on the bed.

Oh, she was so ready for this. She was ready for everything they could give her.

Hale looked like the most decadent treat ever lying there on the soft comforter.

"Go on, baby," Van whispered in her ear. "I want to watch you ride him. I want to watch you come and know I'm going to make it happen all over again."

She climbed on the bed, all her inhibitions banished. She wouldn't need them with her men. She started to straddle his waist when the wickedest grin came over Hale's face.

"No." His hands came out to guide her.

"He doesn't want you to ride his cock yet, baby," Van corrected. "He wants you to ride his face. Do it. Don't hesitate. He wants to taste your pussy, and then we'll show you how good it can be to have two men who love you."

It seemed wrong, but she wasn't going to argue with them, wasn't going to let her awkwardness creep back. If Hale wanted her to sit on his face, then she would. She moved into position, trying to keep her weight off him, conscious that Van was undressing behind her and getting himself ready.

Hale gripped her hips and pulled her down, his mouth covering her like a starving man.

Her eyes closed from the overwhelming heat he sent through her. He fucked her with his tongue, spearing deep while his lips caressed and his hands urged her into a rhythm that had her writhing on him.

She held on to the headboard as she rode Hale's tongue, his hands moving from her hips to grip the cheeks of her ass.

The orgasm rushed through her, and she gave over to it, letting the world fall away as pleasure swept through her body.

And then Hale was pushing her down, guiding her to move. There was another part of his body he wanted her to ride. She felt boneless as she somehow found her way down to his hips. She could feel the hard length of his erection at her pussy, pressing against her and seeking entrance.

Before he thrust up, his hands came out, circling her neck and the back of her head to drag her down close. "I love you, baby."

Those words felt so right coming from him. "Love you, too."

She realized she'd never meant them before she'd met these two men. Her first marriage had been about convenience and the idea that it was what she should do. But this time was right. This time was real. He hauled her in for a kiss, and she could taste her arousal on his lips.

"Hey, don't forget me." Van stood beside them, his gorgeous body primed and ready for sex. His eyes were on her as he grasped her head and gently turned her his way.

"Never, babe." They were both hers, and she intended to show them how much she loved them every single day.

His head dipped down and he kissed her, lips playing over hers while Hale's cock moved against her pussy, sliding around and dipping inside before playfully pulling out.

They were going to drive her mad with desire. She'd had an orgasm moments before and was already feeling the need for another.

"I'm going to make sure you never do." Van had the sexiest grin on his face. "Now you handle him while I get you ready."

"I'm ready." She couldn't possibly get more turned on. She was pretty sure every bit of moisture in her body was currently pooled in her pelvis.

"Not even close, but you'll get there," Van promised.

"Let me take your mind off things," Hale offered.

Before she could protest that the only thing her mind was on right now was sex, he pressed his cock up, filling her and taking her breath away.

It felt so good, and she knew she was ready for even more.

* * * *

Van watched as Hale started to fuck Elisa, and he worried his cock would go off long before he wanted it to. They had all night, but this first time was special. It would be the first time they were all together, and he realized he'd been waiting for this all of his life.

All of his life he'd looked for a home. Even when he'd been a kid. But what he hadn't realized was home wasn't a place. It was the souls his own meshed with, the ones that seemed to complete him. All of his life he'd been searching for something, and he'd found part of it when he'd met Hale, but she was so necessary to them. She was the sun they could circle around, the one who would warm them and give them purpose.

And they would give her everything they had.

He watched for a few seconds more, loving the way they moved together. He grabbed the condom he'd put in place and managed to roll it over his unruly cock, then he climbed on the bed behind them, getting into position. He hadn't thought his arousal could amp up, but the sight of that glorious ass of hers in the air and waiting for him did the trick.

"Hold her still for me," he commanded.

Hale stopped moving, his hands on her hips, controlling her.

Elisa groaned. "I'm so close."

She wasn't getting another one without them right there with her. "You're going to have to wait for me. This is a job that requires both of us. I wouldn't want to let you down."

He was going to feel that tiny hole around his cock. It was almost enough to make him blow then and there. He grabbed the lube he'd brought along with the condoms, though she was a glorious mess already. Elisa was a sensual woman, and he loved how hot she got for them. Still, he parted her cheeks and dribbled the lube over her.

She squirmed against Hale.

He probably should have warmed that up. Well, he was going to be more thoughtful next time, but for now, he couldn't wait.

The time was right and so were the people. And the place. It was only right that they make this stand here in Bliss. Their home.

"I'm going to go slow. You stay still," Van ordered. The last thing he wanted to do was hurt her. She'd taken the plug pretty easily, but he was bigger.

He pressed his cockhead to her little hole, rubbing the lube all around.

"Stay still, baby." Hale's hands had tightened on her hips, holding her in place. "He needs a minute to work his way in. Did I tell you how good it feels to be inside you? You're so tight around me. So fucking hot."

She was almost too hot. He rimmed her with his cockhead and then pressed against it, trying to ease his way in. The sensation sizzled along his skin, sending anticipation through his veins.

Elisa groaned and laid her head against Hale's chest. "It's going to be too tight."

"It won't," he promised. "But you can stop me at any time. We can take this slow and easy. This is all about your comfort, baby."

He wasn't sure what he would do if he had to stop.

Her hips tilted back, letting his cock slide just inside. He had to fight to breathe.

"Give it to me," she demanded. "I want it."

He wanted it more than he'd ever wanted anything in his life. His whole world seemed to shrink down to this one bed and these two people. He didn't need anything else. He would take what the world offered, but they were the only things required for his happiness. His best friend and their wife.

He'd never thought he would get married, had thought he would float through his time here on Earth, but now he wanted to be grounded, to settle into life with them.

He eased his cock in and out, gaining ground with each careful thrust while Hale held her still, allowing him to do the work he needed to do. Every centimeter he gained brought him closer and closer to the edge, but he wasn't giving in. He was going to make sure she loved this, got addicted to it. This was how they would spend their nights. The days would be for working and friends and family, but the nights would be for them.

Slowly he worked his way into her, feeding her his cock in gentle passes. And then he was as far as he could go, her heat surrounding his dick, blanketing him in warmth and pleasure.

He looked down and Hale was kissing their girl, easing the way for her. His hands stroked along her sides, and she was relaxed and ready.

"You okay, baby?" He held himself still inside her, wanting to know she was right here with him.

"I'm better. It was tight at first but now I'm curious." She wiggled her ass, tempting him. "I want to know how it feels when you really get going."

He could do that for her. He steeled himself because this was going to feel like heaven. "I don't want to make you wait a second more."

He pulled his cock back almost to the rim and thrust back in.

He dragged a breath in, letting himself feel every sensation from the heat of her body to how tight she was, to the feel of his cock sliding along Hale's. It was perfect and it couldn't last, but he had to make it good for her.

She moved against him, seeming to find the exact rhythm that had he and Hale riding her body in harmony. Every twist and turn and thrust of her body threatened to send him flying, but he held back.

He let the moment stretch out, riding the wave until she shouted out her orgasm, shaking in his arms.

And he let himself go. He fucked her over and over, working back and forth until he felt that tingle at the base of his spine, and the world seemed to blast to pieces in the absolute best of ways. Pleasure exploded through him as he sent her wave after wave.

He finally dropped to the side, rolling her with him.

A deep sense of peace settled over him as they lay there all three of them, just breathing and letting themselves simply be together.

"You okay, baby?" Hale twisted so he was facing Elisa and Van.

"I'm perfect," she whispered back, cuddling against Van while Hale crowded her front.

They were taking up very little space on this ridiculously big bed. He was okay with that. "You are perfect."

"Remind me of that in a couple of months," she replied with a satisfied chuckle.

"Years," Hale vowed. "I'll still think you're perfect years from now. I rarely change my mind once I've settled it."

This was everything he wanted. His friend. Their one-day wife. "Forever. We'll think you're perfect forever."

Van settled against her, the whole world in his arms.

Chapter Eighteen

Elisa poured herself a big mug of coffee and wished she didn't have to go into work. She wondered if the Bliss County Sheriff's Department allowed personal discomfort days for first time anal sex. Given how most of the county lived, she thought they should.

They should meet new women residents with an ice pack and one of those donut pillows. Welcome to Bliss.

"How do you want your eggs?"

Of course there was a reason all the women stayed, and this was one of hers.

Van stood at the stove. He wore only a pair of PJ bottoms and looked so delicious she might be willing to forget how sore she was.

Might. But then she had a whole shift to work. "Can you stay close to Hale today?"

She didn't want him alone for a minute. Finding the lawyer was the key to everything, she'd decided. Hopefully she could talk to the lawyer today and figure out how all of this was connected. Because she was sure it was. The asshole who was trying to kill Hale, the private investigator, and the lawyer were all pieces of the puzzle, and when she connected them she would be able to see the path out. She would be able to do something.

"Yeah, I've got the day off so I'll stay here and help him.

He's working on the tile. Even I can manage to help with tile," Van promised.

"As long as I make sure he doesn't decide to get too creative." Hale was up and dressed for the day, wearing jeans and a sweater and boots. He looked younger than normal, happier, as though the night before had released something dark inside him. "Sometimes he likes to color outside the lines, so to speak. Staying in the lines when laying tile is incredibly important. Also, we're going to help Jake and Adam set up the security system. It's the last bit of Taggart's plan to transform this place from a cabin to a high-security prison."

"Really?" It looked like a perfectly normal cabin.

"You are surrounded by high-tech security." Hale walked up to her and dropped a kiss on her lips. "Like that door that looks normal is actually bulletproof and difficult to kick in. You would need a battering ram. That fucker was heavy."

"I think what Hale is saying is we're safe here." Van pulled down three plates. "You, my love, can go about your business protecting the citizenry of Bliss while your lovers are safe in Taggart's fortress. Also, we're never telling that dude we had a threesome on his bed. He's scary."

Hale snorted at that thought. "Like your brother didn't text him last night. Maybe he'll wait until this morning, but one way or another that man is going to know there's some kink going on in here. Adam has some weird prank situation with that guy. When do they want to get started?"

She wouldn't admit it, but she did feel so much better knowing Jake's brother and partner were across the road. Of course so were a bunch of her clothes, but she would deal with that later. She hadn't spent a single night in that cabin. It was time to admit she was living with them and would for the rest of her life.

"It'll probably be closer to afternoon," Van admitted. "He texted me that he was taking Serena, Adam, and the kids to Stella's for breakfast, and then they'll probably hit the Trading Post for supplies. They're staying the whole week, and Serena wants a proper Christmas. When is your sister getting in?"

She hadn't even thought about the fact that Sabrina was going to be here in two days. Two days. Forty-eight hours and her sister would be standing at the door to the cabin where she kind of lived with two men. She had to explain that to her sister. "Soon. Where are we going to put her?"

Her sister was coming for the holidays, and more than that she was coming to see if she might want to move here. She was planning on finishing out the end of the school year, but her sister could be living here next summer. Of course she might run when she realized the plans had changed.

"Wow. She is freaking out." Van had his hands on his hips, staring at her.

Hale was studying her, too, his head tilted slightly as though trying to diagnose what was wrong. "She is. I've never seen her so upset. Her left eyebrow moved."

That was such bullshit. "You've seen me more upset. Want to talk about that morning at the Movie Motel and how they're not that bad?"

Hale immediately flushed. "Nope. Hey, do you want me to make some cinnamon rolls? I've got a tin in the fridge. I think I can make them."

Van snorted. "Coward. And you are upset. You worried baby sister is going to take a look at the two of us and run the other way? I'll have you know I'm excellent with families. I keep my crazy at a low boil until I get to know a person."

He so did not, but if it made him feel better she wouldn't argue with him. "I don't think she thought I would become involved so soon."

Hale's eyes narrowed. "Does she know about us?"

"Of course." It wasn't like she'd held back on her sister. She'd absolutely told her everything about the guys, but last night had fundamentally changed things. Her sister thought Elisa was just starting to date these guys, and she'd giggled over the idea of her stalwart, never-do-anything-wild sister having a fling with two men. How would she feel when her big sister was serious about living what most people would call an alternative lifestyle? "She knows you exist. She doesn't know I'm basically living with you. Maybe I should stay at the Movie Motel with her."

Now she had two sets of judgmental eyes on her.

That felt like a no.

"She'll like us." Van shrugged as though the discussion was

finished. "Besides, sometimes we get freak winter storms and the Movie Motel is miles away. Do you want to eat popcorn and licorice for Christmas dinner? Or do you want to eat whatever my endless bags of money sister- and brother-in-law bring in. Note I don't add Jake in there. He can still eat an MRE, but Adam has left his military days behind. He's the single fanciest motherfucker you will ever meet."

"What fancy stuff can he find in Bliss?" The food was great here, but from what she could tell it wasn't elevated, unless one counted the weekly specials at Stella's. And she'd been too afraid to try those.

"He will fly in a Christmas feast for the ages if he has to," Van promised. "You don't want to miss it. Besides, Sabrina will likely feel comfortable in a family situation. My brother is here and he's supporting us, and he's in a weird threesome, too. For a long time. They'll make her see this kind of relationship can work."

"She's not a prude." Sabrina was one of the most open people she'd ever met, and she knew her sister would support her no matter what. But Elisa also understood it could be awkward for Sabrina.

"No, but she's lived in the normal world her whole life," Hale countered. "I had to wrap my head around it in the beginning. Now I'm here and it feels perfectly acceptable to me, and I have no idea why anyone would have a problem with it."

"There are plenty of rooms in this cabin," Van allowed. "If you want to stay in the big bedroom with your sister, Hale and I will stay in the kid's rooms. Or we'll sleep in the big room and you and your sister can have private rooms."

This was all ridiculous. She was overthinking the whole thing. Sabrina knew she was involved with two men, and she also knew her sister. She would know she wouldn't get involved with them physically if she couldn't care about them emotionally. "It's fine. She'll be fine. I have no intention of sleeping apart. Not in my own…in someone I don't know's house. By the way, after you finish the sheriff's place, we're looking for our own space. I know it's easier for you to live where you work, but I want a cabin that we can make ours."

She wasn't even going to pretend they were floating through life, living for today. She wanted all the tomorrows—no matter what they brought.

"I don't know that…" Van began.

Hale held out a hand. "We'll sit down and figure out our finances. Mine tend to come in big payments that I have to use to buy supplies and such, and we'll have costs associated with starting up Van's business. I need a system to help me make sure I'm making the most of my money during a job. The good news is we have a guy who's good with numbers."

Van nodded, obviously shoving some unnamed emotion down as he looked at his best friend. "I've got some thoughts about software that will help you estimate a job. We'll make it work."

It was such a relief that they'd both lost the pessimism and they were all on the same page.

"But until then, we need to talk about cars," Hale said with a sigh as he moved into the kitchen to grab a mug. "Because we are now three adult humans with one car between us, and it's owned by the county."

At least she could help out in this way. "The good news is my sister and I have three. We never sold my mom's Jeep. It's in great condition. We can pay my sister for her part of the car. She's got her own. All we have to do is drive it and my truck out here from North Carolina and we're set."

"Road trip." Van grinned. "That'll be fun."

There was a knock on the door and Van started moving toward it. "I guess Jake got back early. I'm probably going to learn a lot about electrician stuff in the next few hours. I'm sure the system is elaborate."

She actually wouldn't mind learning some of that, but she was due at the station house in half an hour.

Hale poured himself a cup of coffee. "You want some toast, baby? I can do toast. I burn everything else."

And Van was actually a good cook. Between the two of them they could do anything around the house. Except chop wood. No one had done lumberjack stuff yet, and she'd been promised. She wanted to watch her two hot guys chopping wood for their fire.

"Hello?" Van had opened the door. "It's you."

A chill went up her spine and she turned, her worst fears confirmed because there was a man standing on the porch. She hadn't seen his face before, but from the way Hale paled, she knew exactly who he was.

"I tried to do this some other way, but I can't let him have it." The man pulled a pistol, leveling it at Van with shaking hands.

Her duty belt was still sitting on the table. She hadn't put it back on yet so she couldn't reach for her gun.

Hale gasped.

And Van slammed the door.

There was a thudding sound, but nothing came through. Van calmly threw the dead bolt and turned back to them. "You should probably call that in."

Her heart had threatened to stop. She strode to grab her gun. "You get back. Call it in. I'm going to deal with him. Hale, what are you doing?"

Hale had moved to stand in front of the big bay window. He and Van were both standing there watching the unhinged man trying to get inside.

"It's kind of funny when you think about it." Hale took a sip of coffee. "He doesn't know the door is fully reinforced. Oh, shit. That's going to hurt."

"Get away from the window," she yelled because the man with the wild eyes was standing right in front of Hale, and he pointed the gun at his head.

He pulled the trigger and then frowned because the bullet hit the glass and then kind of bounced off and hit the porch.

Hale reached out and tapped the glass. "It's so new I had to have it shipped directly from the manufacturer. It's regular bulletproof glass but with an extra coating that's not even on the market yet. Taggart did this dude a favor or something. Works well. Not a scratch."

She took a deep breath. "Are all the windows that strong?"

Hale nodded, super calm for a dude who had a killer readily stalking him. "Yep. And the back door is reinforced, too. Some bad shit will happen if he tries to come through the chimney. Henry thinks it goes against like human rights laws, but I just think that maybe no one should climb down another person's chimney."

"I'm not climbing down Big Tag's anything." Hale's head shook, and he put a hand to his ear. "Dude, I can't hear you. We're not coming out so you can murder us. Good luck with that."

She grabbed her radio. It was good the guys were calm, but she had a job to do. She would send this Taggart guy a thank you note because his paranoia had likely saved them all. "This is Deputy Leal. I need backup out at the old Jones' homestead." She already knew the lingo. "We've got an armed man outside."

"I'm on my way." Nate's voice came over the line. "Be there in five. You keep those men in the cabin. They should be safe there."

Everyone knew she was living in a fortress except her.

She heard another ping as the man tried again. Or maybe he was mad because Van had found his phone and was rolling video.

"My brother is going to find out who you are now, asshole," Van shouted. "Once Jake has a face, it's only a matter of time. You fucked up, buddy."

Hale frowned as he watched him. "I want to know why."

They didn't have time for an interrogation. She wanted this asshole in the jail cell and then she would ask him questions.

The man turned as though ready to run off and then stopped, his whole body freezing and a look of pure terror coming over his face.

"Oh, shit." Hale's jaw dropped. "That's Maurice. He pulled a gun on Maurice."

Motherfucker. That was not happening. Maurice wasn't going down on her watch. She'd heard endless stories from her dad and stepmom about how Maurice was the town mascot, though her dad used some mythical words to describe the animal. The town loved Maurice. Her first couple of weeks in her new home were not going to be marred by moosicide.

"You two, stay inside," she ordered and threw open the door, training her Glock 22 firmly on the suspect. "Get on the ground. Do not shoot that moose. You shoot that moose and I shoot you."

The moose looked pretty reinforced though. Like as reinforced as the cabin. That moose was solid.

The man turned, and the minute he saw the gun on him, he dropped his. And it looked like he'd peed himself. She hoped urine came out of designer jeans.

"Down on the ground."

His hands were up in the air, his whole body still as Maurice began to walk by.

That fucker was huge. And beautiful in his way. His stately antlers rose from his head, spreading out over his big dark eyes. She stood on the top step of the porch, putting her eye to eye with the large bull as he began to walk by. He sniffed the air and then huffed her way, steam coming from his large nostrils. He turned his head toward the cabin across the way and huffed once more before he made his way over.

She took the opportunity to deal with their would-be attacker. Though she supposed he had totally attacked the cabin. "On the ground."

The man had tears running down his face. "But it's cold."

"It'll be colder in hell, buddy. I'm not joking." In the distance she could see the red and blue lights coming down the road. She could also see that they'd attracted some attention.

"Morning, Elisa." Marie Warner was standing at the edge of her property, and she had a shotgun in her hand. She held it casually, as though it was merely an accessory to her normal wardrobe. "You need any help? Looks like you might need to shoot a son of a bitch."

He got on the ground real fast, holding his face over the snow. "I'm on the ground. I'm on the ground."

Nate chose that second to turn onto the driveway they shared with Jake's place. He stopped the SUV and had cuffs in his hands as he approached the man now crying on the ground. Nate sighed. "I hate it when they cry. It gives me a headache. All right, buddy. You are under arrest. Let's hope I remember how to do this because most of the time guys who do what you did end up in the morgue, not my jail."

"You should mirandize him," Elisa encouraged. She hadn't been on the job long, but she already knew that much. "He has rights and stuff."

Nate hauled him up. "Yeah, well, good luck with that. Elisa, get down to the station with Hale and Van. I've got a nice lady lawyer who's been looking for them. I think she's got a story to tell."

He turned, dragging their would-be assassin with him as the SUV Jake was driving pulled in. The kids had their faces pressed to the windows, eyes wide.

"You have the right to remain silent," Nate began.

Jake pulled the car to a stop, hopping out with a worried look on his face. "What the hell happened? Is everyone okay?"

"We're good." Van stood on the porch. "That glass works. You should think about putting some in."

Hale stood beside him, but his eyes were on the SUV where Nate had settled the prisoner. He looked so lost, like nothing made sense. She hustled up to get beside him.

"Why is there a moose in our yard?" Adam stood by his wife, Serena, staring at Maurice, who was standing next to their porch, his head down. It was obvious he'd found something fun to eat.

"We leave him Snickers bars," Brianna proudly announced. "Mel told us if we want Maurice to like us, we should leave him candy."

That was her dad. He was always giving out helpful advice. She threaded an arm through Hale's and leaned against him. "We're going to find out what's going on now. It's going to be okay."

He leaned in and kissed her right above her ear. "Yes, it is. No matter what."

"No matter what." Van was on his other side, surrounding Hale with their love and support.

"I don't think moose are supposed to eat chocolate," Adam said with a frown. "I'm also pretty sure they shouldn't be so close to the porch."

"Maurice is a magical moose," Tristan insisted.

Then Maurice proved he was a biological moose and chocolate probably did upset his belly, and there was a lot of arguing about who cleaned that up.

But there was no doubt that Bliss was a magical place.

* * * *

Hale stared at the lawyer. She appeared to be in her mid-thirties and was dressed for vacation. Which apparently she was on. She'd explained that she'd taken the job of finding him for the simple reason that she wanted to have some fun ski time with her husband. She sat across the conference table in the sheriff's department wearing activewear and a puffy vest, having come in straight from a ski run up at the lodge. But that wasn't the information that had made

Hale's jaw drop.

"I have a brother?" He had a brother. He had Van. But according to the woman who'd introduced herself as Anna Kaplan, he had a biological sibling.

The lawyer glanced back toward the jail cells, though they couldn't see them from here. "That will take a DNA test to prove, but the resemblance is there. And you look almost like a twin of the man I believe is your biological father, Harrison Jeremy. Here. I brought along the file."

She slid a manila folder his way, and both Elisa and Van leaned in to get a look. Those two hadn't left his side since the moment they'd taken the man who'd tried to kill him into custody. The man who was his brother. Probably. Maybe. Hopefully not.

He opened the folder and all hope fled.

"Holy crap," Elisa said. "That looks like you but older."

"The younger pictures of him are dead on," Anna assured them.

"I don't know. This guy looks mean." Van was on his side. "Hale's not mean."

Anna shrugged. "Well, probably because he didn't grow up in the Jeremy family. There's a reason his brother's such a shitbag. His name is John. John Jeremy. He didn't have a chance."

The lawyer had a dry wit. "I still don't understand why he would want to kill me. I didn't know about him. I would never have known about him."

The sheriff leaned in. He sat at the head of the table, Gemma taking notes at his side. "Why don't you explain how you got involved in this case, Ms. Kaplan?"

"Oh, it's just Anna," she corrected. "I'm not one of those stuffy formal lawyers."

"Amen," Gemma agreed. "I hate those douchebags. Do you do family law? Is that why you work with the probate court?"

"Yes." Anna turned his way, thankfully recognizing he did not understand all the lawyer stuff. "I'm with a small firm outside of Houston. I deal with family law, so it's a lot of wills and advanced directives and custody cases. I personally specialize in wills. If you don't have one, get one or you'll find yourself in Harrison Jeremy's position. Well, he's dead, so I guess he doesn't care, but he left a mess behind for his kid." She frowned. "I'm so sorry. Your dad passed away four months ago."

"I didn't know him, so it's all good. I still don't understand what this has to do with me."

"Well, in the state of Texas if you don't have a will, the court system has a lot of discretion with how they handle the case," Anna began. "It can be simple. If a man dies and he's survived by his wife, it doesn't matter if they had children, the wife gets everything because we're a community property state. It's more complex if there isn't a spouse. In this case Harrison Jeremy's wife died over a decade ago, and he didn't remarry. He only had one acknowledged child, so the court could have made it simple. But it's a small town, and the judge pretty much hated that whole family. Like really hated them. So he followed the absolute letter of the law, which in Texas means when a person dies without a will, the court must do everything it can to insure all possible heirs are identified."

"Ah," Gemma said knowingly. "So you were brought in to look through records to make sure there wasn't another family hanging around in the background who would have a claim on the man's estate."

Now it started to make sense. "So he thought I would take some of his dad's money?"

"Half," Anna corrected. "If I can prove you are Jeremy's biological child—and I don't think that will be a problem—you get half of the estate."

Van sat back. "Wow. That's unexpected."

"You don't even know how much it is." Hale wasn't counting any chickens. None.

"I know he killed one person for it and was willing to kill all three of us," Elisa pointed out. "He didn't show up this morning to talk to us. He was desperate. He's not desperate for a couple grand. Anna, do you know how much the estate is worth?"

"Five million," the lawyer replied. "Your portion would be two point five, but it could be a bit more or less depending on how the assets sell. It's not the largest estate I've worked with. From what I can tell the Jeremy family was good at looking wealthier than they were. I think John Jeremy is in serious debt. He thought he could pay it off with the inheritance. He got nervous when the court ordered me to look for other possible heirs. He hired a private investigator, and she got there first. I'm afraid this kind of work takes a while because lawyers don't prioritize it."

"It's practically pro bono," Gemma added. "The courts don't have the funds to pay lawyers their full rates when they hire them. I bet the PI got paid better. Well, until she was murdered."

He shouldn't forget that this man who was his biological brother was also a killer. He hadn't cared about anything but getting his hands on the money. "How did you find me? I never knew who my dad was."

"Did I mention he lived in a small town?" Anna's eyes lit with amusement. "I know I could have looked through a couple of records and called the people John Jeremy gave me to vouch for the fact that his dad didn't have other children. It's pretty simple. But there was something one of the cousins said about a woman named Margaret Galloway."

"She was my mom. My biological mother." It was hard to think of her. He didn't even know if she was alive. She'd walked out so long before and never looked back.

"Yes, and she was from the same town as Harrison Jeremy," Anna explained. "She was many years younger than he was, and when she graduated high school, she got a job as his secretary."

Elisa gasped. "She had an affair with her boss."

"Obviously," he replied, but stretched his arm around the back of her chair. Normally he would be anxious about all of this. It was a lot of drama and change, and he preferred things calm. He definitely preferred to not be the center of attention, but it was all okay now. He'd found the person who truly centered him, and he could handle it. "Now that I think about it, my aunt used to say things would have been different if my mom had never taken that job. I didn't ask what she meant. I guess she meant I wouldn't have been born."

"I was able to find financial records proving that Jeremy paid the hospital bills for your delivery, though no one put him on the birth certificate," Anna continued. "From there, Margaret Galloway disappears from life in that small town. She left town with her baby and twenty-five thousand dollars, which from what I can tell, she went through pretty quickly. Within a year she was living with one of her sisters in Ohio, and according to the people who knew them, the sister was eventually left with the kid."

"Yes." He knew this part of the story well. "She took off when I was seven. I went through a lot of homes after that and ended up in foster care in Nebraska. I know some of the family services workers over the years tried to get into contact with her, but they couldn't find her."

Anna's expression dimmed, and he knew what she was about to say. "She died a few years after she left you. I'm so sorry to tell you that, but she was killed in a car accident."

Elisa's hand found his.

He squeezed it, but all he could feel was some distant ache for what could have been. "It's an old wound. It's okay because I have a good family now. So you knew my name and basically where I'd been left. I was pretty good at staying off the grid."

"Your friend wasn't, though," Anna countered.

Van groaned, and his head fell forward. "Because I couldn't stay out of jail. Damn. This is my fault."

"Yes. It's your fault we're probably getting two point five million dollars, which will set us all up for success," Elisa pointed out.

Hale grinned. He had not thought of it that way. Two point five million wouldn't allow them to live like the rich and famous, but if they used it right, they could have their cabin and build their businesses, and if they ever chose to, they could adopt and give some kids a good home. It might be the exact right amount of money to make them all content. "She's kind of right."

Van's head came up, his expression brightening. "My anger issues actually made us money."

"Well, they certainly made it easier to track you." Anna sat back, seemingly more comfortable with this part of the story. "So I figured out you were close to Mr. Dean when I searched arrest records in the Midwest and your name came up three times as the man who bailed him out. I was actually looking to see if you had been arrested, but some of those places keep excellent records and even had your driver's license on file. So I knew you were alive and that all I had to do was find Mr. Dean and you would likely be there. I'm going to admit. I kind of thought you were a couple."

"They kind of are," the sheriff said with a lopsided smile. "I mean here in Bliss they are."

Anna's eyes went wide. "Is this what they were whispering about up at that lodge? I can't tell if they're talking about threesomes or aliens because sometimes I'm certain they're talking about aliens. A man wouldn't let me ski through part of the cross-country course because of mating rituals."

"It's the Neluts," Elisa said like it was a perfectly normal thing to say. "It's their wintertime mating. You do not want to interrupt that. It's messy. My dad saved you some serious dry-cleaning bills."

Oh, she was going to fit right in here. "Relationships are different in Bliss. Van and I have been best friends for years, and now we share this gorgeous woman. That's all. How did you track us to Bliss?"

"I asked the sheriff in Oklahoma if he had any idea where you'd gone and he told me the last he'd heard you were in a town called Bliss, Colorado," Anna replied. "Apparently Sheriff Wright called him to make sure you weren't some hardened criminal."

Nate had the grace to flush. "I had to ask."

"I knew you had my records. I didn't realize you called around," Van said with a frown.

"Bliss is a delicate place," Nate admitted. "I had to make sure you wouldn't throw off that balance. And you didn't. If it helps, I vetted your brother, too. And Ian Taggart, and if he hadn't turned out to be a tolerant man who doesn't mind donating to local charities, I would have found a way to keep him out. You'll be happy about that the next time some asshole shows up thinking he can change us for the better."

He probably would. "So you decided to come to Bliss yourself."

"Well, no one would talk to me." Anna's brown ponytail shook. "I found employment records for the Elk Creek Lodge, but you'd moved on. I didn't think you had gotten far though. Van started working full time at Trio, so I knew you would be somewhere close. And I love to ski, so I packed up my husband and the kiddo and we checked into the lodge. I spent a day asking around Bliss and getting nowhere. I was going to come back one last time before we head home, but then the sheriff found me and here I am."

"What do we have to do to get the money?" Van asked. "Do you need some DNA? I can pull some hair out for you."

"Van." Elisa made Van's name sound like the fiery wrath of hell could come down on him.

"Sorry, baby." Van sat back.

But he had a point. "How do I prove I'm an heir? I know I should be above taking money from the man who abandoned me, but we could use it. I think John will be using his part for lawyers."

Nate chuckled at that thought. "He'll need a good one since apparently the whole thing was caught by your brother's security camera. They have an excellent tape of that idiot trying to kill you. And it won't take long to prove he murdered the PI. He's looking at life."

"Good," Van said. "Because I don't think he would leave us alone."

"I doubt he'll be out any time soon. Once he's arraigned here, Denver will probably be ready for him." Nate pushed back from the table and stood. "He won't be bothering anyone for a long time."

"But we'll keep tabs on him." Gemma joined him, closing her notepad. "I don't usually have to do this. Elisa, you should have shot his ass. It would have gotten you an invite into the club and saved me a whole lot of follow-ups. See, that's why we shoot sons of bitches here."

He thought Elisa had handled things perfectly. He turned her way, kissing her cheek. "You were great, baby. You keep right on not killing people you don't have to."

"Good work, Leal." Nate gave her a salute. "Now get to work. It's your shift."

"I didn't even have breakfast," she groused.

He could fix that. "Van and I will run over to Stella's and get you some breakfast."

She smiled at him, lighting up his whole world. "Make sure you get pancakes and syrup."

He winked down at her. "Will do."

When he and Van walked out, he didn't even look back at the jail cell that held the man who might have been his brother.

He had a family who loved him. It was all he could ever ask for.

Epilogue

Two weeks later

Elisa looked around the town hall all decorated for the holidays.

Including the beautiful beet garlands her father had made.

"Our new dad is very talented." Sabrina stood beside her, inspecting the intricately carved garland. "How are his hands not purple?"

The minute Mel and Cassidy had figured out Sabrina's father wasn't in the picture, they adopted her, too. Almost a week into her visit, Sabrina was soaking up all that weird, magnificent love they could give.

"He says something the aliens did to him made it so beets can't permeate his skin. That's why he has to drink so much juice." It was odd how easy it was to accept her dad's eccentricities. Or maybe it should be normal to accept that not everyone was normal and reality could be different for other people.

Her reality was kind of awesome.

"You know he's a legend in my business," a now familiar voice said.

She'd spent a lot of time with Jacob Dean and his family over the last few weeks, including an amazing Christmas day with a feast she still dreamed about. Adam Miles was a fancy fucker, and she appreciated him for it. But Jake was the one she clicked with. "In the missing persons business?"

Jake took a sip of the apple cider Nell Flanders had assured everyone harmed neither environment nor human labor force workers. "No. I was talking about intelligence. My friends and I worked on a special ops team for a long time and then we helped out the Agency on occasion. Your dad has one of the highest security clearances I've ever seen. I think the man has actually met with the president."

"Seriously?" Sabrina asked. "Why would he advise the president?"

There was another explanation for her dad's eccentricities. They could be true. "He's an expert alien hunter."

Sabrina's lips kicked up. "Come on."

Jake's big shoulders shrugged. "There are more things in heaven and earth…"

There were definitely more things in Bliss than she'd ever dreamed. She glanced over as Sabrina and Jake began to discuss the possibility that her dad had saved the world on more than one occasion, but Elisa's eyes found Van. He was talking to Stefan Talbot near the kid's play station, which was completely devoid of children. The kids seemed to be having way more fun climbing on things. Van was speaking with an animation she'd come to realize meant he was talking about taxes or spreadsheets or some other numbers geek thing. Since he'd made the decision to change his major, his freak flag had been flying high. He was no longer pretending to be the cool dude. He was a full on mathalete. And he talked about statistics a lot.

She loved him so much.

"Hey, gorgeous." Her other man walked up carrying two mugs of apple cider, one of which he held out for her. "It's only got a nip of your dad's whiskey in it. I'm taking that slow, allowing my body to acclimate to the special alien deterrent properties."

It was a good idea. Her dad's whiskey had apparently brought low many a Bliss citizen who imbibed too much. She took the mug and said hello to Max Harper, who had walked up with Hale. "I've been told I'm genetically protected since I was conceived after Dad's first couple of alien encounters. His DNA was changed so he could survive in alien climates, so I don't have the same trouble with the whiskey."

Oddly, she didn't. It tasted good to her. The first night they'd sat around her dad's fire pit and made smores and drank while he told the craziest stories, both of her men had passed out. She'd stayed up until early morning laughing with her dad and stepmom.

She loved it here so much. Loved having parents again. She loved it so much she'd even started thinking fondly of her mother. Life had been hard for her, and she hadn't had a Sabrina to take some of the burden. She hadn't found a person who loved her. Her mother's life could have been different if she'd found the courage to take another path.

Being angry with her mother no longer seemed helpful, and she was getting rid of everything that didn't bring her some sense of peace.

"Max, she's looking at me." Hale breathed the words as though he didn't want anyone outside their small circle to hear.

"I told you. Laser eyes." Max had leaned in, whispering as well. "She knows what you did."

Elisa followed their line of sight and ended at Nell Flanders, who was wearing flowy pants and a sweater and had her baby strapped to her chest. Poppy Flanders was an adorable moppet of a kid who always seemed to be smiling and embracing the world around her. Except now she was frowning and staring their way. "Are you talking about Poppy?"

Hale nodded. "She looks at me like that every time she sees me since I tried to save you from my bio bro."

If anything that baby's eyes narrowed more.

"I think she heard you," Max said. "You need to appease that baby. I think she might have witch powers."

"Faery powers." Nell could tell some fun stories of her own. Elisa had been introduced to Nell and Henry's sweet baby, who Nell swore came about from faery magic and a whole lot of love. Honestly, between the aliens and the sasquatches, she would take the faeries every time.

Hale turned to Elisa, his voice rising. "Elisa, I would like to sincerely apologize for being a dumbass who allowed societal norms to squash your far more impressive knowledge of security matters.

From now on any time a brother of mine tries to kill me so he doesn't have to share the inheritance, I will allow you to handle it fully and will be waiting for you to come home with flowers and some kind of food treat."

Every eye was suddenly on them.

"That baby is not trying to kill you," Van called out.

"She's not now because he properly apologized," Nell corrected and looked down at her baby. "See, they can change."

"Well, at least he only tried to kill you. One of the sisters I didn't even know I had erased my mind and tortured me for a year and a half," a big guy with blondish hair said. Jax Lee had an arm around his wife, River's shoulders.

"True story," River said.

"Show off. See, you had it easy, Hale," Max added with a nod of his head. "Hey, Poppy's happy now."

Sure enough, the baby was suddenly fascinated with Long-Haired Roger's baby, who happened to be a dog named Princess Two.

Hale breathed a sigh of obvious relief. "Excellent. Maybe now I can get some of that cake Henry made. It looks good. Well, if I can get through the hellions."

The kids were wreaking havoc. Rachel Harper stood up from her table as one of her kids started hanging tinsel on Marie, who was snoring in her chair. The fact that her wife was holding the tinsel didn't help.

"Kids, come on," Rachel ordered.

They ignored her completely.

Laura Kincaid-Briggs had her hands on her hips, trying to explain to her daughter that the floor was not in fact lava.

It was chaos.

And then a loud whistle split the air, the sound so commanding even the music stopped playing.

Her sister stood in the center of the hall, her best teacher face on. "Children, we're going to sit down and do crafts now. Let's move it. Paige, no more cookies until after. Cookies are for crafters. We have to make decorations or the holiday season is over. Let's go."

She watched as all the children stopped what they were doing and made their way to the craft table.

Sabrina gave the crowd around her a bright smile. "Don't worry, folks. I've been teaching elementary for years. Carry on. The kids and I will be over here for a bit."

Rachel watched as Sabrina walked by. She watched Elisa's sister with the longing look of a woman who was truly in love.

Laura had the same look in her eyes.

Serena Dean-Miles had watched the whole thing happen. Her kids had happily followed Sabrina as well. "Well, that's the mark of a good teacher. Hey, didn't someone say y'all were starting a school?"

Rachel turned and yelled across the hall. "Stefan! Stefan, I'm going to need your checkbook. Who has Stef's checkbook?"

It looked like her sister would do just fine.

"Want to find some mistletoe and heat this party up? I've made up with all the judgmental babies and now the kids are under control," Hale whispered.

Van was suddenly at her other side. "Damn, baby. I think Stef's about to buy your sister. Not in a bad way though. Oh, hey. Are we getting sexy? Because there's a certain broom closet I've heard is fully stocked."

She laughed and let them lead her away.

The entire town of Bliss will return.

Author's Note

I'm often asked by generous readers how they can help get the word out about a book they enjoyed. There are so many ways to help an author you like. Leave a review. If your e-reader allows you to lend a book to a friend, please share it. Go to Goodreads and connect with others. Recommend the books you love because stories are meant to be shared. Thank you so much for reading this book and for supporting all the authors you love!

Love the Way You Spy
Masters and Mercenaries: New Recruits
By Lexi Blake
Coming September 19, 2023

Tasha Taggart isn't a spy. That's her sisters' job. Tasha's support role is all about keeping them alive, playing referee when they fight amongst themselves, and soothing the toughest boss in the world. Working for the CIA isn't as glamorous as she imagined, and she's more than a little lonely. So when she meets a charming man in a bar the night before they start their latest op, she decides to give in to temptation. The night was perfect until she discovers she's just slept with the target of their new investigation. Her sisters will never let her hear the end of this. Even worse, she has to explain the situation to her overprotective father, who also happens to be their boss.

Dare Nash knew exactly how his week in Sydney was going to go—attending boring conferences to represent his family's business interests and eating hotel food alone. Until he falls under the spell of a stunning and mysterious American woman. Something in Tasha's eyes raises his body temperature every time she looks at him. She's captivating, and he's committed to spending every minute he can with her on this trip, even if her two friends seem awfully intense. His father will be arriving in town soon, and he's excited to introduce him to a woman he could imagine spending the rest of his life with.

When Dare discovers Tash isn't who she seems, the dream turns into a nightmare. She isn't the only one who deceived him, and now he's in the crosshairs of adversaries way out of his league. He can't trust her, but it might take Tasha and her family to save his life and uncover the truth.

If you'd like to read Jake, Adam, and Serena's story, check out The Men With the Golden Cuffs!

The Men With the Golden Cuffs
Masters and Mercenaries, Book 3
By Lexi Blake
Now available

A woman in danger...

Serena Brooks is a bestselling author of erotic fiction. She knows how to write a happy ending but hasn't managed to find one of her own. Divorced and alone, she has no one to turn to when a stalker begins to threaten her life. The cops don't believe her. Her ex-husband thinks she's making the whole story up. She has no one left to turn to except a pair of hired bodyguards. They promise to guard her body, but no one can protect her heart.

Two men in search of love...

Adam Miles and Jacob Dean are halves of a whole. They've spent their entire adult lives searching for the one woman who can handle them both. Adam is the playful, indulgent lover, while Jacob is the possessive, loving Dom. When Serena comes into their lives, Adam is certain that she's the one. But Jacob's past comes back to haunt them all. He is suspicious of Serena's story, and his concerns are driving a wedge between him and Adam. But when the stalker strikes, they will have to come together or lose each other forever...

* * * *

"Who is Master Storm?" a low voice asked.

She shrieked like a five-year-old girl. Jake Dean had somehow gotten into her bedroom and behind her when she wasn't looking. "You have to stop that! God, you're going to give me a heart attack."

"He's good at that. It's one of his great life skills." Adam leaned negligently against her doorframe. Mojo sat beside him, their enormous bodies blocking her escape route. Mojo's tail thumped and his mouth hung open, tongue panting. At least her dog found them amusing.

They were both here in her small bedroom. It was the most straight-man attention this bedroom had gotten in years.

"Don't sneak up on me like that." She forced herself to look at Jake. Between the two of them it was obvious Adam would be easier to deal with. Jake was the hard-ass. She didn't deal well with hard-asses.

A single brow arched above his model perfect face. "I didn't sneak up. You weren't paying attention to your surroundings. You were far too busy telling your agent to fire us."

Adam's face fell. "What? But we just got here. Look, sweetheart, I know the whole breaking-in thing was scary, but we did have a point. Your security system sucks. And, in our defense, we did call and ring the doorbell. We can't do our job standing on your front porch waiting for you to finish with the dancing thing. That was adorable by the way."

She flushed. God, she hated the fact that a part of her wanted to believe he wasn't insulting her. His teasing tone was soft and cajoling. When he smiled, the most gorgeous dimples showed up on his face. Adam Miles was just about everything she could want in a boyfriend. He was charming and smart, and he came with a built-in alpha-male partner.

Stop right there, Serena Brooks. Your imagination is running wild. The world doesn't work that way.

"I don't think this is about the break-in. She said we were making fun of her." Jake's brows drew together in a serious expression as though he was working through a problem. "I didn't make fun of her. I told her to stop yelling. I have excellent hearing. I can't stand yelling."

And he apparently thought she was dense. "You know I wasn't talking about you." She turned to Adam. It had really hurt coming from him. She'd expected someone like Jake to think less of her for what she wrote, but Adam had seemed more tolerant.

"What? Me? Are you serious? How did I make fun of you?"

319

He seemed to really struggle with the idea.

"You obviously read some of the titles of my books. Look, I get that you wouldn't read a book like that, but I won't listen to anyone denigrate the choices I've made in my lifestyle. You might not understand or accept it, but I will demand that you respect it."

Jake actually laughed. "The little sub thinks we have problems with BDSM."

Adam's eyes rolled. "Yeah, uhm, you do have some problems, sweetheart. How long have you been in the lifestyle? Or are you a little tourist who likes to rage against the machine?"

"I had to take off my leathers to come here. I was at a club called Sanctum." Jake's face had softened a bit. "Adam knows my limits. I don't like pretty subs spouting filth at me in anger. He has a smart mouth, but he would never ridicule you. Lightning would strike."

Adam smiled at her. "And the earth would shake. Seriously, we don't think that way. We're far too odd on our own. And I haven't read any of your books, but I would like to."

Jake's whole body went on wary alert. "We actually need to. From what I understand, this is about your books, correct?"

She was caught between relief and a dangerous joy. She believed them. They really didn't care. In fact, Jake seemed to be involved in the lifestyle. She didn't know many men outside the lifestyle who would use the term leathers when talking about a pair of pants. The thought of Jacob Dean in a pair of leathers, his cut chest on display as he nodded to the floor, silently requesting that she kneel at his feet, made her heart pound. About a million questions popped into her brain, but she forced herself to keep to the questions asked.

About Lexi Blake

New York Times bestselling author Lexi Blake lives in North Texas with her husband and three kids. Since starting her publishing journey in 2010, she's sold over three million copies of her books. She began writing at a young age, concentrating on plays and journalism. It wasn't until she started writing romance that she found success. She likes to find humor in the strangest places and believes in happy endings.

Connect with Lexi online:

Facebook: Lexi Blake
Twitter: authorlexiblake
Website: www.LexiBlake.net
Instagram: www.instagram.com